*"I don't say what I don't mean."*

Firelight and the lavender scent of perfume, or blood loss and the beginning of fever—Aidan couldn't be sure, but the result had him captured within the depths of Cat's jade gaze. And while his brain still seethed, the rest of him responded with a sweep of heat and a bone-deep ache that had him shifting uncomfortably.

"Very well . . . Aidan," she said, her voice low and uncertain. She stepped forward, the air charged with all the potential of a summer storm. Just as he'd thought, the woman was a walking thundercloud. She held out a hand. "Whether you meant to or not, you saved my life. Thank you."

He didn't want to be thanked. Not with a handshake. Not even with a chivalrous graze of her knuckles. Not now. His traitorous body craved more. His gaze raked the long slenderness of her, the coral pink of her lips, the graceful column of her throat where her pulse fluttered, begging to be kissed.

D1018280

# Earl of Darkness

## BOOK ONE

# ALIX RICKLOFF

*Pocket Books*

New York   London   Toronto   Sydney

Pocket Books
A Division of Simon & Schuster, Inc.
1230 Avenue of the Americas
New York, NY 10020

This book is a work of fiction. Names, characters, places, and incidents either are products of the author's imagination or are used fictitiously. Any resemblance to actual events or locales or persons, living or dead, is entirely coincidental.

First Pocket Books paperback edition January 2011

POCKET and colophon are registered trademarks of Simon & Schuster, Inc.

For information about special discounts for bulk purchases, please contact Simon & Schuster Special Sales at 1-866-506-1949 or business@simonandschuster.com.

The Simon & Schuster Speakers Bureau can bring authors to your live event. For more information or to book an event contact the Simon & Schuster Speakers Bureau at 1-866-248-3049 or visit our website at www.simonspeakers.com.

Designed by Esther Paradelo
Cover design by Lisa Litwack. Illustration by Gene Mollica.

Manufactured in the United States of America

10   9   8   7   6   5   4   3   2   1

ISBN  978-1-4391-7036-6
ISBN  978-1-4391-7058-8 (ebook)

*To Georgia, who wanted one of her own*

# Acknowledgments ❯❯

To all those who helped this book find its way to completion, my greatest thanks.

Those desperate writers out there and especially Maggie who, as usual, went above and beyond.

Kevan Lyon and Megan McKeever, who took the final product and made it even better.

Bethan Davies for coming to my rescue when I needed to know Welsh at a moment's notice.

Those wonderful members of the Beau Monde who were there to answer any and all questions about the Regency period. Any errors or anachronisms are mine alone.

And finally, my eternally patient family for all their support.

Thank you. Thank you. Thank you.

*Deep in the Cambrian Mountains, Wales*
*April 1815*


Kilronan's diary had resurfaced.

Máelodor tapped a gnarled finger against the edge of the letter as he considered the implications of this latest correspondence from his Dublin contact. For six years he'd assumed the diary had been destroyed. Confiscated during the same *Amhas-draoi* attack that left the old earl dead, his network broken and scattered.

Of the Nine who'd formed the inner circle, only Máelodor remained. And he'd been forced into a life of hiding and running until time and rage were spent and the *Amhas-draoi* found new prey.

He spat his loathing for those self-proclaimed guardians of the divide between *Fey* and Mortal. Interfering meddlers was more accurate. Did they think their misguided strike against the Nine could destroy an entire movement? They'd hacked the head from the Hydra. That was all. But resentments continued to smolder. Bitterness flared as each passing generation of *Other* was forced to deny its *Fey* blood in a superstitious world. So if it had become impossible to move forward among humanity's current small-mindedness, perhaps the time had come to turn back the clocks.

To the Lost Days. A disappeared world where magic reigned, and *Fey* and *Other* passed with ease between the mortal and faery realms.

He glanced to the window, where the sun sank through dirty clouds to be clutched by the black, reaching trees, but his mind's eye envisioned a far different scene. A golden-haired king, ambition stamped upon every chiseled feature. His *Fey*-forged sword beating the air as he rallied followers to his banner. Claimed his rightful place in a history that had relegated him to myth.

A rare smile touched Máelodor's lips. If the *Amhas-draoi* had overlooked the diary, then perhaps the brotherhood did not know everything. Perhaps there remained a chance to fulfill the Nine's purpose. To bring to fruition the dream that had bound them together until murder had shattered it.

Murder and treachery.

His thoughts turned black with a hate unalleviated by the distance of years. One man had destroyed it all. One man had bought his life by betraying the Nine. An easy death would not be his if Máelodor ever found him.

"Summon Lazarus."

A young page flinched under the crack of command, but his hesitation was momentary and then he sped off to find the man Máelodor trusted above all others to complete the task taking shape within his mind.

Máelodor heaved himself up out of bed with the aid of the stick at his side. Maneuvered his wooden prosthetic into place before levering himself to stand. It wouldn't do to give an impression of weakness. Authority rested as much in perception as reality.

He shuffled toward the window. He would have his audience there, where the setting sun might wreathe him in an aura of brilliance. Where the light would be always in the other man's eyes, while Máelodor's own shattered features remained hidden in shadow.

He'd just dropped into the thronelike chair when the door opened. No knock. No announcement. Máelodor would deal with the page later. Such a lapse would not happen again.

"You sent for me?" Lazarus shouldered his way into the room with the stalking grace of a tiger. Everything about him speaking of prideful conceit, from his wide-legged stance to the set of his jaw as his sinister gaze passed over the room with the curve of one arrogant brow. His eyes settling finally on Máelodor.

Máelodor couldn't help the flush of satisfaction at this living proof of his magical skills. It had taken years of failure and had cost him his health, but he'd finally achieved the impossible. Created life from death. "I have a job for you, Lazarus. You will sail for Ireland to retrieve a book and return it to me."

"As you wish, Great One." The man's agreement came without argument, as it should; yet he rested a casual hand on the pommel of his sword in a bold pose of intimidation.

Máelodor's hand curved around his stick, though it would avail him nothing in a battle between them. Only mage energy held this ancient in bondage to him, as it would another far superior.

This time, he would not be denied his victory. This time, if all went as planned, Máelodor would forge out of the bones of the Lost Days a new halcyon age of *Other*. And leading the charge—the legendary King Arthur.

# One

Kilronan House, Dublin
May 1815

Cat crouched in the bushes below the window. Branches poked her in places best left unpoked, and nervous butterflies queased her stomach, but she willed herself to relax just as Geordie had taught her. No use getting bothered. It would be the work of a minute to nip in and filch the goods. Nothing to it.

Hoisting herself up onto the sill, she scrambled for purchase on the slick, mossy granite. Turned her attention to the window, sliding the thin metal of her betty between the casement and sash.

She swallowed a contemptuous sniff as a jiggle and a twist of her wrist released what passed for a lock. Committing this sorry excuse for security to memory, she dropped soundlessly into the room. It might be worth her while to return another night. Not too soon. But if she needed a bit of something to pawn, it was good to know where a ready supply of pocketable trinkets might be found.

She cast a quick glance around. In the dark, furniture

stood humped and unrecognizable, though the desk was easy enough to spot—an enormous black shape at the far end of the room, facing the window she'd just come through. But it was the rows upon rows of shelves that caused her breath to catch in her throat, squashing her earlier optimism.

Was she insane? What had she been thinking when she'd offered to come here in Geordie's place? This was a job for a professional, not a novice with more bravado than skill. She'd never find one book among the hundreds rising from floor to ceiling on every wall.

She gave a passing thought to returning home and explaining her failure. Discarded the idea almost immediately. Geordie needed her. He'd asked so little over the years they'd been together, the least she could do was complete this one small job.

Plucking a candle from a low table nearby, she mumbled the words to set flame to wick. She'd learned over the last few years to hide even the small bits of household magic she'd been allowed at home. Survival meant being normal. Passing as one of the non-magical *Duinedon* in a world where to be *Other* meant persecution and worse. But she was in a hurry, with no time to waste searching for flint and steel. Not when she had a much bigger and more frustrating search ahead of her. Magic would have to serve.

Yet the futility of her task was simply made more clear to her in the light of the tiny flame. Had she said hundreds of books? There must be thousands. And more spread out on tables. Heaped upon the desk. Some even stacked in corners for lack of other space. She'd never seen so many in one place. Not even in her stepfather's library, the coveted symbol of his newfound wealth.

Cat started at the shelves, browsing the titles and spines, hoping against hope the damned thing would jump out and holler, *here I am!* Found nothing even remotely resembling the diary's description Geordie had given her.

She moved to the tables. Plucking books up. Leafing through them. Putting them back disappointed. Scowling, hands on hips, she surveyed the bibliophilic excess. This was getting her nowhere. And time stood as her enemy. The longer she remained, the greater the chance she'd be caught. She needed a plan of action.

So, if she had a diary, where would she keep it?

Simple. Close at hand. Easily accessible. That meant the desk.

She focused her attention on the volumes scattered there. A book did lie open. But a quick scan showed her columns and rows of tiny, carefully written numbers. Sheet upon sheet, with little to show for them at the end if she were any judge.

Pushing it aside, she took up the next in the pile. And the next. A third followed. Then a fourth.

She gave up. Started rifling through drawers. Ledger books, receipts, correspondence. She'd progressed as far as the bottom right-hand side when she encountered a lock. Out came the betty. With a practiced flick of her wrist, the lock gave way. *And . . . success.* A book lay at the bottom of the drawer. A drawer empty but for this one item.

Carefully, she withdrew the book. Placed it on the desk, her breath coming jumpy with excitement.

Old?

Frayed at the edges. A cover of tooled leather, supple from handling. So far, so good.

A crescent pierced by a broken arrow in gold leaf?

She studied it in the weak light. Turned it one way, then the other.

Here was a funny squiggle rubbed to a dull brown, but if she squinched her eyes almost shut, it sort of resembled the sketch Geordie had given her to memorize.

The final test. The stamped personal crest of Kilronan.

Cat smiled. That was easy to see. A spread-winged bird atop a crooked sword had been pressed into one corner. *Fortuna ventus validus.* Luck favors the strong.

Latin. A straightforward language and one she'd learned the secret of long ago, despite Mother's gimlet eye on her every moment she'd not been at her needlework or helping with her half sisters.

This was it, then. She could taste success.

Curiosity set her fingers leafing through the pages.

Her heart beat sharp as a bird's, her mouth going dry, her throat tightening. Not Latin this time. No language she'd ever seen.

She lost herself in the hand-inked marks upon the vellum, in the swirl and slice of each faded letter. Strung together like beads upon a string. She studied their weight and shape. The emptiness between. They fell into her head like stones into a pool. Rippled and struck. Bounced back until they met their echo in the still center of her. And from the unintelligible came meaning.

This was what she'd been sent for. She'd bet her only farthing on it.

She smiled, shifting on the balls of her feet as success lit her insides. Clutched the diary to her chest as if embracing a baby.

"Did you find what you were looking for?" A deep baritone voice punctuated by the snick of a cocked pistol.

Cat froze.

———o———

Aidan studied the woman as he might some rare new species.

*Womanus Exoticus.*

Black hair swept up and accentuating a delicate jawline, the pale slash of a scar down one cheek. Wide green eyes round with panic. And a body disturbingly contoured in a snug jacket and a pair of hip-hugging trousers.

"Put the book down and step away from the desk," he ordered.

Her eyes flicked to the open window.

"Don't even think it." Exhaustion edged Aidan's words. His head hurt from a long day spent sparring with lawyers, bankers, and the occasional family member. And sleep beckoned with the arms of a lover. The only lover he'd had in more months than he could count.

Something he needed to remedy soon if his reaction to this woman leaned more toward lust than rage.

His eye fell upon the book she still clutched. Coincidence she chose this item instead of shinier, more tempting baubles? Aidan had long ago decided there was no such thing as coincidence. Even more disturbing, she'd actually seemed to be reading the impenetrable text, something no bookseller or scholar in Dublin had been able to do. And he should know. He'd been to them all.

The woman stiffened, her gaze falling beyond Aidan's shoulder to something or someone behind him. Her eyes widened, her mouth rounding into an "O" of astonishment.

An accomplice? Servant?

Aidan turned. A moment only for his concentration to stray, but all it took for chaos to break loose.

A book came hurtling toward Aidan's head, catching him in the arm; his pistol going off with a report to wake the dead. The recoil jarred his shoulder while smoke stung his eyes.

The woman took that moment to bolt for the window, hitching herself up with a moan of desperation. Scrabbling at the latch with nimble fingers.

Aidan sprang, catching her by the ankle. Dragging her, kicking and flailing, back into the room. "Neat little trick," he hissed.

"You fell for it, didn't you?" she snarled. "Just shows what a stupid prat you are."

A knee caught Aidan in the groin, sending agony curdling along every nerve in his lower half. He resisted the urge to drop into a fetal curl, but the gloves came off. She may have been female, but she was dangerous.

Ignoring the upbringing that taught him not to lay a hand on women, Aidan staggered her with a hard slap to the side of her head. Grabbed her by the arm, ignoring her cry of pain and white-lipped grimace. Twisted her other behind her back, all while avoiding the wriggling kicks and thwarting the clever maneuvers designed to slither out of even the tightest holds.

"Careful how you toss the insults," Aidan cautioned, guiding his captive toward a chair. Shoving her into it.

"I was being careful," she sulked, clutching her upper arm, lines grooved white in her already pale face.

With no hope of escape, the woman seemed to shrink in on herself, and what features Aidan had been able to distinguish earlier blurred and faded. What he'd taken for green eyes were blue now in this light, but a flicker of the candle and golden hazel might be more accurate. And though at first she had appeared slender, hunched shoulders broadened her frame, her face coarsening so that Aidan questioned his first impression. That or—

He blinked, and the woman's image settled like sand in a glass.

A *fith-fath*? Not exactly. This was a more subtle shifting—a clever manipulation of awareness leaving the victim doubting his own observations. An obvious asset in her chosen profession.

Aidan grabbed her roughly by the collar. Dragged her close so they stood nose to nose, trying to avoid her all-too-obvious curves. Her lavender scent so at odds with her boyish costume.

"Who are you? Answer me, or so help me god, I'll have you in front of a magistrate by dawn."

She swallowed, eyes wide, bottom lip bit between her teeth as she struggled against Aidan's grip. "Hired," she gasped.

"To do what?"

She shook her head in denial.

"I said, hired to do what?"

Still nothing.

"You leave me no choice." He dragged her toward the door, her heels scrabbling against the carpet. "What I can't get out of you, perhaps your gaolers will."

"Wait! Please!"

He slowed his steps. "Changed your mind?"

"I . . . that is . . . they might . . ."

He kept his expression purposefully bland. "A definite risk. The keepers at Newgate aren't known for their chivalry. A female on her own . . ." He shrugged.

Her face blanched white.

"So what's it to be? Answer to me or answer to them?"

If looks could kill, he'd be dead thrice over. "You," she spat.

Aidan eased his stranglehold. "I knew you'd come to see it my way. Well?"

"I was hired to find a book. A red cover. Funny picture on the front." Her words came fast and shaky.

"Who hired you? What was his name?" Aidan prodded.

"Said his name was Smith. Said to steal the book. Leave it at Saint Patrick's. That's all I know. Honestly."

He tossed her back into the seat with a muttered oath. He'd two choices. Summon a constable and write the episode off as one more instance of Dublin's pervasive crime. Or lock her in a windowless room until morning when daylight and a few snatched hours of sleep might make sense of a situation that hinted at more than simple housebreaking. A jangling unease tickled the base of his skull. Made the first choice untenable.

"Come." He yanked her back to her feet. Took grim pleasure in the bitten-off groan as she staggered against him. "I've got the perfect place to hold you for the night."

The two of them headed down into the kitchens, the passage growing narrower and dustier the farther they walked.

"Here we are." Aidan swung a creaking door wide.

The woman ducked inside, studying her surroundings. A row of shelves, empty now but for a few mismatched pieces of crockery. No windows. One door.

Still clutching her upper arm, she looked questioningly back at Aidan, those damn green eyes blinking back tears.

"You'll stay here tonight," Aidan said, hating the heavy knot settling in his chest, as if he tortured a kitten or tore the wings from a butterfly. Pushing the thought aside, he growled, "Enjoy it. It'll be the cleanest cell you'll have for a good while I expect."

Before he could change his mind, Aidan slammed the door on his prisoner, turning the latch to lock it behind him. Made it halfway down the dark passage before an idea struck him with such force that his bad leg buckled beneath him. Sent him lurching for the door like a drunkard.

A wild, stupid, ridiculous idea. It wouldn't work. Couldn't work. But once the thought had planted itself in his brain, it refused to be shaken.

If this woman knew enough about her *Other* abilities to manipulate perception, who knew what else she might be capable of? Aidan had been sure he'd seen not only interest but comprehension in her eyes as she'd flipped the pages of his father's diary. Something he would have thought impossible had he not witnessed it for himself. But there it was. A thief who could read the headache-inducing writing that had stymied all his attempts at translation for months.

Once again Aidan dragged back the lock. Felt the grudging give of the ancient metal. Pushed wide the door. And stopped dead in his tracks, the air rushing from his lungs in a gasping string of curses. Great bloody goddamn. *Womanus Exoticus* had shed her plumage.

If there was any mercy in the world, let the gods strike her to cinders right now.

Cat fumbled with her shirt to cover her nudity, the gash in her arm throbbing with every pound of her heart. Prayed for the bolt that would end the humiliating torture of his shocked stare. His curses ringing in her ears like a death knell.

Nothing. She was doomed.

He recovered almost instantly, his gaze darting from her blood-soaked shirt, now draped near her lap, to the bloody score running across her upper arm where the pistol ball had raked her with the sting of a hornet.

"You're hurt."

His statement of the obvious snapped her out of her daze. She dragged her shirt over her head as if somehow he'd unsee what had been staring him in the face moments before. If she'd had her wits about her, she'd have made a dash for the open doorway while he stood gawking. That chance had vanished. He shouldered his way into the room, his tall, rangy frame effectively blocking escape. His bronze brown eyes pinning her where she crouched with the force of a spear point.

"It's naught but a scratch," she argued.

"I've seen men sicken from lesser wounds." He knelt beside her, easing her clamped hand away from her arm. The combined scents of bay rum and cheroot smoke tickling her nose. "Let me take a look."

Was this his way of getting her to drop her guard? And once it was down, what then? She went rigid in his grasp. "I'm no man's whore."

His dark eyes crackled. "Don't add fool to your list of crimes."

Heat scalded her cheeks. Humiliation overriding her earlier sense of panic.

"Do you have a name?" His manner held a gruff kindness.

"Aye."

A long pause followed, punctuated by a rumble of laughter. "And that name would be . . . ?"

She flushed again. Toyed with the idea of giving him a false name, but gave it up as being of little worth. "It's Cat." She skimmed her gaze over his stern profile. Heavy-lidded eyes. Long, narrow nose. Chiseled, stubborn jaw. The man couldn't have looked more aristocratic if he'd been carved in marble on some Roman column. She bit her lip. Amended her answer. "Miss Catriona O'Connell."

A preoccupied grunt met her response as his hands probed the cut, sending flashes of pain radiating down her arm until even her fingers hurt. "It's not deep. A good cleaning and you should be thieving again in no time, Miss O'Connell."

The cool amusement in his voice fired her like no harsh words could. How dare he? Who was he to hold her in contempt? Did he know what it was like to feel the press of desperation and futility always at your back? To spend every moment alert? On edge? Watchful for the one second when a dropped guard would spell disaster?

This second came to mind.

She lurched to her feet. Fury lending her courage. "What do you care whether I live or die?" she shot back. "What's one less of my kind in the world to you?" Fear, embarrassment, and desperation passed like a knife through her stomach.

He unfolded from the floor to tower over her, barely ruffled by her manner. Exhaled on a deep sigh.

Cat noticed for the first time the shadows hovering beneath those impenetrable eyes and in the hollows of his cheeks, the stubble darkening his angular jaw, the ink stains purpling the fingers of his left hand.

He rubbed the back of his neck as if pondering a weighty decision and the glint of a smile lit his dark eyes. Or was that the flicker of their guttering candle?

"A fair reading of the situation thus far," he said, "though if my hunch is right, your kind and mine might not be so different."

Lazarus leaned against the packet ship's rail. Spray needled his face while the wind off the sea raked him like a claw. Left his lungs frozen, his skin flayed raw. Yet he remained topside. Spurned the claustrophobic, overcrowded hold. The suspicious and half-terrified glances from the other passengers. They sensed the truth about him, even if they didn't understand that truth. Who in their right mind would? It was beyond comprehension.

He flexed his hands. Curled them into fists.

Beyond evil.

A throat cleared behind him. "The cap'n says to tell ya if the winds keep up, we'll be makin' port with the dawn tide, sir."

So quickly? Lazarus had hazy memories of counting the crossing from Wales to Ireland in days not hours. But that had been another life. A different existence. He nodded without turning around. Heard the man's muttered oath. His scuttled retreat. He'd be in Dublin tomorrow, retrieve the book from Quigley as ordered, and return to Máelodor within a fortnight.

Scanning the horizon, a slice of midnight against the blood-water of the Irish Sea, he felt as if he could already see the tangled lanes and streets of the Irish capital, the curve of the Liffey. But it was a mirage. A memory. The Dublin he knew was long gone. Transformed through time from the hardscrabble fortress to a metropolis as grand and light-filled as any European city.

The men he knew were gone too. Wilim. Grifid. His brothers in arms. His comrades. All dead. Naught left of them but a few dusty bones. Scraps of cloth. Bits of moldy armor.

That had been all Máelodor needed.

# two

The library held little more than the desk, a sofa, a few comfortable chairs, and an avalanche of books. The combined remnants of the collections from Belfoyle and Kilronan House. Refugees from countless auctions and private sales. Those volumes too esoteric or too unimportant to entice the steady stream of buyers who'd passed through his doors since his father's death. Selling them off had been painful, his father's lifelong passion computed in pounds and pence. But it had been that very blinkered passion that had put the family's finances in this predicament. There had been no choice. Anything unentailed became fair game.

Cat O'Connell's intelligent gaze fell everywhere at once as she stepped lightly across the floor. Took in the blank walls where selected artwork had been sold off. The mantel cleared of its most expensive items, the spaces where prized family pieces once stood. The rest of Kilronan House was much the same. A sad witness to all that had been lost.

Aidan motioned to a chair near the fire. "Have a seat, Miss O'Connell."

"Cat works well enough."

She was right. It did. She walked with a feline, sinuous grace only intensified by those damn trousers. He shook his head. Thank the gods women wore gowns. Men would be reduced to blabbering idiots if they spent every day subjected to the spectacle of women's legs. The male species wasn't up to that kind of continuous temptation.

First thing on his to-do list. Something to cover those long legs and that sweet, round ass. A solution? Doubtful. She'd need a damn sack to completely disguise that lissome allure. But it would definitely help.

"You don't speak like any thief I've ever heard."

She stiffened, her chin jerking up in a thin show of defiance. "And how many thieves are you in the habit of speaking to, Lord Kilronan?"

"Fair enough, yet you haven't answered my question."

"You haven't asked me one."

He handed her the victory with a flick of his fingers. "Let me correct that at once then. Who are you, Miss O'Connell? And what were you doing in my library?"

Uncertainty flickered over her face before hardening to stubborn resolve. And from the porcelain elegance emerged the steely features of the thief who'd broken into his home and fought like a tigress. Two sides of a very interesting coin. "It's not Miss O'Connell. Not anymore. It's Cat now. And I'm whatever I have to be to survive."

"No angry father beating the streets looking for you? No brother with a blunderbuss and priest in tow?"

Her lips compressed until white lines bit into the hollows of her cheeks. "No one."

"Fair enough." He shrugged, reluctantly letting his curiosity go. A burglar who spoke and carried herself like a queen tantalized with possibilities, but he'd reached his quota of mysteries already.

"As for your library," she continued, "I was stealing." She crossed her arms. "Now are you going to send for the Watch or not?"

He bit back the retort on the tip of his tongue. Settled for, "Not."

She sat up, clearly confused, but also clearly relieved. "So if you don't plan on sending me to Newgate, I can go?"

"Not quite."

She slumped back in her chair.

The answers he sought were in the diary. They had to be. Why else would it have been hidden away and not with Father's other personal papers? And not just hidden away but warded and written in a language every scholar he'd contacted had labeled gibberish? The diary contained the keys to finally understanding the truth about his father's death. Perhaps even clues to his brother's disappearance.

And he sat across from the only person he'd found who could decipher it. Newgate would wait. Cat belonged to him now.

He drummed his fingers against his leg. Paced the rug in halting steps while he chose his words. "I've a deal to set before you."

She fidgeted with a raveled thread on her sleeve, her wary gaze never leaving his face. And just like that, jade green eyes faded to gray. Darkened to blue. Was her hair dark brown? Deep claret red? Did it curl at the nape or was that a trick of the light?

He closed his eyes. Counted to ten. Sent his answering spell floating on a whispered breath. *"Visousk distagesh."*

As usual, his stomach shifted, moving into his throat as if he'd drunk too much wine. But when he opened his eyes, her fluid features had settled back into place, her mouth hanging on a startled oath.

"How did you do that? No one's ever been able to—" She clamped her lips shut, sullenness hardening her delicate features.

"I used a *nix* to break through your charm. Crude but effective." He allowed himself a cool, satisfied smile. That particular bit of magic had been the devil to learn. But he'd done it. Not that Father had been particularly impressed. It took more than mastering a minor spell to win his praise. "But I was right." He perched on the edge of the desk, using the casual pose to mask the growing ache in his leg. "You and I have something in common."

Her mouth remained pursed in a surly line. She was going to make him fight for every inch. Very well. He'd been fighting for the last six years. Had perfected the art of banging his head against a wall. "You've heard of the *Other*?" he asked.

She gave a jerk of her chin that could have signified anything.

He continued, undaunted by her lack of response. "Men and women who bear the blood of both *Fey* and human. They range in power from the mightiest *Amhas-draoi* warrior to the fisherman whose nets are always full or the artist whose ability seems almost . . . magical. Or should I say *we* range in power. You're one of them." He let fall a pregnant pause. "As am I."

"So we're both freaks," she grumbled. "Good to know."

"Some might call us that," he replied smoothly. "Others label us witches or devils. Creatures of the dark."

She gave a mocking bark of laughter. "Fools with straw for brains and those that wouldn't know one of the *Fey* unless it tipped its hat to them and introduced itself."

He raised a brow. "So you do know what I'm talking about. Good. That makes things easier." Leaning back, he plucked the diary from the desktop behind him. Opening it to a random page, he crossed to where she sat, hunched and waiting. Shoved the book into her hands. "Read it."

She jumped; her eyes passing over the writing. "I told you, I can't." She tried handing it back, but he'd already walked around to the other side of the desk.

"And most people believe your story, don't they?"

She shrugged, the diary lying open in her lap.

"I'm not most people, Miss O'Connell. I think you can read it. In fact, I bet you can read just about anything I put in front of you." He motioned to the surrounding shelves. "Any book in any language."

She bit her lip, her gaze and her hands moving over the page as if she could pull the words out by touch. Her arched brows drew into a frown of concentration, her mouth silently forming each sound. She looked up. "It's just an old children's story. A fable. I heard it often at"— she swallowed whatever she'd been about to say—"at home. Growing up, I mean."

A rush of excitement cruised along his skin like a static charge. He exhaled slowly to calm the wild hope. "I'm prepared to forgive your crimes, and more than that, I'll hire you. You'll have a place to stay. Meals." He eyed her outfit, trying not to envision what lay beneath. Hard to do since he'd seen what lay beneath. "Proper clothes."

She flushed. "And what would I have to do for this largesse? You've already said I'm not fit for your highbred self." Her gaze remained fixed and unwavering.

Noting the trim athlete's body and the delicate oval of her face, he'd have revised his opinion if he didn't think that would scare her faster than anything else. If he needed talents of a carnal nature—and by his disturbing reactions tonight, he did—he'd join Jack on one of his nightly romps. His cousin had a knack for collecting women of a certain sort. A devil-may-care style women found irresistible and men sought to copy.

He'd possessed that same self-confident bravado once.

A lifetime ago.

He ran a hand down his face, suddenly drained of energy. Frustrated. Despondent.

"All you have to do is translate this one book. From beginning to end."

"I do this," she spoke slowly as if mulling the idea over, "and you'll not turn me in to the Watch for thieving?"

"That's right."

She traced the cover's faded design with the tip of one finger. Looked up, suddenly all business. "And what's to keep me from leaving any time I choose? Are you going to chain me to a desk in my room?"

"No, you'll be free to go where you will within the house or garden. I'll trust to your honor to keep you here."

She gave a derisive snort as if he'd just confirmed her opinion of his gullibility. But really, what else could he do? He wasn't a gaoler. He'd made the offer. Sweetened the deal. She'd either take him up on it. Or she wouldn't.

"Well, Cat?" He tried to keep the keenness from his voice. Best she not know his desperation. But since the idea had first struck, it had dug its roots deep into him. Her refusal would chop him off at the knees.

She glanced down at the closed book and back up.

No need for the *nix* this time. Her gaze met him square on and unflinching, jade green eyes slashed with shards of lightning. "I must be mad, but you've got yourself a deal, Kilronan."

Cat lay on top of the covers, watching the dance of the flames in the hearth. Fighting sleep as she waited until the only sounds she heard from beyond her door were the creak of a settling floorboard and the Watch calling the hour.

If Kilronan thought she'd be bought by some paltry clothes and a warm fire, he'd been much mistaken. She was hardly a beggar off the street, accepting any scrap to fall her way. Between her and Geordie, they made a good living. And if it didn't match the luxuries she'd lost, it wasn't the workhouse squalor or the cheek-by-jowl tenement living of her first desperate months alone.

And as for Geordie, he'd be worried at her continued absence. Best to get back and warn him the job was a bust. Swinging her legs to the floor, she tugged her jacket into place. Slid her feet into her boots. Chafed her hands in nervous anticipation before taking a deep, fortifying breath.

And heard the death rattle click of a key in the lock.

She froze, knowing no amount of shouting or banging would bring Kilronan back to let her out.

She was well and truly caught.

A flare of light and a stage whisper punctuated by muffled laughter dragged him back to consciousness. Had Jack returned already? Or had Aidan slept longer than he'd thought? It felt like mere minutes since his head had touched the pillow.

"Are you awake, coz?" The sour, claret-coated question turned Aidan's empty stomach.

He thought about feigning sleep in hopes his tormentor would give up and shuffle off to bed. But the space behind his eyelids burned bright red, followed by heat enough to scorch his nose hairs as the lit candle wavered inches from his face. If he didn't respond, he'd not put it past the drunken fool to set him on fire.

He opened his eyes. "I am now. What do you want?"

Jack's hovering countenance broke into a snozzled smile. "Missed you tonight. Barbara Osborne attended. Asked after you."

"Did she?"

"If you're not careful, Aido, old man, you'll lose your chance at her. Not to mention that enticing marriage portion."

Aidan drew the covers over his head. Jack sober and nagging was bad enough. Jack drunk and nagging was more than he could bear. "It won't matter if Sir Humphrey doesn't give his consent. He thinks I'm only after her money."

"And aren't you?" Jack's voice came muffled, but come it did. "With a bit of the old Aidan Douglas persuasion, her father's objections could be a thing of the past."

"Ruin her, you mean?"

"I prefer to call it introducing her to the joys that await."

Aidan snorted into the quilts, almost suffocating beneath the heavy layers. "Why are we having this conversation again?" he mumbled, emerging long enough to send his cousin a dirty look.

Jack shrugged. "Not tired yet." Changing tack, he continued, "Heard you've had a bit of excitement here tonight. Sorry I missed it." He beamed down at Aidan with glazed eyes and a stupid smile. "A woman. I heard she's still here." As if Cat might be hiding beneath the covers, he made a quick scan of the bed.

Aidan squirmed with the memory of his last and very vivid dream, blinking away a pair of inviting green eyes and a taut, quicksilver body.

Dragging himself up against the headboard, he plowed a hand through his hair, knowing he'd never rid himself of his drunken cousin if he didn't come clean. "Miss O'Connell has been hired to do some translation work for me. I've decided it's best if she remain here for the time being."

"Translation work. Good one." Jack's brows waggled in appreciation. "I'll have to remember that."

It was like talking to a rambunctious sheepdog. Aidan wished for the thousandth time he'd not given in to a moment's madness and invited his cousin to visit Kilronan House. That had been two years ago, Jack managing to turn a fortnight's stay into a permanent posting.

He straightened. "Right. Well, see you in the morning, coz." He started for the door, far too easily satisfied with the bullshit story for Aidan's peace of mind. He'd expected quizzing. A cousinly interrogation peppered with snide innuendo. Even a drunken harangue. This instant acceptance was completely out of character.

The reason struck him with the force of a backhand. He kicked himself out of his covers. Lurched across the room. Shoulder slammed the door closed before Jack could depart. "Miss O'Connell's under my protection. Off limits. End of story. Do you understand?"

Jack glowered, holding his fingers, the tips of which had come close to being crushed by the heavy door. "I just wanted to introduce myself. She probably doesn't realize she's staying with two of the most sought-after bachelors in Dublin."

"Oh? Invited guests in, have you?" Aidan couldn't resist.

"Touché." A smile quirked Jack's lips, but the bullish jut of his chin told Aidan he wouldn't be put off. "Heard you caught the chit trying to make off with Douglas heirlooms. Not exactly a Trinity scholar in languages. Come, Aidan. I'm not stupid."

"She's *Other*." There. Let him chew on that one. "And as I said before, off limits."

Jack scraped his knuckles over his chin as he digested this bit of news. "Well, that changes the outlook slightly. So she's an *Other* chit. Really, Aidan what are you trying to do? Have us murdered in our beds?"

"She's a thief, not a murderess. And right now she's neither. She's in my employ."

"You sure she didn't land you a crack to the skull?" Jack asked, worry beginning to cloud his otherwise glassy gaze.

Aidan started to defend himself, but arguing would only prolong the conversation. And right now, he needed sleep more than understanding. "Let me worry about her. You just forget she's even here."

Jack shot him a doubtful look, but his offhand nod seemed genuine. "Right. Well, I'll leave you to her then." He headed down the corridor with the hangdog air of someone losing his buzz, pausing only to focus his thoughtful gaze back on Aidan. "She must be something, to drag you out of your shell."

Aidan closed the door, his hand white knuckling the knob, his bowed head pressed against the wood. Not a shell.

A prison.

But if he'd judged correctly, Cat O'Connell held the key.

# three

Shoving aside the hated accounts ledger, Aidan took a swallow of tea and grimaced. Stone cold.

Out of habit, he'd risen at dawn. Spent the past hours bent over the labyrinthine convolutions of his financial picture. Only in the last year had his parsimony paid off. His revenues finally eclipsing the pile of inherited debt. But he still didn't take anything for granted. As surely as the wealth accumulated, it could drain away.

An advantageous marriage to a woman of birth and fortune would put the final stamp on six years of hard-fought struggle. Barbara Osborne fit very nicely into that category. Sir Humphrey blustered at his only daughter tossing away her chances on an impoverished earl whose family had for generations possessed a reputation for being not quite *bon ton*. But a title, no matter how tarnished, was still a title, and a baron couldn't be too picky where a countess's coronet stood in play.

On the other hand, Aidan couldn't assume her partiality.

A note and flowers sent with his regrets at being otherwise occupied the previous evening would go a long way to assuring his continued place in her affections. Women loved that sort of thing. Coming to a decision, he pulled a piece of stationery out of his top drawer. Chewed the tip of his pen as he pondered what to write.

A discreet cough broke into his reflections.

Cat O'Connell wavered upon the threshold like a flame. Her skin shone pale as marble, smooth black hair framing her narrow face and a waif-thin slenderness masking what he knew from painful experience was a wiry tenacity.

In a borrowed gown whose bodice had been hastily pinned, Cat looked like a child playing dress up in her mother's clothes. But not like any child he'd ever known. Hauteur sparked along her limbs. Flashed in her lightning-sharded green eyes like a challenge.

He pushed aside the unfinished note as if he could push away his uncomfortable reaction to her appearance. Hid his momentary discomfort in another swift glance at the clock. "I'd wondered if you'd thought better of our agreement."

She saw the track of his gaze. "I overslept," she offered in a grudging tone that dared him to argue.

He noted the faint smudging beneath her wide, doelike eyes, the chalky undertone to her milky flesh. Did she think he scolded over a few minutes? He'd not begrudge anyone a dreamless night. He'd had too few of them himself over the years. But perhaps with Cat's help he'd find an answer to the questions that had long plagued his sleep.

He glanced at his father's diary brooding at the edge of his desk. What had his father worked so hard to keep hidden? Clearly something of import. Why else would

Cat have been sent here to steal it? Two reasons. Someone wanted to read it for himself. Or didn't want it read at all. "Have you eaten?" he asked.

"A bite in the kitchen." A mischievous glint lit her eyes. "The servants watched every clack of my jaw. I think they expected me to swipe the silver if they so much as blinked."

He laughed, the sound loud in the solemn tomb of a room. "And did you?"

A shutter came down over her face, the light doused. "I don't double-cross, Kilronan. Nor do I go back on my word."

Was that an accusation? A veiled response to her locked door? He'd caught her in the act of theft. She could hardly complain if his trust was lacking. "You only vowed to stay and help me with the book. Robbing me blind while you did so was never part of our bargain."

She blinked, chewing on her bottom lip. A mannerism he'd grown to know in just the few hours they'd spent in each other's company. Then, with movements unconsciously provocative, she reached into the gaping bodice of her green muslin. Pulled forth one teaspoon. Placed it on the desk before him. Squared it up so its bowl pointed at him like an arrow.

"Anything else residing in there? The rest of the set? The pot, perhaps?"

Downswept lashes hid her eyes, giving him no hint of her thoughts. "I've room for it, I suppose. But no. There's naught but me left in here."

Had he been the youthful scoundrel who'd played London like a game he'd have teased her with flirtatious innuendo. Had he been the undisciplined rogue who'd hopped from scrape to scrape and bed to bed with a youthful exuberance his older self both scorned and envied, he'd have asked her with sly gallantry to prove her innocence.

His skin prickled as if too tight for his bones and a sudden heat raised a sheen of sweat across his shoulders. The knotted muscles of his leg throbbed with every push of blood from his heart.

He did neither of those things. Feeling as ancient as the volumes surrounding him, he rose. Dusted the breakfast crumbs from his breeches. Ushered Cat to a chair. And handed her the diary.

Cat tried not to dwell on the humiliating withdrawal of the pilfered teaspoon from her bodice. Nor on the inexplicable urge that had her confessing to the crime almost before she'd been accused. What had she been thinking to rummage about in there as if panning for gold? Had she been testing his honor? Had he been testing hers? And who'd come out the winner?

It had been such a minuscule event, but for some reason, it solidified the arrangement between them like a contract.

"Why is knowing what's in this book so important?" she asked. *That you would stoop to bartering with a thief,* hanging unspoken between them.

Kilronan plowed a hand through his thatch of auburn hair, and Cat found herself transfixed by the tanned face beneath the arching brows, the austere, angular features. He held himself with all the bearing of one born to privilege and power. Confident. At ease in his own skin. Shoulders erect. Eyes piercing.

Something that even with all his wealth Jeremy had never been able to achieve.

Only Kilronan's plain coat and leather breeches, the

smell of cheroot smoke clinging to the folds of his clothes, and the shrewdness in his keen gaze gave a hint there might be more to this earl than the typical wastrel playboy who spent his days in extravagant, aristocratic boredom. His nights between the legs of his latest mistress.

A frisson of excitement or foreboding danced across her flesh, and she felt as if she'd stumbled from danger into catastrophe.

"Why? The book belonged to my father," he answered. "I found it among his things after——" He crossed to the window, twitching the curtain aside to scan the street. Turned back. "My father was murdered, Cat. Six years ago by members of the *Amhas-draoi*. You've heard of them?"

"Warriors of Scathach. Guardians of the divide." Cat had even seen one once, albeit from a distance. A giant of a man with the dense muscles of a fighter and a gaze like a razor. He'd radiated violence and magic in equal measure. "What did the last earl do to have the *Amhas-draoi* after him?"

Kilronan paced the room with a strange, half-halting gait as if an invisible wire stretched from his spine down his leg. But at her question, he pulled up short. "Do?" He paused as if deciding how best to answer her.

She tilted her head in question, but he didn't finish his thought. Instead, pulling a cheroot from his pocket, he lit it from the hearth fire. Inhaled on a long, slow drag before tossing the whole into the grate. Straightening, he lost the stony implacability, but a grim light still crouched in the corners of his eyes. "I lost everything the night my father was murdered."

"Except a title. Property. Rents——"

"Cold comfort while I watched my family splinter

before my eyes," he snarled, though his anger seemed directed inward rather than at her.

Did he notice the nervous tapping of his fingers against his thigh? Or was it habit? Was his limp due to an old injury or a recent accident? She wished she dared ask, but the hard-edged lines of his face forestalled questions. He may have used the carrot up to now, but she didn't doubt he'd apply the stick if needed.

She'd decided in the long, empty hours of last night to play along until she found an opportunity to run. So far, despite Kilronan's assurances to the contrary, she'd been well watched if not outright guarded. But she'd be ready when the time came. And if she didn't return to Geordie's with the diary, at least she'd have her freedom.

"Your attempted theft only confirms what I've suspected all along. The diary is the key to unraveling what happened. And why," he continued.

He leaned against the desk, arms crossed over his chest. His gaze settled on her with a look that could curdle milk. The ruthless nobleman of last night. Imposing. No-nonsense. All together too much in control. She felt the sharpness of his gaze straight to her center. And again, that same jolt of electricity jumped through her. Roused long-dormant sensations she'd thought buried in the same grave as her infant son.

"Someone hired you, Cat. He'll wonder what's happened when you don't show up. And likely come looking for answers. Is he someone I should fear?"

She hunched her shoulders, pinpricks of nervousness needling her skin.

Kilronan bore the toughness of a fighter in his lean, muscled height. His rangy, rough-shouldered arrogance.

His capable, work-scarred hands. But the light of humanity still danced in his brown eyes. The same could not be said of the heavy-jowled arch rogue she'd seen talking to Geordie. What would he do when he came to collect his prize and found Geordie laid up with a bad sprain and no diary?

She shivered, for the first time afraid of what freedom might mean. "I'd fear him if I were you."

The man slopped into the breakfast parlor in a loose banyan and trousers, the glow of bare chest glinting from his open collar. Under normal circumstances, she supposed he'd be handsome in a sleek, practiced way. But not this afternoon. Chin peppered with stubble, face hangover gray.

A smile broke over his carved features. "So I wasn't dreaming."

She self-consciously straightened in her chair, wishing Kilronan was here to intercede. And wasn't that ironic? The man had held a gun on her, locked her in a cellar, threatened her with prison, and now she saw him as a protector.

"You must be Aidan's"—he raked her with an appraising stare from the top of her head to the tips of her toes, the smile never leaving his face—"translator." Dropping into a chair, he poured a cup of tea. Held it in both hands, inhaling the steam as if it were the elixir of life. "Though if Miss Osborne hears . . ." He shook his head in some private regret. "You don't look like a resident of the Liberties. What's your story?"

"I could be asking you the same question."

Again the flash of white teeth in a smile that could boil water. He pulled himself to his feet. Sketched her a ballroom bow. "Mr. Jack O'Gara. I live here on my good cousin's sufferance. So what's Aidan got you translating? Some moldy tome unearthed out of his father's library?"

Cat couldn't be sure about O'Gara. A cousin to the earl, it stood to reason he shared his bloodlines and his power. But if he didn't, and Cat let a long-held secret out of the bag—

She picked her words carefully. "You mock the earl's scholarly endeavors?"

"No, I despair of his sanity." His benign expression hardened. From lapdog to wolf in the blink of an eye. She'd have to be careful around him. He might act the part of jester, but if she wasn't mistaken, that was exactly what it was. An act.

"Aidan's relentless," he continued. "He searches for answers, but I've found answers always come with strings attached. And even the ones you think you want aren't always the best for your health."

Cat twisted her napkin through her fingers before catching O'Gara's eye upon her. With deliberate slowness, she placed the napkin on the table. Smoothed it out. "I'm only a translator. Not Kilronan's conscience. Mayhap you should be talking to him."

He bared his teeth in a grim smile that never reached his eyes. "What makes you think I haven't?"

Pushing a curl behind her ear, Cat bent her attention to the diary. Opened it to the flyleaf where the cover's same crescent and broken arrow swooped across the spotted vellum. Tips of bold writing smudged the bottom edge, but there was no telling what it said. Someone had ripped out half of the page. She thumbed to the next.

"Well?" Kilronan's excitement churned the air like an ill wind.

She fought to ignore his eyes fixed upon her. The blunt-fingered, calloused hands clenching the back of a chair. The strength of his lean, muscled body as it hovered, waiting on her words as if anticipating an oracular event.

Instead she forced her concentration back on the strange swirl and slice of the language before her.

Cat knew Latin. Read Greek. French. Spanish. Italian. German. It had always been this way. Her father had been proud his *Other* blood flowed in his offspring. Her mother, less enthusiastic. And after her father's death, Cat had been charged never to flaunt her abilities for fear of what people might say.

Still, this language wasn't like any she'd ever seen. It moved and flowed like water, the bold writing like the chop of waves, a splash of ink from time to time drawing her eye away, the words curling and eddying into new images and new thoughts by the time she'd refocused.

She traced the line of the writer's pen as a way to train her mind. One word at a time. One sentence at a time. Letting the language crystallize in her mind. Harden into meaning. Her head ached with the strain of translation, the muscles of her neck and shoulders snarling into angry knots. *"The word of Ercaidu is like the tongue of the serpent. Forked and flickering. The seeker of his knowledge must bear its weight. Must put aside the life he has known and become one with Ercaidu. As like him as makes no difference to the pure bloods."*

"What the hell's that supposed to mean? And who is Ercaidu?" Kilronan interrupted, jolting Cat out of the moment. She squinted, but the words curved and shifted. Ran like rain through a brain scratchy and tight.

She slammed the diary closed. "I don't know. I didn't write it. But it doesn't sound pleasant. Not if you have to walk about with a forked tongue."

Kilronan pulled up a chair. Straddled it, resting his arms along the back. The relaxed pose at odds with a body tense with anticipation. His implacable gaze locked on hers. Again came that quicksilver slide of emotion. What was it about this man that he sparked such an answering sensation deep within her? She clamped down on the slow heat seeping up through the hard, cold layers of her suspicion. Hadn't she learned anything from her mistake with Jeremy?

"Read on. What else does it say?"

Scattered by the blunt force of Kilronan's stare and her reaction to it, she stumbled to find her place. Scanned the next few lines, though it cost her in a renewal of the pounding in her head. This time the text spoke of a lord named Toth. The breadth of his power. The quickness of his temper.

After he'd lopped off his tenth head, Cat blinked. Tearing her eyes from the page with great effort. She rubbed her temples, hoping to stop the bass drum behind her eyes. "Sounds a horrid sort of monster to me. Do you think he actually ate the poor man's entrails?"

Kilronan's mouth twitched. "Wouldn't doubt it. Though sounds as if the fellow deserved it. Slaking his thirst with rivers of blood and smiting his enemies with that lightning strike stare of his. Poor old Toth may have just come to the end of his patience."

Cat pursed her lips over a nervous laugh. What a nonsensical sort of conversation to be having here in this dusty, cloud-shrouded room. But for a moment as she'd been reading, the old stories had come alive. She'd seen Toth swinging his great axe. Seen his enemies struggling to flee as he cleaved his way through their falling bodies, gore streaking him like war paint.

She'd looked upon a face that for the space of two heartbeats had been the grim, blood-soaked visage of Kilronan.

"No excuses. You either have the Kilronan diary or you don't." Lazarus's words cut through the babbled justifications and finger pointing like a scythe.

Immediately silence reigned as the men looked to one another before glancing fearfully, first at the arsenal strapped to his waist, then up into his face, purposefully empty of expression.

Lazarus settled his gaze on the leader. His hand twitched with murderous intent, but he concentrated on the beat of his heart. Let the slow expand and contract of his lungs bring him back from the brutal edge of no return. "What went wrong?"

"I had it in my shop. In my hands," Quigley whined. "But Lord Kilronan wouldn't give it up. Not even when I suggested he let me borrow it in order to find him a translator."

Lazarus must have shown his confusion, because Quigley hurried on with his explanation. "The old earl must have wanted to keep the contents of his diary safe from prying eyes. He wrote it in a language I've never seen."

"So it's useless to Kilronan," Lazarus surmised.

"Precisely." Quigley smiled, but it was an anxious, half-hearted attempt not returned by Lazarus. "Mr. Smith has assured me he'll obtain the diary. Haven't you, Mr. Smith?" Quigley said, drawing attention off himself and on to the twitchy bear of a man loitering by the door.

Lazarus speared Smith with a look. "Does he speak truth?"

Smith broke off scratching the stretch of grimy waistcoat encasing his midsection with a startled grunt and an uneasy shifting of his eyes. "Aye," he grumbled. "I'll get your book. But then I want what's owed me. Payment in full. Quigley's promised . . . a hundred quid."

"I . . . I . . . never—" stammered Quigley.

"Done," Lazarus interrupted, already tired of this conversation. "Quigley will pay."

The bookseller gave a mew of protest, instantly quelled by a glance from Lazarus.

Smith's brows drew into a beetle black frown as if he realized he'd underpriced his services. But he recovered his composure with a nervous jerk of his head. A quick clearing of his throat. "Right, then, if you're through with us, me and mine will be off to get that diary for ya."

"Go," he ground out.

"And when I retrieve the book, I'll be findin' ya here?" Smith asked.

Lazarus's reply came as a chilling whisper. "Or I'll find you."

# four

Aidan leaned back in his chair. Stared up at the portrait over the library mantel. A pastoral setting, the west fa-çade of Belfoyle in the background. Mother with impish Brendan, one hand resting on her shoulder, his other upon the shaggy head of the family hound. Sabrina, already a little lady at four, leaning against Mother's skirts. And he and Father side by side. The earl and his heir. Both tall. Both confident. None gazing upon the domestic scene would ever suppose how great a distance truly separated them.

They had been a young family at the height of their glory. Strong. Powerful.

Their descent had been precipitate.

A light rap upon the door drew him back from his melancholia. "Yes, Mrs. Flanagan?"

The housekeeper shifted uncomfortably, guilt-ridden dismay written all over her. "It's about that girl, milord. She's gone."

Aidan lurched to his feet, his gaze automatically falling on the diary. "Damn it—"

Her face crumpled. "It's my fault, milord, I know. I left her alone for only a moment. When I returned to the kitchen, she'd bolted."

"Have you checked the garden? Her bedchamber?"

"I beat the bushes, milord. Scoured every room in the house, but it's no use. She's slunk back to whatever sewer she crawled out of."

Her tone of voice said plainly—*What did you expect from a slum doxy out of the Liberties? We're just lucky we weren't murdered in our beds.*

"Should I call a constable?" the housekeeper asked.

His gaze moved from the diary back to the portrait, the ghosts of his broken family awaiting his decision. Cat could read the journal. So far, the only person he'd found with that ability. He refused to let her escape stymie his efforts.

He shrugged into his coat. Brushed past Mrs. Flanagan on his way out the door. "No. I'll bring her back."

"You, milord? How on earth will you find her?"

He bared his teeth in imitation of a smile. "Search house by goddamned house if I have to."

Cat slipped through the filthy back lanes and mud strewn alleys of Saint Patrick's deanery on an unerring course. She'd done it. Slid into the anonymity of the city to be swallowed unseen.

She shoved her hands deeper into her jacket pockets. Kilronan would never find her. Probably wouldn't even look. For some reason that thought didn't make her feel better. In fact, it made her feel worse. And how ridiculous was that? Kilronan didn't care about Cat O'Connell. He only cared about his damned diary. He was a user. Like Jeremy. Like her stepfather. Like all men with their wily double talk and false promises. All men but Geordie.

He'd be worried sick, wondering what had happened to her. Her first real friend in the terrifying new world she'd fallen into, he'd sheltered her in those delirious weeks when she'd been out of her head with grief and fear. Coached her in the thievery that kept food on the table and a roof over their heads. Two misfits against the world, he'd told her more than once.

He'd be disappointed at the loss of the diary's income—the promised payment had been outrageously extravagant. But Geordie had a nonchalant outlook on life—take it as you find it. To be too up or too down meant you cared too much. Had invested too much of yourself. He'd tried instilling that same casual disregard in Cat. And to some extent succeeded. Cat wouldn't make the same mistakes again. There would not be another Jeremy to destroy her a second time.

Fending off the overfriendly hands of a bearded man in bloody apron and rolled shirtsleeves, she rounded the corner onto Crooked Dog Lane. Clambered up the last alleyway, the boards laid across the mud bowing beneath her feet. Took the stairs two at a time.

"Geordie? I'm back," she shouted. "It's me. Cat."

No answer.

She slowed her steps, a slithering apprehension curling up her spine. "Geordie?" Her voice came low and uneasy.

Reaching the landing, she pushed the door wide.

"Cat! Run!"

Geordie's warning shattered the unnatural stillness, leaving Cat but a moment to take in the scene—the glowering features of Smith and another man, Geordie lying prone on the rug, his undersized, misshapen body no match for their bearlike strength.

"Go!" he screamed again just before a meaty fist struck him a knockout blow to the side of the head.

Cat spun on her heel, tearing back down the stairs. The heavy booted feet of her pursuers matching beat for beat the pound of her terrified heart. She swallowed back the panic coating her throat like bile. Making her yearn for the first time in years for the claustrophobic security of her stepfather's town house in Ely Place.

Smith's threats echoed off the walls of the narrow, crooked passage. Dogged her heels. Slipping, she fell to her knees, allowing them to gain ground. She scrambled back to her feet, expecting any moment for a hand to clutch her collar. Snake around her neck.

Even as she ran she conjured the confusion of the *spyrel visouth*. Used the spell to disguise her hair. Her clothes. Prayed it would be enough to lose herself among the throngs clogging the streets.

She tore back onto Canon Street. Doubled back down a covered close, ducking laundry lines and dodging market stalls. A stitch cramped her side, and blisters already stung from her ill-fitting boots.

And then they were there. One in front. One behind. Closing the gap from either direction.

What had she gotten herself into? What was so blasted important about that damn book? And where was Kilronan with his bloody great pistol now?

Where the hell was she? Saint Patrick's Cathedral, she'd said. Cat had been instructed to leave the diary at the cathedral, the epicenter of his search. He'd crisscrossed the streets leading away in every direction. Tramped up and down for hours, braving suspicious glances and outright hostility. Only boneheaded stubbornness kept him searching when every other instinct told him to give up and go home. He'd found one person who could read the diary, he could find another. Unfortunately a louder voice chided that, in point of fact, Cat had found him.

He kept at it.

Tobacconist. Warehouse. Knacker's yard. Tenement. Tenement. Stables. Alehouse. All achingly familiar. They ought to be. He'd passed them at least four times already.

Bloody Patrick bloody Street again.

Once more he strolled up the street, his gaze passing over the pinched, desperate faces. Hoping to recognize Cat's dark hair and clever features. Hoping she wasn't using the *glamorie*'s enchantment to hide in plain view. On a whim, he whispered the *nix*. The burst of released mage energy was like a struck note at the base of his brain, the scream that followed dropping him into a flat run.

He'd found her.

It must be how a snake felt shedding its skin. Exposed. Defenseless. With a jolt like a body-wide static shock, Cat's blurred, indistinct features dissolved. So too did Smith's final hesitation. The man lunged for her, his burly fist clutching air where she'd been only a moment before. He cursed but kept his patience. His accomplice had her cut off. She'd nowhere to run, and they all knew it.

Cat's frantic gaze took in the suddenly empty alley, the dead end stairs, the locked doors.

"Look at the pretty bit, Neddie. What do you think she looks like out of them clothes?" Smith jeered. "You and your partner thinkin' we're a couple of gulls? We showed him we meant business. Now it's your turn unless you hand over that book."

*Oh gods. Geordie. Be all right. Please, be all right.*

"I haven't got it," she stammered.

Smith stepped forward, flashing a knife. "No more tricks, girl. The book. Now."

Cat took a step back for every ominous movement made in her direction. "I tried. I did. It wasn't any use. Lord Kilronan had the place guarded. Tighter than a tick."

"Our employer isn't wantin' excuses. He's wantin' the Kilronan diary. Now."

"And who would your employer be?" From the shadows to her left came a familiar deep voice, dripping with patrician arrogance and the calm assurance of easy authority.

Cat's puddling relief came tempered with butterfly nervousness. Not exactly a rescue. More like exchanging one pursuer for another.

Smith's eyes traveled between Cat and Kilronan as if weighing this new development. "This isn't any of your concern. Just a cheating street rat what needs to be taught a lesson."

Kilronan stepped around Cat and into the field of battle, his eyes never straying from the weapon-wielding attacker as if he could sway him with the power of his gaze alone. "I'll ask you once again, who wants the diary?"

Understanding finally lit Smith's face. "Kilronan," he spat.

The earl inclined his head. "Neither the diary nor the girl are your concern any longer."

"The hell they aren't." Smith lunged, his knife coming within inches of Kilronan's ribs.

Kilronan answered with a quick dance sideways and a follow-up fist to the jaw.

"Neddie! Get him from behind!" Smith hollered between dodging feints.

The earl closed in, clamping down on Smith's weapon hand, and with a quick twist tore the dagger free. It spun with a clang across the alleyway.

Smith sought to dive for the loose blade, but Kilronan punished him with a fist to the jaw before swaying under a blow to his stomach. Another to his ribs. He responded with a move that had Smith back on his heels. At least for the moment.

What Kilronan possessed in training and finesse, Smith made up for in street fighter cunning. Fists. Feet. Teeth. He used them all to hold the earl at bay while Neddie advanced, murder in his piggy eyes. The deciding factor in this up-to-now evenly matched life-and-death struggle.

Cat jumped into the fray. Caught Neddie's arm to drag him away from the pair still locked in a tit-for-tat rain of blows.

He shrugged her off with the ease of swatting away a fly. Followed it up with an open-handed slap knocking her flat into the alley's quagmire, ears ringing.

"Kilronan. Watch out!" she squawked, spitting blood.

The earl spun and ducked just as Neddie sought to stab him in the neck, but his feet slid from under him, his body falling sideways into a stack of boxes.

Neddie and Smith took the opportunity to end it, but it was Kilronan who struck first.

The spell he uttered came fast and furious. A vicious swathe of mage energy catching even Cat in its riptide. She clutched her stomach, her breakfast in her throat while

Smith and Neddie doubled over, the sour odor of fear and then vomit rising from their grubby clothes, their eyes rolling to spear the earl with twin gazes of hate and horror.

"Holy Mary, Joseph, and John. 'E's a devil, he is," Smith spat. "Workin' Satan's evil."

Climbing to his feet, Kilronan snatched her hand. Dragged her away, ignoring the curses following them up the alley. They made it as far as the next doorway before Kilronan swayed, his body convulsing in a jerk of broken magic that had him stumbling against the frame.

"Damn, that's done it," he muttered as the spell dissolved and the men recovered.

Smith uncurled, pounding toward them. Neddie close behind.

They bulled into Kilronan, dropping him to his knees. Raining blows and kicks until the earl could do little but suffer through the attack. Curling his body into a protective ball. Protecting his kidneys. His head.

Cat shouted. Tried pulling them off, but they smacked her aside, their original purpose forgotten amid their need to destroy what they didn't understand.

Frantically she searched the alley for a weapon—a brick, a broken piece of wood, anything.

There.

In the doorway they'd only just passed.

A gleam of metal. A bent wooden handle.

Smith's knife.

Cat dove. Grabbed the blade up, holding it before her as if it might bite. Shouted to be heard over the curses and the sickening thud of fists on flesh. "Get off him!"

They paused as she took a reckless step into the fray. Pricked Neddie in the ribs.

"Now," she hissed.

His eye fell to the knife, and he gave a rough snarl of laughter. Moved to wrestle it from her hand.

She lashed out with a wild thrust that bit deep into his arm. Followed it up with another that grazed his ribs as he yelped, backing out of range.

Smith, too, had abandoned his thrashing of Kilronan and now watched her with a leery eye. "Careful, bitch, afore ya hurt yourself."

"Your concern's touching." She followed Smith's movements while trying to keep one eye on Neddie.

Smith lunged while Neddie sought to attack from behind. She sliced Smith hard on his wrist, squirming at the feel of his flesh parting and crunching under her cut. He screamed, yanking his arm away.

Neddie never reached her.

Kilronan had fumbled himself up onto his feet and crushed Neddie a blow to his side, punching the wind out of the man. Sending him reeling.

Straightening, he faced the men down. Eyes feral bright in a face carved of stone. "Who sent you?"

Neddie, clutching his side, splashed back up the alley while Smith, a hand clamped on his bloodied wrist, wavered. Cast Kilronan and then Cat a long, fuming look. Plunged past them to fade into the market crowds.

Cat's limbs shook, a woozy feeling in the pit of her stomach. Though because of the blow from Neddie or because of the man standing stiff with fury before her, she couldn't say.

"I can explain—" she began, the sheepish pleading sounding ridiculous to her own ears. What could she explain? The naive, romantic notions that had triggered her avalanche fall from a life of respectability? The blood and the pain and the terror as her child entered the world? The crushing weight of grief as he departed?

His gaze flicked over her, and she knew none of it would matter to him. He would judge her as the others had. Nothing she said in response would matter.

"Let's go," he said.

She straightened in surprise. "But . . . Geordie . . . he . . ."

He blinked, pain replacing the impenetrable, bronze brown stare. Pushed aside his coat. Touched a hand to the spreading stain across his waistcoat, his fingers coming away tipped in red. "Save your arguments, Cat, unless you wish to carry me back to Henry Street."

"Oh gods," she squeaked.

"My thoughts exactly," he said, his voice unsteady. Almost surprised. "I don't feel so well."

Cat caught him before he stumbled, his weight almost burying her. His face white, his breathing shallow and rapid. She glanced over her shoulder. Geordie was just a few streets away. Had those men . . . had Geordie . . . should she. . . .

"Cat?"

Biting her lip, she turned back. "You're going to be all right. I'll get you home, Kilronan," she murmured as if she spoke to a child.

For a moment, clarity sharpened his unfocused gaze, and a smile twitched the corner of his mouth. "Aidan works well enough."

# five

Blake fussed around Aidan like an old woman, murmurings of infection and pending death an incessant melody to the bass line throbbing in his side. To be fair, his valet was more at home starching cravats and polishing boots, but his whimpering was beginning to grate.

"Stop your god-awful weeping, and send for the bloody surgeon," Aidan finally barked.

Blake obeyed, relief at being cast out of the sickroom evident in his rapid withdrawal.

Aidan shifted, wincing against the agony slashing up his rib cage. Tears springing to his eyes. "Great bloody goddamn," he swore through clenched teeth. "I hope you appreciate this. It hurts like the very devil."

Cat started with a guilty flush from where she'd been hovering by the doorway, trying to be invisible. "I didn't think—"

"I heard you slink in? I'm starting to sense your presence. Like an approaching thunderstorm." He touched a tentative hand to the shiner adorning his right eye, compliments of Smith's well-aimed shoe. "Next time I'll step back and let the lightning strike someone else."

She crossed her arms in a huff. "I saved your life, thank you very much."

"Yes, but only after I saved yours."

Her chin came up, her jaw thrust forward. "Your spell casting almost got us both killed."

She had a point, but damned if he'd admit it. He returned fire. "Well, I wouldn't have had to cast a spell if you hadn't run away."

Her scar stood out white against the creeping stain of her cheeks, her eyes hot as green fire. No telling what thoughts flitted behind that belligerent mask. Finally, "I didn't ask you to come after me."

"We had a deal."

"There's a difference between a deal and a threat." She looked away. Turned back, her face rigid with fury and something else . . . something resembling startled bewilderment. Somewhere along the way, he'd not acted according to her plan. "If you'd just let me go—"

"You'd be floating in the Liffey right now."

That sank beneath her veneer of swagger. She bit off whatever mulish comment she'd been about to make. Instead, ducked her head, shrugging deeper into her jacket. "You've no right to keep me here."

"I have every right." He inhaled on a sharp breath against the pain. By tomorrow he'd be black, blue, and every shade in between. "Someone's willing to kill to get their hands on my father's diary, Cat. I want to know who. And why. We'll start with who hired you."

Her gaze shifted to the windows, where a drizzly

rain grayed the skies, then settled back on him, the piercing green of her eyes dulled with sorrow. "The man's name is Smith. Or at least that's the name he gave Geordie."

All right. Now they were getting somewhere. "Who's Geordie?"

She hesitated before finally answering, "A friend. He and I have rooms off Saint Patrick's Close."

She pursed her lips, clearly waiting for his appalled reaction to such an arrangement, but he kept his silence. It was nothing to do with him. She was a thief. Why not a light heel as well? But he didn't really believe it. Her grace held none of the rehearsed air of the practiced courtesan. Too artless. Too unaware.

He watched her stalk his room like a caged animal in those goddamned formfitting trousers.

Too disconcerting.

"They didn't tell Geordie why they wanted the diary," she continued, "only that it was worth a fortune, and he'd be paid well. Then at the last, he sprained his ankle and couldn't manage. I volunteered to go instead."

Now that he had her talking, he didn't want to give her time to collect her thoughts. "And you disappeared this morning because?"

"Why do you think?" She gave a shuddering breath, her eyes bright with angry tears. "But Smith was there. Waiting for me. And he—if I'd succeeded, Geordie wouldn't have suffered. Those men would have left us alone."

"And the diary would be in their hands, not mine."

Her face hardened. "I don't care about your damned diary. It's nothing to do with me."

He held his temper, though it took much grinding of

teeth and internal blaspheming. "You're involved whether you like it or not. Those men won't stop searching for you. And as long as you're the only one who can figure out what's so important about my father's diary that people are willing to kill for it, you don't leave this house without me glued to your side."

She folded her arms over her chest in a last-ditch attempt at defiance. "And if I refuse?"

He offered her an acid stare. Or at least the best one he could muster through a rapidly swelling eye. "You're smarter than that. You won't."

She bit her lip, the open rebellion bleeding out of her with each passing second, but her words when they came seemed to be choked out of her. "You win, Kilronan. I'll stay."

"It's Aidan. Remember?"

Her mouth rounded in a moue of surprise. "But you and I—you didn't mean it."

"Unlike some I could mention, I don't say what I don't mean."

Firelight and the lavender scent of perfume, or blood loss and the beginning of fever—Aidan couldn't be sure, but the result had him captured within the depths of Cat's jade gaze. And while his brain still seethed, the rest of him responded with a sweep of heat and a bone-deep ache that made him shift uncomfortably. What the hell was it about this damn woman that had him randy as a tom on the prowl?

"Very well . . . Aidan," she said, her voice low and uncertain. She stepped forward, the air charged with all the potential of a summer storm. Just as he'd thought, the woman was a walking thundercloud. She held out a hand. "Whether you meant to or not, you saved my life. Thank you."

He didn't want to be thanked. Not with a handshake. Not even with a chivalrous graze of her knuckles. Not now. His traitorous body craved more. His gaze raked the long slenderness of her, the coral pink of her lips, the graceful column of her throat where her pulse fluttered, begging to be kissed.

What the hell was such a woman doing wallowing about in the back alleys of Dublin? And why did he suddenly want to punch Geordie in the nose?

He forced his lust back into a dirty little corner of his mind. Imprisoned it as if chaining a rabid animal.

"Don't thank me yet. Before it's over you may wish I'd left you to Smith," he snarled, hating this unintended reaction to her closeness. She was trouble with a capital "T." If he wanted a quick bang, he'd find another. He gave a bark of nonlaughter. Professional, unemotional ecstasy. That was his usual approach. He flashed her a menacing glare. "Send me Blake." His gaze scoured her. "And for my sanity's sake, get out of those bloody trousers and into something decent."

She backed away before darting like a harried rabbit from the room.

And just like that, exhaustion undermined his guilty burst of anger. Closing his eyes, he sighed back against the chair. Concentrated on the steady pain in his side to exorcize the sudden pain in his heart.

Aidan leaned heavily against the corner of the house, trying not to double over. Perhaps Blake had been right. Perhaps he should have listened to the surgeon and waited to rise from his bed until tomorrow. But tomorrow might be too late. He needed to act now, stitches and multiple contusions be damned. His work was almost finished. One more laying of the ward, and he could crawl out of the drizzly rain and back to his mattress. Until then, he inhaled through his teeth in shallow pants. Kept his voice to an even, uninterrupted tempo as he released the spell. *"Dor. Ebrenn. Dowr."*

The power speared him with a wrenching violence. Seared nerves already raw. Punched him with a breath-stealing whiplash that had tears collecting in the corners of his eyes. Mage energy had always claimed him in this way. A blistering volcanic burst of power seeming to suck the very essence from him. He'd learned to control it—no Douglas would be a prisoner of his *Fey* inheritance—but every draw upon his magic brought with it a moment's unreasonable fear that this would be the spell to finally send him up in flames.

*"Tanyow. Menhir. Junya."* He closed his eyes, focusing only on the words. On the need driving him to complete the house's perimeter warding.

Whoever sought the diary knew it for what it was. A window into his father's life and work. Into the secretive circle of mages who'd clung to the family's seat at Belfoyle like malignant satellites. That had to mean he was dealing with *Other*. And to barricade himself against the magic of his own kind meant more than locked doors and primed pistols.

Mage energy flared in a chain of green and yellow light before dissolving into the early dusk. And Aidan slumped rain soaked and shivering against the house's foundation. The remnants of his power curled back along his veins inch by fiery inch toward his heart. He lifted his face to the sky, hoping to cool the fevered burn, but the heat lay too deep within him. Only time and rest would calm the tempest boil.

"You know better than to fiddle about with magic while you're ill," a familiar voice scolded. An arm braced him upright.

"I'm fine, Jack," Aidan answered through chattering teeth.

His cousin cocked an unconvinced eyebrow. "Well, let's be fine in our bed, shall we?"

Aidan set his jaw against the clash of warring agonies as Jack helped him up the steps and into the house. "You're treating me like a child."

"And you're acting like one."

Aidan's strangled laugh smothered the stream of swearing that followed. "That's always been my line."

Jack flicked him a sardonic glance. "Which says what about this situation?"

Trapped, Aidan knew better than to answer.

Jack folded his arms across his chest, eying Aidan with a scolding big brother air that set his chattering teeth on edge. This was wrong. All wrong. Not only was his wastrel cousin younger by a full three weeks, but giving unwanted advice was Aidan's job. Ignoring it was Jack's. Anything else felt unnatural.

"Well?" Aidan growled. "Say whatever it is you want to say and be done with it. Or were you planning on simply glowering your displeasure?"

Jack huffed his annoyance. "You want me to say it? Fine. I'll be quick and concise. Are you trying to get yourself lynched? What if a neighbor saw you casting spells out there?"

"Is that all?" Aidan lay back, wrapping himself deeper in his blankets in a vain attempt to get warm. "No one saw me, Jack. Give me credit for a bit of sense."

"I would if I thought you hadn't had every bit of it knocked out of you by those ruffians. That in itself should have warned you it's not safe to be flaunting your powers."

He was ill. He was exhausted. His wound hurt like the very devil. Did Jack have to pick now to rake him over the coals? "So I should have simply let them kill me?"

"No, but—" Jack ran a tired hand down his face. "All I'm saying is that times are uneasy. People are nervous and looking for a scapegoat. Don't give them a reason to make it you."

That caught Aidan's attention. He gritted his teeth as he struggled to sit up. "Have you heard something?"

"Nothing specific, but rumors abound. An old woman in Kildare was burned out of her home after her daughter-in-law denounced her as a witch. A family living near Rathnure simply disappeared. Neighbors not saying a word, but the stories talk of strange doings by the son and daughter catching the attention of the village leaders. The devil's work and all that."

Almost Smith's exact words. "Bloody hell," he muttered.

"The *Duinedon* are nervous, Aidan, and the *Other*, at least those who understand the warning signs, are lying low. It's well to watch your back under the circumstances."

Rain smacked against the windows in a renewal of the earlier downpour. The room thrown into a gray half light. Cold. Gloomy. A sudden yearning for Belfoyle set him shuddering. It had been too long since he'd ridden his fields. Stood at the edge of the Burren's rippling barrenness, feeling the pass of invisible *Fey*, hearing the chime of faery bells. A magical world just beyond the limits of his vision.

Aidan touched the tightly wrapped bandage round his ribs. "Do you think it will ever be easy between us, Jack? *Other* and *Duinedon*, I mean."

His cousin dipped a shoulder in a noncommittal shrug. "I'd not wager on it."

And for Jack, that was saying something.

Cat sat at the drawing room window. The passing rain shower had been replaced by a pale, milky sun and a stiff breeze hurrying the people down Henry Street like a chivying hand.

She scoured their faces as they passed. No Smith among them. In fact, no one she recognized at all. As if in the three years she'd been gone, the world had moved on. Left her behind. The Miss Catriona O'Connell they knew expunged from the record. A fallen woman. A whispered warning for other young debs at their coming out. Be careful or you'll end like her.

But had they truly known her?

Had she known herself?

Did she now?

She'd reinvented herself so often she didn't know who Cat O'Connell was anymore. And now she was being asked to do it again. But could she? Or in slipping so casually from one form to the other had she finally lost her core? That part of her that remained unchanging and eternal? Was she as much a spirit as any wraith doomed to *Annwn's* underworld?

Thoughts of death drove her to Geordie. Had Smith taken his frustrations out on the dwarf? Or did he live to question and worry over Cat's survival? She hated not knowing. Dreaded certainty even more.

So many people important to her had come and gone in her life. Her father had been the first to vanish. Swallowed by the sea in a gale off Gibraltar. Then Jeremy with his silver tongue and laughing eyes, who chose duty to another over devotion to her. Her child, whose existence could be measured in days yet whose pale face haunted her dreams with unfailing regularity. Now Geordie. All lost to her as she tumbled from one life to another like some jumbled piece of flotsam.

Unable to sit any longer with naught but the tangle of her thoughts for company, Cat rose and left the room. Climbed the stairs, the upper corridors dimly lit and chilly. Paused in front of the first closed door, its brass knob a shining temptation. Her hand reached for it. Turned it. The door opening a crack. Wide enough for the warmth of a stoked fire to heat her face. For the faint tang of cheroot smoke and bay rum to tease her nose. For the slow, easy breathing of the man in the bed to assure her that despite her stupidity she'd not killed him. This man had yet to disappear.

Even swimming in a laudanum haze, Aidan sensed Cat's presence. A quiver of the air. A pensive, weighted silence. Storms brooding on the horizon. He felt her stare in the prickling of his skin and a sweep of heat separate from the spiking fever. He pictured her flashing green eyes. The sleek polish of her hair. The flush of her pearl skin. He wanted to reassure her. Tell her everything would be all right. But his drugged mind had divorced itself from his body. He could only lie there. Feign sleep.

And even long after she withdrew, dreams plagued him with visions of Cat, not as the thief he'd hired, but as a woman brilliant and courageous and vivid as a queen. A woman to understand him. A woman to love.

# Six

Cat sat surrounded by parcels. Some opened for inspection. Others still wrapped in string and brown paper. Aidan's barked sickroom command becoming reality within days. Apparently a perquisite of being an earl. Even one hanging to his wealth by his fingertips.

She'd long since given up combing through the packages, much to Mrs. Flanagan's grudging surprise. For some reason, the abundance hadn't lightened Cat's heart. Rather, the display of Kilronan's patronage hung like a stone around her neck. A weight pinning her to this place and this man when common sense told her to run.

She trailed a bored hand over the empty tables. Picking up then discarding the few magazines tossed about. With Aidan laid up, she'd nothing to fill the empty hours and had forgotten how to be idle with any kind of composure. Having nothing to do and nowhere to go was downright dull.

A knock at the front door drew the bustle of Mrs. Flanagan. A purr of muffled voices in the hall. Then louder.

Shriller. And the drawing room door opened on the coifed and coutured figure of an elegant young woman Cat's age, or a bit younger, with eyes of deep blue and hair like late summer wheat. She stood in company with Mrs. Flanagan and an older, nondescript lady whose features faded into the background next to the vitality of her companion.

For a moment, panic clogged Cat's throat, and she made a desperate wish for the carpet to swallow her whole. She speared Mrs. Flanagan with a look, but the housekeeper seemed immune to her silent plea. Or perhaps she was too flustered on her own account to worry over Cat's anxieties. She certainly looked a bit gray around the gills.

"Miss O'Connell, I—" she began in an almost apologetic tone.

"You see?" the young woman spoke over Mrs. Flanagan's attempt at an announcement. "I knew she'd be here, Stow." She floated forward in a cloud of expensive scent and muslin, her curves undulating in a sultry writhe that in the right company must draw every eye.

Cat was not the right company.

She fell back on the tattered rags of her upbringing long enough to bob a curtsey and offer a chair, but Miss Osborne seemed in no hurry to take a seat. Instead she did much as Cat had just done. Took a slow turn about the drawing room, her eyes roaming every nook and cranny as if mentally categorizing the contents. Her shrewd gaze lingering for long minutes on the clutter of packages. A morning gown spilling from one. Another parcel's tissue folded back to reveal pairs and pairs of stockings and three petticoats.

Cat flushed with angry humiliation.

"Such a well-appointed room," Miss Osborne commented, stepping around a ribboned hatbox as if she were avoiding a pile of dog waste. "A bit dull, but nothing a woman's touch couldn't fix in a trice. Don't you agree, Stow?"

Stow simpered her agreement as she boggled at the wrapped bundles, less skilled than Miss Osborne at ignoring Aidan's generosity.

Her audit apparently complete, Miss Osborne's attention fell back on Cat, who'd remained silent and waiting and sick to her stomach.

Mrs. Flanagan tried once more. "I'm sorry, but His Lordship is not—"

"At home to visitors?" Miss Osborne interrupted. "Oh, I know." She turned to Cat. "Mr. O'Gara told me all about Lord Kilronan's run-in with those horrid footpads. I would have rushed over here immediately, but I was asked to sing at a charity concert last evening. And then this morning I was due to meet with some of the committee members for the Magdalen Asylum." Her pointed gaze narrowed. "Perhaps you've heard of it."

Cat's hands curled to fists. "No, but it must be an admirable cause. I'm sure nothing less would have kept you from your betrothed's side."

Miss Osborne frowned, her lips pursing in a quick moue of distaste, obviously unsure whether she was being ridiculed. "Just so. But really, I wouldn't go so far as to label him my betrothed." She tittered with false modesty. "I mean nothing's official. Yet."

The woman couldn't have been more obvious had she knocked Aidan over the head and dragged him back to her cave.

"Normally, Miss O'Connell, I wouldn't pay a call on a

gentleman's establishment. People will gossip, you understand. But I felt I must put aside the potential harm to my
reputation in order to speak with you." She offered Mrs.
Flanagan a radiant smile. "Run and find us some tea, won't
you? That's just the thing to accompany a good woman-to-
woman chat. And take Stow with you. She can help butter
the toast."

The authority behind the gentle suggestion had the
housekeeper and Miss Osborne's silent companion nipping
to the kitchens, leaving Cat alone. A toy on which Miss
Osborne could sharpen her dainty claws.

"Please, don't remain standing on my account, Miss
O'Connell."

Cat all but collapsed in a chair, nerves battering her
insides. "If you're not here on His Lordship's behalf, what
brings you to Kilronan House this afternoon?"

"When I heard rumors of Kilronan's dear cousin being
newly arrived in town, I knew I must make my introduc-
tions. And then when Mr. O'Gara explained about your
poor mother's unexpected illness, I felt it behooved me to
come and offer my sincerest sympathies." Her blue eyes widened in mock horror. "To think, coming down with plague
on the eve of your departure. I do hope she's out of danger."

Plague? Of all the illnesses in the world, Jack came up
with plague? Why not just accuse her imaginary mother
of flying to the moon? But Cat let none of her irritation
show. Instead she offered a regretful lift of her lips and a
heavenward raise of her eyes. "Yes, thank you. The doctors
assure us it's a mild case of . . . plague, so she should be up
and about very soon. I'm only grateful my cousins"—she
accentuated the word—"were able to house me as they'd
originally planned."

"Yes, that was fortunate, wasn't it?" Miss Osborne's fluttery sweetness dissolved with every passing second, and Cat tensed for a hair-pulling, face-scratching brawl. Miss Osborne had weight and height on her side, but Cat had experience and a mean left hook.

The woman settled herself upon a sofa, gloved hands resting in her lap, chin tilted at the perfect angle to showcase her elegant profile. Only her eyes glittered with a flinty stubbornness. "Can we stop pretending to each other, Miss O'Connell?"

Cat's knots doubled. "I don't know. Can we?"

Miss Osborne's lips curved in another vixen smile. "I think so. You look like an intelligent woman. And of course, I'd expect no less from Aidan. When all is said and done, he does have standards."

Ah. There was the proprietary use of his first name. She was leaving no doubts as to her future plans. Cat wished her all the gods' good fortune.

"I understand a man's animal nature." Miss Osborne colored as she spoke, a beautiful blushing pink that made Cat's teeth ache. "And as a bachelor, it's only natural Aidan would seek the company of someone like you to sate his base needs." Someone like Cat being, in Miss Osborne's eyes, two or three steps below leper. "But once we're married, any connection between the two of you must end. Do it. Or I will do it for you." Spoken with all the cool assurance of one used to getting what she wanted.

Cat defused her menace by laughing outright. "Let me reassure you, Miss Osborne, I wish you much joy of him. By that happy day, I can only hope I'm settled as far away from Lord Kilronan as Ireland will allow."

Clearly prepared for a fight and discomfited by Cat's

cheerful acquiescence, Miss Osborne seemed deflated by her quick success, but it lasted only a moment before she regained her earlier poise. Cleared her throat. Even that managing to sound melodious. "I don't blame you. It's easy to see how one in your position might fantasize. It would be only natural. Aidan's shaky finances. His family's odd reputation." She dismissed them with an airy wave of her hand before resting her palm on her heart as if preparing for martyrdom. "Temporary obstacles to overcome. They mean little to me when placed against the venerable consequence of the earldom. That is truly forever."

In other words, she didn't care if she wed Attila the Hun as long as she gained a title out of it.

A serving maid took that moment to enter bearing a heavily laden tea tray. Stow following behind, a nervous smile on her waxen face.

Cat waited through the girl's clinking bustle and withdrawal, her jaw clenched against what Miss High-and-Mighty could do with her earldom. Instead, she merely smiled until her cheeks ached. "Kilronan is lucky to have gained such unwavering affection, but I can assure you I harbor no fantasies toward His Lordship. He and Mr. O'Gara are family. Nothing more."

Her warning imparted and the tea forgotten, Miss Osborne drifted toward the door. Stow a gremlin shadow dogging her heels. "I'm so glad we were able to come to a suitable arrangement, Miss O'Connell." Pausing with a dramatic flourish, she offered Cat another piercing stare. "Do give your mother my best."

Cat waited until the drawing room door closed behind them before falling into a seat on a furious exhale. "Gods above, Aidan. What the hell have you gotten me into?"

———o———

Aidan found Cat in the library, muttering obscenities more at home on the tongue of a sailor.

"Plague. Of all the harebrained, idiotic—what was he thinking? Why not just come out and say I'm the household's communal trollop? It amounts to the same thing in the end."

"Flan told me about Barbara Osborne's visit."

She spun around. Desperation and fear darkened her eyes, making empty pools within the chalky pallor of her face. "You're out of bed."

"After two days, staring at my ceiling was growing a bit dull." He reached for her hand, but she flinched out of his grip. Glared up at him. "Don't. Just don't touch me. That's what she thinks. What they'll all think once they discover me here."

A crack in the impenetrable mystery of Cat. He probed with a delicate touch. "They?"

"It doesn't matter. I have to leave. Now."

She stalked ahead of him. Back and forth. Back and forth. Her long stride hampered by the sweep of her new skirts.

He'd been far off the mark with that one. Not even the primmest of gowns fully disguised the silky, seductive way she moved. A shame he'd wasted so much blunt to no purpose. But he could admire. And imagine. From a safe, celibate distance.

He did just that. Remaining calm amid the human eye of the hurricane pacing in front of him. Letting her work off her angst until her frantic gyrations wound down and she sank onto a sofa, her head in her hands.

"We had a bargain," he began.

"That was before. Don't you see?" she mumbled.

He leaned against the mantel as if patience was his middle name. "No, but you won't let me."

"Let's just say I'm painfully familiar with accusations of immorality."

He waited on a held breath for her to continue, but she clamped her mouth shut, any confession at an end.

"If you want to leave, let's get to work."

"And Miss Osborne? She did everything but plant her flag in you."

"Now there's an image to get the blood moving faster."

"Don't tease. It's not funny," she grumbled, but at least her earlier outrage seemed to be diminishing.

"If you like, I'll speak to her. Explain that if she'd only waited she would have met your very proper and very ugly chaperone, Miss Grimm, who locks you into your chastity belt every morning and guards your door with a brace of pistols every night. And if that doesn't do the trick, I'll reassure her of your close family connection and explain about your poor ill mother, bless her soul. The plague can be nasty this time of year."

She snickered. "You're making fun of me."

"Would I make fun of someone whose mother lies deathly ill?"

She chewed her lip, humor dancing in her eyes. "You're ridiculous."

"The dear woman's only wish as she lay suffering with pustules—to see her daughter safe in Dublin with her very proper and platonic cousins."

A full-fledged giggle escaped her. "She never thinks of herself, does she?"

He smiled. "A martyr to her core, your sweet mother.

I've often said so." He drew her up from the sofa, her hand resting in his. Trust replacing her earlier desperation. That and something else. Fellowship? Camaraderie? Would he go so far as calling it friendship?

"Leave it to me, Cat. Barbara Osborne's no coldhearted ogre. I shall soothe her ruffled feathers, and your honor will be restored."

She stiffened. Withdrew her hand, stepping back. The moment of solidarity gone. "If only it were that easy."

Cat closed the book, stretching her arms over her head. Feeling the pop of unkinked muscles down her back.

Daylight had become candlelight as heavier rain moved in, darkening the room. She closed her eyes, enjoying the sensation of being warm and comfortable inside while the booming echo of thunder rolled overhead. It had been long years since she'd been able to take luxuries like these for granted. Long years since she'd been driven from her stepfather's house, the marks of his rage on her face, his pilfered coins wrapped in a knotted kerchief banging against her side. The first theft in a slippery slope that had landed her here.

Her momentary contentment faded. She'd still had no word concerning Geordie's fate, despite Aidan's promise to investigate.

Their lodgings had been ransacked and abandoned. None asked could say whether the dwarf had escaped or been taken. Not even the promise of a reward loosened tongues either too suspicious or too fearful. She'd had to settle for a message entrusted with the publican at the Red Lion on New Street. An especial haunt of Geordie's and the one place where he might go in a pinch. If he lived, he'd know she hadn't forgotten him. He'd know she was safe. He'd know she was sorry for making a complete mess of everything.

Kilronan sat in a deep window embrasure. The effects of the ambush in the alley had slowly diminished. His black eye faded to a sort of sickly puce gray. The scratches on his face mostly healed. Unconscious of her scrutiny, he leaned his head back against the wall, eyes raised heavenward, muscles in his jaw jumping. Tension shivered off him. A coiled intensity barely contained.

She'd witnessed the explosion that came upon the release of that taut spring. The effortless transformation from polished aristocrat to hardened fighter as the instinct to survive took hold. It had been beautiful and terrifying and thrilling to watch. And if she hadn't been scared sick she would have lost herself completely to the fantasy that he'd been fighting to protect her.

He stretched stiffly and rose. Like a sailor's first tread upon dry ground, his steps came unsteady before his limbs loosened. Yet even then, his gait contained that slight half-halting stride she'd noticed earlier.

Catching her eyes upon him as he rubbed his thigh, he quickly defended himself. "It's an old injury, so you can stop looking at me as if you want to bundle me back to bed."

"Are you mad? I'd not even suggest it."

Grim features brightened to boyish mischief, and he laughed. "Then you've already won my eternal gratitude. Between Blake's whining and Jack's advice, I'm all suggested out."

He took a turn around the room, his gaze passing over the portrait above the mantel, an unreadable expression hardening his eyes. "You'd not know it to look at me, but in my day I had the women swooning over my favors. Their husbands gunning for my back."

He sounded like an octogenarian recalling a faded past, yet he couldn't be more than thirty, the muscles moving beneath his skin still supple, the razor-keen edges hardening his features still glittering sharp.

"Is that how——" She motioned toward his leg.

"Aye. A lesson for you. A drunken cuckold and a loaded weapon are not a good mix. You should have heard my father. The surgeon's digging for the ball was a jaunt compared to the haranguing I received from the old man." Bitterness tinged the dark amusement. "I don't know whether he was angrier at my dishonorable behavior or at my losing the duel to a mere baronet." His gaze lengthened into memory. "Ahh, but she was worth it. A grand beauty with——" he caught her derisive look. Quickly changed the subject with a shamefaced smile that suddenly made him seem years younger and far more vulnerable. "And you, Cat? Were you the apple of your father's eye? Your mother's little helper?"

Cat thought back to her mother's convenient blindness when it came to her new husband. The blame. The cajoling. The jealousy. But that scene shifted to her stepfather's short temper and acid tongue. His seeking hands. His smarmy threats. Jeremy had been as much about running away as running toward. She just hadn't realized it at the time.

"They weren't anything special," she mumbled.

He leaned over her shoulder, examining her progress. She found herself staring as he turned each page. The strong, capable fingers, the heavy bones of his wrists, the solid chunk of an emerald adorning his pinky. His breath came soft against her bare neck. His sleeve brushed her shoulder.

Was it the cozy snap of the fire? The patter of rain against the windows? The effects of too much claret? Whatever sparked this bewildering fascination, it quickly grew until the smoky warmth of his body lit an unwelcome flame in the inches between them.

She cursed her rotten luck. She couldn't be marooned with a scrawny, horse-faced clod who picked his nose or wiped his mouth with the tablecloth. Oh no. She had to be trapped with every woman's most sinful fantasy. A man who radiated enough sexual energy to fell a roomful of females.

She tensed, hoping he didn't notice the hitch in her breathing, the quiver of nerves trembling her limbs. She fought back with recollections of his disdain when she'd worried over his intentions. The dismissive way he scoured her with his eyes as if she were dirt to be scraped from his heel. Miss Osborne's prior and very emphasized claims.

It worked.

Her body's mutiny subsided, leaving behind a dull ache in her chest, pressing against her ribs, and a new realization that she needed to remain vigilant or she might forget the truth of her stay here. Be it within the comfort of Kilronan House or the misery of a Newgate cell, she remained a prisoner.

Night hung thick in the room, cut only by the meager halo of candlelight surrounding his desk, the red gold glow of the fire. Cat had already done so much. Pages and pages in her tidy handwriting lay scattered across his desk. He scanned one as he paced, his hand nervously tapping his thigh, his brows raised in curiosity. "My sister doesn't write half so legibly."

She looked up, startled, from where she hunkered in

a chair, the diary propped against her knees. "Huh?" she grumbled.

"I asked about your education. Where did you tell me you learned to write such a neat hand?"

One shoulder dipped in a half shrug, half rebuff. "I didn't."

Another nonanswer. He let it go.

He returned to his study of the pages. Anecdotes, expenditures, daily family events. Aidan laughed out loud, reading about the day his father had caught him and Brendan on Belfoyle's roof. And the culmination of ladders, footmen, nursery maids, and attic windows it took to get two oblivious young boys down. His father's vexation was clear even at this far remove.

"Let me guess. The roof story?" Cat asked.

"Dead on."

"Your parents must have had their hands full. It's a wonder you made it to adulthood."

"Looking back, I'll admit there was a definite pattern of danger seeking. But my father promoted it to an extent. He never wanted his sons to flinch from a challenge."

"Stand fast or die trying?"

He met her eyes, baring his teeth in a roguish smile. "Something like that. I rode. I fenced. I boxed. I shot . . ." His voice trailed off into a stilted silence.

"But?" she coaxed.

He shrugged. "In the end none of that seemed to count against the one thing at which I didn't excel."

She lifted her brows expectantly.

"Magic. If you hadn't noticed, I'm not exactly proficient."

She looked as if she might say something. Her eyes

widened, her lips parted, but she must have thought better. She dropped her gaze back to the diary, and the opportunity passed.

Just as well. What could she possibly say to mitigate a lifetime of not measuring up? What would she know of the tangled web of love and disappointment, pride and expectation that made up the memories he held of his father?

He raked a hand through his hair, put his maudlin thoughts aside, and focused back on the translation. Or tried. His temples bulged with the throb of an anvil clang, and yellow black swirls swam across his vision. They'd been translating for hours, and he'd yet to come across anything seeming to be the stuff of murder.

The page he held contained notes from a meeting. One of the mysterious gatherings that seemed such a large part of Father's life. And Aidan's childhood. Men and women who arrived stern lipped and grim, disrupting the household as they lurked in the corridors and treated the normal inhabitants like intruders. Mother would flutter uselessly as Father barked orders for meals to be prepared and rooms to be readied. The stream of commands ending only when the group disappeared into Father's study, doors locked against all comers. Except for Brendan. He'd been the only one of the children to warrant an invitation.

Aidan remembered seething with jealousy until his younger brother had confessed the nature of the meetings. Astronomy, he'd claimed. Mathematics. Ancient languages. And like a dolt, Aidan had believed him.

Or had he wanted it to be true so badly he'd disregarded all the clues pointing to a more sinister purpose? Only emerging from his blindness after it was too late.

Scanning Cat's translation, he read names, dates, an

agenda of sorts, though even translated it made little sense. One name stood out among the others. Aidan read it with a twinge of recognition. Daz Ahern. A man he'd once known with the intimacy of a favorite uncle. A man last known to be residing outside Knockniry in the moorland isolation of the Slieve Aughty Mountains. He'd send an inquiry by post. Discover if Daz still lived and what he knew.

None of the others mentioned rang any bells. A hodgepodge of Irish and English surnames. A few foreign sounding titles thrown in for good measure. But nothing to explain why unknown hands would be bent on gaining the information contained within these up-to-now mundane pages of trivia.

"Here's something interesting." Cat's voice broke into the endless circle of questions. "*October seventeen. Eighteen-o-three. One of our own has sought to break with the group. Un . . . unfor . . . oh no, I have it— unacceptable.*"

Aidan crossed to her side, his stomach knotting in unexplained dread as Cat continued reading the entry word by stammering word.

"*M. suggests we*"—her face scrunched in concentration—"*persuade him to return. As if we all don't know what he means. I'm not . . . not . . . a . . . averse to his suggestion, but how dare he undercut me with the others. I brought him into the council. I made him one of the Nine. And he repays my interest in his . . . schooling . . . knowledge . . . no that doesn't*"—one finger traced the page as if understanding involved the whole body—"*studies by suborning my closest friends.*"

Aidan followed the progress over her shoulder. The writing spilled across the heavy paper in bold, violent strokes. It jumped and swooped as if Father had sought to assuage a black fury here within the privacy of his diary. Even Cat's colorless translation was unable to mitigate the blast of emotion worked into the ink. It transferred itself to Aidan as an immediate lance of agony. Glowing auras outlined the room and everything in it, pulsing with every rapid beat of his heart.

*"It does not sit well with me to prolong . . . strife that can only under-mine our . . . our . . . energy for greater things. But M. cannot assume I will allow him to continue this blatant bid for dominance."* She shifted in her chair so that she faced him, strain tightening her mouth, clouding her eyes. "Who do you suppose M. is?"

Aidan shook his head. Immediately regretted it as the pain curled down his spine. Slid along his ribs to the gash in his side.

"You look odd," she said, rolling up and onto her feet in one fluid movement, a queer look passing over her face. "How many fingers am I holding up?"

She wore the same golden glow as the rest of the room, her black hair haloed, her skin pearlescent. Even her lips burned scarlet, pulled now into a frown, slanting her dark brows over eyes sparkling like green gems.

He yearned to crush that sex red mouth to his. To comb his hands through the feather fineness of those inky tresses. To cup the small, upthrust breasts, rubbing them to pebble hardness. Another side effect of the diary's archaic language? A result of a sexual itch left too long unscratched? Or something else? Something he wouldn't even name for fear of giving it life. There was no future there. This was only Cat. He'd do better to save his pining for a female who could bring him wealth, not simply steal it. Someone like the incomparable Miss Osborne.

So why did he want to taste those lips to discover if they were as berry sweet as they looked, or whether that lithe body would fit as perfectly against his as he imagined?

A hitch came in her breathing, her cheeks flushing to a beautiful rose pink before her eyes darkened to storm cloud black. "I said, how many fingers am I holding up?"

He blinked, focusing on the fingers wiggling under his nose. "Three," he answered.

She nodded. Backed away.

But instead of letting her go—what his head told him he should do—he followed her retreat. Stepped into the space between them.

The shimmer of golden light surrounding her flared bright. A heady warmth washed over him, sizzling along his nerves. Frying away the last hesitations. He reached up to tuck a strand of hair behind her ear. Trace the line of her scar with a touch as light as breath.

She swayed toward him as he brushed her lips with his before dragging in a harsh breath. "No." She broke away, eyes dilated and hazy with desire, yet betrayal lurking there also. And the shadow of another embrace. Another kiss. One whose memories brought fear and anger and shame. "I can't. Not again." Shudders wracked her thin body, the muscles in her neck working as she fought tears. "Don't ask it of me. Please."

His clenched hands dropped to his side, shame freezing him into shocked immobility. *Bloody fucking brilliant, Aidan. You fucking randy dumbass. You've cocked it up now.*

The auras had lessened to a blue-white outline, but Cat still remained damned tempting, those knowing eyes in that oval face, the sheen of her hair. He shifted in painful frustration. He'd hired her to translate, not to satisfy his body's mounting demands, but did she have to be so . . . desirable and so . . . available?

"Go to bed, Cat," he said through clenched teeth.

She dropped the diary onto the chair. Backed away as if he might jump her should she turn her back on him. Only when she reached the door did she hesitate and turn back.

He waved her out, knowing nothing she said would make him feel less a fool and anything he said now would only confirm his stupidity in her eyes.

Alone, he lit a cheroot to steady his shaking hands. Took a restorative drag. Tossed it onto the fire. Cat. His father. Street thugs bent on murder. And now a mysterious M.

*Bloody fucking brilliant* didn't even begin to cover it.

Blake had been sent to bed, leaving Aidan to complete his undress in privacy. Solitude in which to sort through the mess he'd almost made with Cat. To firmly attribute it to exhaustion and the insidious mage energy given off by the diary's wards. It had nothing to do with her spirited self-reliance or her quick humor. The courage in her lightning gaze. Definitely not the way she moved with the grace of a dancer or that smoky purr of a voice. No. Mage energy completely. Had to be.

A halfhearted rap on the door and Jack slouched into his dressing room, wineglass in one hand, bottle in the other. "You awake, coz?"

Aidan paused in shrugging out of his shirt. Opened his hands in a what-does-it-look-like gesture. "Thought you'd be out carousing. Weren't you expected at Daly's tonight?"

Jack flopped into a chair. Downed his drink. "Decided to attend a musicale at the Campbells' instead. Went for the food, but spent the evening listening to a recitation of your charms by the lovely Miss Osborne. Don't know what she sees in you, Aido. You're grouchy, overbearing, and far too dull. You'll bore the poor woman to death within a month of your marriage."

"If there's a marriage. Miss Osborne's gotten wind of Cat as well as a story about a mother come down with plague." He arched a cynical brow. "Ring any bells?"

Jack flushed scarlet. "I can explain."

"I'm all ears."

"She cornered me over the canapés a few nights ago. Said there were rumors circulating about a young woman residing with us here. I panicked." He offered a roguish smile. "But then, the Aidan I remember had women stashed all over the city. Hell, two cities if you count your years in London."

Aidan rubbed a tired hand across the back of his neck. "Yes, but the Aidan you remember wasn't concerned over outstanding loans, interest payments, estate maintenance, advances on purchases of seed, machinery, and stock—"

"Enough. Sounds horrid."

"So now you know why I don't need Barbara Osborne thinking me a libertine, pursuing her while blatantly enjoying a mistress."

"So, you mean to court her in earnest? I began to wonder if it was all one-sided on her part."

"Once these bruises heal. She can hardly want me at her side looking like this."

"You'd better heal fast. They're queuing up at her door. The figure. The dowry. Perfect hips for bearing sons," Jack cajoled.

Aidan couldn't help the laughter in his voice. "Who told you that? No, forget it. Don't answer. Should I worry you'll sneak your way into her affections while my back is turned?"

"Not likely. Her father may mistrust you, but he hates me."

"Owe him money, do you?"

Jack grinned. "A bit overextended when it comes to the gentleman, but nothing worrisome. You know me. Just when things look blackest—"

"If you could distill that luck of yours."

Jack offered him a bland look of innocence. Poured himself another drink, stretching his legs out in front of him, examining the toes of his boots. Apparently this was to be a prolonged visit.

Aidan gave up good manners and shucked off his shirt. Tossed it on a nearby chair.

Jack's gaze took in the swathe of bandages, tracked the route of Smith and Neddie's fists across Aidan's multicolored chest and arms before traveling up to meet the gleam of challenge in his eyes.

He braced himself against Jack's forthright, familial stare. A harbinger of trouble.

"Is this all worth"—Jack waved the bottle in the direction of Aidan's bound ribs—"being beaten within an inch of your life?"

Aidan reached over and removed it before its contents ended on his carpet. At least they'd turned from the subject of his marriage situation. "You have to ask?"

"Aye, I do. It's been six years, Aidan. Six long years. What can it possibly matter now? Let the past bury its dead."

Aidan's hand fisted around the neck of the bottle at Jack's familiar recital. "And Brendan? Is he dead? Or living? How about Sabrina moldering away in a damned convent? She barely returns my letters. We've all been ground between the millstones of not knowing. But that ends with the discovery of Father's diary. This"——he waved a hand over his bandages——"is the clearest sign the diary holds more than the sum of Father's days. I want to know what he hid in there that's important enough to warrant hired assassins."

"I, uh——" His cousin wore a cringing, expectant look as if he might be shoring himself up. Aidan waited. "Have you thought about speaking to the *Amhas-draoi*?" Jack asked anxiously.

"Is that what you came in here for?"

"Hear me out. It's clear there's more to the diary than a collection of old family anecdotes. Can you trust your wards and a few measly spells to protect it? And you?"

Aidan drew himself up. "I think so."

"The *Amhas-draoi* may know more about the diary than you guess."

Aidan took a fortifying swig from Jack's bottle. Wiped his mouth with the back of his hand. "Even if they did, do you think they'd share it with me? Not bloody likely. I'm on my own and prefer it that way."

"And if those thugs return to finish the job? Or the man who hired them? What then?"

"I'll handle it, but don't expect me to grovel for help from the very people who destroyed my family. It's not going to happen."

"More hope than expect." Jack sighed his resignation. "Then if you're resolved to keep at it, just——be careful, Aidan. I know you. You throw caution to the winds. Especially when you've got the bit between your teeth. Just look before you leap in Miss O'Connell's case."

Aidan cocked a quizzical brow at the odd coupling of so many clichés. "You think she set me up?"

Jack rubbed a speculative hand over his chin. "I think we don't know anything about her. I think you caught her in an attempted burglary. I think she was also the reason you were almost murdered by a gang of cutthroats. What I think is the woman is trouble."

Just when he thought he'd put the disastrous night behind him, Jack dredged it all back up. She was trouble all right. Trouble he'd wanted to experience firsthand, damn it. "Give me credit for having a little sense. I'm keeping the diary locked away. Not even Cat knows where. That should keep it safe."

Jack wouldn't be placated. "Should, but we don't know what kind of abilities she holds beside this talent for language. She might be able to breach a ward. Ensorcell us with a spell—" He ground down at Aidan's look of skepticism. Reached over to retrieve his claret. Took his own fortifying swig. "Fine, she won't, but who is she? Where does she come from? You have to admit she piques a person's interest."

Oh, Aidan would definitely admit that. Though "piqued" didn't seem to cover the realm of feelings she provoked in him. Insane, reckless feelings that would only lead to trouble on too many levels to contemplate. "There's definitely something that doesn't add up about her, but that only heightens her allure. I mean—" He cleared his throat as he bent to pull off a boot.

Jack's amusement rang clear through the claret haze. "Careful, Aidan. Your lust is showing."

Aidan stiffened, a hand still holding the boot he'd pulled off, tempted to heave it at Jack's head. The fool probably wouldn't even feel it, as much alcohol as he'd pumped into himself.

Putting down glass and bottle, Jack stood to shaky feet. "Piece of advice."

"What's that?"

"Bed her and get her out of your system. Always works with my infatuations. I mean they're all the same in the dark, aren't they? Soft flesh, a few maidenly whimpers, and boom, the itch is scratched."

Aidan sighed. Why had he even bothered having this conversation? He should have bundled his cousin out as soon as he'd shown signs of nesting. Exhaustion and his own laudanum hangover had loosened Aidan's tongue more than he'd expected. He sought to repair the dam. "Thank you for that lovely image, but I think I'll stick to my own plans. And Cat's bed does not figure in any of them." He'd said it. He meant it.

Jack made his way toward the door, only the cautious way he carried himself a hint at how drunk he was. "No Miss Osborne. No Cat." He sighed dramatically. "Just remember, all work and no play . . ."

This time Aidan gave in to the temptation. The boot hit the wall where Jack's head had been only moments before.

Lazarus straightened, slamming his dagger into its sheath. Breathed slowly to calm the shaky jags trembling his hands.

Already the battle madness ebbed, that endless, impossible abyss of hate and evil seeking to pull him into its fiery vortex. Claim him as it had so many others before him.

If he thought it would end the pain, he'd give in. But he knew it for the chimera it was. There would be no end. Not as long as he remained trapped in this living hell of slavish bondage. For one of the mage-born *Domnuathi*, not even death came as a relief. After all, death had been the origin of his creation.

He tried remembering that other self, the warrior who'd found honor in battle, pride in a skill few challenged. But the memories came as through a dream, fragile as smoke, dissolving before he could capture the illusion for truth. Instead, his eye fell upon the carnage before him, the bodies strewn across the room. Quigley with a sword thrust through the heart, the bookseller's final expression almost defiant as he called for aid that had never come. Smith and his cronies had fallen only seconds apart, their criminal cunning no match for Lazarus's dual lifetimes spent on the attack.

No trail, Máelodor had ordered. No way to trace Quigley back to Lazarus and thus back to Máelodor.

Even if he'd not been compelled to follow his master's commands, these less-than men deserved the death they'd received. They'd failed him. The whole lot of them. The diary was no closer to his hand than it had ever been. Máelodor would be angry. Máelodor would blame him.

Lazarus closed a fist over his sword's pommel. Felt his fingers fall into the well-worn grooves of a weapon that had become an extension of his very self. His whole self, for wasn't that what he'd become—a living, breathing weapon?

He studied the cooling broken corpses with envy. Wished with whatever tattered remnants of soul left to him that he lay among them.

# Seven

Spring found its way even into the neglected garden. Sunlight poured through branches heavy with green, and huge, blowsy peonies nodded in the warm breeze. Here, removed from the suffocating pages of the diary, Cat could imagine away the worst moments of the last days. Pretend Geordie waited for her with a bottle of claret and a good laugh. Pretend she wasn't being hunted by a gang of cutthroats. Pretend she hadn't almost kissed a man who made her feel hot and cold and nervous and eager all in the same instant.

As she strolled the paths, the soupy mental fog accompanying every reading of the diary slowly faded so that the landscape's graceful unfolding stood out in richly defined clarity.

Something every other part of her life at this moment lacked.

Pushing through overgrown shrubbery, she discovered a secluded grotto. A sheltering stand of laburnum surrounding an abandoned and unappreciated statue of Leda and her swan. Sinking onto an iron bench, Cat took in and quickly dismissed the passionate coupling of the woman and her avian lover. Closed her eyes, lifting her face to the healing sun.

A rustle of boxwood, a muttered, "Ouch! Blasted branch," and she found herself face-to-back-of-the-head with the man she'd come out here to escape. He looked up from untangling his coat. Started with another muttered oath.

He couldn't have found his own secluded piece of garden? He had to invade hers? She rose from the bench, smoothing her skirts.

"I'll leave," she said before he could do more than blink his astonishment at being in her company.

He recovered with fluid ease. "It's all right. I'm just not used to encountering anyone out here. Jack's not much on communing with nature, so I tend to have the garden to myself."

His gaze flicked to the statue. Back to her. And what had been mere pleasing artistry suddenly took on looming significance. The swan's magnificent wingspan combined with Leda's arched back radiated eroticism with the blunt force of a hammer. Cat clenched her jaw until her teeth ached. It couldn't have been a rendering of some spear thrusting warrior exterminating a lion. Oh no, she had to be trapped with Aidan amid seduction on a mythic scale.

"My father had it commissioned for my mother as a wedding gift," he offered, strain running through his voice.

"It's beautiful," she replied, knowing she sounded insipid.

"He always teased that his love for my mother rivaled the passion of the gods."

A feeling she thought long past tightened her throat. "Now, that's beautiful."

His gaze traveled over Leda's very evident charms—wide, rounded hips, long legs spread in tantalizing invitation, head thrown back in obvious desire—before he lifted his eyes to hers. The mesmerizing intensity in them pushing past her formidable inner defenses. "Yes, isn't she?"

A queer fluttery feeling beat against her insides. Sent unwanted heat pooling deep in her center. She felt his long, slow scrutiny of the sculpture as hands upon her own body. The sure yet gentle touch of a new lover. His increasing arousal. His growing boldness. She welcomed his reckless longing with a spreading fire of her own. Her skin beneath the sturdy gown flushed in anticipation. Her lungs working frantically to keep pace with her heart.

The outside world shrank down to the space of the secluded grotto, the powerful, stern-faced man in front of her, the measureless depths of his stare. His hands flexed at his sides. His breathing as jagged as her own. The bronze light in his eyes darkening with every passing second they remained locked together in this neverending, crystalline moment.

He escaped first. "Last night—"

"It wasn't your fault—" she interrupted.

"I should never have—"

"It's just—"

They spoke over each other in their haste to clamber off the shifting sands beneath their feet. To pull free of a quagmire that had cataclysm written all over it.

Aidan stepped into the breach opening between them before she could drag herself completely clear. His hand found her cheek. Traced the silver line of her scar with a touch that had already claimed her in a thousand secret places before he'd ever laid a finger to flesh. His lips parted as if he meant to speak, and she found herself leaning in to hear. Instead, he lowered his head. Slanted his mouth against hers, his warmth as welcome as the May sunshine.

This was wrong. All wrong. The Earl of Kilronan didn't steal kisses from women like her. He could have anyone he wanted. Could snap his fingers and have them lined up awaiting his choice. Her head knew it. Her heart knew it. Her body didn't give a damn.

If Leda could surrender, so could she.

Take that, Miss High-in-the-Instep Osborne.

Cat answered Aidan's kiss. Opened to him, letting his tongue dip within. Swirl and tease in a playful exuberance that conflicted with his usual sober caution. His hand found her hair. The other curving around the back of her neck. Drawing her closer until the buttons of his coat bit into the fabric of her gown. Until the rise and fall of his chest rested beneath her own open palm.

He lifted his head, the slow burn of his gaze illuminating a glimpse of her past. The alluring beguilement of forbidden fruit. The desire to be loved so fierce within her that any scrap resembled a feast. And waiting at the end, the empty, gnawing hunger when reality hit.

She stepped back, his hands falling away, his features blurring behind a wash of idiotic tears. She wiped them away with her sleeve.

"Excuse me," all she managed through lips still tingling from his kisses.

He let her go without comment. Watched her push back through the boxwood in silence. Never once tried to follow her.

At the terrace steps, Cat met the housekeeper. "Have you seen His Lordship? I've looked all over and can't find him anywhere within." She scanned the garden, her hands fluttering uselessly at her apron. "He has guests. Lady Osborne and Miss Osborne are here."

"There he is." Cat pointed toward the shrubbery, the secluded stand of laburnum, Leda and her god hidden away in eternal orgasm.

Aidan emerged, his body stiff, face set in rigid lines.

As Mrs. Flanagan descended to impart her news, Cat slipped within. Made her way with steady steps to her room where she could contemplate the perfection of his kiss in solitude. Slow her frantic heart. Regroup.

She would take it as she found it.

Geordie would have been proud of her.


Aidan watched her lips move. Caught the play of eye and toss of head signifying interest. The adroit movements of her body assuring him of her attraction while hoping to ascertain his own.

And Barbara Osborne was attractive. Hair the summer yellow of wheat. Eyes clear and blue. A body that enticed from the point of her dimpled chin to the sleek length of her legs. Not that he'd seen her legs. It had been Cat's limbs he'd been fantasizing about ever since he'd seen them encased in those damned sexy trousers. Asking—no, begging—to be skimmed with a lover's touch. He cleared his throat. Focused on Miss Osborne's smile. The symmetry of her face. There was no denying the gods had been good to her.

He swallowed, slapping a mental hand to his forehead.

Gods led to Zeus led to Leda led to that thrice-damned

statue. The kiss it inspired. The flare of luscious heat it ignited. He shifted in his seat.

When had he begun thinking with his lower extremi-
ties? Here sat his future. Equal to him in rank, in background. Possessing the drive and ambition and energy as
well as the sizeable dowry to fully restore his family's wealth
and rightful place in society.

Miss Osborne was everything he wanted and needed
in a wife. So why was it Cat who kept provoking him into
one awkward situation after another? What impulse had
him seeking her out just to be near her? What elemental
urge kept overriding good sense? Whatever it was he needed
to get a grip on himself. He was no longer the immature
scoundrel led by his cock.

Miss Osborne tipped her head in expectation. Damn.
Had she said something? Was he supposed to answer? He
looked from her to her mother, praying for inspiration.
Settled for, "I defer to your judgment. As always."

It worked. She sat back, pleased with herself. Her
mother preening as if the marriage banns had already been
read.

So what was he waiting for? What kept him from forming the words "Will you marry me?" and taking the final
steps to securing his future? It was honor, surely. Pride, certainly. Until he'd freed himself from the chains of the past,
he didn't feel comfortable declaring himself.

That meant deciphering the diary.

For all that her presence disturbed him. For all that
those vibrant green eyes and sexy sweet body sparked an
attraction harder and harder to ignore. For all that every encounter left him seeking out cold baths and a stiff drink—
that meant Cat.

———o———

He absently pitched a pebble into the fountain. Then another.

After playing host to Miss Osborne and her mother for a good hour, he'd shown them out to their carriage. Miss Osborne's lips curled in a seductive pout as she sought to coax him into joining them at the Rimshaws' card party later. Her mother beaming her agreement. At least he had one parent's approval for his courtship.

He made his regrets, pleading the lingering effects of his attack, which seemed to satisfy her for the moment. But it was clear he would need to act soon or risk losing her interest.

He tossed another pebble.

His eyes followed the contours and curves of the statue as if drinking in the flesh and fire of the real thing. But whereas Leda remained cold and untouchable, the arc of her spine, the hollow at the base of her throat, the moment of ecstasy all rendered in endurable marble, Cat's thunder-cloud personality and mercurial temperament made every moment fraught with cliff-scaling thrills. A pulse-pounding sensation he'd not experienced for longer than he liked to admit.

He flicked a last pebble into the water.

But excitement didn't feed the bulldog creditors hounding one's door. Money did. And that remained the purview of Miss Osborne and her well-heeled father.

Rising from the bench, Aidan dusted off his breeches. Wiped his hands. Took a deep, careful breath. And deliberately turned his back on a statue built in honor of love.

A last sparkling shaft of evening sun streamed through the tall library windows. Fell across the page Cat read, picking out one single sentence near the bottom.

Her gaze dropped to the swirling clash of letters, forcing her mind to pick apart the strange pairings of vowels and consonants. Unstressed. Stressed. Long. Short. The diary resisted her translation, seeming to squirm and writhe against her grasping for its meaning. Every word fraught with a double dose of illness and a headache like a drill to her brain.

But in the end, sense came from the foreign gibberish inked upon the paper.

She read it. And again. And even a third time. Disbelief giving way to shock. Then finally—

Horror.

"Oh gods," she gasped. "He couldn't. Not his own son."

# Light

———————➤

"You read it wrong. It's a mistake. It must be."

Aidan fought his panic with a long, slow drag on his cheroot. It didn't help. He tossed it in the fire, unable to even look at the paper Cat had shoved into his hands.

"I translated it twice more. No mistake."

Aidan forced himself to read the words Cat had carefully written out for him. His stomach rolled, cold sweat breaking out upon his skin, and he looked away. "Father would never have gone through with such a plan."

"That's not what it says here." Cat tore the paper from his limp fingers. Read it out loud. *"It's decided we need a blood sacrifice. Brendan has been suggested as one with the required power."* She scowled, eyes flashing. Her shoulders tight, motions jerky and quick-tempered. "Not even a spark of outrage, Aidan. What kind of man blithely agrees to murder his child in the name of . . . of . . . what? We don't even know. It doesn't say."

"It must." He strode to the diary, lying open upon the

desk. Scanned the pages as if through sheer willpower he could decipher the crazy slant and jump of his father's writing. Immediately, his stomach rose into his throat and he bent double, clutching his gut.

Cat was there. Slamming the book closed. Shoving him into a chair until the worst passed. Giving him time to recover before she slid into the seat opposite, features brittle with determination. "I looked already. I read ahead a dozen pages and more. There's no reference to a sacrifice other than these few passages. If it's in there, I haven't found it. Or he hid it in meanings inside of meanings. It certainly wouldn't be the first riddle I've uncovered."

"Damn it, Cat. What's the point of translating the damn thing if I end with more questions than when I began?" Tightness banded his chest, whirling nausea dragging him like an anchor.

"Could that account for your brother's disappearance?" Her voice came low and uneasy. "Could your father have—"

"No." He flinched, coming up hard against the edge of the desk. "And don't even suggest it."

Her brows rose in unvoiced cynicism. "If your brother were still alive, wouldn't he have gotten in touch with you after your father's death? Six years is a long time to stay away without any word whatsoever."

An argument he'd held with himself many times. If Brendan lived, why no letters? Visits? Why had he cut himself off so completely from his family? There had to be an explanation, but he refused to consider Cat's. That Father had—no. Impossible.

Closing his eyes and pinching the bridge of his nose between his fingers, he tried gathering his scattered thoughts.

Shifting the few puzzle pieces they had, but no picture emerged beyond the one Cat had produced with her outrageous suggestions.

"My father couldn't have done it. He loved Brendan."

She stood close behind him. Her cheek a soft curve at the corner of his eye. "Maybe so. But it's clear he also planned a sacrifice. Could this be why the *Amhas-draoi* marked him for death?"

He breathed in her lavender scent. Felt the pounding rush of his blood settle as he traced the faded marks of the crescent and broken arrow on the diary's cover with one slow finger. "I don't know." He lifted his eyes to her worried gaze. "And for the first time, I'm not certain I want to."

Curled like her namesake on a chaise lounge, Cat's head ached with a buzzing tightness, so that any flick of her eyes sent the pain flexing down her spine and into her stomach. The diary lay open on Aidan's desk to the page where she'd left off, her corresponding sheet of translation trailing from the comprehensible to near chicken scratch as the sickness increasingly turned interpretation to torture.

But no more references to the ritual sacrifice of Aidan's brother. No more clues as to why it had been planned and whether it had been achieved. One more mystery to add to the growing list.

Closing her eyes, she snuggled deeper into the cushions. It had been an interminable day with no end in sight. She'd been locked away with Aidan since after supper and now all she wanted was the sweet oblivion of bed. Alone.

She slit her eyes to take in the strong-jawed features, lips she now knew could tease her into stupidity, a stare with a hypnotist's stun power. She curled tighter into her seat.

Yes. Definitely alone.

Thankfully, he'd made no more mention of their kiss. And, both grateful at his discretion and perturbed at his nonchalance, she'd settled into ignoring it too. Or as much as she could when forced to spend every waking moment in his somber company. She sank back.

The soft weight of a lap rug across her shoulders broke into the troublingly delicious vision of Aidan that had survived every attempt to exorcize it. She opened her eyes to catch him watching her, the concerned look on his face adding kindling to the dream spinning.

"You look awful," he explained.

She fought her fantasy with sarcasm. "Just what every woman wants to hear."

Laughter teased his mouth into a rare smile. "I only meant you seem wrung out and tired."

A squirmy feeling that had nothing to do with the diary shivered her stomach, and she offered him a more gracious "Thank you."

That should have been it. Quick. Over. Back to work. Instead, Aidan's mesmerizing stare speared her in place, enough heat within it to make the lap rug irrelevant. Her skin flushed, her body going uncomfortably warm. How did he do that? One glance in her direction and she went stupid for him. It was embarrassing.

"Cat, I need to—"

She leaned forward, held her breath.

"That is, we—"

His stare burned a hole straight through her.

Then just like that, he blinked. Cleared his throat. And

dropped his gaze to the pages in his hand. "Yes, well I suppose we should get back to it."

A mental sigh deflated the growing excitement. She scrubbed her eyes with the heels of her hands. Wished she could scrub her mind as easily. "I suppose we should."

Silence resumed as they retreated to neutral corners. She settled deeper into the cushions, wrapping the rug tight about her shoulders. Tried erasing the pulse-pounding memory of his kiss from her mind. Stripping away the image of that fathomless bronze gaze.

"Here. Now this looks interesting." His tone overly brisk and businesslike as he slid into the chair behind his desk. Scanned the page greedily.

"*Yn-mea esh a gwagvesh. A-dhiwask polth. Dreheveth hath omd-hiskwedhea.*"

She recognized the words. She'd stumbled over them earlier, her mind frantically scrambling for a hold upon their slick black sounds. But they remained infuriatingly elusive. Not even her *Other* abilities granting her a window into the harsh vowels and rasping consonants.

But now on Aidan's tongue, their meaning seemed all too clear.

"*Skeua hesh flamsk gwruth dea.*"

"Aidan, don't. Please."

He lifted his head, his gaze turned inward upon some image only he could see. He bore a quiet intensity, eyes alive with an inner fire turning the dark brown orbs gold as suns. But this wasn't the stare he'd given her moments earlier. Instead it was as if the man within had been shunted aside by another. A creature of razor-edged cruelty. A being who fought tooth and claw to emerge.

"*Drot peuth a galloea esh a dewik lya.*"

"Stop, Aidan!" She clapped her hands over her ears, her head threatening to split with the sudden pain, stomach rolling in sour waves, throat closing around a cold knot of fear. Terror had Cat out of her seat and across the room before conscious thought kicked in. She grabbed his arm. Sought to shake him back to awareness. He tore free of her. Shoved her away, sending her sprawling over a stool. Her elbow banged the floor, her wrist twisted painfully beneath her.

*"Drot peuth a pystrot esh a dewik spyrysoa."*

The creature gained supremacy. Aidan's grave, pensive features giving way to a violent evil. A blood thrill lit his eyes, a leer of greedy defiance twisting his face into a mask of hate.

She scrambled to her knees. "Aidan! What are you doing? For the love of the gods, stop!"

As the spell reached its crescendo, the air within the library thickened to a greasy haze, the fire leaping from its grate to claw at the hearth rug. Within the smoky miasma, a form emerged. A squat, muscled torso with a wrestler's low-slung gravity. A face that might pass for human should it remain hidden by twilight or shadow.

It craned its short, thick neck as it surveyed this new plane. Settled a milky, opaque gaze on Cat, its mouth peeling back in a snarl before latching its eyes on the man who'd summoned it.

It approached the earl, Aidan meeting the unblinking malevolence of the monster with no sign of fear upon his face.

Cat watched horrified as the beast slid one fist and then another into the earl, his flesh parting then sealing around the monster's limbs.

Aidan flinched but made no move to fight back. Instead,

he almost seemed to welcome the monster's possession. His features sharpened over the angular bones of his face, even as his skin faded gray as death.

She'd one final hope to break the possession before Aidan was lost to the *Unseelie* demon.

On her feet, dashing for the desk, Cat snatched up the page Aidan had been reading. Tossed it onto the fire.

Both the creature and Aidan screamed their agony as smoke thickened around them. Keening ripped through her skull like claws across a thousand slates. Her eyes burned with a sickly yellow fog. It clogged her throat. Filled her ears.

The house rocked upon its foundation, a grinding of stone and plaster, a shattering of glass, the shrieks of frightened maids and the housekeeper's bellow for order.

And the monster disappeared.

The library door burst open. "What the bloody hell?" Jack shouted. "Are you trying to bring the house down around us?"

His puzzled gaze took in the dissipating fog, the tumbled books and scattered portfolios, the globe upended in its stand, the floor dirtied with chunks of frescoed ceiling, and Aidan slumped on the floor, gray-faced and shaky.

He shot Cat an accusatory glance as he shouldered Aidan upright and helped him to a chair. "Damn it. Can I not leave you alone for a few hours without worrying you'll try to kill yourself? Again?"

"It was incredible, Jack," Aidan muttered.

Incredible? Try incredibly horrible.

Jack looked from Aidan to Cat. "Will one of you please explain what happened?"

Cat shook her head, pointing at the space where the

creature had stood only moments before. "Something. Something stepped through."

"Something stepped through what?"

Aidan straightened, the man once again in control, though his eyes still glowed with success. "A spell from the book. It . . . it worked. I made it work."

Jack's grim features moved over Aidan as if seeing him for the first time. Flashed Cat a silent question.

But she couldn't answer. What would she say that would make sense to anyone who hadn't watched the change in Aidan as he read those horrible words? Who hadn't witnessed a creature surfacing behind his eyes? Dragging Aidan toward a possession. A domination.

Yet something of what she'd seen must have been evident in her face. Jack nodded as if he understood. She wished *she* did.

"Aidan, listen to me. You need the *Amhas-draoi*," Jack said.

"We've had this discussion. I'm fine."

"This is magic beyond your ability. You have to see that."

Aidan's expression hardened to stubborn anger. "Thank you for pointing out my deficiencies—"

"Aidan, that's not what I meant. But your father was meddling with dark magic he shouldn't have touched. And in the end it killed him."

"No!" Aidan slammed his hand against the desk. "The *Amhas-draoi* killed him. And I'm not going to crawl to them for help. That's final."

"Then if you're intent on destroying yourself, can you at least refrain from spells that threaten to destroy the house and terrify the servants?" Jack pleaded. "I'm having the devil of a time trying to convince them it was an extremely localized earthquake. Dublin isn't exactly known for its tremors."

Aidan waved him off with a dismissive gesture of agreement, though even now he seemed only half-aware of his surroundings. "No more fireworks, I promise. Cat will keep me honest. Won't you, Cat?"

Startled at being addressed, she flashed a worried nod in Aidan's direction, but her eyes held Jack's for long moments after.

He answered with a half nod. A decisive look in his cousin's direction. Tense lines tightened his mouth. "I begin to pray for your sake, she does."

Lazarus collared a man stepping from a hackney. In the light of the lamps, the man's supercilious gaze melted into bewilderment then fear.

"Kilronan House?" Lazarus growled.

The man pointed back up the street. "North of the river. Henry Street. You can't miss it."

The coachman shouted down from his box. "Here now! What ya on about pesterin' folks?"

Lazarus settled his grave stare on the coachman. Felt the unnerving ripple of mage energy like the stirring of a serpent within him. It slithered from its resting place. Glided with deathly intent along limbs that had once stalked the forests of Gwynedd. Fired blood that had once pounded in battle allegiance to Prince Hywel. Sustained a body that, but for the Great One's black magics, would have remained buried and forgotten.

The mage energy charged the air. Crackled with a heat and light only he could see, but all could feel.

Frozen in stupefied horror, the gentleman at his shoulder and the coachman upon his box could do nothing but watch the creature in front of them and wait for their destruction.

It never came.

Lazarus fed the evil before it overpowered him. Turned it inward to feast upon his few tattered yet precious memories. And sated, it retreated to sleep.

But only for a time. When it woke it would be angry. Starved for destruction. For killing. He'd not be able to deny it a second time. Didn't want to. He had few memories left. He clung to them with the strength of two lifetimes.

Lazarus released his captive with a shove, sending the man stumbling back into the sanctuary of the hackney. Even before the door slammed shut, the horses had been set to. The coachman barreling down the street as if pursued by the devil.

He let them go. And with a steady, unerring tread, made his way toward Henry Street.

Kilronan would feel the strike of deadly force. Fall beneath the foul weight of Lazarus's mage energy.

Nothing would stay his hand this time.

No memory would be enough.

# Nine

Everything hurt. Down to his hair. His mouth felt as fuzzy as his brain, wine sour and gritty. And even the faded smell of the evening's cooking was enough to roll his stomach. To combat the nausea, he sat with a cup of black coffee. Dry toast. More black coffee.

Hunched over the kitchen's scrubbed worktable, head resting in his hands, he heard the swish of skirts. The drawing back of a chair.

"Jack told me I'd find you down here. And he was right. You do look like death on a mop head."

Aidan looked up into Cat's solemn green eyes. "As usual, Jack's choice of phrase is so complimentary." He winced as his voice reverberated through his paper skull "Spot on, nonetheless." He sipped at the coffee in front of him. "You couldn't sleep either?"

She offered him an are-you-insane stare, and he glanced to where her hands rested on the closed cover of a slim, leather-bound volume. Raised a curious brow, but waited for her to initiate.

"Not exactly easy to drift off after tonight's events . . ." Her words trailed off into an accusatory silence.

Aidan nibbled the crust of his toast. Tasteless and burnt on one edge, but at least it stayed down. "I told you before, I was excited. And perhaps a bit too self-confident, but the spell worked. Did you see it? The summoning brought—"

"A demon. Here." Her hands and her voice convulsed before she brought both under control once again. "You pulled an *Unseelie* across the divide, Aidan. You almost joined with it. Let the creature take over your skin. Inhabit your flesh."

"It would never have gone that far," he said quietly. A sharp knot wedged in his throat. He'd blame the toast, but he knew for a fact it was something more. The same thing that had kept him awake most of the night. Memories of Father had battered him hour after hour. The daring sportsman who'd taught him to climb the sheer, rocky cliffs around Belfoyle. The caring parent who'd read to his children from a great book of stories, transforming the night nursery into a fabulous wonderland spun with words. The professorial academic who'd tried to instill a love of learning and a pride in being *Other* in his offspring. He'd been stern at times. Demanding when it counted. But never before had Aidan questioned his motives or his morality.

The diary had opened a window on a different man. A complete stranger. A ruthless *Other*.

Cat blurted, "Your father toyed with dangerous magic."

Aidan's face went stiff; the knot in his throat grew. Threatened to choke him. "Father was a dedicated mage and scholar with a desire to learn. To stretch boundaries. To push his mind and his magic as far as they could reach." He could barely get the words out.

"Summoning *Unseelie?* Sacrificing his own child? That's not pushing boundaries. That's sailing right off the edge of the map."

"You don't know anything about it." His chest ached as the knot expanded. Sank into every part of him until the lancing pain of tonight returned a hundredfold. "You weren't there. You didn't know him . . . before . . ."

He sounded like a child standing up to the schoolyard bully. Shaking. Scared.

"Neither did you apparently. But the *Ambas-draoi* must have. They executed him. They must have known he was abusing his powers. Look. Just read this." She pushed the book across the table at him.

"What is it?"

"It's a treatise on the nature of *Unseelie.*"

He flipped through the book, though his eye barely registered the flicker of passing words.

"It documents everything," Cat explained. "Or as much as the author knew or could surmise from the limited contact between the *Unseelie* void and the mortal world. Though it would seem by some of the footnotes that the contact was more than anyone had dared before. The author had opened the door. Not once or twice. But dozens of times. Maybe hundreds. He talks about the summoning. The fatal possession. *Unseelie* can't survive on this plane. Not without a host." She paused, letting the import of those words sink in. "It's a temporary bond. Death is certain. The fragile human shell can't handle that kind of parasitic power. And live."

He looked up. "Are you going to tell me my father wrote this book? He wasn't like—"

"No, Aidan. Not your father. A man by the name of Máelodor."

Bloody hell! The elusive M.

Unable to read any more, Aidan closed the book, queasiness souring his stomach. If half the pages he'd read were true, the author had been a master mage of incredible power and charisma as well as immense brutality. Along with being a nutter of the first order. His writings hovered somewhere between brilliance and madness. His hypotheses reached so far into the realm of impossibility, Aidan would have discounted them if he hadn't seen the *Unseelie* take shape before his own eyes. Sensed the elusive vastness of eternity hovering just out of reach as the creature attempted to merge with him. Akin to a death experience or a birth experience. A total and irreversible passing from one form into another.

"Well?" Cat prodded.

"What do we know about Máelodor? Did you find anything else?"

She shrugged. "A book of essays recounting obscure *Other* history. Another of natural philosophy that I couldn't make heads or tails of. But nothing that revealed more about Máelodor than his contempt for the *Duinedon* world and an overweening desire to return to—in his words—'the last Golden Age of *Other*.'"

Aidan didn't get as far as answering. Instead, mage energy cruised his skin like ice. A moment later the ice plunged like a frozen knife into his gut. Doubled him over with the force of a sucker punch. Congealed the blood in his narrowed veins until his limbs went numb.

"Aidan!"

Cat's frightened scream bounced through his skull. But he'd passed beyond words of reassurance. Whoever just breached his house wards had the power of lethal sorcery behind him. A power Aidan could never match.

He speared Cat with a grim stare. Choked out one hissed word. "Run." And clutching the table for support against the menacing weight of panic and mage energy, straightened to meet the attack.

The door burst in on a wet draft of air, rain puddling on the threshold, the familiar city smells of coal fires and damp stone overlaid with a brimstone burn rising off the man towering before him.

A colossus in black. Black hair. Black eyes. A face black of purpose. And a blade glittering with wicked, obsidian light.

He stepped through the door, slamming it closed behind him. The world of *Other* and *Fey* crashing into Aidan's carefully constructed *Duinedon* persona with deathly violence.

His gaze searched the room, head up as if scenting a trail. "It's here. I feel it."

"Who the hell are you?" Aidan choked through a throat gone tight and dry.

The man offered a nod of mock solemnity. A chivalrous gesture in an otherwise cold-blooded killer. "The Great One names me Lazarus. I am death undone." The man raised his sword, the tip grazing Aidan's jugular. "The diary. Now."

The prick of the blade acted like a goad to Aidan's numbed senses. His own powers flooded him with a thawing heat. Sparked along his nerves. "Not in a million years."

Lazarus's gaze narrowed, and if Aidan had thought

the man's eyes black, he now saw he'd been mistaken. They glowed with a hell-born, inhuman light. Death reflected back on his victim a thousand times. "I have a million years, Kilronan. You don't."

The neat sweep of the blade had been meant to sever Aidan's head from his neck. But Lazarus hadn't counted on Aidan's bad leg buckling beneath him. Dropping him to the floor. The sword's keen edge whistling over him. Sweeping the table clean in a crash of china.

With the instincts of the survivor, Aidan twisted and jinked, using the close confines of the kitchen to dodge the follow-up attack. Lazarus's frustrated curses sounding like the fevered screams of a million lost souls.

Rolling to his feet, Aidan blindly grabbed anything and everything that came to hand. Pots, pans, trivets, and utensils. They bounced off the man's chest. Clattered across the floor in a silver shower of cookware. Less a threat than an irritation.

Aidan found himself backed against a shelf. Reaching behind him, his hand found the knife box. Gripped a handle. Turned and threw. Again and again. Paring. Chopping. Cleaver. The smaller knives did little more than nick Lazarus's war-toughened hide. A boning knife bit into his arm. Another sliced him a wicked wound across his thigh. He never faltered. Beyond pain. Beyond fear.

Aidan risked a glance, but the knife box was empty. He'd run out of arsenal.

Lazarus's mouth gaped in a sadistic smile. "And now the diary."

"Get away from him!"

The crack of a gunshot shivered the smoke-blackened air. Felled the man with spine-shattering accuracy. His sword clanged and spun across the bricks, coming up against Aidan's boot.

Aidan reached down, his fingers fisting around the pommel. Falling into the worn ridges as if he'd been born to it. Leveraged himself up against the grinding of screaming tendons.

"I told you, Cat," he growled, "to get out. You—" Stopped himself with a disgusted snort. Was he really going to argue with her over saving his life? Again? This was getting to be a habit with her.

Cat lowered the pistol, her gaze riveted to the body. Her face wore a blank sheen of terror, but her eyes gleamed with a ruthless ferocity. He'd caught that look in cornered animals. Convicted felons. Those pushed dangerously close to the edge.

"I came across the gun in your desk a few days ago." Her voice came hollow of emotion. Weak and fluttery. "I wasn't sure it was loaded."

Aidan pulled it from her lax fingers. Tossed it on the worktable. "I put it there on a hunch." Nudging the body with the toe of his boot, he swallowed against an instant gag reflex. "One that proved correct."

As if pulling herself back from the brink, Cat took a deep cleansing breath. Her shoulders squaring. Her face losing that pasty, vacant expression. "He came for the diary, didn't he?"

Aidan didn't answer. Instead, he knelt. Rolled the man over onto his back, searching his pockets. Who was he? For that matter, what was he?

He looked human enough. More so now without the ghoulish flame flickering behind those empty black eyes. But for a moment, he'd sensed a difference about the assassin moving beyond mere *Other* sorcery. A savagery born at the witching hour when monsters stir. Death undone, the man had claimed.

Blood pooled beneath the body. Spread in a growing morbid circle.

Well, *Annwn* may have spat him back once, but Cat's crack shot had returned him to the underworld.

Nothing came of Aidan's search but a ticket booked on tomorrow's packet for Wales. Not a local then. He'd been imported for the job.

Aidan pocketed the ticket before straightening.

Cat stood hunched and forlorn at his side. He led her out of the kitchen. Nudged her unresisting body toward the warmth of the library fire. Made it as far as the hall when the same arctic blast that had preceded the first attack shivered along his flesh. Bit through muscles. Sank bone-crushing fangs into the well of his powers until he cried out against the ice cold agony. Swung around to face once more an undead and unkillable killer.

"You're wasting time, Kilronan. The diary. Now."

The man's voice fell like lead into the silence that had descended over the house. A horrible, enveloping silence holding an echo of the grave.

But how? She'd killed him. She knew she had. She'd heard the shot. Watched the corpse crumple to the floor. Seen the sticky, red blood crawl over the bricks.

Aidan's grip crushed Cat's shoulder, his body sagging against her as the mage energy tore through him, the over-spill burying itself like needles in her brain.

The appropriated sword dropped to the marble floor. Followed by Aidan. Hatred edged his expression. Glittered with animal intensity in his eyes.

The man stepped forward. "Don't make me harm your lady."

His gaze swung to her, the triangulating stare enough to steal her breath. Hold her captive. Motionless but for the frenzied rise and fall of her chest.

"Go to hell," Aidan cursed.

That seemed to amuse the man. The corner of his mouth curved into a smile, his hands flexing in a spasmodic jerk. "I'm already there."

Lazarus's curse smashed into her. An avalanche of cascading, pummeling, body-crushing battle magic trapping her beneath it. The spell's force pushed the air from her lungs. Tore through her like a scythe. She struggled, but like a snare, the poisonous mage energy coiled and twisted itself around her. She couldn't breathe. Couldn't swallow. Her vision hazed and dimmed.

She tried screaming, but there was no time. No time for anything but a final reassuring thought—*I'm coming for you, my son. Mama will see you soon.*

Cat's body lay curled in a ball as she attempted to shield herself from the spell's lethal force. A tangle of hair curtaining her face. Pale arms hugging her body.

Lazarus's jaw jumped, his body as rigid as if he suffered alongside his victim. And his gaze held a grief almost as great as Aidan's. But then that gaze hardened to a diamond brilliance, any second thoughts eliminated through sheer force of will. He gave a regretful shake of his head. "Stay my hand, Kilronan. Give me the diary."

"Fuck you," Aidan snarled. His grip tightened on the sword's hilt, but without the strength to fight, it was useless. At least he wouldn't make it easy. If the bastard wanted the diary, he'd have to search every bloody nook and god-damned cranny of Kilronan House to find it.

"As you will." Lazarus's evil stare held centuries of de-struction. His dark magic crude, but effective.

Aidan's agony as the man's curse ripped through him was like a roaring, living thing. The will and then even the ability to move were stripped from him. His body began to unravel strand by strand. Tingling and then numbness spread inward from his fingers and toes. Racing to his heart. Leaping from nerve to nerve until, all senses dead-ened, he collapsed. Felt death reaching for him in the bitter, frozen cold of Lazarus's magic.

A yell came from outside. The calls grew louder. Oh gods, Jack was home. Aidan needed to shout a warning. Call him off. But he couldn't move. Couldn't speak. His body unresponsive, his mind clouded and sluggish.

A door slammed back on its hinges. Shouts echoed off the plastered ceilings and columned hall. Reverberated through his body with the jangling shock of a tuning fork.

He caught sight of booted feet. A tilted glimpse of Jack's horror. The gowned figure of a mesmerizing woman.

A shimmer of color danced in front of him, the air running like water. His eyesight narrowed to a pinprick. Then the world went black.

# ten

Aidan tossed back the brandy. Poured and tossed back a second. Let the cauterizing fire slide through his insides. Calm the restless tension jumping just under his skin. It didn't work. He poured a third.

Jack watched him from his place by the window, his expression grave but cautious. "Aidan, perhaps you—"

He flinched. Downed the brandy. "Don't say it."

Jack held up placating hands. Settled back into anxious silence.

Aidan ground his teeth against the throbbing pain in his leg. Kept up his impatient pacing. Lit a cheroot from a nearby candle, inhaling on a lung-soothing drag. Stubbed it out, tossing the whole into the grate. Kept pacing. His mind all for what went on upstairs. Off his last image of Cat draped in Jack's arms, a death pallor cast over her already ivory features.

"She sleeps."

Aidan staggered to a halt. Lifted his gaze to the woman

at the door. The reason Lazarus had been prevented from gaining a final victory. The cause of his own continued survival, though it grated to admit.

A sloe-eyed beauty, Miss Helena Roseingrave was denied perfection only by the corded strength in her arms, the broad shoulders, the squared-off jut of her chin. In all other respects, she was amazing. Jack obviously agreed. His eyes ate her alive, a foolish smile hovering at the edges of his mouth.

Her gaze swept over the two of them, the usual *Amhas-draoi* arrogance in full view. "She'll sleep for the next twenty-four hours. That's normal. When she wakes, she may or may not remember what happened. That too is normal. Don't push her. Memories will return in time."

Aidan felt the first unclenching of his innards. The first stirring of a warmth stolen from him after the glacial freeze of Lazarus's attack. He hadn't lost his one chance at completing the diary's translation. At understanding what secrets it harbored that would warrant murder.

The woman's sphinxlike stare remained fixed upon him as if she read his thoughts. Saw his self-interested relief. His refusal to linger on any emotion softer than expediency.

He wanted to wipe that smug reproach from her face. Tell her what she could do with her disdain. Instead, he reminded himself she had saved him. Saved them. He stood in debt to the *Amhas-draoi*. A disturbing idea, but enough to banish the misery wrought by Cat's lifeless body, the chalky gray of a face whose contours he'd traced only days before, the curve of a mouth his lips still remembered.

Jack crossed to the door, bowing to Miss Roseingrave as if in the presence of royalty. "Forgive my cousin. He's stunned to speechlessness with gratitude."

Amusement lit her dark eyes. "I see that." She sobered. "But I understand his reluctance to accept our help. The history between his family and the brotherhood does not make for easy confidences."

Aidan broke his stubborn silence. "If you want to gain my trust, you can begin by telling me who or what just attacked us?"

She offered a curt campaigner's nod in return. "His name is Lazarus, just as he told you."

"Cat killed him. I saw her do it. No human could have survived that shot."

Miss Roseingrave's face dropped into solemn lines. Unsettling even to one accustomed to the freedoms allowed women among his kind. Freedoms were one thing. A female who wielded magic and weapons with a soldier's ease was something completely different. Again, unsettling.

"Not a normal human, no. But Lazarus isn't a normal human. Not anymore. He's a soldier of Domnu. One of the *Domnuathi.*"

Jack and Aidan exchanged mirroring expressions of confusion.

"A creature whose original humanity has been twisted into something unnatural," she clarified. "Whose soul has been drawn back from the land of the dead to inhabit a body created from the bones of its former self. As *Domnuathi*, he is in thrall to his maker. Compelled to follow his commands."

"A slave," Jack offered as if he'd passed some kind of test.

She answered with another quick nod. "Aye. Though we're speaking mainly in theory. None within the current order of *Amhas-draoi* have encountered a soldier of Domnu before. The magic it takes to create one is staggering. None have ever survived the attempt."

Aidan kept up his mad pacing as his mind grappled with this new scenario. "So how do you kill something already dead?"

Her gaze flicked to the sideboard, Jack jumping to fill her a restorative glass. Aidan watching the interplay with an eye roll and impatient drumming of his fingers.

She let out a resigned sigh at the first sip of claret. "He's not dead. He's as alive in his own way as you or me. Just in an altered state."

"That's not an answer to my question. How do we kill him?"

Jack shot him a pained glance, but Aidan's impatience grew. His thigh and his head hurt. His body ached. Cat lay insensible upstairs. And he was no closer than before to discovering what all this had to do with the diary or his father.

"If I can't kill him, what's to stop him from returning and trying again? Do I have to watch my back from now on? Jump at every shadow? Are you planning on camping out in my drawing room?"

This time it was Jack and Miss Roseingrave who exchanged pointed looks. She straightened, a stance one took when meeting an enemy head on. "Give us the diary, Lord Kilronan. Give it to the *Amhas-draoi*, and Lazarus will have no reason to return. That's what he wants. That's his directive."

Her words landed like stones on his chest. Tore the answer from his mouth in a chain of sailor's swearing even Jack winced against. "Who told you about—" the red haze of his vision landed square on "—Jack?"

His cousin leapt to his own defense. "I warned you that

book would lead to trouble. And I was right. Only Miss Roseingrave's arrival drove that hell spawn away. Only her abilities kept you and Cat from death tonight."

"I can handle it."

"What more needs to happen? This fellow, Lazarus. The *Unseelie* summoning. Hell, the damned brawl in that alley. Your father's obsession is threatening to pull you in just as deep."

"Enough!" Aidan's barked command stunned Jack to silence. He turned to the *Amhas-draoi.* "If I'd risk death to keep the diary from him, why would I hand it over to you?"

"You may despise our actions, but you know we act in good faith and for the good of all *Other.*"

"You do what's advantageous to your cause. Having the diary locked away serves you. Not me. My family's future is tied to that book. To learning what really happened." He met her stare for stare. "To knowing the whole truth."

"And if I offer you truth, would you believe?"

"Try me."

"Lazarus is a slave to his creator. Do you wonder who that man might be? Who has the power and the motivation to capture your father's diary for himself? Who would eliminate anyone standing between himself and gaining the knowledge therein?"

Aidan sat in silent fume, refusing to surrender an inch. He'd been trapped into this confrontation. Hated every minute of it.

Miss Roseingrave speared him with another unnerving *Amhas-draoi* stare that burned with brandy intensity. "Lord Kilronan, what do you know of your brother's recent movements?

———o———

She woke, remembering.

Not where she was or how she'd come to be lying muffled beneath quilts in a bed large enough to fit ten of her. Instead she recalled the tight, searching pucker of her son's mouth, the wispy black hair, the clean baby smell of him. Even things she'd since forgotten were newly etched on her waking consciousness with indelible clarity. The way he had of patting her breast as he suckled, the incalculable wisdom in his newborn eyes. For one glistening moment she'd traveled back in time, and he remained a soft weight against her heart.

She lay completely still, hoping to cage these recaptured memories before they faded, but already shadows clouded the perfection of the images. Gaps punctuated the picture she'd conjured, leaving her with naught but sensations of helplessness, grief, and a loss as great as when they'd torn her dead son from her arms.

Tears leaked from the corners of her eyes. Slid down her cheeks to drop salt bitter past her lips.

She slept.

Brendan was alive. That was Aidan's first and overriding thought.

Father hadn't gone through with it. His brother hadn't been led like a lamb to slaughter.

Somewhere out there, Brendan was alive.

Aidan stood within the shadowed bedchamber. Surveyed the stripped bed frame, the furniture swathed in Holland covers, the yawning, cold hearth. He'd not been in here for years. Not out of any childish sentimentality. Simply because a lack of guests meant a lack of need to open extra rooms.

He ran a casual finger over the dusty mantel, a corner of his mouth twitching at the stain above where an errant thrown egg had marred the expensive Chinese wallpaper. All right, six thrown eggs, but Brendan had deserved it for swiping Aidan's birthday half crown. Father had summoned him to the library where a dripping, eggy Brendan had run to tattle. Aidan had been given a sharp lecture on the nature of self-restraint. But now that he thought about it, he never had gotten that half crown back from his little brother.

Aidan hadn't thought about that incident in years, yet the *Amhas-draoi*'s insinuations had stirred all sorts of similar slights and strange oddities to the surface—Brendan's tight-lipped silence whenever questioned about the meetings with Father and his friends, his unexpected fury at catching Aidan in his rooms unaccompanied, his dismissive rebuff of Aidan's invitation to join him in London. That last one still stung. He'd not realized at the time it would be the final letter he'd receive from his brother.

But did those things alone point to the menacing conclusions drawn about him? Hardly.

"Aidan?" came a tentative voice from behind.

"What do you want?" he answered, startled by the renewed sense of loss these memories dredged up. Brendan's absence had been a grief long healed over. Or so he'd thought until the discovery of his father's damned diary. The resurrection of numerous buried hurts.

"I came to make sure you were all right."

Aidan finally turned to face his cousin, the pathetic hangdog expression on his face almost humorous. Or it would have been had Aidan not been in his current black temper. "As well as can be expected." He jerked his head in the direction of downstairs. "Has she gone?"

"Aye." Jack's own troubled gaze circled the room before coming to rest on Aidan. "I know you said to keep the *Amhas-draoi* out of it, but you have to admit if I hadn't—"

Aidan offered a chilly, humorless smile. "If you hadn't, you'd even now be preparing to pack to make way for the new earl."

Jack shuddered. "Bite your tongue."

"And loath as I am to admit it, you saved my sorry backside with your bungling interference. Thank you."

"So all's forgiven?"

"On that score, yes." Aidan took a stiff and painful turn about the room, his thigh one big knotted ache throbbing all the way to the bone. Pausing at the window, he twitched back the blinds. Looked out on the garden as if he could pierce the gloom. See what lurked beyond the meager light of his taper.

The night breathed like a great animal. And he shivered, imagining the creature Lazarus. The hollow, pitiless stare as he struck, but for that split second's regret.

What sort of devil would create a man from the dust of his former life? And what sort of hell would that existence be for one who found himself enslaved beneath a madman's spell?

"Have you reconsidered Helena's advice? Will you entrust the diary to the *Amhas-draoi*?"

Aidan smirked. "Helena is it?" Resolve stiffened his mouth into a grim line. "No. The diary stays with me."

Jack joined him at the window. "That creature is still out there, Aidan. And you heard her, it won't give up. Besides, you don't know what more harm that bloody book will do before it's all over. There must be a good reason Brendan wants it so badly."

"Not Brendan!" Aidan snarled.

"You heard her—"

"I heard her offer a convincing argument, yes. But not convincing enough to change my mind. Brendan's no black sorcerer conjuring living nightmares from dead bodies."

"I know you don't want to believe it," Jack argued. "But it does make sense. His disappearance right before your father's murder. His continued absence after so many years. And who else would know your father kept a diary?"

Aidan had already battled his way through those arguments within his own mind. Come to conclusions he sought now to explain to his skeptical cousin. "If he'd wanted the diary, why didn't he simply take it with him when he vanished? Why wait six years to come after it? Or why not come himself and ask for it? He's my brother, not some stranger. He should know I'd let him look his fill. He doesn't have to kill to gain it." He shook his head. "Someone else is behind this. It has to be."

Jack shrugged his grudging acceptance of Aidan's persuasions.

"No, I keep the diary. Cat and I have barely scratched the surface."

"And how do you plan on remaining alive long enough to finish the translation?"

Aidan had already figured that one out. "By leaving," he replied. "Kilronan House is all yours."

"So I'm left to fend off your unwanted and undead visitor?" Jack offered a grim twist of his lips. "I'll try to contain my enthusiasm."

The scratchy starch of clean sheets. The comforting weight of a blanket. The quick chirrup of birds beyond her window. The faint scent of bay rum. These were Cat's initial impressions upon waking.

She opened her eyes to a world streaming in sunshine. Squinted against the blinding vividness as she scanned the room. Tried to piece together recent events.

As everywhere else within Kilronan House, this bed-chamber suffered from a lack of funds. Nothing jarring, simply a sense of chronic neglect—plasterwork left unre-paired, a spiderweb crack running jagged down one pane of window glass, drapes frayed and left to fade in the sun.

All right, so she knew where she was. A mark in her favor. She also knew why. To assist Aidan in translating the diary. So far, so good. Things were returning to her mushy, befuddled mind.

Cautiously, she sat up, expecting . . . what?

The bone-grinding pain of broken limbs? Her body ached like one big pulled muscle, but nothing more.

A stomach somewhere in her throat? No, actually she was ravenously hungry.

A brain sloshed and foggy with vague recollections of a fight and an enormous man with murder in his eyes, his mage energy crushing her like an egg?

One out of three.

Her blood went cold as the events of last night felled her like a hammer's blow. But she lived. The intruder hadn't suc-ceeded in turning her into a puddle of nothing on the floor.

How had she survived? Had Aidan struck a bargain? Had he handed the diary over? Was her time trapped within the limbo of Kilronan House at an end? Would Aidan re-turn her to the streets where he'd found her? And why did that thought make her want to curl even tighter into her bed and never emerge?

To combat the unwanted sensation, she forced herself up. Swung her legs out of bed. Tested her strength with a wobbly rise to her feet. Immediately, the room took on the whirling aspect usually accompanying a bad plate of oysters. Nausea, cold sweats, pins and needles. She sank back onto the mattress with a shut-eyed moan of pure *ick.*

So much for hungry.

Flopping back onto the pillows, she stared up into the bed hangings. Wished the answers to her questions would suddenly appear there as if by, well, magic.

While she searched for solutions in the damask, a shadow fell across her. Aidan's lean, noble features and bronze brown glare bursting her illusion of control. She remained a mere puppet in a larger game. A game she began to wonder if Aidan even understood.

"You're awake."

She tipped her head in his direction. Offered a cynical curl of her lips. "Yes, but beyond that, I make no claims."

Amusement brightened his eyes for a moment before his face settled into grim lines. "Can you travel?"

She shot him a you've-got-to-be-joking look. "I can barely stand."

He sized her up with a long, deliberative stare that had her squirming. "Be ready to leave Kilronan House in three hours."

Anger flared through weakened muscles. Quickened a mind spinning in futile circles. All her pent-up frustrations finding a target in the arrogant condescension of this overbearing earl. "The hell I will."

He blinked and for a moment she thought she saw again that glint of amusement. But so quickly did it pass that she couldn't be certain, leaving only hard-jawed annoyance and disbelief that someone like her might actually thwart the plans of someone like him. "Excuse me?"

Being flat on her back was a disadvantage. She struggled up, meeting him eye to eye and scowl for scowl. "I said I'm not going." Before he could offer a retort, she plowed on, her blood stirred now she'd begun. "I've done everything you've asked and been almost killed in the process. Who's to say I won't end up dead if I stay with you? And despite how it appears, I like living, thank you very much. I'd like to continue doing it for a bit longer."

"Which is why we're leaving," he explained in a tone of voice normally reserved for small, stubborn children. "Lazarus won't give up until he's gained the diary. And now that the *Amhas-draoi* know it exists, they'll be just as persistent if not just as treacherous about laying their hands on it. I can't fight both."

He hadn't done such a grand job of fighting one, but she didn't say it.

"Kilronan House isn't safe. We need to get away from here. Out of Dublin."

Leave the city? Travel alone in company with Kilronan and his magnetic gaze? His body-luring kisses? His sensually charged charisma working at her indifference with a sapper's doggedness? Definitely a very, very bad idea.

Now she was on her feet. A finger jammed repeatedly into his unyielding chest. "And where would we go that's safe?"

Had she said we? Had she actually agreed to this?

"West." He ignored her finger. Admirable in someone who—now she looked closely—appeared as battle-scarred as she. The tiny fatigue lines gathering at the corners of his eyes, the pastiness underlying the bronze of his skin, the tension humming along jumpy muscles. He may have survived, but it had been a hard-won battle. "There's someone I must speak with. Someone who knew my father."

She flung herself away from him to stomp like a madwoman about the room. "I can't just go haring off with you to some unknown destination on an insane hunch."

"Social calendar full?" he responded wryly. "Of course you can go. Must go. Or have you forgotten Smith and his associate? They're still out there. No doubt nursing a dangerous grudge. Your friend Geordie's yet to turn up living or dead. You've no home. No work." He ticked off his reasons one by one. Each like a nail in the coffin of her justifications. "There's nothing left for you here, Cat. And everything to be gained by traveling to Knockniry. As I said before, we leave in three hours."

"I can't—" Stopped, consternation wiping away the last vestige of argument. She was vertical. Ambulatory. And in naught but her chemise with Aidan's eyes burning a hole right through it. With a groan, she swept the quilt off the bed and around her shoulders.

"Miss Osborne won't be pleased."

His mouth thinned to an irritated line. "No, she won't," was all he answered.

A malicious spark pushed her into final agreement. "Fine. Three hours."

Aidan crossed to the door. "I'll send someone to assist you in dressing."

He'd made it to the top of the stairs before Cat came to her senses. Shouted after him, "Who's Lazarus anyway, and what has any of this got to do with the *Amhas-draoi*?"

# Eleven

"What's to stop Lazarus from catching us out here?" Cat asked the back end of Aidan's horse. "What makes you think we aren't walking right into an ambush?"

She scanned the dripping trees as she asked the question. Peered through the tangled overgrowth lining the river of mud calling itself a road.

"We may well be." Aidan swiveled in the saddle to answer, hat pulled low over his brow, a blue tinge to his lips. "But that was guaranteed if we hadn't left the city. I'm banking on speed and secrecy to keep us safe until we reach Knockniry."

She tensed as her own mount tossed its head at the crack of a twig, the squawk of a startled jay. "And then?" she persisted, wiping the rain from her eyes.

Aidan didn't answer.

Or couldn't.

After all, as he'd explained it to her, Lazarus couldn't be killed. Or at least, no one had figured out how to do it yet. Brilliant.

She shrugged deeper into the heavy cloak he'd tossed her as they slipped up the area steps to be met near Henry Street by a groom leading two horses. It had been the last notice he'd taken of her before reverting to stone-faced reserve throughout the hours that followed. As they made their circuitous way out of the city and onto the road toward Edenderry. As they paused just long enough to rest the horses and snatch a hasty bite at a roadside tavern outside Kilcock. As the rain moved in, turning a merely interminable trip to one downright dismal. It had only been in the last miles that she'd ventured conversation. That or go stark staring mad with boredom.

"Jack was only acting out of concern for you, you know. Perhaps it would have been better to give the diary to the *Amhas-draoi*. They could protect it." She peered over her shoulder into the veil of drizzly mist closing in behind them. "And us."

Aidan's whole body went stiff in the saddle. "Protect us? Is that what you think they'd do? Hardly. They'd feed us to the wolves if it suited them. They want to use my father's diary as bait. Dangle it in front of Lazarus and his master to flush them out."

"And is that wrong? I've met Lazarus. The *Amhas-draoi* are welcome to him. Dangle away, I say."

Aidan never turned around. Instead, his voice carried back to her on a ribbon of silver cloud. "And the man who controls him? Lazarus's master?"

She tightened her hands on the reins, a razor reminiscence slicing right through her. She choked down the momentary panic. "Anyone who can control that monster must be a monster in his own right. The *Amhas-draoi* can have them both, and good riddance."

Aidan didn't answer at once. Cat wondered if he would. But finally, he spoke. His words rough with confusion. "I won't believe it. Lies. It has to be."

And with that enigmatic comment, a fresh downpour sent her burrowing into the cloak like a turtle into its shell. The wool smelled like Aidan—a musky combination of scents sparking a tingling heat in her belly.

For a moment, she found herself back in the garden of Kilronan House. Aidan's heartbeat steady beneath her palm, his lips moving against hers in a slow seduction, the track of his fingers upon her face loosening the hard core of her anger.

But this time, she did not step out of reach. This time, she did not allow Jeremy's ghost to insinuate itself between them. This time, she gave in to the temptation of Aidan's touch. Surrendered to the honey swell of sensation drugging her body. And found release in his arms upon the soft grass beneath the sheltering laburnums.

An explosion of wings and croaking squawks jerked her back to reality with the heart-stopping force of a gunshot. And the molten slide of orgasm gave way to the slippery muck of the road, unceasing rain, and thigh muscles stretched to the breaking point.

She glanced at Aidan's uncompromising back from beneath the soggy hood of her cloak.

Had she said this trip would be very, very bad? Try horrible times infinity.

Aidan woke, blinking up into the gray of predawn, confusion at his whereabouts making him question the heavy oaken beams above his head, the draft from a rattling set of windows, and the dampness in the smelly blankets covering him. But with the acclimation of his vision came clarity of thought. A sparsely traveled road. A rickety inn chosen for its unassuming façade. A bedchamber that under normal circumstances he'd have handed over to his manservant with reservation.

He watched the creep of shadows over the floor as night faded into another rain-weary day. Shifted on the thin, straw-filled pallet. Felt the tendons in his thigh give with a snap akin to the original gunshot. The pain slicing from his leg to his brain, dragging a groan from dry lips.

". . . Jeremy . . . nowhere," came a grief-stricken entreaty.

Aidan froze. What the hell was Cat doing in his room? And who was Jeremy?

Leaning up on his elbows against the lingering strain of overused muscles, he found his translator and traveling companion curled in a threadbare blanket on the floor in front of the dying remains of the fire.

"Cat," he hissed.

She roused with a bleary, confused shake of her head.

"Cat."

This time she heard him. Came fully awake with a startled sailor's oath.

He raised a curious eyebrow.

A flush of scarlet creeping up her throat, she drew her knees to her chest. Dragged the blanket up over her shoulders. Her hair lay tousled with sleep. And from beneath the hem of her chemise, bare toes peeked. An innocent vulnerability that had Aidan shifting uncomfortably in his bed. The agony moving from his leg to his groin.

"How did you get in here?" His gaze shot to what he was sure had been the locked door.

She answered with a proud sniff. "Anyone with half a brain and a hairpin could have gotten past that lock."

"All right, then. Next question. Why"—he motioned toward the nest of blankets, the fire, her current state of dishabille—"the midnight visit?"

"The roof leaks in my chamber."

He glanced to the window and the gray misty veil of rain.

"Sieves have fewer holes," she complained. "When an ominous drip started over my bed, I surrendered to the flood and decided to camp in here."

Skepticism must have been written all over his face because a glittering scowl lit her jade stare. "Why did you think I'd come?"

A rusty smile curled a corner of his mouth. "Let's just say I had a theory."

She scowled. "Oh, really? And what would Miss Osborne think of your theory?"

Their eyes met. Cat's green gaze as luminous as river stones. A shift and shimmer of emotion he felt all the way to his bones. It made him bold. Reckless. And gut-seethingly jealous.

"Who's Jeremy?" he blurted.

He knew he'd made a fatal error as soon as the stupid question left his lips.

Instantly the shutters came down. Inscrutability replacing the scorching heat he knew he'd seen racing over the surface of her features. So much for the dirty little fantasy he'd been conjuring.

"What does it matter to you?" Her tone regally cold.

"You spoke the name in your sleep." He backtracked like mad. But the damage had been done.

Cat rose. Padded toward the door, her thin shoulders erect, back ramrod straight. "Jeremy was my first mistake." Paused on a shaky, indrawn breath. "I won't make a second."

"Miss O'Connell? Is that you?"

As if conjured by Aidan's earlier heart-stopping, horrible question, the past rose up to smack Cat right between the eyes. William Danvers shook the rain from his greatcoat. Peeled off his gloves. Ran hands through hair damp from the day's drizzly rain before sauntering toward her table, his curious gaze searching her for any sign of recognition.

Normally, veiling her features took no more effort than breathing. But right now, inhaling and exhaling seemed like monumental tasks. She hid behind her cup of chocolate, scalding her mouth on an ill-thought swallow while she steadied her shaking limbs. Concentrated on the visage forming in her mind—lighter hair, rounder face, weaker chin, paler eyes, a body just a touch on the plump side— felt the minute changes as pins and needles tightening her skin, and knew she'd succeeded when his assurance turned to uncertainty.

"I'm sorry. I thought—"

She offered him a confused smile and a shrug of her shoulders. A quick shake of her head. "Sono spiacente, signore. Non capisco l'inglese."

Prayed Danvers didn't know Italian.

His immediate dismayed tug at his cravat told her she'd chosen well.

He began again. "You look very much like someone I knew once." Shouted as if volume might overcome the language barrier. Drew inquiring looks from the few ill-kempt patrons sharing the taproom.

"Can I assist you?"

Cat and Danvers both turned at the smooth inquiring tone, but Cat heard the thread of cautious edginess behind the upper-class condescension.

Aidan's gaze held every drop of the world-weary nobleman, his demeanor as crisp and correct as if the three of them met at the Castle for a ball. He studied her distorted features with a flicker of confusion before turning to Danvers, whose eyes widened with recognition then pleasure.

She sent up a silent prayer. *Please, Aidan.* Don't give her up. Not to the biggest busybody in Dublin.

Danvers cleared his throat before sketching a bow. "Your servant, my lord. My horse threw a shoe, and I've had to kick my heels here while the smithy fits a new one." He paused, apparently expecting Aidan to explain his own surprising presence at such a seedy and out-of-the-way establishment.

But Aidan remained completely in character. The aloof and achingly proper peer of the realm.

Danvers plowed on, unfazed by the silent set down. "I was speaking with Miss—"

"Have we met?" Aidan interrupted while continuing his smoldering staredown. Cat had felt the force of that gaze. Knew it for the quelling confidence squash it was.

"Oh yes, Lord Kilronan." Danvers graced Aidan with an oily smile. "Once or twice at Daly's in the company of your cousin. And I believe we both attended a dinner party at the Barnwalls' last fall." He darted another searching glance at Cat, who was trying to be invisible behind her chocolate.

"I approached when I recognized the young lady." He frowned. "Or thought I had."

Cat bit her lip as she ran a finger around the rim of her cup. "Pensa che parli soltanto italiano. Gioco avanti. Per favore."

Aidan answered with a very bewildered shake of his head. "Are you speaking Italian, C—"

Aidan leapt, but too late. "Damn it! Are you mad?" Chocolate dripped hot and sticky across his coat.

Cat jumped up, apologizing in babbling Italian while mopping at Aidan with her napkin.

He grabbed her elbow. "May I speak with you for a moment?" he chewed through clenched teeth. Guided her away from the table without sparing Danvers a single backward glance.

In the stairwell, he rounded on her. "What was that?"

"He recognized me. I had to do something."

"You know that man?"

She twisted the soggy napkin between her hands. Hated the panicky sense of her life unraveling. "Yes. A long time ago."

Aidan cocked a curious brow, a gleam she didn't trust sparking his dark eyes. "And so you hid."

She grabbed his sleeve. "Please, Aidan. Let it go. Go back and tell him I'm some long lost Italian cousin of yours. Tell him I'm your crazy Aunt Mary just released from the asylum. Tell him I'm your latest mistress trained in foreign erotic arts. I don't care."

Aidan acted as if he hadn't heard her. "Someone who knew Miss O'Connell from her days prior to a Saint Patrick's deanery tenement," he mused to himself. "Who knows why she hides. Why she runs." He met her frightened gaze with his own impenetrable stare. "What she dreams."

"It's not important," she pleaded.

His questing gaze searched her out as the tip of his finger skimmed her cheek. Pushed a tendril of hair behind her ear.

She fought back the shiver answering that gentle caress. Knew he'd not been fooled.

"Are you certain?" he whispered. "Because, for some reason, I find it very important."

After sending Cat to their room, Aidan strolled back to Danvers, now seated with a bottle of claret and a plate of boiled beef and potatoes.

Of all the thrice-damned things to have happen. To come across someone they knew when he'd worked so hard to remain invisible. At least he might gain something from the debacle. A window to the woman who intrigued him more and more with every passing moment. Much to his growing consternation.

And the detriment of his clothing.

Upon seeing Aidan's grim-faced approach, the man rose to his feet. Offered a chair. "I hope you weren't too hard on the girl. I'm sure she didn't mean to uh, hurl her chocolate at you."

Aidan accepted the invitation, still dabbing at his waist-coat. "Carlotta is new to the country," he lied. "She's a trifle excitable." He peered over at Danvers. "You made her nervous."

Danvers adjusted the cuffs of his bottle green coat, rubbed at an invisible spot on his buckskin breeches, clearly both ill at ease in Aidan's company and eager to push himself into the earl's good graces. It would be almost too easy to pull information out of this unctuous jackanapes.

"I apologize for approaching her in such a forward way, my lord. For a moment I was certain . . . you see, she was so very like . . ." he broke off. Took a hearty swallow of his wine.

"She was so very like who, Mr. Danvers? I'm curious. Who did you mistake Carlotta for?"

Hesitation passed over Danvers's features. But only for a moment before his obvious desire to please won out. He leaned forward. "I knew a young woman a few years ago."

Aidan kept his gaze as bland as milk.

Danvers hurried on. "Our fathers served together in the Mediterranean, you see, and she and I spent much time together growing up. For just a second, I thought your"— he stopped, apparently unsure of what to label Aidan's companion and not wanting to get it wrong—"but I was mistaken."

Aidan leaned back. Steepled his fingers beneath his chin, regarding the man with his most supercilious stare. "And just out of curiosity, what happened to the young woman in question?"

Danvers's gaze went flat, his face pulled to a taut mask of disappointment. "I can only pray she has died, my lord."

Aidan's brows shot up. "A remarkable statement."

"I mean it only in the most sympathetic way, Lord Kilronan." He rushed to clarify. "Miss O'Connell and I were close once upon a time. But there was a scandal with a young man. Her disgrace humiliated her family and shocked her friends. She disappeared shortly after it became known. None have had word from her since."

"That's quite a story." Aidan masked his surprise in bored cynicism before forestalling the queasy stomach churn of questions by lighting a cheroot on the candle flame. Inhaling on a nerve-calming drag. Grinding the remainder out.

"And what happened to the gentleman involved?" His tone held a whiplash violence that had Danvers cringing, the wrinkled nose and disapproving glare at the unfashionable cheroot wiped from a startled face.

"No one knows, my lord."

"You mean he disappeared too?" Aidan growled.

"I mean Miss O'Connell refused to reveal his identity. It's still a mystery."

A muscle jumped in Aidan's clenched jaw. Not quite a mystery. Aidan had a name.

Jeremy.

Lazarus prowled the town house from attics to cellars, knowing he'd arrived too late. Kilronan had fled, no doubt taking the diary with him. The only inhabitants remaining, a handful of terrified servants who'd scattered like chickens upon his assault.

He searched anyway. Tearing through rooms. Upending furniture. Emptying drawers and chests and cupboards in a smash of splintered wood and shattered china. Using the pretext of his hunt to ease the roaring fury howling through him like a northern gale wind.

Chest heaving, muscles jumping, he dropped into a chair. Hung his head until the worst passed.

The *Amhas-draoi*'s attack had weakened him more than he would admit. Even now, he sensed the lingering damage from the magic unleashed upon him. A slowing of his reaction time. A grating shift of tendon against bone as if she'd knocked his entire skeleton off balance. But not even that catastrophic force of mage energy had been enough to stop him completely. He'd suffered. Felt the chill of mortality slide like needles through his veins. Hovered in the white light of eternity for hours or days or weeks. But in the end, it hadn't been enough to send him back. Send him home.

Sinking to his knees upon the floor, he threw back his head. Raised his fists. Roared his hate and his fear and his desperation to the empty room.

He remained bound to the hunt. Bound to Máelodor. Bound to a life where death could be meted out but never claimed.

# twelve

The house stood off the main road. Down an overgrown lane shaded by rowan and snarling gorse. A far cry from the wide avenue and rolling park he remembered. Back then, there had been woods to roam and streams to wade. Tracks leading up into the scrubby, windswept highlands of the Slieve Aughty and down toward silty creek beds and swift rivers flowing south and west toward Lough Derg and the Shannon.

Daz had been a presence in Aidan's life forever. A big, barrel chested, laughing giant with a scoundrel's tongue and a childish sense of mischief that charmed the Douglas children. Even when the shadows began to form and the golden idyll of childhood faded to an edgy awareness of growing storms, Aidan relied on Daz to bring a bit of the sparkle back. To remind him of a time when he didn't feel the press of unknown fears weighing him down. When guilty suspicions had yet to take him over.

After the murder of Aidan's father, Daz had vanished

into his mountain holding like a badger to his hole. Returning no letters. Welcoming no visitors.

Absorbed by other worries, Aidan had endured that silence. Until now. Now he wanted answers. Answers that, according to the diary, Daz could give.

Beside him, Cat swayed bleary-eyed and silent in the saddle. They'd been riding without a break since noon, pausing only to rest the horses. Stretch their legs. In the days since their unfortunate encounter with Danvers she'd said no more about the mysterious Jeremy. And Aidan had never again awoken to find her curled sleeping upon his floor.

But he'd watched her from beneath hooded lids as the miles and days passed. Her stubborn chin, her body's sylph-like curves, her hands fisted with tension on the reins. And jealousy had tightened into a hard, angry knot in his chest. Envy for the man who'd held Cat's heart. Fury for the man who'd broken it.

"Will Mr. Ahern be able to tell us why the *Amhas-draoi* believe Brendan sent Lazarus?" Cat asked.

"He's the son of the notorious Earl of Kilronan. That would be proof enough for Scathach's trained assassins." Miss Roseingrave's accusations still grated. Almost as much as Jack's willingness to believe. Brendan had been a victim. Not a perpetrator.

"But didn't he sit in on your father's meetings? He must have known about the dangerous lines they were crossing. Their experiments with dark magic."

He gave an angry shrug. "My brother was no participant in an insane *Other* conspiracy. Brendan was a damned pretty-boy bookworm. Cried like a baby at the slightest bruise. Hated fencing, cricket, boxing. Loathed cliff climbing. About the only activity we both had in common was riding. He rode hell-for-leather. Could manage any half-broke rogue mount my father brought home."

"People aren't always what they seem," she said quietly.

He shot her a look, but her face remained veiled in shadow. Only the ghostly curve of her cheek suspended amid the folds of night.

A rabbit erupted from the bushes, frightening her horse, loosening her tongue on a well-phrased oath. And the charged moment passed.

The overgrown avenue opened into a sweep of weed-choked gravel before the stately stone house, now swallowed by ivy so that only the upper windows remained completely free of the tangled jungle of green.

Cat pulled up. "Are you sure he still lives here?"

She was right to be skeptical. No light shone from the windows and shrubbery had overtaken the front door. Damn. He'd made no provision in case Daz was gone. Or worse—dead. The diary had so far yielded up no other clues.

Aidan slid to the ground. Looked up at the darkened façade with something akin to hopelessness. Banished it before it took root. "He has to."

"Who is it, Maude?"

A raspy whine sounded from beyond the crack of the garden door, the churlish housekeeper planting herself on the threshold and refusing to open it wider.

Cat tucked her hands beneath her cloak. Cast a doubtful glance around her. This isolated house was Aidan's sanctuary? Except for the beefy-knuckled brawler of a housekeeper, Cat had yet to see any defenses that might hold back an attack by the nightmarish Lazarus.

"A gentleman," the housekeeper shouted over her shoulder. "Says his name's Kilronan. Says he knows you."

"Kilronan!" The whine rose to a shout. "It can't be. Kilronan's dead. They're all dead. Get rid of him, Maude. He's an imposter. One of them."

The housekeeper started to shut the door, but Aidan jammed his foot in the crack. "Tell him it's Aidan."

Maude rolled her yellow eyes, sighing with enough force even Cat, standing a foot away, smelled the sour odor of gin on the housekeeper's breath. "Says his name's Aidan."

A pregnant silence from the inside of the house. Someone heard. Someone considered. "Aidan Douglas?" came the same whiny voice. "Kilronan's oldest boy? Let him in, Maude. Let him in, you horrible strumpet."

The housekeeper cackled, smoothing a hand down her apron front as she curtseyed them in. "Have it your way, ya old grump-necked curmudgeon. Come in, milord. Milady."

"In for a penny . . ." Aidan murmured as he ushered Cat ahead of him with an encouraging smile.

A man stood at the far side of the room, dressed in the style of an earlier century—clocked stockings, knee breeches, and a frock coat that had once been a beautiful midnight blue, now faded with wear and age. Evidence of former strength was still visible in his huge hands, broad shoulders, but age had shrunken his frame, leaving him hunched and crooked.

Lank, gray hair hung to his shoulders while spectacles perched on a red-veined nose, enlarging a pair of rheumy eyes. Crumbs spotted his front, stains blotted his rumpled breeches. And—Cat looked again to be certain—he wore only one buckled shoe.

He studied Aidan through a narrowed gaze before his

haggard face broke into a relieved smile. "Dear me, it is you. Come in, lad. Come in."

Aidan seemed as startled as Cat by the man's odd appearance though he hid it behind a polite bow and a smooth courtier's smile. "I apologize for not waiting for an invitation. I wrote but never received an answer to my letter. Decided to risk it."

Ahern harrumphed away Aidan's apology. "Always welcome. Always welcome." Before mumbling, "Thought you were one of them. Never rest. Never give up until it's done. Until we're all gone." He began rummaging through his pockets. "Maude? Look alive. Prepare rooms for our guests, you bitter old shrew. Can't you see they're exhausted?"

Maude shook her head. "No use shouting at me, you old fool. I'll see to it. Never you fear," before shuffling out of the room on muttered curses.

Cat shot Aidan a sidelong look, but he ignored her. Tightened his grip on the saddlebag slung over his shoulder. "I came to ask your help, Uncle Daz."

Ahern never paused in searching his pockets. Pulled out a piece of string. A stone. A shriveled, green leaf. "Don't know what help I could give a young sprig like you. Why don't you ask your father? Always was right brilliant when it came to things like that."

"My father's dead, Daz," Aidan answered smoothly. Tossing his saddlebag onto a table. Unbuckling the flap. "He was killed six years ago."

"Kilronan? Dead? Of course he is." Out came the broken half of a bird's egg, a crushed flower bereft of most of its petals, a feather. "Scathach and her cursed *Amhas-draoi* killed him."

Aidan paused while Cat gave a don't-look-at me shrug.

"That's why I came to see you," Aidan plowed on. "I thought you might be able to help me." He withdrew the diary. "With this."

Ahern finally looked up. Gagged on a wheezy breath, his face blanching to a ghostly white. "Kilronan's diary." Met Aidan's eye with a gaze sharp as a blade. "It's no wonder you're running, boy. You've got a devil by the tail, for certes."

Aidan stretched his bad leg toward the parlor fire, hoping to ease the cramps knotting his muscles. Endless days in the saddle had worsened the plaguey effects of the old wound.

Daz watched him with an unflinching stare. "Still bothering you, is it?"

Aidan lifted a brow in surprise.

Daz merely smiled. "I remember the night your father received word you'd been wounded. Your mother burst in despite all his warnings never to intrude. Shoved the damned letter beneath his nose and told him to hell with his warnings, his son and heir was dying." He shook with wheezy laughter. "Never saw your father so flummoxed— or so scared."

"Scared I might die?"

"Aye, that for certain. But scared of what the others might think—thought they'd see it as a weakness. Fear for one measly son when the entire fate of the world of *Other* hung in the balance. Perhaps if it had been Brendan, they'd have felt differently. They respected him. You?" His hands opened palm up in a surrender gesture.

"Not at all," Aidan finished the unspoken thought.

Daz leaned back in the chair. Closed his eyes. "You lacked the qualities they admired."

"In other words, I didn't have Brendan's abilities with magic."

He'd always known it, but hearing Daz admit his father's partiality stung. Even now.

Daz opened his eyes. Stared Aidan down, no trace of madness in his pale gaze. "It was Brendan finally made your father see reason. Called him the worst sort of coward if he didn't ignore their disapproval and go to you. I'd never seen your father so wroth with the boy." He cackled, slapping his thigh. "But he went."

He'd come all right. All the way to London. Burst into Aidan's rooms on Henrietta Street like a force of nature, his cold fury obvious even through Aidan's agony-laced laudanum haze. Taken the first opportunity to rake him over the coals for the scandalous affair, going into great length about Aidan's stupidity, his disastrous lack of discretion, the folly of his immature behavior.

He'd never stopped regretting that ill-fated duel. And not solely because of the lameness still afflicting him after so many years. But because of the final wedge it had driven between him and his father. A gulf that never had a chance to be repaired.

But if it took Brendan's rebukes to rouse his father to attend what could very well have been his son's deathbed, what did that say about the strength of that relationship? Had the bond between him and his father been more one-sided than he'd thought? Had Father truly cared about any of his children? Or were they mere pieces to be used and discarded as needed?

Aidan sought to make sense of it all while fighting the dull press of old regrets and new questions. Felt the stab of a headache erupt behind his eyes. He sought escape in the facts he did know. The diary. Lazarus. His father's emerging villainy. The accusations of the *Amhas-draoi*.

Daz had risen to stab at the fire with a poker, the sparks crackling up the chimney. The light etching his face into harsh lines of light and shadow. The glow of the flames reflected in his haunted eyes.

So far, Daz's confusion at their arrival had given way to an encouraging lucidity. But would it hold? Or was it as ephemeral and changing as the flickering light from the hearth? With no way to tell and no other place to turn, Aidan ventured to brave the subject he'd avoided so far this evening.

"Earlier tonight, you recognized the Kilronan diary."

Daz stabbed the grate, sending up a new shower of sparks.

"Someone's after it, Daz—a *Domnuathi*."

The man's hand tightened around the poker handle, his face twisting into a grimace of pain or fear or both.

"The *Amhas-draoi* are after it too. They want to use it as a lure to capture whoever is manipulating this creature."

"Not over. Not over," the man mumbled, one hand on the poker, the other diving into his pocket. "I knew it wouldn't be over. Not until all of us were dead and gone. Not until he was dead and gone." Daz pulled out a stone. Tumbled it in his hand. "Not over. Not over."

"Who?" Aidan asked, barely breathing for fear of breaking the spell. "Who still lives who knows about the diary? Who has the power to raise a soldier of Domnu? What's so special about this diary?"

"We ran. We hid. Escaping like rats from a sinking ship. They found us. They hunted us. One by one."

"Who?" Aidan interrupted. "Who ran?"

"He survived by cunning. By stealth. They pitied me. Spared me. I wasn't worth much. Never worth much." Daz's breathing came shallow, his chest heaving as if he was being chased by evil memories. His eyes fixed and glowing like coals upon the writhing fire. "And young Brendan?" he hissed. "Where is he? Did he survive? Or did he meet the end they planned for him?"

Aidan leaned forward, heart thundering. "What end? What did they plan?"

"The Nine agreed. The Nine are no more. The High King remains lost so long as the diary remains lost."

With a clang, Daz tossed the poker on the hearth bricks. Tore his gaze from the fire with a shivering groan before stumbling toward the door. Dropping the stone where it rolled unheeded under a table.

As if she'd been eavesdropping, the housekeeper stepped into Daz's path. Took him roughly by the shoulder in a comforting embrace. Whispered soothing words too quiet to hear before stinging Aidan with a look of reproach. "You've upset him. You and your badgering questions."

"I need to know," he persisted. "There's someone out there hunting for this diary who—"

She spat her disgust. "Can't you see what your questions do? How the memories hurt him? Leave it be. What's done is done. The Nine are gone. Let's leave it that way." With her arms firmly around Daz's hunched shoulders, she began guiding him out of the room.

"Are you so sure?" he shouted after her. "Or does one still live who seeks to begin the madness all over again?"

And the gods help him, he didn't want to even think it—was it Brendan?

—o—

*The man's a blasted magpie.*

Cat stared around her bedchamber, hands on hips and jaw set against the curses knotting her throat.

Crates and barrels. Trunks and bags. Piles of books and bundles of magazines and newspapers. Broken tables. Straight-backed chairs in need of recaning and armchairs with torn cushions. A suit of rusted armor complete with a deadly looking pike standing at attention in the corner.

The bed rose up from this sea of refuse like a small island of tidiness. Fresh sheets. Clean coverlet. Pillows plumped. And a basin and ewer on the only unbroken table in the room.

At least Maude had tried.

Shedding her cloak on the nearest pile, Cat threaded her way through the jumble. Crawled up into bed, enjoying the idea of not having to rise before dawn for another day in the saddle. By now, every bone felt shaken out of place and she'd discovered muscles she never knew she had. All of them sore.

She closed her eyes, but the disturbing image of William Danvers and Aidan in close conversation swam up to jolt her alert. What had that blasted tattle merchant said? Aidan had never again brought it up, his silence more unnerving than any confrontation. At least if he accused, she could defend. But how could one fight back against an attack that never came?

Her shredded nerves had frayed to the point where she almost wanted Aidan to ask. Jeremy had shown himself to be unworthy of her loyalty and speaking of her son might shore up frayed memories—allay the fear she harbored that one day she'd wake and recall nothing of his face or his smell or his cry. And he'd truly be gone.

But would Aidan look upon her child as gift or sin? Her loss of maidenhead as a sordid crime or the naiveté of a young woman in what she thought was love? And why did it matter to her what he thought? He was all but betrothed to Miss Osborne.

Her mind too full for sleep, she rose. Pushed through the mess to rifle among the cast-off treasures. An Indian silk scarf from one trunk. A cache of gaudy necklaces from a chest with two missing drawers. A gold-framed miniature depicting a young boy with dark hair and sad eyes.

The pile of books she left for last. Works by Swift and Richardson. A travelogue of India by John Henry Grose. Two books of sermons written by a pair of Erskines: Ralph and Ebenezer. Any relation?

But here was something interesting. Midway through the pile. A slender volume in red leather. Loose papers stuffed willy-nilly among the pages. Cracking open the stiff binding, she thumbed through. Taking only moments to recognize the familiar diatribe of *Other* persecution and victimization at the hands of the *Duinedon*. The need for action on the part of the faithful before it was too late. She flipped to the flyleaf.

Máelodor. The author of the book on *Unseelie*.

A torn page slid free. Drifted toward the floor before she snatched it back. Scanned it, her fingers trembling the paper, a knot forming in her throat. The ever-shifting currents of language. The slow uncurling of each thought as she sought meaning among the swooping shift and eddy of each letter. Exactly like the diary.

She focused, letting the amorphous words and images harden within her head. Every sentence making the next come easier. Faster: "The tapestry is safely hidden, and

Brendan's left with the stone." She jumped lower on the page. "If my suspicions are correct, they'll be here before the week is out . . . time to prepare if not time to escape. I write this to you as a warning and a farewell."

Down to the scrawled "K" of the signature.

And back to the top.

Not meant for Ahern at all.

This letter was addressed to Máelodor.

# thirteen

Cat's brisk knock echoed up and down the empty corridor.

No answer.

She lifted a hand to knock again just as the door was flung open by a rumpled Aidan in his stocking feet, shrugging into his waistcoat. Neckcloth askew. "What the devil—oh, it's you."

"Good morning to you too." She didn't wait for an invitation. She'd been sitting on her news since last night. Passed sleepless hours as a consequence. It was Aidan's turn to worry. "I've found something I think you should see."

"Do come in," he offered, a smile hovering at the edges of his mouth. He bowed her into a bedchamber as cluttered as hers. Removed a tarnished silver set from a chair and motioned her to sit. "I apologize for the mess."

"Never mind that."

Picking her way through the piles, she averted her eyes from the unmade bed. Reprimanded herself for the images flashing through her lascivious little head. Shameless, that was what she was. Shameless and pathetic. She'd seen the kind of woman destined for the Earl of Kilronan—beautiful, elegant, virginal. If he looked at Cat it was only as a snack to hold him over until he could savor the main meal.

Her stomach growled for breakfast.

Angry with herself and—now that she thought about it—a tad annoyed with him, she shoved the letter at him. "I found this among the things in my room. I thought you ought to see it."

His curious gaze lingered on her face just long enough to make her uncomfortable before he dropped his eyes to the page. Back to her. "My father . . . what does it say? I can't . . ."

"I wrote it out for you." Into his hands went the second piece of paper. "It's addressed to Máelodor."

His gaze went diamond hard; a muscle jumped in his jaw. "Where did you find this?"

"Among a box of papers and books. I spent most of last night reading through them. Most are simple correspondence. Deadly dull." Anticipating his next question, she added, "This was the only one of its kind."

"Have you seen Daz yet this morning?"

"Maude says he doesn't usually rise until much later." She bit her lip before deciding full disclosure was best. "And he's not always coherent when he does wake. She says our coming might jolt him into lucidity or he may not even remember us." She shifted from foot to foot before blurting, "Aidan, the man's mad. Maude says he addressed a cow by his sister's name. Spent three days asking why Alice had been given rooms in the barn. He passed a week once hiding in a wardrobe, claiming the *Amhas-draoi* were after him.

Made Maude test all his food before he'd eat it. These are not the actions of a man in full control of his mind."

"He's old."

"If by old you mean touched in the head, you're exactly right."

"Leave Daz to me. Your job is translating the diary. The rest is my problem."

"You arrogant bastard." If she needed solid evidence the spark between them had been classic male strutting, here it was. She'd one function in this twisted relationship—linguist. Fine. "Then if you're done with me, my lord, I'll just get back to my job." Swung around to go, hating the lump trying to force its way into her throat. He wasn't worth it. No man was.

He grabbed her by the arm. "Wait, Cat."

She stopped but didn't turn around.

"I didn't mean that the way it sounded."

"Didn't you?"

"You shouldn't even have to ask. If anything good has come from this insanity, it's been you."

That did it. The lump choked off her breath. But not the hot tears blurring her vision. "No, let's be clear. It's my talent you admire. Once the translation is complete, I'll be out on the street without a second thought."

Why was she having this silly argument? What admission was she trying to force from him? He'd kissed her. So what? She'd had plenty of randy gents try their luck once they knew her history. Geordie had sent them packing in quick order. But Geordie wasn't here. She was on her own. And instead of sending Aidan packing, she was playing as if a kiss meant for keeps. She, of all people, knew that for the fallacy it was.

"Cat?" He tipped her chin toward him. Searched her face. "What's going on? Or should I say, *che cosa sta accendendo?*" His eyes crinkled with laughter, the burning intensity brightening to a sunshine brilliance.

She wrenched away from him. "I knew it. I knew you were only biding your time. What did that wretched jaw-me-dead tell you? I have a right to know."

Aidan didn't even flinch. "He told me your father was a naval man. Captain of a thirty-two-gun frigate stationed in the Mediterranean. "

She blinked back tears. Wiped them away with the back of her hand. Crying for a father she barely remembered. A lost future. Would things have been different had he lived?

"His ship was lost during a storm. My mother remarried. A brewer. He lives in eternal hopes of a knighthood for exemplary service to the crown."

"Supplying them with the best ale in Ireland?"

She laughed. "Something like that," before sobering. "Did Mr. Danvers tell you the rest? I'm sure he couldn't wait to fill you in on the sordid details. He was always an enthusiastic tattler of tales."

"He said there was a scandal involving a gentleman. You disappeared soon after."

Damn Danvers's wagging tongue. May his journey be fraught with bad weather, poor roads, and rotten meals.

"Was his name Jeremy?" Aidan asked quietly.

"You're like a dog worrying at a bone." Hands on hips, she faced him down. "You want to know? Truly? Then, by all means, let me enlighten you once and for all. I was twenty-one. He was twenty-five. I met him at a dinner. He was charismatic and handsome, and he made me feel special. A sensation I experienced rarely in my stepfather's household." She squared her jaw in defiance. Met Aidan's gaze dead on, daring him to speak. Or even flicker a shocked eyelid. "When he said he loved me, I believed him. And later when he said he could never marry me, I believed that too." She paused, her heart fluttery as a bird's beneath his hand. "He was never anything but truthful."

Aidan's eyes were round with shock, a stricken look upon his face.

"So there you have my tragic tale," she challenged. "Are you satisfied? Relieved you have the virginal Miss Osborne waiting for your return with trousseau packed?"

Loss stabbed beneath her breast, a gnawing hollow despair that had nothing to do with the dark-haired charmer she'd given her body to. All to do with his son.

"I don't know what to say," he answered.

"Don't say anything," she said, laying a hand upon the door. "I don't want your pity nor do I care about your disapproval."

"One more time, Daz. And this time, slowly. Who is Máelodor?"

Aidan clutched the letter while he paced the drawing room. Crates and boxes rose up on either side of him. Old furniture. A pianoforte draped in a pair of tasseled velvet curtains. A space directly in front of the hearth had been cleared, leaving room enough for two chairs and a table set with the remains of breakfast.

The old man shifted in his seat, fingers nervously toying with his lap rug, eyes darting from the congealed egg on his plate to the smoking fire to Aidan. "Found the name in an old book, he did. Did I ever tell you that?" He gave Aidan an expectant look before continuing. "Found it and decided he'd take it as his own. Said his real name carried too much of the *Duinedon*. Who ever heard of a master mage named Henry Simpkins?" Daz's nervous worrying intensified. "What he said, not me. Mind you, I'd no problem with his name."

Simpkins . . . Simpkins. He'd no recall of any Simpkins prowling Belfoyle. The name Máelodor didn't strike any sparks either. But it was obvious by the letter Cat found that not only had this man been an intimate of his father, but he also understood the indecipherable language of the diary.

Thoughts of the letter and Cat sent his mind spinning off course to this morning's bungled questioning. He'd all but cornered her into confessing her disgrace. Should he be surprised she was angry? Or assumed he'd view her ruin as cause for either pity or scorn? No doubt she'd experienced large helpings of both. But it was impossible to pity someone who so obviously refused it. And though he dug deep, he unearthed neither disdain nor contempt in the welter of feelings Cat produced in him. Exasperation certainly. Irritation occasionally. Frustration definitely.

He rubbed his face, forcing his mind back on Daz, the letter, and the topic at hand. Forget Cat. He had bigger worries. Her offended sensibilities would have to wait. "What happened to Máelodor after my father's murder?" he asked. "How did you get this letter?"

Daz's gaze fell on the paper in Aidan's hand. "Don't know about a letter. Never saw it. Brendan brought me things. Warned me to keep them safe."

"Brendan's been here?" Aidan almost shouted.

Daz jumped. "Aye. Brendan Douglas." He squinted. "Do you know him?"

Aidan struggled to master a calm he didn't feel. "A long time ago."

"A good lad, Brendan. Gifted with the kind of powers I've only ever read about. Never came back. Did he survive? Do you know?"

"I don't know, Daz. I haven't heard from him in years."

"Tempted, he was. We all were, weren't we? Tempted to do things we shouldn't. Lured by the darkness. By the power it gave us. Kilronan made it seem so right. Made it seem so . . . bloodless." He paused, his knobbed fingers pulling out thread after thread. "It wasn't, though. Blood flowed. Deaths. More than I could count. Funny, how callous we grew. We didn't start out that way."

Aidan sought to redirect the conversation back to the letter. "What does my father mean when he talks about a tapestry? A stone? They must have been important if he sent both away ahead of the attack."

Which meant he'd known the *Amhas-draoi* were coming. He'd known he had little time left and had the presence of mind to prepare. Prepare. Not run. Had he thought he stood a chance against Scathach's brotherhood of warrior mages? Had it been pure hubris, or had his father been stronger than Aidan had ever imagined? Yet in the end, not quite strong enough.

"Years and years, he hunted. And in the end the tapestry and the stone both came to his possession. Worth a king's ransom for those who understood what they were," Daz answered.

"What are they? What do they do?"

"I would have kneeled before him. Had he returned as they promised, I'd have followed the High King's standard. He'd that kind of power."

"Who, Daz?"

"The kind of natural charismatic radiance that made men follow him."

"Who did they promise was returning?"

"I always imagined him like Brendan. Young. Golden. Alive."

"Damn it, Daz. Who reminds you of Brendan? Tell me."

Daz's vacant stare sharpened to almost-sanity. "Arthur, of course."

The gardens stretched in a wild riot of green, though the bones of a once well-ordered series of parterres and pathways, avenues and orchards, existed still. One just had to look for them. Inhaling the pungent smells of loam and the damp woodsy smoke from some gardener's fire, Cat felt years of city living slough off her in the space of minutes. Felt the tension thrumming her body ease.

Slightly.

After all, she remained caught in an insane limbo between lives. Hunted by a killer whose cold-blooded viciousness was matched only by his apparent invincibility. Trapped with a man who snuck beneath her guard at every turn. Who caused her not only to remember her past but to dream of a future.

She'd not breathe truly easy until she was rid of them both.

Coming to an impenetrable bramble fence, Cat doubled back to where she'd last caught sight of a path. Struck out toward the sloping green roof of a folly or summerhouse or pavilion. Sensed the surge of charged air and the inside-out feeling of mage energy like a brush of silk across her skin, a lurching of her stomach.

Someone else walked these paths. Someone else rambled this verdant jungle. She froze, aware the house lay east, though hidden from view. Too far to scream. Too far to run.

She was on her own.

"Damn it to hell." Words followed another prickling rush of mage energy. "Thrice-cursed damn magic. Bloody pain in the bloody ass."

She let out a terrified breath on a half giggle of hysteria. Aidan.

She followed the chain of blasphemy to a small clearing amid a profusion of wild-growing rose elder.

He stood, shoulders squared, back straight, a hand up as if he attempted to ward off the tree in front of him. The flash of his emerald caught the sun. *"Treusfurvyesh goea dhil dowsk. Nerthyoest dhil gwanndesk."* This time the mage energy released by his words sank beneath her skin. Sent a flush of heat through her body. Flip-flopped her stomach before evaporating.

*"A lest tarenesh dhil*—ugh." He doubled over, knees buckling, head bowed as if he'd been struck a knife blow.

She ran to kneel beside him, trembling with fresh memories of the horrible, vicious-eyed creature unleashed by his last stab at spell casting. "Are you all right?"

Lines bit deep into either side of his mouth, his hair damped against his skull, face ashen. Straightening, he drew a deep, ragged breath. Cocked an embarrassed and disgusted look in her direction. "Do I look all right to you?"

The aggrieved-little-boy tone drew the sting from his words. Cat rocked back on her heels. Smothered a smile. "No, actually you look completely awful."

"Thank you." He staggered to his feet. Held out a hand to her.

She slipped her fingers into his grasp. Met his eyes, and this time the charged rush of sensation had naught to do with magic. Everything to do with the warm, callused grip of the man holding her. She swallowed. Pulled away. She'd burned that bridge. There'd be no going back. "What were you doing?"

The color slowly returned to his face, though he held his side stiffly. "Practicing."

"To kill yourself?"

"No. To protect you," he snapped, jolting both of them into an awkward silence. Aidan quickly sought to mend the fence. "And the diary. When—not if—Lazarus returns, I need to be ready for him."

"But just then, you—"

He went rigid, the nobleman's arrogance in full view from the darkling light in his eye to the grim jaw. "Failed? Is that what you're trying to say? Don't bother pointing out the obvious. It's not the first time I've bolloxed up a spell. It's just a wonder I haven't incinerated myself yet."

This bitterness carried the weight of years. A lifetime's shortcomings in the acid tones and harsh admission of defeat. How did she combat a statement like that? Should she even try? Perhaps it would be best to simply walk away. Leave him to his self-pity without a backward glance. She took a few dragging steps before reluctantly turning back, her words pulled from some hidden corner of her soul. "We all have flaws, Aidan. That doesn't make us any less worthy."

"Or any less treasured," he murmured in agreement, his stare trapping her in place.

Was this his way of telling her he didn't hold Jeremy against her? Didn't despise her? Or think any less of her? She focused on a bird perched on a branch beyond his right shoulder. It kept her from having to look him in the eye. Experience the pull of that scorching bronze gaze. Succumb to the growing ridiculous need to carve herself some small place in his life that didn't revolve around the diary.

"I'll leave you to it then." She swept past him, her body alive to his presence, her skin prickling and gooseflesh springing up her arms.

"Perhaps I should have done as Jack suggested and let the *Amhas-draoi* have the diary. At least they don't suffer from ridiculous seizures every time they use their powers."

She turned, catching the rueful twist of his mouth. Bit her lip as she sought to find words to soothe, knowing she'd never been good at conciliatory speeches. "The *Amhas-draoi* are the best of the best. Warriors and mages of the highest order. That's what they do. Who they are. You can't compare yourself to them."

Aidan limped to a log. Sank down on it, kneading his thigh, wincing as he worked. "Brendan could have been one. He even asked Father once to send him to Skye to train with Scathach. Father refused. Brendan sulked for a month."

She leaned back against a tree. Used the rough dig of the bark to counteract the dangerous quicksand feeling his candidness elicited. This was suddenly Aidan and Catriona speaking. Not the Earl of Kilronan and Cat the thief.

"Did you ever want to go to join them?" she asked, knowing she'd waded in over her head. Risked being dragged under by emotions that didn't make sense. Could never be allowed to emerge.

"Join the brotherhood? Me?" Surprise flitted across his face. "No. As the heir to the earldom, I knew my future. And thankfully my awkward reaction to mage energy didn't alter that inheritance."

His easy answer emboldened her—that and a desire to seize this brief intimacy. Be the one asking the questions for a change. "Have you always been affected this way?"

He shrugged. Snapped off a dead branch. Swiped at the shrubbery. "More or less. Father declared it was all in my head. Assured me training would correct it. I just wasn't working hard enough. It was always a bone of contention between us."

A well-traveled argument. Familiar to her, though in a different form. Her mother had used it whenever Cat and her stepfather argued. She was imagining things. Mr. Weston was a good and respectable gentleman. Cat was being difficult. Stubborn. Not trying.

"It wasn't in your head though, was it?" A cloud crossed the sun, throwing the glade into shadow. Cat hugged her arms to her body. Gritted her teeth against the ache of betrayal. Why hadn't her mother believed her? Why hadn't she listened? Why hadn't she cared?

Had she truly loved her new husband so much? Or had it been that she loved Cat so little?

And then Aidan was there. His body warm and solid, the beat of his heart steady beneath her ear. She tensed, but only for a moment before accepting the embrace. Relaxed into the feel of him pressed against her, the hard-muscled strength of him cradling her.

"No, Cat," he answered, the rumble of his baritone

rippling along nerves raw with an overload of emotions. "What I feel is not all in my head."

"Oh, excuse me. I didn't know anyone was in here."

Cat began to back out of the room, but Daz Ahern stopped her with a raised hand. A watery smile from behind thick spectacles. "No one but me, Miss O'Connell. Come in, come in."

In a moth-nibbled coat with elaborate gold-trimmed cuffs, breakfast-stained silk knee breeches, and his hair pulled back neatly with a velvet ribbon, he almost looked presentable. Just so long as you didn't notice the high-heeled yellow pump paired with a black leather dancing slipper. "Actually, I've been hoping to have a word with you."

That sounded ominous.

"Just make yourself at home while I finish looking for a volume I've mislaid. I filed it away, I'm sure of it. I just have to remember where."

She cast a skeptical glance at the heaped stacks and paper-filled crates before lifting her eyes to the overflowing shelves. Filed? There was a system behind this clutter? This she had to see to believe.

As she watched, he scanned the shelves first. "It's not under authors I know, nor authors I think I know." He dropped to rummage through a box. "Nor under authors I detest—an especially large category, by the way."

He straightened, casting one more puzzled look around the room. "Perhaps it's filed under authors as insane as myself." He tapped a thoughtful finger to his chin. "That's a definite possibility."

Cat bit her lip, torn between amusement and distress.

Aidan really expected this man to be of help? "Perhaps I should leave you to your search." She started for the door.

"No, please stay, Miss O'Connell."

She subsided onto a lumpy sofa. Folded her hands in her lap before raising a passive face to her inquisitor.

"Aidan related how he met you. Quite extraordinary. A female thief. And a jolly good one the way Aidan told the story." He adjusted his spectacles, examining her through great bug eyes. "Yet you speak and act with the elegance of an aristocrat. I saw it myself as soon as I met you. Told Maude even, 'that is a young woman of breeding, that is.' Ask her, she'll tell you. So how is it you came to be lurking about in Aidan's library with malicious intent?"

"Circumstance can make anyone act in unexpected ways. And desperate circumstances call for desperate acts."

"Yes, yes. Very true," he muttered as he fumbled in his coat pocket. "But surely you regret your criminal activity." A somber note crept into his voice. "It presses upon your soul with the weight of chains." Out came a marble. "Haunts your dreams." A pair of dice. "A guilty stain that never washes away." A chicken bone.

Her hands clenched to fists as she fought outrage. "I do what I must to survive in a world all too quick to condemn a young woman's folly while admiring that same inclination in a man."

His brows rose into his wrinkled, liver-spotted forehead as he considered her words before nodding as if in agreement. Dropping his eyes to study his left shoe. "One moment's weakness changes everything. There's no going back. We bear our guilt forever. And only our victims can give us the absolution we seek."

Her victim? She hoped he wasn't referring to Jeremy.

Anyone less victimized she couldn't imagine. He'd gotten everything he wanted. And with little inconvenience.

But perhaps he referred to someone else. Someone completely innocent of any wrongdoing, whose only fault was being born to a stupid, weak girl who'd loved both unwisely and too well.

# fourteen

Cat put aside the diary with a sigh. Massaged her throbbing temples in a vain attempt to ease the blinding headache. Obviously Aidan's father had used the impenetrability of the language as well as the unappealing side effects to keep snoopers away. And for good cause, as Cat found with every fresh entry. Spells ranging from innocuous to lethal riddled the margins. Potions an apothecary would run from shrieking in horror. And descriptions of creatures whose existence seemed conjured from nightmare. These, coupled with the day-to-day entries of a man more than slightly fanatical about the close-knit circle of scholars under his titular head, made for dense reading. Denser translation.

As weeks and months passed under her thumb, the diary's tone grew angrier. Hostility and resentment filled the pages, coinciding with more sinister magics. A spell that could devour a man from the inside out. An experiment in reanimation that begat a walking, stinking corpse that had to be hastily unreanimated. She still gagged over that one. An entry detailing a meeting where someone was "disciplined." She'd mentally added the quotation marks after she'd read two entries later about the second experiment in reanimation. Also a failure, thank goodness.

Through it all, the network of mages grew. Stretching like spider legs out from Belfoyle to places as far reaching as Dublin, London, Edinburgh, Paris. Surely they didn't simply gather to complain about *Other* persecution and experiment with dark mage energy. Men didn't collect conspirators without a purpose. So why?

Tonight she and Aidan had been working through an entry that spoke of the High King's final resting place and the unearthing of the Sh'vad Tual, describing the stone as the final key. Though the key to what was left decidedly vague.

She rolled her neck. Stretched to relieve the knots in her shoulders. Wished she could untangle the knots jumbling her insides as easily. Aidan's careless gesture of comfort in the garden had lit fires she'd hoped long since extinguished.

It was Jeremy all over again. A handsome man. The desire to belong. The need to be loved. She'd read this book before. She knew how the story turned out. A weak woman. A willing man. Heartbreak to follow.

But would it? After that one veiled comment, Aidan had never again referred to her shocking ruination. And though she'd studied him covertly at every opportunity, he never showed the slightest discomfort or embarrassment in her company. As if he didn't care. As if it truly didn't matter to him. A thought only adding to the wild roundabout of emotions.

"It doesn't make sense. The words tease at a reason, but they don't explain anything." Aidan broke her from the useless circle of her thoughts. Pacing the room like a frantic automaton, hand tapping a rapid beat against his leg, he'd long since discarded his coat. Loosened his neck cloth. "What was my father doing?"

She cupped her chin in her hand. "You knew him. Was he always so secretive?"

He threw up his hands in frustration. "He was a scholar with a scholar's amazement that what he found easy might in fact be bloody incomprehensible." His words grew harsh with long-held anger. "No doubt Brendan would understand Father's riddles. Brendan had the same Byzantine personality. Wheels within wheels. But Brendan's gone. And I'm left to figure out what the man was trying to get at."

"So that would be . . . yes," she replied, keeping her tone light. Doing her best to ignore the undercurrents of old pain and remembered betrayal.

He caught her attempt at lightheartedness. Offered her an apologetic laugh. "Aye, a definite yes." He rubbed a thoughtful hand over his chin. "And you're sure that's what those last paragraphs say?"

Cat nodded. Wished she hadn't. "Take my word or don't. I'm not reading it again. Feeling like I've had my innards stirred with a stick wasn't part of our deal."

Rubbing the back of his neck, he cast her a compassionate look. "It does take some getting used to."

"I don't want to get used to it," she grumbled, wrapping her arms more firmly around her torso, wishing she could go to bed. Make up for the hours she'd missed last night.

"The letter mentioned a stone too," Aidan said. "That must be the Sh'vad Tual referred to here. And Daz spoke of the High King. He said Father and the others promised Arthur would return."

"As in King Arthur? As in Knights of the Round Table? Excalibur? Camelot?"

"As in all of the above."

"I hate to throw cold water on your theory, but Arthur's a legend. He's just stories to pass a winter's evening." She faltered under Aidan's solemn gaze. "Please say he's just stories to pass a winter's evening."

He shrugged. "Some believe he existed. That in fact Arthur was the last in a line of great kings of *Other*. Ruling over a world that not only accepted the *Fey*-born powers of our race, but admired them. That once upon a time our kind walked this earth without fear of persecution. Without the shadow of superstition clinging to our every breath."

Did he know his eyes lit up with pride when he spoke like this? A new, razor-sharp arrogance crept over his features? A battle brilliance emerging with each lengthening stride?

"During the Lost Days, the walls between the faery kingdom of *Ynys Avalenn* and the mortal realm remained open with both sides able to pass as needed. Blood ties strengthened between *Other* and *Fey* as a result. There have even been theories the mage Merlin was the product of one such liaison between a mortal woman and her *Fey* lover."

"So what happened to end the idyll?"

"Arthur's death. Some say with his passing, that bright age ended, and magic fell into the shadows to be hidden and feared."

"Some?"

"My father believed." His gaze focused inward, his words coming faster now. "He used to regale us with stories of Arthur's court. But he treated them like history. Our history. Making sure we understood where we'd come from while explaining how modern writers had twisted the truth to suit their slanted agendas. The incestuous coupling between Arthur and his half sister, the adultery of Guinevere, even Arthur's bastard conception—all of it was designed to blacken the High King and cast darkness on a time of *Other* dominance."

"Why would they do that?"

"Because to them, we're naught more than devils. You heard those men in the alley in Dublin." Anger deepened his voice. "The *Duinedon* have always feared what they don't understand. They're frightened and envious of what we can do. Of what we are. And so they seek to destroy us. Or at least drive us so far into obscurity we'll never recover."

His features hardened, his eyes burning with a fearsome energy as he stalked the room in ever more agitated circles.

"My father was proud of his *Other* heritage to the point where to be *Duinedon* was a failing in his eyes. As if *Fey* blood and mage energy alone made you more of a person. To him, Arthur's world must have seemed like the embodiment of everything he dreamed. A world that accepted you for who you are. Not who they think you are."

The yearning in his voice pushed through Cat's exhaustion. Did Aidan seek such a world? It sounded too good to be true. A place where the people accepted you without comment. Without restrictions. Loved you no matter what you'd done. What so-called sins you committed.

She threaded her fingers together to stop them from shaking. Focused on Aidan. And off the rush of her own yearning for such a dream existence where she could speak of her son. Where her memories of him would no longer be colored with her own shame.

"So your father collected a stone and a tapestry," she

said, hating the shaky vibrato in her voice. "For what purpose? What do they have to do with King Arthur?"

He plowed a hand through his hair. Gave a frustrated shake of his head. "Daz said they promised the High King's return . . . Arthur's return . . . they promised—" he stopped. She could almost see the gears turning. "Could they have actually wanted to restore Arthur? Begin a new reign of *Other*?"

She straightened. "By bringing Arthur back to life?"

"Daz said he'd always imagined Brendan as Arthur."

"Could that be why he's after the diary?"

"It's not Brendan," Aidan insisted. "Besides, the letter says Brendan knows where the stone is. He doesn't need the diary."

"You don't know what else is in here. There could be any number of things Brendan might need."

"I won't believe it. They promised his return. Not a new Arthur, but Arthur's return."

"You can't bring people back from the dead," she argued.

Green eyes met brown. And Cat knew exactly what Aidan was thinking. Because she was thinking it too.

The *Domnuathi*. Lazarus.

Aidan finally broke the heavy silence. "Can't you?"

Snapping the half-cocked pistol's frizzen in place, Aidan wiped his hands on a cloth. Carried the loaded weapon to the hall, casting his eye about for a convenient hiding place. The chest of drawers tucked under the lower landing looked a perfect spot. Near the front entrance, yet out of the way of nosy housemaids.

Successful, he returned to the library. Lit a cheroot to

stave off exhaustion. Stalked the room as he inhaled on an energizing drag before stubbing it out. Tossing it into the fire. Settling himself once again with notes and diary.

He'd sent Cat to bed, but the lavender scent of her lingered. Teased him with ungallant thoughts. Lusty imaginings. He shifted in his seat. Fought to concentrate on the collection of transcripts she'd left and ignore the pair of spring green eyes and the reed-supple body alive with anticipation. What would have happened if he'd ignored his good angel and done what he'd wanted this afternoon? If he'd freed the long-suppressed seducer who, if given a chance, could not only drive the memory of Jeremy away, but obliterate it completely?

The answer was obvious from past experience. A knee to the groin followed by a fist to the jaw. Subtlety and Cat weren't exactly friends.

He sighed. Blinked her away. Forced his mind to an image of Barbara Osborne's buxom good looks. What on earth did she make of his sudden disappearance? Did she assume he'd taken off with Cat to continue their liaison in the privacy of the country? Had she taken such rogue's conduct as reason to shift her attentions to another? No, surely she'd wait to hear his explanation before jumping to conclusions.

But did he really care?

Of course he did.

Didn't he?

He was giving himself a headache. Trying not to dwell on the problems he'd left behind or the problems he'd brought with him, he picked up the next page in the scattered stack, and found himself chuckling over the recounting of Sabrina's sudden interest in the healing arts. Not even the dogs had been immune to her mad scramble to bandage anything that came within ten feet of her.

That had been in the summer of her fifteenth year. The last one she'd spent at home. Father had met his death the following November, Sabrina choosing to remain with the *bandraoi* sisters rather than return to Belfoyle. Her most recent letter had spoken of her apprenticeship to the order's infirmarian. Apparently her interest in medicine was more than a girlish fad.

The next page had obviously been recopied from another work. A recounting by the master mage Garaile Biteri of his first successful passage between worlds. Descriptions of the cold, the pressing weight of emptiness, the creatures inhabiting the abyss. Cat had even translated his father's margin-scribbled annotations. References to testing the hypothesis at their next gathering when the family would be conveniently absent.

One entry stung even at a distance of years: "Aidan's hopeless. I gave him the simplest of spells—Brendan mastered it within hours—and what does my firstborn do? He sets the greenhouse on fire and nearly destroys a small fortune in exotics. When I taxed him with it, he merely shrugged it off as of little consequence. He's my son, but, by the gods, his lack of interest is infuriating. He may be my heir in body, but it is Brendan who inherited my soul."

Aidan read and reread that indictment, resentment riding closer to the surface than expected. Dredging up old hurts and old slights forgotten in the chaos of keeping his head above water. He took a deep breath, exhaling slowly in a bid to calm himself.

His father wrote only truth. Brendan had been the special one. The one whose *Other* gifts had shown the greatest promise. Aidan's interests had always lain in the land, the green fields, the rocky moorland and crumbling cliffs, the overgrown stands of blackthorn and ash. They were his. Every blade of grass and every animal crouched in hiding from the poacher's snare. Hell, every poacher when it came to that. So from where did his resentment spring? Perhaps it lay more in his father's neglect of Aidan's birthright than of Aidan himself.

He turned to the next entry and another reference to the Nine. He'd seen this more and more as if the amorphous group his father had gathered congealed into something permanent and official enough to need a name. But for what purpose?

His father's thirst for knowledge and pride in his talents came through loud and clear. A clarion call to all *Other* to embrace their *Fey*-born inheritance, to strive to turn even the least gift to its greatest use. But to be used for what? The *Other* could never risk exposure. They had nothing to gain and everything to lose should the *Duinedon* world rise up in answer to what they would surely see as witchcraft and devilry. Did he truly expect Arthur's return to tip the scales in their favor? Usher in a new era of *Other* dominance?

"Still awake?"

Aidan jerked at the creaky rasp of words inches from his ear. How the hell had Daz snuck up on him?

"I'm light on my feet, lad," Daz answered in response to Aidan's unspoken question, shuffling his feet in what appeared to be a jig. "I move with panther stealth."

If that was Daz's idea of panther stealth, Aidan had to have been dozing. That or stone deaf.

"My neuralgia is acting up. Can't sleep. Thought I'd join you, lad." He dropped into a chair with a glance around the room. His eyes bright, but not wild. His movements holding none of the frenetic tendencies of the madman. He'd even managed to clothe himself in banyan and—both—slippers. "Your young lady gone up to bed, has she?"

"Hours ago." His young lady. It sounded so possessive. So permanent. So completely the opposite of what he needed. Barbara Osborne would be his young lady. She would. Really. Once he returned to Dublin, it was as good as done. So why did the thought of tying himself to her seem more and more odious, yet opening himself to Cat came natural as breathing? Or should he say, panting.

He grimaced against a renewal of his earlier lecherous aches.

"Sweet lass." Daz levered his leg onto a padded footstool. Settled deeper into his seat with a satisfied grunt. "She's had a difficult road."

Aidan shot him a pointed look. "She's told you of it?"

Daz returned the glare with a knowing smirk. "Doesn't take the gift of the seer to see the child's been hurt. There for anyone with eyes. Even you." His gaze grew worried. "Maude says you came back from a walk about the grounds looking as if you'd been kicked between the eyes by a mule. More than once." Shook his head. "Working the mage energy, weren't you, lad?"

Why did Aidan have the sensation of being caught with his hand in the biscuit jar?

"And if I was?"

"You know you and the magic don't get along. Never have. Why risk injuring yourself?"

"Because if I don't I may as well stake myself out for Lazarus and let him have a nice easy go at me," Aidan answered, sharper than he'd intended, but the reproof stung.

Especially after reading his father's indictment. "I refuse to let my deficiencies win. I need every weapon at my disposal to defend myself. And this damned diary."

Daz rubbed a thoughtful finger alongside his nose. "Ah yes, Kilronan's diary. The trouble in a nutshell." His pale gaze raked Aidan with the blistering power of a torch. Seemed to strip him down to bone. "What do you seek among its pages? Your father's motivation? That's easy. He was driven by pride. Misplaced arrogance. Thought he could remake the world the way it should be. Ignore the way it was." He flicked a careless hand in Aidan's direction. "Do you look for approval? You won't find it among those pages. He loved you. But he despaired of you. Your lack of skill. Your lack of ambition."

"Loved me? Are we speaking of the same man?"

"Aye, but he wanted more from you than you could ever have given. Your complete devotion. Your undivided loyalty. And your unquestioning enthusiasm. He gave up on you when he saw you for the flawed vessel you were. When he finally admitted to himself your powers would never rival his own."

"I tried. Hell, I damn near turned myself inside out trying."

Daz ignored him. "Brendan had it all. Gave it all. In the end, Brendan turned out to be just as flawed—in his own way—as you were."

"How do you know this?" Aidan's voice came raspy with emotion, his throat closed around the lump. "How can you say these things?"

"I was your Uncle Daz, wasn't I? Kilronan's best friend. His trusted confidant. I may not have been one of the Nine, but I saw it all. Knew it all."

The Nine. There was that term again. "Who were they, Daz? What really happened to make the *Amhas-draoi* come after them? Tell me the truth."

The air seemed to thicken around the older man. Aging his features. Deepening the wrinkles in his face, the worry in his eyes, trembling his hands as they clutched the arms of the chair. Had Aidan gone too far? Would his question send Daz back to that shadow-filled world of delirium? He worked his jaw as if chewing his words carefully.

"What really happened? What did we do to have the *Amhas-draoi* after us?" Even his voice creaked, his stare turning inward to a time and place Aidan could not follow. "The true question, lad, is not what did we do, but what did we not do?" He shuddered, licking his lips. "The diary can tell you some of it. The meetings. The experiments. The speeches and posturing. But it can never bring to life the real terror of those days."

He paused, leaving Aidan stretched and waiting. Frightened. Sick at heart.

"Your father originated the idea—organize the *Other.* Unite them in common cause against the *Duinedon* oppressors. A rope of many strands is always stronger than a single thread. That's what he used to say."

Luck favors the strong. His family's motto. His father's battle cry.

"The Nine grew from there. A spreading menace threatening to devour us all. We ignored the warning signs. We were justified. Had right on our side. But when words weren't enough to advance our cause, we turned more and more to violence and murder. Our dream had become our obsession."

"I don't understand."

"Don't you?" Daz's harsh, level gaze speared Aidan to his seat. "I think you understand all of it, even if you won't admit it to yourself. Your father. Your brother. We washed ourselves in the blood of anyone who stood against us. Disagreed with us. All in the name of our *Fey* inheritance. Our race. We sought to use our powers to unleash magics locked away in the void of the *Unseelie*. Imprisoned for good reason. No human can control those forces. They act according to their own will. They do not ally and they do not supplicate."

"Father had to know he could never hope to achieve such a victory." Now his voice came as quick and shaky as Daz's. "The *Duinedon* far outnumber the *Other*. A hundred to one? A thousand? Even if we resorted to using our powers, the mortal world would crush us as easily as breaking an egg. We bleed. We die. There's nothing special about us that way."

"Yes, but if we had a leader. Someone to rally our scattered numbers and show us what we could be."

"Arthur," Aidan murmured.

"Brendan's idea. He came up with it. Followed it through. Fought for it. Was even prepared to sacrifice himself on the altar of his cause." Daz slumped back, his face as gray as his hair. "It never got that far, though. Instead of a grand and glorious end, Brendan found naught but an ignoble death."

Or had he only made it seem so?

Light-headedness. A frenzied horror. A sweep of gut-churning heat followed by teeth-chattering cold. Aidan slumped against the wall of the upper corridor. Squeezed his eyes against the pictures in his head.

He and Father scaling the cliffs below Belfoyle. Brendan laughing as he and Aidan thundered neck and neck down the gallop. Father, a stern disciplinarian, yet always willing to take the time to listen to his children. Brendan, a rival in so many ways, but a friend as much as a brother.

Plotters in a scheme to rearrange a world order? Evil conspirators in a plan to raise a dead king? Ignite a brutal war of supremacy between *Other* and *Duinedon*? Bloodthirsty, conscienceless killers leaving a trail of bodies behind them as they worked their dark magics?

He couldn't believe it even as he knew it for fact. It was what he'd feared. And so much worse.

He shoved off the wall. Stumbled like a drunk down the narrow passage. If he could just get to bed. Fall into oblivion and wipe out the incessant drumbeat of Daz's voice, killing off cherished memories with the downward stroke of the executioner's axe.

He made it ten paces before his damned thigh gave out. Sent him reeling to his knees on an anguished moan born of poorly healed muscles and an ache grinding his tendons like a millstone.

Rage boiled through him like a sick, black cloud. Anger tensed his arms. His shoulders. Squeezed his brain. Set him on fire. Father's crimes had not only crushed him and those friends who'd joined him, but whole families had been torn asunder. Lives ruined. Futures blotted out with the finality of an *Amhas-draoi* sword thrust.

He dropped his gaze to his hands, the heavy weight of the Kilronan emerald on his hand like a stone pinning him to the dragging fortunes of his house.

His family. His life. His future.

Propped against the wall, his leg stretched in front of

him, he rested his head back against the wall. Fisted his hands at his sides and let the grief and pain pour out of him in dry, wracking sobs.

"Aidan? Are you all right?"

The familiar lavender scent. The smoky, sexy boudoir voice sliding like honey along nerves shattered to the breaking point. He opened his eyes. Lifted his arms. And kissed her.

It was grief. Exhaustion. Pain.

Not desire. Not tenderness. And definitely not love.

Cat knew it. Ignored it. After all, she suffered from the same rampage of emotions.

His mouth on hers came warm and brandy laced. His hands cradled her face, skimmed her throat, threaded through her hair. His body shuddering from some inner maelstrom.

"We can't . . . the corridor . . . the floor . . . it's cold . . ." What she meant to say was "no, we can't because it was absolutely, positively, no-doubt-about-it the wrong thing to do. They'd regret it. It would complicate an already complicated relationship. She'd promised herself not again . . . never again."

Somehow it hadn't come out that way.

"Aidan . . . someone will come . . ." She spoke between kisses, between trembling caresses as she responded to his attentions with embarrassing eagerness.

He grunted in a typical male answer. Drew himself up, dragging her all-too-compliant body with him in an iron embrace. As if she might run if he released her. A wise idea if she could only get her legs to work. Tear herself away from the drugged heat of him.

He backed her the few paces to her bedchamber door. Nudged it wide. Steered her unresisting body toward the bed, kicking the door closed behind them.

Moonlight glanced off the dented suit of armor. Picked out the trim on a broken gilt-rimmed platter. Highlighted Aidan's auburn hair with strands of gold. Bounced off the green of his emerald ring. These snatches of observation buried themselves within her. Points in time she knew she'd remember long after the physical acts of the night had faded. Long after she'd come to her senses.

His gaze swept the cluttered room. The flickering candle. The book turned facedown upon the pillow. "You were reading." He picked it up, checking the title. Flipped her a smile that never reached his eyes. "Not exactly a comforting bedtime story."

She pulled the book from his hand. Closed it, setting it aside. "I wanted to know more about this Máelodor."

His mouth thinned to a snarling whiplash, the harsh angles of his face hardening to granite fury. "I know more than I care to. About all of it. Oh gods, Cat. Father and Brendan—" he looked away, swallowing the rage and sorrow that had brought him here. To her. To the point where any solace would suffice.

The mattress sank beneath their weight, Aidan coming over her, his hungry, desperate stare sizing her up her. Making her all too aware of her thin chemise, her chilled body, and all it implied. She sought to cover herself, but he captured her hand. Threaded his fingers with hers. Refused her attempt at modesty.

No wonder.

Modesty at this point seemed a bit too little too late.

And anyway, he'd seen her before. Dismissed her as not his type. But that was then. This was now. And his type was a willing female with all pertinent parts. Escape without the hangover.

"Don't," he murmured. "I want to see you. Need to see you."

"If you're expecting luscious curves and ample flesh, you're in for a shock," she joked, though neither of them laughed.

"I know exactly what I'm getting, *a chuisle*."

He lowered his mouth to hers in another bone-melting kiss. Clasped her other hand so she lay imprisoned and exposed under his triangulating hunter stare. The casual endearment skewered her with dangerous precision. A vulnerability she'd thought long callused over. But now, her skin prickled and flared, heat warping the barriers she'd erected after Jeremy, need battering the walls built stone upon stone upon the lifeless body of her son.

She looked inward for repulsion. Panic. A sick memory to dull the sharp crush of desire, but no images assailed her with gut-freezing horror. Instead a hole had opened, a chasm where life poured in. Drowned the past.

He tasted of brandy and smoke, his velvet tongue teasing her with the promise of what awaited if only she had the courage—or the stupidity—to accept it.

Off went the waistcoat. The neck cloth.

"Catriona," the rough-edged purr of her name ignited long dormant passions.

She arched into the hard-packed muscles of his chest. Desire like a physical pain between her thighs. A greedy craving for fulfillment.

She rubbed against the bulge in his breeches, thrilling

to his hiss of pleasure. To the knowledge of her own sexual power.

He released her hands on a groan. Dragged her chemise up and over her in a slick rake's move that had her naked and quivering, her body one giant exposed nerve. His eyes and then his hands glided over her in lush seduction—the column of her throat, her pebble-hard breasts, the flat of her stomach. Ending at the junction of her legs.

Her breath caught on a strangled whimper as she pushed up into his touch. Willed him to satisfy the wicked, pressing urgency vibrating through her. Once committed, her inhibitions burned off in a dirty passion, swamping her with a wet, throbbing heat.

She fumbled with his breeches in a desperate move to have him inside her. Shoved them down over his hips, but he was quicker. Kicked himself free before dragging his shirt over his head.

His gyrations rocked the bed. Knocked the table. The book hitting the floor with the explosive power of a gunshot. Startling them both out of their inescapable whirlpool descent into sex. He remained poised above her, Cat reading second and third thoughts on his face. Hesitation in the tension stringing his body.

And what a body it was.

No extra flesh or rich man's excess marred the lean strength of his chiseled frame. The whipcord slide of honed muscles. The packed ridges of a stomach begging to be caressed.

Washed in silver blue moonlight with dark pools beneath his candlelit eyes, he seemed something out of fantasy. A lover born of her wildest, most erotic imaginings.

If he stopped now, she'd shatter.

She pushed a flop of hair off his brow. Lifted her head to trace the seam of his mouth with her tongue. Splayed her hand over the marbled coolness of his chest. "Don't you dare come the prude on me now."

A grim smile flashed in the reaches of his gaze, a wicked greed suffusing his face. His hands and his mouth creating a twisting torture spiraling up through her. Liquid fire running with her blood. The beat of her heart thunderous in her ears as he tightened his hold upon her soul.

He sheathed himself in her heat. Lowered his mouth to hers, sweeping her along on a kiss, claiming her as his own. She rocked forward, taking him deep into her. Gasping back a trembling moan. He thrust again and again in a fierce bid to outrace memory. To find release from a past holding the killing strength of a weapon. She knew, because she did too.

Pleasure-infused destruction.

Desire's sweet tension tightened. Crushed her under collapsing wave after wave of orgasm. She cried out, clutching his shoulders. Spine arched. Head back. Felt his shuddering ripple as he found release. As he spilled himself into her. As his sated weight pressed her into the mattress's smothering cocoon.

She closed her eyes on what she'd done. Struggled to feel shame or guilt. Some emotion signaling she wasn't completely lost to propriety.

Couldn't do it.

The corpse lay facedown in the mud, his bottle green coat twisted up around his chest, mud and blood spattering his buckskin breeches, a spent pistol clutched in his cold hand. Lazarus wiped his blade on the grass before shoving it back into its scabbard. Pushing aside his coat to check his own bloodied side.

The man's bullet had broken a rib when it hit. Slashed its way through muscles. Grazed a lung. Spent itself deep within him. Pain squeezed Lazarus until every breath he took sent a shock wave reaction through his whole system. It wouldn't last. It never did. The agony would dull. Fade. Leave nothing but the echo of its force behind. A memory of pain. Of death. Of peace.

Mage energy would have sufficed to end the man's life. A clean kill. Murder woven with words and released on a breath of air. A coward's way. No, he preferred to close with his quarry. Blade on blade. To scent a man's fear. See the cleverness in his eyes. Hear his labored breathing and his curses as they struggled. To exercise the skills and training he'd learned on the tilting grounds and fortress yards. Murder might be his purpose, but he could pretend. He could remember.

He moved to catch the man's skittish horse lurking just out of reach. Smelling death in the air, it sought to escape him as it would a predator. Lashed out with teeth and hooves, its nostrils wide, its ears flat against its head.

Lazarus allowed it to fight. Allowed it to tire.

West, the man had said. Kilronan had been traveling west, though he'd offered no more specifics than that. Belfoyle lay west, the principal seat of the Earls of Kilronan standing watch upon the coast. Could they have been going there? No, the man had seemed certain. He'd overheard His Lordship speaking. Had heard the word Killeigh. They planned to turn off at Killeigh. That way lay the mountains. The craggy sweep of the Slieve Aughty. And Kilronan was no fool. He had to know Belfoyle would be the first place Lazarus would search.

Exhausted by fear, the horse finally let itself be caught, its sides heaving and trembling as Lazarus smoothed a hand down its neck. Crooned to it until it calmed beneath his hand. A memory blossomed from the barren soil of his consciousness. He'd owned a horse like this one once. Same steel blue coat. Same fathomless black eyes. Same fiery temperament. Neirin, he'd named it.

He pushed aside his shirt one last time. No shredded flesh. No gaping hole. Nothing but a puckered scar where death had been turned aside. Even his movements came easier, the sharp edges of this recent pain receding to be lost amid a groundswell of deep-rooted anguish.

Swinging into the saddle, he lengthened the leathers. Gathered the reins. Turned the gelding's head to the west. "Walk on, Neirin."

# fifteen

————————◦➤

Aidan woke from a tumultuous dream where Barbara Osborne's pillowed curves and soft valleys writhed beneath him, nails digging like talons down his back. As he climaxed, her face changed. Became elven-narrow, high cheekbones, delicate jaw, flashing jade green eyes. Raven hair spilling across his chest in a shining wave. A body supple as a bow with moves to make a man weep.

He ran a shaking hand down his face. Sought to erase the disturbing vision even as his cock throbbed in frustration. He rolled onto his stomach. Buried his head in the pillow. Let loose with a string of muffled curses. He'd bolloxed it up. That was for damn sure. And what was worse, he'd do it again. Wanted to feel Cat close around him. To watch her face go bright with ecstasy. To chase her ghosts away.

His ghosts? They'd never leave. But he could bring her relief even if he found none for himself.

He flopped onto his back. Stared into the gray blue of

dawn. Listened to the rattle and hiss of rain beyond his window. And rode the memory of Cat's lovemaking from the cliff edge of Daz's revelations.

"You need to eat, miss. You're wraith thin."

Maude shoved a plate under Cat's nose. Crossed her meaty arms as if daring Cat to argue with her.

The smell of food turned her attention from the part of her cringing at the thought of facing Aidan. Habit kept her eating long after she was full. It was something to do.

More mistress than maid in this odd household, Maude shuffled as she refilled platters. Checked the tea. Scolded the housemaids chattering in the hall on their way upstairs. Finally, she huffed her bulk into a chair. Pulled a flask from her apron pocket, pouring a share into a bone china cup. Topped it with tea from the pot. Swigged it down before turning her attention toward Cat. "He's not worth your fretting yourself to the grave. No man is."

Cat froze with a fork halfway to her mouth, her meal settling like a stone in the pit of her stomach.

Helping herself to a piece of toast, Maude chewed with loud smacking noises. "I've put three in the ground. Left the fourth after he struck me with a shovel handle. Can't say as I ever mourned for one of 'em. Full of their own bluster and not a one with the sense the gods gave a loon."

"He's different," Cat answered without thinking.

Maude offered her smug sympathy. "And you said that about the first one too, didn't you?"

Cat went rigid, a new awareness of this quivering mountain of a woman in her soiled apron and heavy wooden clogs, her frizzy, hennaed hair pinned in a lopsided mess beneath a wrinkled cap. "You're *Other*."

Maude plucked another piece of toast from the rack. "Did you think Daz Ahern would have any about the place who didn't carry the blood of the *Fey*? The grousy old coot's powers wax and wane along with his madness, but he understands that well enough."

"Were you here when—"

She puffed up like a proud broody hen. "Aye. Been here going on twelve years." Smoothed a hand over her apron as if she preened in her best silk gown. "I seen the rise. Cleaned up after the crash. Always been like that for us women. We're there to mop the spills and dry the tears. It's what we're best at." Her pointed stare flamed Cat's cheeks. "Am I right?"

Last night. Being drawn from her reading by the horrible sound of Aidan's grief. Finding him prostrate and sobbing like a child. That's all it had been. Sympathy sex. She'd felt sorry for him. But one didn't go around sleeping with every person one felt bad for. So why had she given herself to Aidan? Why had it been so easy?

"The boy what broke your heart. He was a right bugger. And this Kilronan?"

Cat's mind slammed shut against the answer floating at the edge of her mind.

No. She'd not let any hint of that emotion see a glimmer of daylight. That way lay destruction.

"He's not like anyone I've ever met," she answered. Truth as far as it went.

Maude uncorked the flask. This time bypassing the teacup altogether. "I'm thinking not. He's a pretty bauble for any woman to catch. Looks. A flashy title," she fanned herself with her apron hem. "I'd have a go at him myself if I thought I stood a gallows' chance."

Cat frowned. "That's not what I meant. I've met handsome gentlemen." Though none with Aidan's turbulent vitality. "And titles never impressed me." Much to the lasting chagrin of her parents. "It's something else. I can't explain it." And why she strained to define her relationship to Maude of all people, she didn't know.

"You don't need to be explaining anything to me at all, at all. The body knows what it wants and there's little the head can do about it when the blood runs hot." Maude rocked forward in her chair, spearing Cat with a wizened stare that had naught of stage farce about it. "As long as you understand how it ends, there's no harm in enjoying the pleasures what come in a lover's arms. Easier in some respects. You can always leave when the shovel comes out, can't you?" She leaned back, cackling at her own joke.

Cat stood to leave this disturbing interview. The old woman may have finagled her way into Ahern's confidences and even into his bed, but that didn't give her the right to treat Cat like some wayward daughter in need of advice. "Good day," she nodded in imitation of her mother's best quell-the-servants tone.

Maude just grinned and shook her head. "You can act the great lady if you like, Catriona O'Connell, but I'll tell you what you be needing to hear for your own good. No man wants to come second to a woman's bed. No man wants to think he's being compared and found lacking. And no man wants another's leftovers. It's just the sad facts."

Had it been said in any but the most compassionate tones, Cat might have bristled. Argued. Defended. Instead the words fell into the abyss of her own insecurities. She knew them for truth. Had known her future as soon as

Jeremy's seed had borne fruit. As soon as her son had slid into the world, blue-fragile and bastard.

Maude gave a passing imitation of a grandmotherly smile, though she was clearly out of practice. "If you're intent on playing with fire, I'll not gainsay you. But I warn you—guard your heart. Protect it like you would a child."

The abyss opened, sucking Cat under. Crushed her with a life-ending grave weight. For in the end, she'd failed at that too.

"Maude says you've been out here for hours. Didn't come in for dinner."

The kitten froze inches away from Cat's outstretched hand before scrabbling under a broken board. A half hour's toil all for naught.

She leaned back against a stall partition, drawing her legs underneath her. "Maude needs to mind her own business."

She felt Aidan sink onto his haunches beside her. His shadow coming between her and the sun. The masculine, smoky, bay rum scent of him filling her nostrils.

Chewing her lip, she drew circles in the dirt with the tip of a finger. It kept her from having to look him in the eye. She'd been here before. Felt the blood rush of attraction. Become stupid with lust. Paid a life-altering price. She couldn't afford it again. But every day she remained trapped in Aidan's company brought a night when she lay awake and frustrated with a need she knew all too well.

"Cat?" He tipped her chin toward him. Searched her face.

She gazed upon those chiseled granite features, the sharp angle of his jaw, the stubborn chin, the hooded eyes whose flinty gaze could penetrate with spearlike precision. Bracing herself, she blurted, "I shouldn't . . . last night . . . it was wrong, but you were . . . and I—"

While he fumbled, "It's not your fault . . . I never meant it to go so far . . . never blame you—"

They spoke over one another in a jumbled rush before coming to a ragged halt fraught with nervous laughter. She started to rise, but he caught her hand. Drew her back down so they met face to face and eye to eye. "I'm no saint, Cat. I've never pretended to be. And what you offered, I couldn't resist. But—"

Of course, she should have expected the *but*. Should have known he'd be quick to extricate himself from a tricky situation. She struggled to rescue her hand.

"Hear me out," he urged.

"Hear you tell me I'm not for someone like you? That it's not for a belted earl to sully his family honor with a whore like me?" Her chest went achy and tight just saying the word. Then anger barreled in behind, spilling out of her in a torrent she couldn't stop. Wrenching herself loose, she straightened with a look that spat fire. "You pulled me into your life with no thought to what it might cost me. Would Miss Osborne have stood with you against Lazarus? Or helped you translate a diary that left her retching into her slops jar for hours after? Does she even know you're *Other*? I wager that'll go down well with her high-in-the-instep phil-anthropic friends. She may be respectable, but she's not half the woman I am. Admit it."

"All right. I admit it."

She sucked in a startled breath. "What?"

A self-satisfied gleam sparkled in his eyes. "I said I admit it. I was selfish to drag you into this mess, but you've taken everything thrown at you with soldier courage. You're a marvel."

"That's not—"

An annoying smile played at the edges of his mouth. "What you expected? I know. I'm full of surprises."

Rising to stand in front of her, he crushed her against him. Silenced her with a kiss. A spine-tingling blaze of heat turning every ironclad intention to a drippy puddle of desire.

It was only hours later that she realized he'd never finished his sentence. What had he been about to say? What "but" still lurked in her future?

The sconces had been doused, lamps turned down, leaving the staircase shrouded in shadows. The quiet, sharp-eyed servants had long since been sent to their attic bedchambers for the night to be replaced by the quieter, sharp-eyed mice who rustled the walls and wainscoting.

Cat paused at the bottom riser, a hand on the banister as she peered up into the long dark tunnel of the stairwell. Not out of fear. Terror of the dark had long since left her. Instead, her eye fell upon the masculine silhouette of the man towering behind her, one candlestick-laden arm raised high, his unruly hair standing around his head like a crown, his burly-broad shoulders and long muscled legs etched in black.

"Let me." The voice rumbled through her like an echo as his arm reached around her to light the way.

She shook off fatigue and fancy. Glanced back with a nod of thanks as she lifted her skirts to climb. But a foot caught in the hem of her gown. Stumbling, she barked a shin on the hard edge of the step. Grabbed for the banister.

Instead her hand fell on Aidan's steadying arm, his body disturbingly close now that she knew the hard muscles that lay under that fabric. The glide of athletic assurance in a body trained for bolder actions than gentlemanly falderal.

Cat bit back the unladylike oath on the tip of her tongue as she rubbed at her leg. Tried to forget the man hovering solicitously beside her. As if that could ever happen now.

"Tipsy on Daz's claret?" came Aidan's wry comment. "I'd have thought a good brewer's daughter like yourself would carry a stronger head for drink."

"Correction. Brewer's stepdaughter. Sailor's daughter."

"So it's not a head for drink but a mouth for swearing. It all begins to make sense."

She was glad he found it so. She was topsy-turvy and tumbled with emotions, feeling as tossed as a juggler's ball. Looking up, she found herself caught in the bronze brown reaches of his laughing eyes. His teasing white smile.

Her heart squeezed with an ache she thought she'd put far behind her while heat burned a face already tired from hours spent reading. Should she? Shouldn't she? Could she walk away when all was over? Would she have to? Could there be a future where no future ought to be?

"Aidan?" she whispered.

His brows quirked in look of half surprise, but then he sobered, his face growing serious. "Come with me, Catriona. I'll not let you fall."

An answer to her thought. A reassurance against the hesitation plaguing her.

At the top of the stairs, he paused. And with a steadying breath and a heart full of doubt, yet fuller of hope, she followed him.

———o———

Aidan drew her into the room, closing the door behind them. Pulling her back against him. A hand at her waist. Another curving around to cup her breast. Brushing her nipple. Nuzzling her neck. Skimming the sensitive flesh just behind her ear. "Gods, Cat. I've been fantasizing about this all day."

She could tell. His erection was very much in evidence, and she ground into him, aroused by his sharp intake of breath.

"Wildcat," he chuckled, the rumble of his laughter a heady vibration jumping through her.

She tried twisting in his arms, but he held her captive, his grip like iron, the heat of his body raising a sheen of sweat between her shoulder blades. Between her breasts.

"Not so fast. Not this time," he whispered.

Pushing aside her hair, he slid his tongue down her exposed neck. Releasing one button of her gown at a time. His tongue following the curve of her spine.

The gown slid to the floor in a muslin puddle joined quickly by petticoats and stays.

His other hand continued to move over her breasts in teasing passes that had her nipples puckered and painful.

She leaned back into him, rubbing herself against the swollen size of him, loving the sizzle of desire burning its way through her like blood on fire.

He groaned, a hand dropping to skim her mound until she responded with a whimper of her own.

Then with a deft sweep of his body, he had her pinned against the door, his gaze devouring the length of her until she felt herself go wet and ready for whatever he had in mind.

Dropping to his knees, he reached up. Untied the

ribbons of one garter. Rolled the stocking to her ankle, his teeth grazing the length of her leg, pressing kisses against her inner thigh. He repeated the procedure with her other leg, leaving her jelly-kneed and throbbing.

And then he was between her legs, his lips and tongue dipping to taste, jolts of pure pleasure shooting through her. He wouldn't let her fall? Think again. She was tumbling head over heels. Plummeting through a sea of lush seduction. Everywhere he touched her, a lit fuse. Everywhere his lips moved against her, a devouring explosion.

Just as she felt herself peak in a spiraling crescendo, he abandoned his sweet assault. And as her knees gave way, he caught her. Carried her to the bed where he tossed her in a laughing, tumbled heap.

She watched in languorous pleasure as he shucked off his clothes in eager haste. And then he stood over her. Gloriously, beautifully naked. She feasted on the sight of him. Wanted to imprint the memory on her brain. The stern bones of his face. The sculpted breadth of his shoulders, the sleek line of his torso, and the hard-packed ridges of his stomach tapering into—*oh, my.*

Her brows raised in admiration, she laughed. "Are you trying to scandalize me?"

His mouth quirked in a wicked little boy smile. "No, simply pacing myself."

"Leave that to me."

She leaned up, taking his hand. Pulled him down to join her on the bed. Swung a leg over him, straddling his hips. Let the curtain of her hair spill over them, shutting out the world. If she could only shut out the accusing voices as easily. They warned her of the evils awaiting any woman foolish enough to get caught in the same trap twice.

Chided her for a monumental stupidity she'd regret forever. And all in variations of Maude's broad brogue.

But though she heard the voices, she'd long ago mastered the art of ignoring them. She'd had to. Only madness lay in wallowing through the "what-ifs" of regret. She'd already been tried and condemned. May as well enjoy her fall from grace.

Firmly beating back the last hesitation, she closed her eyes. Impaled herself on his thick shaft. Stretched to take him inch by excruciating inch. He shuddered and was still. And with a smile every bit as wicked as his, she withdrew. Sank back onto him, the tempo as she rode him slow, steady, and designed to drive him as far over the edge as she'd been only moments before.

Her success was obvious. He groaned, his hands kneading her breasts before sliding down to curve around her ribs. The callused rub of his palms sparking new tremulous spasms. Intensifying the already orgasmic sensations pulling her toward climax.

She was deliciously and horribly lost. A harlot of the worst kind. And she didn't care. Aidan Douglas was worth damnation.

He lay with one arm behind his head, one snuggling Cat close, as yet unwilling to release her. She curved into the crook of his arm, her silky flesh still a dangerous temptation as he quickly and painfully found.

Had this scoundrel Jeremy claimed her body with the same savagery? Had Cat lost herself to his lovemaking with the same sinful delight? And why the hell did it matter, so many years later? It didn't, he told himself firmly and repeatedly.

"Describe Belfoyle to me," she whispered, breaking him from the pointless speculation that could only complicate matters further.

"Why would you want to hear about that? It's not exactly pillow talk." She raised her eyes to his in such a beseeching way that he laughed. "Very well, if you insist on hearing about the ancestral pile, I'm happy to oblige."

She snuggled into him like a child awaiting a story.

"It's in County Clare. About twenty-five miles northwest of Ennis, if you know where that is. It's a bit over eighteen thousand acres, devoted mostly to sheep and cattle. Some acreage set aside for corn and other grains. We have a mill and a—"

She shifted onto an elbow, her brows wrinkled in amusement. "I don't want to purchase it."

He laughed. "Very well. Let's see." He smiled with inspiration. "All right, once upon a time there was a house that stood in a green park surrounded by beautiful views, the sea a shining dazzle through the trees, breathtaking cliffs where puffins nested and seals basked in the sun."

"Sounds delightful."

"This house had stood for hundreds of years. Never changing. Always there," he continued, warming to his theme. "A sanctuary for the family that sheltered within its protective heart. A heaven for mischievous little boys."

"I can only imagine."

As he spoke, his heart ached for Belfoyle. For the comforting solace of its aged strength. For the sharp sea salt air and the endless cloud-raced sky that made up his earliest memories. He'd been away from it since autumn—an eternity. Since he'd discovered the diary among an overlooked box of his father's papers. Since his determination to find the truth had driven him to Dublin. Straight into the waiting arms of catastrophe.

But could he call it so? His search had brought him Cat. A glimmer of precious light in a world suddenly topsy-turvy with every memory called into question.

"What happened then?" Cat's sleepy murmur drew him back to the story.

He tightened his arm around her. "And then a great storm came. A tempest that threatened to destroy the house and the family. It pounded at the foundations. Scattered the family. All seemed lost until . . ." His voice faded.

"Until what? How does the story end?" Barely audible. Naught more than a whispered breath.

He glanced over. Eyes closed, her lips parted in a wistful smile. She slept.

Sighing, he looked for the answer in the ceiling's tangle of shadows. His duty remained with Miss Osborne. But his heart lay nestled beside him. Squeezing his eyes shut against an ache tearing at his insides, he brushed a kiss upon her damp brow.

"I wish to the gods I knew, Cat."

# Sixteen

"I think I've found something!"

Cat's excited shout broke through the thunderous silence. Jerked Aidan upright in his chair. Hours spent staring at the ceiling last night had made today one long sleepy, nap craving. Coffee had brought temporary relief, but the effects wore thin. And he didn't think he could stomach another gut-griping cup of Maude's vile brew.

"Listen. It's an entry from seven years ago: *Those chosen to guard these sacred objects held them in trust for all generations of* Other. *Not as dry artifacts to be kept in dusty vaults or locked away in dazzling treasure houses. But to be cared for until such a time as there were those to use the knowledge locked within them. Now is that time. And we are those people. And someday those who revile us as murderers will laud us as heroes.*" Cat massaged her temples, wincing as she did so. "The tapestry. The stone. Those must be the sacred objects he's talking about."

"But what are they? What do they do? We still don't know."

"There's a snippet of an entry a few pages earlier talking about the High King's resting place. He refers to it as the hidden tomb." She licked her thumb. Leafed back through. "What does Daz say?"

"I tried asking, only to have him tell me a story about my mother's cousin and a man by the name of Lawrence with a thing for feathers. I interrupted before he got too descriptive."

"Now how on earth would he know—"

Aidan held up a hand. "I didn't ask and I don't want to find out."

"So it's up to the diary to tell us."

Aidan pinched the bridge of his nose. His whole body was one strained muscle, and he hadn't had a restful night since . . . since the night before he walked in on Cat in his library. The more they sought to tease meaning from his father's words, the deeper the swamp shifting beneath him. His father's life had been a sham. His brother, a mirage disappearing with every revelation. What else would he find out if he kept digging? What new horror waited to spring out at him?

"Maybe it's best to leave this for now," he suggested. "After all, we're just assuming that's why Brendan wants the diary. We don't know for certain. There might be a whole chapter of death spells or a thousand and one ways to kill your enemies and destroy your friends."

"You've changed your mind about Brendan?"

"It makes sense, doesn't it? The *Amhas-draoi* certainly seemed assured of his guilt. Who am I to argue with the logic of Scathach's brotherhood?"

"You're his brother," she answered flatly. "You knew him better than anyone. Could Daz be mistaken? Could he be lying to you for some purpose of his own or simply not remembering correctly? We've already established his less-than-firm grasp on reality."

"Not when it's counted. Then he's been sharp as a damned knife through the heart."

"I've found it!" Daz entered the dining room, triumphantly waving a thick leather-bound book, the corners of which looked gnawed, the binding broken and split. "And the last place I expected. Under 'authors who died under mysterious circumstances.'"

Maude looked up from her third cup of gin-laced tea. "What are you prattling on about, you chatty old scalawag?"

"The book. It's in the book," he shouted, shuffling about the table in a rickety dance.

Aidan mouthed the word "feathers," leaving Cat snorting into her napkin.

"Sit down before you break a hip, you musty old fool," Maude scolded.

Ignoring Maude's unusual way with endearments, Daz fell into a chair. Opened the book to a dog-eared page. Pushed it across to Aidan with a dazzling smile. "I knew I'd a seen a mention of it somewhere." He pointed to a paragraph halfway down that had been heavily underlined. "See? The Rywlkoth Tapestry. That's the one."

Aidan scanned the entry, his face hardening into grim lines. He looked up. "And you say this"—he flipped to the flyleaf then back to the proffered page—"Dudley Squires met a sticky end?"

Ahern nodded, his smile dimming. "Found dead in his bath."

"What's so mysterious about that?" Cat asked.

"He was fully dressed and missing his head."

Cat grimaced. "Sorry I asked." She turned her attention to Aidan, who remained stone silent, his gaze dark with some inner demon. "May I?" She slid the book from under his fingers. Read the underlined passage. And then a second time—more slowly—trying to take in the implications of Squires's hypothesis. "The High King's hidden tomb." She glanced up. "That same term was mentioned in your father's diary."

"Apparently not so hidden if one has the tapestry," Aidan said, coming out of his trance to top off his claret. Tossing it down as if it were water.

"A sort of a treasure map?" she asked, frowning her distaste. "Follow to where 'X' marks the spot and *voila*— Arthur?"

"It's not as simple as that, Miss O'Connell. It's a riddle. Instructions woven into the fabric only those with the knowledge might decipher."

"Cat's an expert at deciphering." Aidan glanced her way with a possessive can't-wait-to-get-you-in-bed stare that had Maude's lips pursing to a white line of disapproval.

Cat felt the woman's warning like a mental slap to the back of the head. A slap she chose to ignore.

"So if the tapestry finds you Arthur's resting place, what's the stone for?" Cat asked, firmly dismissing Maude's intrusion.

Ahern snatched the book back from her. Flipped pages to get to the second bookmark. "Here." Shoved it back into her hands.

Cat scanned the page, her turn to grind her teeth in growing fury. "The stone's the key that releases the protective wards. Why such safeguards?"

Ahern cast her a look like she'd taken leave of her senses. Not so far off. Here she sat discussing the reincarnation of a king as nonchalantly as if she were conversing about a visit from some family friend.

"It was Arthur," he said in a tone clearly implying she was daft to even ask such a question. "Those who attended his death and saw to his burial knew the importance of the last *Other* king and his legacy to our race. To protect his eternal sleep, they hid the tomb. Warded it against any trespass."

"Then why keep a map and a stone as if tempting someone to use them? Doesn't seem an intelligent idea on the part of those so-called protectors."

"According to the legends, an attendant kept eternal vigil within the tomb," Daz explained as if she were a rather slow-witted convalescent. "Every year the guard changed in a ritual handover. The map and the stone would be the only way to gain access."

"But if the map and stone are lost—"

"Somewhere there's an attendant left unrelieved," Aidan ended her sentence on a solemn intonation.

Ahern fluttered. "It's a hypothesis only. No one knows if the tapestry and stone are anything more than grand hoaxes or if they lead to anything."

"My father believed it. So did Brendan. And they managed to convince plenty of others."

"But they're dead. All of them. The *Amhas-draoi* ended it. The Nine are gone."

"Not all of them. You said it yourself, Daz. One of them survived. And he's set his killer on our trail. He wants the diary, and he's prepared to kill to gain it. Now we know why."

"But Brendan has the stone already," Cat reasoned. "It

said so in the letter your father wrote. Brendan took the stone and your father took the tapestry."

"So Brendan's back to find out the tapestry's hiding place. He must think Father wrote where he hid it in the diary."

"Brendan?" Ahern asked.

"It seems as if my brother's not so disappeared after all."

Daz's face crumpled, his fingers trembling but his eyes feverishly bright. "Brendan's alive? Could it be true?"

Aidan scowled before fisting his hand around the stem of the wineglass as if throttling it. "Very alive and very dangerous."

He approached as close as he dared, the presence of the estate's wards a tangible ribbon of mage energy stretching north and south in front of him. He'd left Neirin tethered in the woods, pawing at the soft ground, the gleam of the horse's bit flashing in the light of a low moon.

Now, crouched at the edge of the boundary, his senses picked through the gloom with little problem. Caught the panicked dart of a hare. The shush of an owl's wings, talons extended like knives. A death scream as the hare was ripped from neck to belly. The hot, sweet scent of blood. He breathed deeply, letting the animal's killing ooze through him like the high of a drug. Strengthen him. Bolster his flagging resolve.

Beyond a line of trees, lights glimmered. Cattle lowed. A dog barked.

Kilronan's diary was in that house. He felt it tugging him forward like a lodestone upon a string. As if the black spells written within it whispered to him, abomination to abomination. He almost heard their dark voices on the wind.

He tested the strength of the wards. A crackling flame raced up his arms, but instead of heat, a numbing buzz jolted him backward like the kick of a horse. Rang in his bones long after.

Leaning back on his haunches, he considered his options. Raised his gaze to the sky, black as velvet and dusted with a pale wash of cold light.

A scene burst into his head. A similar night to this one. Chilly. The wind sighing like a lover. The moist tang of spring growth filling his nostrils.

He'd sat in patient silence just as now, the campfires of the English just beyond a ridge. Nudged Ivor, motioning to the picket line where a beautiful white stallion glowed scarlet in the light from the flames. "He's mine," he'd whispered, his eyes never straying from the elegant-boned destrier.

Ivor smiled, whispered back, "That one's fit for no less than a prince. Not a simple soldier like you—"

He strained to catch the name on the man's tongue. His name. But just like that the memory vanished as if he'd doused the light. As if witnessing the sword stroke that ended that long-ago existence, he shivered, his fingers slick and a cold sweat damping his shoulders.

And instead of charging through the faulty wards, he chose to wait. Watch the slow spinning of the heavens, searching the sky for that past life. Wishing he could fly up into the darkness and be back there among his friends. Feeling that if only he remembered that lost name, he could leave Lazarus and his slavery to Máelodor far behind.

# Seventeen

⎯⎯⎯⎯⎯⎯⎯⎯⎯⎯⎯►

Aidan trailed a lazy hand down Cat's side. Cupped the perfect weight of her breast, thumbing the nipple before taking it into his mouth. Laving the sweetness of her skin. Drowning in the musky sex scent of her body. Reveling in the way her panting, gasping moans aroused him all over again.

With an enigmatic smile, she curled her hand around his member. Guided him into her with a clever expression hinting at a wicked waywardness he'd never find in a proper marriage bed. But who said his marriage had to be proper? He'd never been a proper anything. Son. *Other.* Earl.

Why start now?

For Belfoyle, his conscience complained. For an estate long owed a master who cared enough to restore it to prosperity. For the scattered remains of a family who looked to him to reestablish honor to the name of Douglas and the title of Kilronan.

Honor. Duty. Loyalty. He thrust again and again, her

velvety, wet heat sweeping him close to explosion. She ground her hips in response, letting him ride this wave of anger to its climactic end. As if she understood. As if she fought her own private battles within their shared bed.

In self-denial, he pulled free. Rock hard and coiled tight. One torturous undulation away from eruption.

She groaned her frustration. Arched into him, purring her demand. Instead, he let her writhe. Lowered his head to nibble and nip his way down her stomach, over the inside of her thighs. Knelt between her legs to lap at the slick center of her.

She bucked, threading her fingers through his hair. Urging him on with every shuddering tremor.

But he refused to give her what she wanted. To surrender, even though his cock throbbed with impatience. Instead he held back just enough to prolong the pleasure. To reel out the tension—hers and his—to orgiastic lengths. He vibrated with a body-wide need. Blood roaring in his ears, heart pounding in his chest.

A throaty, ragged gasp signaled her tip over the edge. And only then did he move over her. Spread her legs and bury himself inside her.

She laughed, and with one of those wanton siren moves, had him on his back. Straddling him. Ebony hair like a river of silk over his chest.

One hand splayed against his chest, she rocked forward. Bent to take his nipple in her mouth. Tongued until he moaned, spasms rippling through him. The rhythm of their joining intensified until he crumbled under the blast of white heat, his climax exploding through him like lightning. She followed him in the toppling ecstasy, her inner muscles closing around him, head thrown back, eyes closed, skin like pearl in the light from a waning moon as she rode him to her own release.

Spent, they snuggled in the bed, their limbs sweat slick but rapidly cooling, their breathing raspy from the race. He pushed a damp tendril of hair from her face. Caught the sliver of the ancient scar on her cheek. Dropped a kiss upon it. "How did it happen?"

She reached up to cover his hand where he touched her cheek, her eyes sleepy, her mind open to sharing confidence. "My stepfather's riding crop."

Aidan stiffened. "What kind of man raises a hand to a defenseless girl?"

A corner of her mouth twitched in a half smile. "You did once if you'll remember."

He flushed. "That was different. And you were hardly defenseless. You about emasculated me with that kick."

She brushed provocatively against him. "Had I only known." She giggled. "But I wasn't exactly defenseless that time either. He received a fist to the face in response. It was the last time he struck me."

"Learned his lesson, did he?"

"I walked out. It was when he learned about Jeremy and the baby. "

Aidan went completely still, her last word dropping like a weight in the quiet room. Repeating with the echo of complete shock. His hand unconsciously found her stomach. Brushed the flatness of it, imagining it stretched and heavy with pregnancy. Envisioning her caught in the throes of childbirth. Images battering him of her and Jeremy together. Impossible to ignore after he'd just experienced her reckless passion for himself.

"Baby? You have a child?"

"Had." She stared long and hard at some invisible distant point, anguish as raw upon her features as pleasure had been only moments before. "He lived for only a few days," she said, interpreting his silence as approval to continue. "I'd not even enough coins to bury him." She sniffled in the darkness. "He lies in a pauper's grave. I try to . . . to tell myself at least he's not alone. He rests among souls as lost and lonely as he."

Aidan closed his eyes against the heartbreak in her voice. Damning the thrice-cursed Jeremy to hell even as his stomach curdled, his fragile peace cracking along a thousand fault lines.

"I worry every day I'll forget him. That some morning I'll open my eyes and the memory of his face, his little wrinkled fingers, his need for me will be gone. And I'll be truly alone in the world."

Why did every syllable congeal his blood to icy sluggishness? This was Cat. She was courageous. Defiant. Displayed the will of a lion, yet conveyed a vulnerability generating unfamiliar knight-errant tendencies in him. Her sins meant less than nothing. He'd told her that. Believed it.

His hand slid away as his head buzzed with questions.

"Aidan?" she asked tentatively.

He couldn't answer, still trapped between acceptance of Cat's tarnished past and shock at the existence of a child. A concrete and very real symbol of that past.

Her breath caught in her throat, her body going still. "You bloody great hypocrite," she murmured in the same sultry sexy voice used only moments earlier as a wanton invitation. "I should have known."

She catapulted from his bed, dragging the blanket with her. Wrapping herself in its folds like some quivering

vengeful Roman goddess, finger pointed in wrathful accusation. " 'You're a marvel, Cat,' " she mocked. " 'I won't let you
fall.' So my bedding another is fine. But bearing his child
puts me beyond the pale? How dare you!" Her jeers came
ugly and hoarse with fury. "You strung me along like some
stupid, senseless female until I trusted you not to judge me.
Until I thought maybe—just maybe—you'd understand,
but you're like all the rest. How many women have you
gulled into your bed with a honeyed tongue then left when
you'd had your fill? How many of your children lie buried
in forgotten graves? Answer me that."

For a split second, his mind retraced a string of name-
less, faceless women whose sole memorable feature was
their willing compliance in his artful seduction. Flinched
from the thought that somewhere out there a child might
cry for a father he'd never known.

He crushed the thought. "No. It couldn't happen.
Wouldn't. And I'd know if it had."

But Cat's scarred face and bruised soul told him it
could and did happen all too frequently.

She fumbled with the blanket, her hands shaking as
badly as her voice. "I've been a fool twice over. And that
makes what we've done here my folly. Not yours. So I can
forgive your seduction. What I can't forgive is your betrayal."

Unable to speak or move or defend against the truth, he
merely lay there in stony silence, left alone with a whirl of
questions, and a gnawing emptiness where his heart ought
to be.

Cat's rage carried her back to her rooms. Through a
clumsy, hurried dressing into petticoat and gown whose
buttons seemed suddenly overlarge, the fabric harsh against

flesh still tender from lovemaking. Stuffing her hair into a loose roll and pinning it with a set of silver and bone combs she'd unearthed from one of the trunks, she sank among the crates and barrels, wishing she could turn to uncaring wood and stone like the trinkets and treasures surrounding her.

She pressed the heels of her hands to her eyes, refusing to give in to the humiliation and anger squeezing her throat. Searing her cheeks. If she cried, she'd never stop. Simply drown in a river of stupid tears taking her nowhere. She knew that from bitter experience.

The world didn't change to suit your dreams. It was your dreams that had to change to suit the world. Another of Geordie's maxims. Thoughts of the dwarfish little thief brought a fresh ache to a throat sore and throbbing.

"Cat, open up." Followed by a soft tap at the door. "We need to talk."

"I think we've said all that needs saying."

The door opened, a slice of Aidan's face appearing in the crack. He'd dressed. She caught the white of his shirt, and a boot slid into the opening, wedging the door open. "Someone will hear. Let me in."

"Afraid they'll reveal your lechery to Miss Osborne and she'll call off the wedding?" A new realization brought her quivering to her feet. "Or is it that you think if you don't play nice, I'll stop translating." She nodded. "That's it, isn't it?"

Discarding his conciliatory pose, Aidan stepped into the room. Closed the door behind him, leaning back against it as if she might flee. His clothes looked as if he'd flung them on in haste, and his uncombed auburn hair stuck out in elflocks. "Don't be daft."

She tilted her chin to meet the annoyance flickering in his eyes. "So now what? Do you lock me in again, Kilronan? Tempt me with proper clothes and coal for my fire as if I were a stray you could toss a bone?"

"Kilronan again, is it?"

"It's a finer title than the one I could be using."

That brought a gruff laugh and a bitter twist of his lips. "True enough." He reached for her. "Cat, if you'll just let me—"

But he never completed his sentence. Instead, his head jerked up as if he'd been pulled by invisible strings, his pupils constricting to obsidian chips in a face suddenly devoid of color. "He's here."

"Who?"

But the space where he'd been had no answer for her.

Not that she needed one.


Aidan plunged down the dark stairs. Beat a path through the house, pausing only long enough to gather the loaded pistol from the chest in the hall. A knife from the kitchens.

What he'd do with them, he hadn't the foggiest notion. They certainly wouldn't stop Lazarus. Barely slow him down if his last encounter with the *Domnuathi* was anything to go by. But he had to try. For the diary's sake. For Cat's sake, even if she wished him to the devil just now. Not that he didn't deserve it. Her revelation still sizzled along his nerves in sickening little bursts, but he'd gotten past the initial lightning shock. And that's just what it was. Cat— the walking storm cloud. The living breathing hurricane force blowing apart every preconceived notion of what he wanted. Who he needed.

He rushed out onto the wide back steps leading down

to the garden. A yellow moon hung just above the trees, a bite taken out of it, leaving it jagged and pale against a sky dark as ink.

Somewhere out there, Lazarus waited. The hairs on Aidan's neck prickled. His skin itched and stretched as if his whole body expanded to seek out the intruder. Fisting the handle of the knife, he descended the steps slowly. Scanning the terraces for traces of movement.

"Lazarus!" he shouted. "I know you're out there. I can smell your death stench!"

Probably not the brightest of ideas to taunt a man who had the ability to kill you a thousand different ways, but what the hell? He rode close to the edge. Half-crazed from a night spinning so out of control, it seemed the very sky tilted on an awkward axis.

"Afraid to face me like a man? Oh, that's right. You're not a man. Not anymore. You're a wraith with no more power than what your creator gave you!"

He worked his way toward the closest grove of trees in an attempt to lure Lazarus away from the house. Made it as far as the first scraggly shrubs when his quarry appeared behind him. At first no more than another shadow among many until the *Domnuathi* separated from the gloom. Stepped into the clearing.

Damn, he'd forgotten how bloody huge the creature was. His head scraping even with the tree limbs, his expression lost in the murk, all except for the inhuman animal eyes. They speared him with the emptiness of the grave. Burned like twin embers.

"For that, a slow and painful death is yours." Lazarus's voice came rough and creaky as if he seldom spoke. His hand fell to his waist where Aidan had been trying not to notice the long outline of a scabbard hanging with menacing promise. "But first the diary."

Aidan pulled the pistol from his belt. Steadied it at Lazarus's chest. The soldier of Domnu smiled, a thin terrible smile full of pity and longing, emptying Aidan of his last hope. This man wanted to die. Would welcome it. And who could stand against a fool who chased death with such naked yearning?

"If only you could, Kilronan," he sighed. "I might just let you live."

And then he struck.

Cat banged on the bedchamber door. Rattled the knob. "Wake up. Please. Get up. Aidan needs you."

She collapsed sobbing against the panels. Almost tumbled into the room as the door was wrenched open to Maude in cap and wrapper, hair in a messy night plait down her rounded back.

Daz sat up in the enormous four poster bed behind her, rubbing his eyes.

"What the devil!" Maude scolded. "You're making enough noise to raise the dead."

"He's already been raised," Cat blurted. "And he's out there now. Aidan's trying to stop him." She looked past Maude to Daz. "Please. You have to help him. Lazarus will kill him."

Daz cocked his head. "Lazarus?"

"Brendan's conjured killer. He attacked us in Dublin. And now he's tracked us here."

"Brendan?"

"He's after the diary."

Daz flinched, his face ashen, his eyes wide and fearful.

"The Nine are no more. Brendan's no more. The *Amhas-draoi* killed them all. They're no more, and the dream is dead. The High King's return stale as yesterday's bread."

Cat crossed to the bed, taking him by the arm. Trying by sheer force of will to propel him up and into sanity. "Stop it. Stop prattling like a damned Bedlamite and do something."

Maude sought to intercede, but Cat was beyond listening. Beyond understanding. Beyond anything but panic and the fear that even now it was too late. Surely that was the steady approach of Lazarus she heard across the boards below. And there was his breathing as he climbed the stairs. The drip of a blood-splattered blade.

"Get up, damn you!" she shouted.

Daz started to move. With agonizing lethargy, he drew on his breeches. Wrapped a banyan about his shoulders. Too slow. Far too slow.

Hurry! she wanted to scream.

Hurry before it's too late.

"Even without your help, I'll find it, Kilronan. And your silence will mean less than nothing."

If Aidan closed his eyes, the earth would devour him. The soil would close over his head. Roots would snarl in his hair, and his flesh would dissolve to naught more than food for the worms. So he kept his eyes open and locked on the fiend striding triumphant toward the house, while his mind fastened on the only answer to this unwavering onslaught of devastating mage energy.

Gulping a fiery breath, he descended. Pulled forth the words he'd read only once, yet which had sat upon his tongue like a bitter taste ever after. Words with the force to summon an *Unseelie*. The only being he could think of with the ability to vanquish the reanimate.

"*Yn-mea esh a gwagvesh. A-dhiwask polth. Dreheveth hath omd-hiskwedhea.*" Just speaking took monumental effort. Placing the emphasis in the right spot. Shaping the harsh vowels and chewing the raspy consonants. Pushing them through cracked lips from a mouth sticky and numb. "*Skeua hesh flamsk gwruth dea. Drot peuth a galloea esh a dewik lya. Drot peuth a pystrot esh a dewik spyrysoa.*"

The words seemed to draw a shadow over the sky, as if some great beast had swallowed the moon. And he shivered despite a heat beginning in his belly. Spreading along his arteries and veins in the usual fiery race to his brain. But something else traveled in the same current as this molten flash flood. Something foreign and potent and bearing the weight of oblivion.

Aidan repeated the phrase. And again. Each time feeling death recede and a new existence beckoning with skeletal fingers. The air thickened, making it difficult to breathe. His lungs worked like a bellows, yet dizziness spun the stars overhead and spots clouded his eyesight.

A form took shape at the corner of his narrowed vision. A creature more shade than substance, yet gaining mass with every passing second. Craning its thick, wattled neck back and forth as if seeking the origin of its summoning.

Laying its gaze upon Aidan, its lips peeled back on a mouth full of razored teeth and a lolling tongue like a lizard's.

"*Hwot gelweth mest, Erelth.*" It spoke in a slithering, hissing speech, its unblinking vertical-lidded eyes pale as bleached stones.

"I called you forth." Aidan heard the words come from

his mouth. But his voice had deepened. Bore the same unnatural reptilian crawl. "Join with me. Take your place within me."

"*Mest akordyesh, Erelth*," the *Unseelie* answered. "*Hwot esh biest mest.*" It punched its fist into Aidan's flesh, his body parting bloodlessly. Again came the pain like a breath-stealing bullet's rip. And the *Unseelie's* other arm disappeared into Aidan's body.

He shifted against a feeling as if his bones had hardened to iron, his blood turned to acid, his brain whirling and overflowing with thoughts and memories not his own.

Fury. Rage. Murder. Hate. Chaos. Destruction. Ruin. Death.

The creature's voice filled his head with a screeching buzz like metal against metal. "*Esoest hwot, Erelth. Owgsk vest. Oa hunot.*"

And like stepping through a door, the creature settled beneath his skin. Controlled him. Became him.

With the *Unseelie's* help, Lazarus would be a dead man. Again.

# Eighteen

Cat stumbled to a crashing halt at the top of the stairs.

Below her, an expression of grim determination upon his upturned face, climbed Lazarus. His gaze settled upon her like a knife at her throat, his steps unfaltering.

Spinning, she fled back toward her bedchamber. Slammed the door closed behind her, sobs knotting her throat, her heart thundering. She scanned the room for a hiding place. Somewhere she could crawl into and become invisible to the searching, killer eyes of the deathless *Domnuathi*.

Steps sounded on the floorboards. Slow. Sure. As if confident none could stand against him. And wasn't that true? How did one kill something already dead? How could one hurt something for which pain was less than nothing?

She'd prodded Daz and Maude to action. Now she prayed the old man and woman huddled safely in their chamber while Lazarus searched. He didn't want them. He wanted the Kilronan diary. She wished she could give it to him. Hand it over and be done with it. All she'd found within it had been sorrow. Sorrow and misery. The pages seemed to bleed these emotions, as if agony had been written into the mysterious language with every stroke of the pen.

"Lazarus!"

The shout erupted in the torpid silence of the house. The footsteps paused.

"Your bravery does you credit, Kilronan," came the grim voice on the other side of the door.

"Abomination of *Annwn*. Your cannibalized half-life is over." Aidan's voice—yet hardly his words. No, these came clipped and enunciated with careful and formal precision. As if the speaker used a language not his own. *"Yntresh esh dea hesh dea tarosvana, not bodsk diwedsk mesk nana."*

Chained rage quivered off every syllable, and Cat's throat closed around a panicked moan. She knew this language. Had heard it once before in Aidan's library the night he'd called the *Unseelie.* This wasn't Aidan. Or at least not the Aidan she knew. This was a merging of man and monster. He must have summoned a being of the Dark Court to aid him against Lazarus. But who could be the victor between two such unspeakable creatures?

A blast of mage energy lit the space beneath the door. Sparkled the very dust hovering in the air. The wood panels buckled, the lock rattling, the nails glowing red-hot.

There came a shout and a scream, and again the mage energy crackled through the air with a sulpherous stench.

"Hold, damn you!" That was Aidan, for certain. But then his words came again with the same odd dissonance as before. "No peaceful sleep, *Domnuathi*, but a wakeful eternity in the deepest pits of *Annwn*."

The sounds of battle rang up and down the corridor and the stairs. The crash of a gunshot. The whistle of arcing steel. The grunts and curses of men locked in a death struggle.

The fight receded in a tumble and rush of boots upon stairs. A scream and a string of furious swearing. And through it all the prickly rush of expelled mage energy bathed in the nausea-inducing miasma of the *Unseelie*.

A slam of bodies. And from the lawn, another blue white flash turning night to day as it expanded in wave after wave of rolling magic.

Aidan's triumph sounded animalistic and wild like a blooded animal crowing over a fresh kill. Then came silence as thick and brimstone filled as the air of the underworld.

Cat fingered the doorknob. Flinched from a heat bursting up her arm before it dissipated.

Ignoring the unsettling sensation, she wrenched open the door. Stumbled down the stairs. Past the broken and hanging furniture, the spilled blood, the crush and splinters of destruction. Out the back to stand upon the terrace stairs.

Below, in the pallid light of a setting moon, Aidan crouched over a body upon the grass.

"Is he dead?" she called.

He straightened and turned toward her. And his eyes shone like pits of fire. "Not yet," he hissed.

The man upon the grass moaned and stirred, reaching for a dagger just out of range. And Cat sucked her breath in over a tongue swollen with horror.

Not Lazarus. Of the dead-eyed *Domnuathi*, there was no sign at all.

This was Aidan.

Battered. Bleeding. And about to be murdered by— himself.

---o---

Aidan touched the dagger's hilt, the cool steel grazing the pads of his fingers. Reality amid a battering nightmare of sensations and images flooding his bruised and exhausted mind. Weakened by his fight with Lazarus, he had no strength left to struggle against the *Unseelie's* domination. The long, excruciating consumption of his existence into the body of the creature standing over him.

Thoughts came slowly. Action slower. The air around him grew heavy upon his chest. Sight came through a prism of flame and smoke and cinders.

He reached for the dagger. Closed his hand around it.

There came a muffled shout from somewhere to his right, the monster's attention momentarily diverted.

With almost the last of his strength, Aidan lurched upward, the blade plunging deep into the monster's chest. Interrupting the parasitic drain with a crackling infernal roar even as it opened a long, jagged wound. Black blood spurted, burning Aidan's exposed flesh, the dagger disintegrating on a sour wind.

The *Unseelie* reared back in surprise and pain, its eyes wide and terrible, Aidan seeing his death mirrored in the crazed fury of the animal.

Surrender would be easy. Let the *Unseelie* have him. Let this struggle end now. He'd no hope of winning against such strength. Yet sheer cussedness kept him fighting.

Father thought he'd never be good enough? Well, he'd be damned if the old man would be proven right.

*"Dehwelea dh'agaa bya!"* The shouted words from the stair above stung Cat to life. Daz's sturdy warmth. His musty old-book and sour-wine smell. His voice, no longer

shivery and ancient, but bold. Confident. Forcing the *Unseelie* away from Aidan's prone body. *"Moa hath ankresyesh not nesh fellesh!"*

It eyed them with a viciousness Cat felt all the way to her bones. Here was evil hiding beneath the cloak of the familiar. The same tousled auburn hair, the same aristocratic bearing, the same large, work-hardened hands ornamented with that heavy emerald chunk. Only this stranger-Aidan remained gray as ash, with a body coarse and stocky and unlike lover-Aidan's long, lean frame.

She shuddered so hard her knees knocked, and she felt she might slump to the bricks beneath her feet if the *Unseelie* didn't turn its gaze elsewhere. But then Maude appeared, her matronly bulk offering reassurance. "Come, child. Strength is needed tonight."

*"Dehwelana dhe'n gwagvesh, dewik spyrya. Dehwelana dhe'a flammsk hesh moth esh ankoest!"* His knobby hand still clutching her shoulder, Daz shouted again. Battering the enemy with his curse. Keeping it from feeding upon its host.

Together the three of them descended the steps.

The monster lurched but remained upright, his tongue running over lips peeled back in a triumphant grin.

Aidan moaned, his fingers scrabbling desperately in the grass. Faded and shrunken. Bones held together by a wrapping of skin pulled until it threatened to split. Spill his spirit upon the ground to be devoured by this creature of the void. Every second Aidan became more insubstantial, like mist struck by sunlight. Even as the *Unseelie* seemed to grow more solid. More confident.

"Daz! Look to Aidan! He's dying! Disappearing!"

But Daz ignored Cat's pleas. Remained focused upon the monster, his words weaving a cage about the *Unseelie*.

The creature twisted, its misshapen limbs jerking, its jaw wide and snapping as it struggled against·the bonds of mage energy holding it fast. Unable to complete the take-over of this host body. Unable to retreat into the safety of the abyss.

The words streamed in an endless rhythm. A background noise like the wind or the scrape of the trees or the drip of a broken gutter.

Aidan's back arched, hands grabbing at the turf as if he might hold himself in this world by digging deep into the earth.

"Go to him, child," Maude shouted over the cacophony. "Perhaps you can hold him."

Cat ran down the final stairs. Crossed the open lawn, though as she passed the *Unseelie,* she forced her eyes to look at Aidan, not the creature, certain its gaze held the power to burn her to ash. Instead, she dropped to her knees beside Aidan. Took up one hand, linking her fingers with his.

No noise came from his open mouth. No light brightened eyes blind to everything but the horror awaiting any mortal who dared switch places with a creature of the Dark Court. His chest rose and fell, his throat worked as he swallowed. His flesh as unsubstantial as cobwebs, veins and arteries, tendons and muscles all clear beneath the ethereal shine of translucent skin.

He turned his unseeing eyes upon her, his grip tightening upon her fingers. His breath coming slower, as if he sensed her presence and was calmed by it.

And like a door flung wide on a candlelit room or a thousand torches being set alight, the night seemed bathed in a fiery green glow. Thunder rolled across a slick, yellow sky empty of stars as the ground heaved and shook, toppling trees and sending slates tumbling from the roof in a violent cascade.

Smoke and dust settled, revealing a void where the *Unseelie* had stood. A fading stench soon blown away by the incessant wind. An oily smear upon the lawn washed away in the tempests that followed.

"Carry him this way. Careful now. That's it."

Arms hooked him by the oxters and under his knees. Lifted him in a dizzying swoop of screaming muscles that left him retching. Jostled him indoors with battlefield tenderness.

"Blighter's dead if'n yer ask me."

"Naw, he's breathing, see? Leastways for now, he is."

A doubtful snort followed this maudlin opinion, then a curse as someone's hold slipped, sending pain shooting along every charred nerve.

Blessed unconsciousness hung like a treasure just beyond reach, and he begged for it, though the sounds he made resembled words only in his own mind.

"That's it. A little farther now, boys."

His shoulder struck a wall, drawing a moan from cracked and bleeding lips.

"Gently, you dolts. Gently. He's had a bad fall."

A whispered snicker met this comment. And no wonder. The cosmic event surrounding the *Unseelie*'s banishment had hardly been subtle.

There followed the soft give of a mattress beneath him. A muttered thanks and coins being handed over.

"Aidan, my boy? Are you with us still?"

He looked toward Daz's voice. Saw nothing beyond a rising sheet of green flame. Swallowing his panic, he squeezed his eyes shut. "I've—" he took a breath laced with the stab of fever—"been better."

A hand rested upon his shoulder. "And will be again, my boy." His voice came raspy with emotion and age. "Methinks he'd have been proud."

# Nineteen

His body withered, his limbs hung weighted and useless. Voices spoke to him in the twilight. Hands reached out. But ghost and flesh became indistinguishable and reality and dream entwined. The bed grew to become the cliff edge below Belfoyle. The walls expanded into a dark, moonless night, a silver cream marking the offshore shoals.

"You won't fall, Aidan. I've got you." Father's voice. And there he was. Smiling his reassurance from a handhold just above, harness clipped to a rope disappearing over the cliff edge, where it had been securely anchored.

Following instructions, Aidan checked his footing before making his next move. The ever-present wind buffeted him as he slowly ascended.

"That's it, son. Slow and steady."

He remembered this day. It was June. He'd turned fifteen the week before. His birthday a celebration of laughter and parties and gifts from friends and family alike. But this had been Father's present. A day spent together. A hike north toward the rocky beaches, culminating in a dangerous cliff ascent—something Aidan had been forbidden to do until this year.

Glancing up, he judged his next foothold. Committed to it with a lurch, taking him out of the safety of the cliff edge and into the wind. It screamed and whistled past him in a *ban-sidhe* shriek. Curled like smoke into a monstrous form—blind white eyes, terrible smile.

"Father!" he shouted in his panic.

But his father's face melted into a grimace of stony hatred. Impossible evil. Reaching over, he slid his knife from its sheath.

"I'm sorry, son. You've failed me," he said, sawing through the rope.

Aidan grappled for a hold, but it was useless. He fell and fell without end, the void swallowing him, the wind's shriek becoming his father's triumphant laughter.

Just before he knew his bones must shatter, he jerked awake. The dream faded into the walls of his room. The folds of his bed curtains. Only the pulse-pounding terror lingered. Only that proved real.

Aidan's chest burned, and jagged razors of pain slashed their way up his throat even as inner visions savaged his mind and tore through him like an illness. He couldn't think. Suffocated under the weight of his agony. And understood now why Daz chose madness. It was easier.

The *Unseelie* lurked. He couldn't see it but knew it remained. Waited for its chance to feast upon his soul. End what he'd started with his unthinking summoning. He felt its empty stare as he slept. Heard its slithery, blood-chilling words.

Sometimes it stood within Belfoyle's great hall. Stretched its neck as it surveyed its new home.

Sometimes Aidan found himself racing Brendan neck-and-neck down Belfoyle's avenue, only to discover he raced an unbeatable nemesis, its steed a red-eyed monster with a serpent's hide and blood-dripping fangs.

And other times, it spoke to him in Father's voice. Explaining. Cajoling. Trying to make him understand.

Those visions were the worst. Those cut close to a wound still raw and bleeding. A past seeming as imaginary to him now as one of Father's fantastical bedtime stories.

The nightmare ended on a scream of terror as a man plunged earthward before being lost among mist-shrouded rocks. Cat woke, heart racing, skin clammy. The deadly rocks disappeared, the falling man faded into memory, but the screams continued. Horrible, furious cries of pain and fear and rage. She pressed her hands to her ears, trying desperately to drown them out. Trying frantically to forget the battle raging in the room down the corridor. The ongoing fight for a man's soul.

Daz had tried warning her. He'd told her to harden herself to all that went on behind that locked door. To ignore the heartrending pleas and choked weeping, the shrieks of animal fury, ominous threats, and fiendish curses.

"It's not him, Miss O'Connell," he'd sought to explain. "The beast's domination was almost complete. To heal Aidan fully, we must draw the evil like drawing poison from a wound. The withdrawal of such a malignant force leaves a great, horrible emptiness in a person. And like an opium eater remains addicted to the drug, so does Aidan remain addicted to the unholy force. Craves to be reunited with the

*Unseelie* demon. We must wean him from that dependence slowly."

Cat started at a shattering of glass and a shouting pounding cry. "Let me out, damn you! You can't hold me forever! Daz, you thrice-cursed bastard, let me out!" His voice held a foreignness in its slippery self-assurance, a haughty scorn that had never been characteristic of the Aidan she knew.

How long would this go on? How long before his strength gave out? The last episode had continued for hours before subsiding into dry, gulping sobs that tore at Cat's heart.

"I know you're out there! I know you can hear me. Cat? Please! I need to get out, goddamn it. I can't take it anymore! Please, Cat!" A crash of thrown furniture. Another earsplitting shatter. "Damn you, bitch! Release me! Get me the hell out of here!"

She threw herself onto her stomach. Pressed the pillow over her head. No use. Even muffled, the tortured struggle carried through. She bit her lip, stifled her own sobs, tried blocking out Ahern's last somber words. "He'll recover, or he'll break. And then there is but one merciful end."

She didn't ask. She already knew. She'd seen the pistol.

"Cat?" he forced out.

Maude pursed her lips. "She's sleeping, milord."

"Send her to me when she wakes," he muttered as he sank back. "Tell her I'm sorry."

"Men are born sorry," was the last thing he heard before he fell into the sweet oblivion of sleep.

It watched him from the end of his bed. A crouched and waiting figure with a milk white, paralyzing gaze. It knew he'd never withstand the agony of withdrawal. Already a clawing ache strained Aidan's stomach and twisted his bowels. His hands shook as if palsy stricken, and thirst parched his desert-dry mouth.

He leaned over the bed as spasms ripped through him. Heaved until he tasted the iron tang of blood in his mouth and on his lips. Flopping back against the pillows, he narrowed his stare upon the patient watcher. Focused every ounce of strength left in him on banishing the creature back to the void. The *Unseelie* merely smiled its intent, as if expecting a pleasant show as the sickness tore Aidan apart from the inside out.

"If you think I'm scared of you, think again," he brazened.

The *Unseelie*'s mouth widened, displaying rows and rows of needle teeth.

"I've bested you once already."

Scorn dripped off it as it worked its jaw, its tongue darting in and out. *"Erelth, merweth,"* it hissed.

*Other.* Die.

Uncurling from its place at the foot of Aidan's bed, it hovered above him, placing its bony hands upon his chest. Its fingers dipping within his flesh as if proving to Aidan how easily he would succumb.

Aidan flinched as frozen fire singed him outward from the point of contact.

*"Erelth. Skoa."*

Soon.

He moaned, coming awake with a start. Staring round him with disbelieving eyes. Same cluttered bedchamber. Same pitcher and glass on a table beside him. Same sputtering fire upon the grate. The gut-wrenching, muscle-seizing illness remained. So too did the pressing sensation of death delayed. But no *Unseelie* lurked. No monster threatened. He was alone.

"Aidan?" Cat's voice, tired and anxious, came from a corner of the room beyond the reach of the candlelight. "Are you awake?"

She swung into his view, hair bundled loosely off her face, mouth pulled into a worried frown. "Do you know who I am?"

"The angel of death?" He tried smiling. Failed miserably.

She sniffed. "I suppose if you can joke, you must be on the mend." She placed a hand upon his forehead. *Tsk*-ed. "Yesterday you called me Miss Osborne. I nearly sent you to the grave for that insult."

Talk about a slip of ill-starred proportions. He winced. "Sorry."

She shrugged, trying to show her indifference, but he saw the hurt and the desolation before she turned away. Even out of his head, he managed to cock things up between them. "Cat, if you'll let me—"

She drowned him out. "The day before was worse. You called me a demon temptress and it took three of us to wrestle you back to bed."

He sought to shift himself farther up the pillows. Fell back with a gasp as muscles cramped and seized. "Cat—"

Again she refused to let him finish. "You've been like this for almost two weeks."

Dear gods. An entire fortnight lost to the endless stretch of nightmare and sickness.

"We weren't sure you'd recover. It was"—she shuddered—"closely run."

"I'm too stupid to know when I'm beaten."

"Or too stubborn."

He gave a bark of cynical laughter. Rubbed at his throat.

"Daz has been fabulous," she offered, a false jauntiness in her voice. "I don't think he's had an episode since that night."

"And you?"

She looked away, her profile tipped in rose and gold from the candlelight. The sorrowful curve of her lips and that pale silver slash a reminder of words he wished with all his heart he could take back.

"Cat, what happened that night—"

She swung back to face him, the momentary weakness shuttered behind a stony façade. "Should never have occurred." She took a deep breath. "You have a future waiting. You belong to Miss Osborne. I knew that and ignored it at my own risk."

"What if it's a future I don't want anymore? What then?"

She offered him a humorless smile. "I'd say you're hallucinating again."

The kitchen lay wreathed in dim shadows, the flickering light from the banked stove and the single taper upon the table her only illumination. She'd retreated here for a quick restorative cup of tea and a slice of cake, but had remained lost in the jumbled round-and-round that was her twisted relationship with Aidan.

He'd called her Miss Osborne.

He may have been out of his head. Fevered and delirious. Pumped full to the brim with Daz's medicinal concoctions, but the truth had been revealed like a crack across the face, reminding her he'd a future she couldn't be a part of no matter how much she pleasured him. A woman waiting for him who hadn't made the monumental mistake of trusting the slick whispers of a fly-by-night lover.

Aidan had fooled her into believing.

No. Take that back.

She'd fooled herself. Aidan had never once promised anything more than he'd given. It had been her with the wild fantasies and a body heart-led by images of a life together. She'd known better even as she'd delighted in the amazing flash fire of their joining.

But to call her Miss Osborne? She tightened her hand around the mug as if it were the lily white neck of that society harpy.

That was just plain mean.


Aidan heard her before he saw her. A soft voice, low and sultry as a tropical sea. Words were lost amid the thick soup of his pain, but the voice never faltered. Always there. Like an anchor, holding him fast when the effort of each breath seemed not worth the trouble. Easier to let go. Let the enveloping black swallow him.

So it was the silence waking him. Making him crack his eyes against the glare. The room tipped and spun. Pinwheels and spots of color burst in front of him, and every sense seemed heightened. The scratch of the sheets. The weight of the blankets. The perfume in the air.

He glanced around, nausea clawing at his throat even at that little bit of movement.

Cat sat beside him, her head resting on her crooked arm, her eyes closed. Against the curve of her jaw, her hair was a shimmering raven black. A sweep of long, sooty lashes shadowed her cheeks.

How had this woman twined herself into his life and his heart? How had he allowed it? Lovers had come and gone with nary a backward glance. None had touched him. None had seen him in anything less than noble invincibility. Detached arrogance perfected over long years of practice. None but Cat. She'd peeked behind the curtain. Witnessed a breakdown of quantum proportions. And hadn't gone screaming into the night.

Cold logic tried convincing him that ending things was for the best. He couldn't marry Cat. It was impossible for a thousand different reasons. He'd be a fool to even contemplate such a move.

Cat stirred, lips parted on a whisper of breath, the faint scent of lavender hanging in the air.

He hated cold logic.

# twenty

Cat stalked the corridors and chambers like a restless shade until Maude chivied her outside under the threat of bodily harm.

"Go, child. Get some air and leave me to my work."

With no excuses left, she ventured out. Followed a narrow lane up into the hills, through groves of trees where deer froze in nervous groups and she stumbled across a hedgehog, scuttling nose to the ground. The wind blustered and tugged at her skirts. Shook her hair free of its pins. A falcon rode the updrafts, its mournful call only adding to her loneliness.

The lane wound off to the north, looping across the hills and uplands before being lost in a purple horizon haze. That way lay civilization. Villages and people. Coaching inns and tollgates. She could follow it to Portumna, score a few guineas off some easy mark, and book herself a seat on the mail coach. Be back in Dublin by week's end at the latest. Lose herself in the Liberties. And this time, remain unfound.

With that thought half-formed in her mind, she wandered farther and farther from the house. A fast-moving stream curved down to meet the track. Trees and scrub crowded close to its banks. Thick brush sheltering the moorland creatures as they paused to drink.

Thirsty, she followed suit. Bending to scoop a mouthful to her lips.

A snap of twig froze her immobile, the icy water sliding forgotten between her fingers. Something else had come to this spot to drink.

Something large.

Without moving, she let her eyes slide to the right. Caught a glimpse of a dirt-encrusted hand. Bloody, broken nails. A stained, muddy sleeve. The fingers trailed unmoving within the stream, the current sluicing around them.

Too frightened to breathe, she rose slowly. Tried backing away without making a sound. Praying the noise of the stream would mask her departure.

"Water? Please. Thirsty."

Too late.

She closed her eyes.

She hadn't heard it. Just the wind. That was all. Walk away.

Her steps slowed. She stopped, straining to hear the whispered plea again.

It was a trap. He was probably waiting with sword raised and mage energy enough to fry her brain.

It came again softly. "Please." A gentle request, and strangely jarring after Aidan's bloodcurdling threats.

She moved to her left, following the stream bank. Pushed through a scraggly thicket of furze, even as she muttered, "You're a complete fool, Catriona O'Connell, and deserve whatever messy end awaits."

Found exactly who she expected. And nothing like she anticipated.

Flies buzzed around the putrid wound in his thigh. Another gash oozed sticky black blood down his arm. He'd sought to bind them both but had lacked the strength and then the will to do so. After all, this was what he'd been asking for. This was death, wasn't it?

Dark against dark. Evil against evil. The *Unseelie*'s power had overwhelmed his defenses, bringing him as close as he'd been to complete collapse. Close, but not accomplished. How long had he lain here unable to move? Days? Years? Time had ceased to matter. All he knew was that though he suffered, he did not succumb. Though his body festered, still it fought to renew itself. Sinew by sinew. Nerve by nerve.

Palm clamped over her mouth, face a sickly gray, the woman stood poised to flee. Instead, she shuddered her recovery and bent to the stream edge. Retrieved a large, dripping stone, holding it up in what she must have thought was a threatening manner.

Seemingly surprised he didn't erupt from his resting place and throttle her, she stepped back, as alert and quivering as the deer he'd spotted earlier. Raised the rock above her head.

"Go on." He sank back against the base of the tree on a sigh. Closed his eyes, awaiting the head-splitting blow.

Nothing.

He risked a look. The rock remained cocked and ready, her brows drawn into a deep frown, her lip caught between her teeth.

He shifted, the flies rising up to swarm about his head, his thigh screaming. "You mayn't get a better chance, my lady."

She braced herself. Raised the rock higher. Swung it down with deadly intent.

He flinched, but the rock never left her hands. Her frown deepened, guilt and disappointment hardening the soft lines of her face.

"Weak," he spat. Angry with her for backing down. At himself for the cringing flash of panic when he thought she'd go through with it. "Like all females."

She stiffened, anger flashing in the depths of her green eyes. Tossed the rock aside. "If death is what you long for then life is the true punishment, is it not?"

Clever, this one. Clever and far too observant.

"Besides, it looks like death will find you soon enough without my help," she continued, her gaze fixed firmly upon his face and off the festering wounds, the dark sorceries bound within the *Unseelie*'s battle spells slowing his healing to agonizing lengths.

She bent again to the stream, but this time came back with a handful of water which he slurped from her fingers with humiliating eagerness. And again and again until he lay back, his parched throat eased, the muzzy light-headedness receding under the sweet tang of the icy water.

"I'd thank you, but the victim rarely thanks his tormentor."

She clenched her jaw. "Jut so long as you see it for what it is."

He stifled a chilly smile. "Merciless as an executioner, my lady."

"Stop calling me that."

"You're Kilronan's lady, are you not?"

She leveled him with a lethal gaze but didn't answer. Instead she studied him as if deciding whether she'd worked enough ill will or whether a few more kindnesses were warranted. The silence hung thick and frozen between them. Even the stream seeming to mute its burbling descent as they stared upon one another in mutual loathing.

His hand flexed and fisted. "Your man gained a short-lived victory. Once called to this world the *Unseelie* are not easily banished."

A cloud settled over her features, her shoulders hunched as if suffering under a blow.

He'd struck close to the mark. Perhaps the creature of the Dark Court had succeeded where Lazarus had not. Perhaps Kilronan was no more, and the diary unguarded and exposed.

Pain succumbed to exhaustion, and he closed his eyes. Let his body renew itself bit by unnatural bit.

When he opened them again, she was gone.

"You'll carry it always," Daz intoned in a grave and sorrowful manner.

Aidan examined the angry, puckered three-inch scar upon his chest. The very spot he'd stabbed the *Unseelie*.

He touched it with tentative fingers. Ran his finger up and down the length of it. Pressed the healed flesh. It didn't hurt. In fact, it tingled with an icy chill.

He looked up to meet Daz's solemn gaze reflected in the long mirror.

"You will always bear a piece of the creature within you," Daz explained. "A splinter of the demon *Fey* to plague you ever more. A reminder of how close you came to being devoured by your own idiotic summoning."

His stern master mage expression quirked into the rolled eyes and shaking head of scolding teacher, and he clout Aidan upon the shoulder with enough force to drop him to the edge of the bed. "What were you thinking, boy?" he scolded. "You know better than to play about with magic of that sort. It's evil. An outrage to call on the Dark Court."

Aidan slid a shirt over his head. Inhaled slowly until the dizziness passed. "I was hardly playing about. It was that or allow Lazarus to steal the diary for Brendan."

There, he'd said it. What he'd been thinking ever since Daz had revealed the depths of his family's treachery and his brother's cold-blooded ambition. It hurt still. A pain he knew he would carry as surely as he carried the scar of the *Unseelie*.

How had they held so much back from him? It was like discovering the two people he loved most were complete strangers.

"You mentioned Brendan once before." Daz stared at him as if he'd grown three heads. After the attack, not completely out of the range of possibility. "Why would your brother be after the diary?"

"Brendan must need it to find the tapestry. To bring Arthur back."

"Why on earth would Brendan want to do that?"

Daz's recovered sanity must be slipping.

"You said it yourself. The Nine sought to resurrect Arthur. To start the wars that would lead to a new order, this time with *Other* dominant over *Duinedon*. And we know it's possible. The creature Lazarus is proof of that."

The old man scratched at his unwashed hair. "It couldn't be Brendan."

His protests merely fanned the dull press of betrayal. "Don't try to protect him. I know you loved him. I loved him too. And in the end, he was rotten to the damned core."

Daz scowled, his ruddy complexion reddening to a deeper shade of purple. "You're talking madness."

"The *Ambas-draoi* were right," he shot back. "They tried to warn me. Even Jack sought to put me on my guard. But I was blinded by a love as faulty as my memories of him."

"It wasn't Brendan."

"Stop trying to keep the truth from me."

Voices rose in volume.

"You don't understand."

"I understand perfectly. Brendan was a bloody criminal. A madman."

By now they each shouted to be heard.

Daz grabbed Aidan by the shoulders. Wheeled him about so they faced each other squarely. "Listen to me, Aidan. It was Brendan who betrayed them to the *Ambas-draoi*. All of them. Even your father." Purple faded to ghastly gray. "Brendan betrayed them and was, in his turn, betrayed."

Aidan gaped stupidly. "What are you saying?"

Daz's grip tightened on Aidan's shoulders until he wondered if he were the only thing holding the old man upright. His fingers convulsed, grief softening his face, dimming his eyes. "It was Brendan who set the *Ambas-draoi* onto the Nine. Who condemned your father and the others to death. Arthur had been his idea, but he knew it would fail. And knew even in its failure it would cost the lives of thousands, perhaps hundreds of thousands, of innocents. He'd had too much of the blood. Of the killing. Of the soul-crushing guilt."

"How do you know all this?"

He released Aidan with a painful wrench before falling into a chair. Shading his eyes with a trembling hand. "Because I agreed with him. We both cracked beneath our burdens. Brendan chose an honorable way out. He sacrificed everything to try and right what he'd wronged."

"And you, Daz?"

"I chose the coward's way."

"You said Brendan was betrayed. What happened?"

Daz looked up, the ghosts of those days clear in the bloodshot gaze. "He chose to confess all to the *Amhas-draoi*. He wanted to go himself, but the others—perhaps suspecting something—kept him close. He couldn't get away long enough to deliver his information. So he sent it to me. Asked me to go in his stead."

"And did you?"

"Aye. I fell upon Scathach's mercy. Told her everything I knew and more."

"And?" Aidan felt he knew where this tale was going. Knew it and dreaded it.

"And afraid for my life amidst the raised swords of the brotherhood, claimed the information as my own. They spared me."

"But executed the Nine." Aidan's voice held a steely note not lost on Daz.

"Brendan escaped," he whispered. "He survives. You said it yourself."

"As a hunted man."

"Yet while there's life, there's hope." The eagerness of someone grasping at straws in the wind.

Aidan swallowed the urge to strike the earnest expression from the old man's face. He'd put him through hell.

Had smashed every image and corrupted every memory Aidan held of his brother. And now the truth came out. A truth almost as gut wrenching as the falsehood.

Brendan betrayed. Brendan hunted. Brendan an innocent victim of *Amhas-draoi* zeal.

He fisted his hands at his sides to keep them from snaking around Daz's neck. The icy tingle deep in his chest spread to become a tightness in his brain. A violent anger seething just below the surface. "Do you know what you've done? They seek him even now. They think he's behind this creature Lazarus. That he's trying to restart the Nine and its network of the disaffected," he snarled between gritted teeth. "If they find him before we do, they'll kill him first and ask questions later."

Daz crumpled, his body folding in upon itself with guilty sorrow. "My fault. All of it my fault. The Nine are no more. The Nine are gone."

Damn. He'd pushed him too far and lost him. "Daz!"

No use. From crumpled to rocking, accompanied by a steady, keening murmur. "The Nine are gone. No more. All of it over. All of it destroyed. The King will never return."

Aidan paced the room, tapping his thigh nervously. Wheels grinding. "If Brendan betrayed the Nine, it couldn't be him seeking the diary."

No answer from Daz. Not that he'd expected one. The wheels kept turning as he talked it through. "Someone else must be after it. Someone else who knows what secrets it's keeping. And someone with the ability to decipher it."

It was there. At the edge of his mind. An impression. A glimpse of the answer.

"The High King's glorious return is for naught." Daz

kept up his rocking and muttering. "The blood was too much. Always the blood. The death."

Aidan ignored Daz. The solution was there somewhere. Locked in a fuzzy corner of his mind. "Someone with the ability to decipher Father's language." Frustration. Irritation. It was there if only he were clearheaded enough to remember.

Daz pressed his hands to his ears. "Brendan knew. Brendan tried. Keep them safe, he said. And so I did. Safe until he returns for them."

That was it. A letter. A farewell. Written in the same headache-inducing language as the diary.

Of course. The answer hit him like a lightning strike.

"Máelodor."

Cat stared out onto a night black with her own fear. Aware that somewhere beyond the pools of washed-out light cast by the house's windows stalked a hunter. Though perhaps "limped" might be more accurate. She closed her eyes, but Lazarus's face, grim and implacable as any effigy, remained burned into her brain.

She should have struck. Should have at least tried to finish him off. He was defenseless. Vulnerable. An easy target. For heaven's sake, he'd lain there and begged for it. And what had she done? Nothing. And worse than nothing, she'd actually given him water. Why not just pat him on the head like a good little nightmare creature and be done with it?

Fool and ten times a fool.

"Cat?"

The easy baritone slid along her raw nerves like the screech of nails over a slate. Whipped her around in a heart-stopping lurch.

"I called your name three times," he said. "You were miles away."

What would Aidan say if he found out she'd seen Lazarus and let him escape? He'd think she was mad, and with good cause. She could try to explain the creature's desire for death, and how her actions were more torture than relief, but she doubted Aidan would believe it. She didn't really believe it herself. For even in that black, hell-smoldering gaze, she could have sworn she saw for the heart's beat of a moment real desperation. A desire for life as great as her own. Just not the life he had.

And how insane did that sound?

She bought time with a wan smile and an adjustment of her shawl across her shoulders. Hated the way her stomach swooped and plunged and her skin went all tight and prickly. But at least the vision of a midnight black killer dissolved beneath the reality of the sleek and panther-muscled former lover.

Aidan cocked his head, concern in his eyes. "We're safe. He can't harm us ever again. We're finished with him."

That's what he thought. And why not? He'd seen the damage inflicted. Damage no normal human could withstand. Not even a human like Lazarus. But he had withstood it. Could be on his way back here already. And this time what would Aidan do? The first attempt had almost killed him.

He crossed toward her, an arm out as if to comfort, but she stepped beyond his reach. Stiffened and turned away. It was the only way to save the refuge she'd built around herself over the last weeks. One touch and all her good intentions might shatter like glass. Aidan was off limits. He didn't belong to her world. And she'd turned her back on his. They'd tested the waters. Found them treacherous and shark infested. Best to remain on shore and dream of the sea.

"I want to leave, Aidan." She hugged the shawl to herself. Cast a desperate glance in his direction. "Tonight. Right now."

A frown appeared between his dark, slanting brows. "Leave? Just like that?"

"Why not?

He opened his hands in a gesture of resignation. "The diary isn't"—his gaze narrowed in thought—"unless you're through with the diary. I suppose I don't blame you. It's been a curse from start to finish."

She shook him off. "That's not it. I gave you my word I'd help you with the diary. And for better or worse, I'll stand by our agreement. But Maude and Daz aren't safe as long as we remain."

"It could be weeks before Máelodor realizes his resurrected killer has returned to the grave. We've time."

"No, we don't," she urged, hoping he'd take the hint. "Time is definitely not on our side."

His frown deepened. "What are you trying to say, Cat?"

She threw up her hands. Strode away from him to gaze out the window, imagining again the *Domnuathi*'s solemn, endless stare. "I'm saying Lazarus is alive. He's out there. I've seen him."

"Dreams can be powerful."

She pounded a fist against the casement. "Not a dream." Spun to face him. "I found him out in the hills. He's hurt. Badly. But not fatally. He'll recover. And when he does, I don't want to be here."

The frown became a scowl. A stormy, dangerous scowl. "You didn't say anything? Not to Daz? Not to me?"

"And you would have done what?" Exasperation and her own guilt sharpened her words. "He can't be killed, Aidan. Not by me. Not by you. You nearly died once trying to vanquish him."

"So that makes your silence acceptable?"

She pursed her lips. How could she defend herself against the truth?

"Damn it, Cat. What the hell game are you playing?"

Stung, she shot back with the first thought that came to mind. "Perhaps I've just found confessions and you aren't my cup of tea."

That drew him up short but didn't stop the irritation from blossoming to full-fledged anger. The transformation obvious in the taut muscles of his face. The furious tapping of his hand against his thigh. "So you would jeopardize everything because I . . . because I might find it a bit troublesome you had not only bedded a man but bore his bastard child?"

She reeled as if struck. Froze him with as glacial a stare as she could muster under the chest-tightening ache of his hurled accusation. Had she really thought anything but disaster could climb out of the wreckage of their tumbled bed? Here was her answer, glaring at her in thunderous outrage. "Damn you!"

He crossed his arms over his chest, arrogance rising off him like smoke. "Don't act surprised, Cat. It's exactly what you knew I was going to say."

"What's that supposed to mean?"

"It means you've got this scene all worked out in your mind. How I'm going to react. How you'll respond to my reaction. All neat and tidy. Makes it easy for you to hide behind your outrage. Push everyone away. Push me away."

How had their quarrel swerved so off course? How had they gone from Lazarus's survival and the need to flee to a rehash of the same tired argument? But not quite the same. Aidan was treading onto dangerous ground. Turning her words back on her. Ripping into wounds never truly healed.

Her hands trembled, a rapid pounding rising from her chest into her head as she defended against this unwanted intrusion into what he could never possibly understand. "I saw the contempt in your face," she fired back. "Heard your stumbling justifications. That wasn't feigned."

"Was I shocked? Of course. A babe was the last thing on my mind. But you saw only what you assumed would be there. Answer me this. Are you more furious over what I might think of you, or what you truly think of yourself?"

The first blow struck him on the chin. The follow-up doubled him over. "Agreement or no, I'm done here," she snarled. "I'm leaving tomorrow for Dublin. Translate your own damned diary."

"Can't," he gasped from his knees, his arm pressed over his stomach. "Need you still."

"Get used to disappointment. I have."

# twenty-one

"You're insane," she spat. "Stark staring mad."

Aidan peered at her over the top of his paper. "Needs must when the devil drives. And my personal devil may already be on our trail. You said yourself we had to leave immediately."

"And this?" She offered him her wrists, bound with thin cord.

He winced, knowing he was killing any hope of a reconciliation with Cat, but seeing no alternative. "I need you."

The whys of that need remained so twisted within his mind that he couldn't separate the individual reasons any longer. It was easier to say it and let it end there.

She worked the cord at her wrists before slumping back against the seat of the coach. Gazing on him with that same injured expression he'd seen on her face the night he'd caught her in his library. He hardened the cracked and bleeding pieces of his heart against the familiar pulling-the-wings-from-a-butterfly feeling. She'd learn to understand.

That or take a dagger to him in his sleep.

First item of business upon reaching Belfoyle—hide all daggers.

He flipped back to his month-old Dublin paper. Pretended he didn't feel her viper glare right through the newsprint.

"And Ahern?" she asked after a silence so laden with guilt and accusation he could barely breathe. "Maude? Has your callous behavior extended to leaving them to their deaths? You owe them after all they did to save you."

His grip on the paper tightened. "Daz and Maude are safe enough. As for what I owe," he paused. "Daz stole my brother's life. He gave me mine. Our debts are clear."

No reply. Hopefully he'd forestalled any further comments long enough to ease his jangled nerves. Swallow the very bad feeling he'd given up the promise of a future before he'd gotten a chance to see what that future held. What might have been between him and Cat would remain just that—what might have been.

Casting away useless regrets as one more victim in this undeclared war, he focused on the immediate—the next days. The next destination.

Belfoyle. His home. The origin of this spider's web and the last line of defense in a struggle that would gain him the truth or lose him his life.

"We're almost there. It's just past this turnoff."

His impatience was infectious. Cat found herself glancing out the coach window despite her resolve to ignore any and all conversations with the odious person seated across from her.

"There now. Just around this bend."

She craned her neck as the coach slowed to make a turn past a vacant and overgrown gatehouse and rumbled through iron gates mounted with the Kilronan spread-winged bird and crooked sword.

The avenue wound past long stone walls covered in ivy, heavy stands of ash and oak, a park dotted with grazing cows. In the distance she caught the blue and silver flash of a river.

"Give me your hands," he said.

She held out her wrists, the flesh red and bruised beneath the cords. A few sharp tugs, a slip of the knots, and she was free.

She forced herself not to rub them, though they hurt like the devil. "And if the first thing I do is scream bloody murder? Tell everyone I'm your prisoner?"

"They'll think the same thing the coachman thought when you tried that with him—that you suffer from a nervous condition. A pity, I'll say, but we're doing all we can to keep you comfortable while you recover." He crossed his arms over his chest. "This is my demesne, Cat. Here, I'm master, and they do what I tell them to do. Believe what I tell them to believe."

"I don't doubt your father thought the same thing," she sneered.

The thrust hit home. He paled and looked away.

The coach slowed as they climbed a hill. And she caught her first glimpse of the house, though house hardly seemed a fitting description for Belfoyle.

Castle. Keep. Stronghold.

Terms more suitable to the monstrosity confronting her.

Beyond the arch, huge towers of gray stone rose straight

up into the sky, topped by steeply pitched roofs and crenellated battlements. Upon cresting the hill, they drove beneath the gateway into a courtyard where additions and wings moved in every available direction. Tudor warred with Jacobean led into Baroque until the whole place was a hodgepodge of styles and periods.

Cat steeled herself for the few moments of freedom she'd get as the doors were opened. She didn't care what Aidan said. She had to try to escape. She didn't belong here. Not with him. Not now. If she could get even one person to doubt his story, she could work her way to freedom. She knew she could.

The coach crunched to a halt upon the gravel.

Stiffening in anticipation, she slid her hand out to grasp the door handle.

Distracted by voices raised in excitement and welcome, Aidan's attention was elsewhere. This was the moment. She'd not get another such.

Holding her breath, she threw open the door. Scrambled from the coach with a cry of distress, awaiting the clamp of a restraining hand upon her shoulder. Catching her back.

But no hand stopped her. No alarm was raised. And panic flooding her, she flung herself straight into the shocked arms of Jack O'Gara.

"I've heard Miss O'Connell's explanation," Jack said. "Now I'm interested in hearing yours."

Aidan looked up from the sideboard. The brandy he'd already drunk had done little to warm the cold, gnawing cramp in his bowels. Instead, nausea squirreled his insides, his balance was off-kilter, and darkness crouched at the corners of his vision. "I can guess what villainy she re-counted into your waiting ears." He poured himself another.

Jack flopped into a chair, stretching his legs out in front of him. Offered a wry smile. "No, coz. I don't think you can." He shook his head. "It was quite a tale. A few cogent details conspicuously missing, but my own prurient imagi-nation filled them in. So much for keeping your hands off the help."

Aidan's fist came down with a crash that rattled the decanters. Shook a tray of glasses. "If you value our friend-ship, Jack, shut your mouth. Cat's a guest. A valued and very precious guest."

Jack remained unfazed. "That's not how she tells it. 'Prisoner' is how she termed her stay here. Begged me to help her escape. What the hell happened between Dublin and here? Did you actually try summoning one of them?" Gravity hardened the playboy perfection of his face.

"I did," he answered. "And bear the scars to prove it."

He turned from the sideboard to stiffly pace the length of the salon, raking the room with a possessive eye. Breathing deeply, he inhaled Belfoyle's freedom like a drug. Surprised at how just being within his own house upon his own land cleansed the lingering feverish tension from a brain scraped thin from sickness.

"Why don't we skip the account of how I've managed to bungle, fail, and otherwise make a mess of this entire debacle, and focus on you?" He tossed back the brandy. Waited. Nothing. Not even a glimmer of heat to tease him back to life. "What are you doing here, Jack? Dublin get too hot for even your *Fey*-given luck?"

His cousin straightened in his chair. "Funny you should use that particular term. Hot was just what it was." He cleared his throat. Shifted uneasily before rising and pouring his own restorative brandy. Tossing it back. "Aidan? How . . . uh . . . how attached were you to Kilronan House?"

Now there was a loaded question if he'd ever heard one. "Why?"

Jack shifted again. Ran a hand over his face. Huffed an uneasy breath. "Well . . . because it's not there anymore."

Aidan didn't explode. Didn't collapse. Barely inhaled on a quick, shocked gasp. Placing the glass on the mantel with exquisite care, he adjusted it until it caught and refracted light from an arched window nearby. Any action, no matter how small, while his mind wrapped itself around Jack's outrageous statement.

Catching his cousin's worried gaze, he nodded. "Explain."

"It happened three days after you left. Started in the library, suspiciously enough."

"What started in the library? You're talking in riddles. And I'm up to my ass in bloody riddles."

"A fire, Aidan. No one knows how it started, though I have my guesses. Guesses I thought it best to keep to myself when people started asking questions. The place went up like a damned box of tinder. Destroyed everything. There's a bit of one wall left standing. A few charred chimneys. That's about it."

Aidan swallowed back the choking knot of rage. "How many perished?"

"None, thank the gods. They all got out. I'd been caught up in a night of gaming with some friends. Won more than I lost so I stayed later than usual. Didn't make it home until almost four. Arrived to find the place engulfed in smoke and the fire spreading fast. If I hadn't—" he let that thought trail off into awkward silence.

"The uncanny O'Gara luck at play?"

Jack shrugged. "Not so lucky for you."

He thought of the drain on his bank accounts to maintain a town house he rarely visited, the stifling atmosphere of Dublin society where the name Kilronan had become synonymous with bizarre and outrageous half-believed tales of murder, sedition, and financial ruin. By now even Miss Osborne must have decamped for greener pastures.

It was his turn to shrug.

"No one knew where you'd hared off to," Jack continued. "I started a story about an unplanned trip to visit your Lancashire estates. Then we hired a chaise and headed here. Figured you'd show up sooner or later. We've been kicking our heels for weeks, unsure whether you were alive or if that creature Lazarus had tracked you down after torching your house."

"We?"

Jack cleared his throat. "Yes, well, I was concerned, you see. And she'd been such a help already."

Aidan didn't know whether to laugh or scream. "You didn't. Please tell me you didn't bring her here."

"Don't get your breeches in a twist, Miss Roseingrave's not here anymore."

The long face accompanying this statement revealed more about the relationship between Jack and his *Amhas-draoi* paramour than Aidan cared to know.

"She's been called away. A messenger arrived a few days ago with a letter and off she went with nary a backward glance."

"Poor Jack, his lady bird's flown the coop. Was it you or the diary she decided wasn't worth the effort?"

"Very funny, but if it's as Cat said, you may be thankful of Helena's help. Tell me the gods' honest truth. Did you really"—Jack shook his head in disbelief—"summon—"

"Yes, Jack. Yes. I summoned an *Unseelie.* Let it take me over. Almost died. Still feel a jagged piece of it within me." He pulled a cheroot from his pocket. Lit it with an unsteady hand, singeing his fingers on the candle flame. Inhaled, the smoke filling his lungs. Easing the cramps within a chest squeezed beneath a stoning weight. "And what did I accomplish with this selfless act of heroism? Not a damned bloody thing!"

Disgusted, he tossed the cheroot on the fire. "Cat informs me that she's seen the monster. Seen him and allowed him to creep away with his tail between his legs. And what happens when he returns, because he will return? Do I summon another *Unseelie?* Perhaps this one will succeed where the last failed. Do I hand over the diary and pray Lazarus doesn't rip my head off just for fun?" His hand drummed frantically against his thigh as he stalked the room. His mind a torrent. "What the hell would you have me do?" Falling into a chair, he raised his gaze heavenward. "What the hell does she want from me, Jack?"

A long pause followed before Jack answered, "Did we change conversations?" His voice sounded on a confused note. "I thought we were speaking of the *Domnuathi* and your continued survival. What's Miss O'Connell got to do with it?"

Aidan shut his eyes against the remembered glare of loathing in Cat's eyes, her expression like a punch to his gut. "I've lost her, Jack."

"Why do I feel as if I've come to the play after the intermission and left my damned program in the retiring room?" His cousin's response was typical Jack and almost brought a smile to Aidan's lips.

Almost.

Cat measured the perimeter of her chamber. Thirty steps by forty-four. The same as when she'd calculated it an hour ago. And the hour before that.

Sunlight moved across the floor in wavering lines. Climbed the papered walls. Slid over the needlepoint coverlet. Shone against the dark woodwork.

She plotted. Pistols? Too dispassionate.

Clouds moved in from the west. Rain followed. A slow, drizzly mist adding a moldy dankness to the chilly air. Depressing an already depressed mood.

She planned. Knives? Too messy.

She'd refused the meals offered to her on the road. Turned her nose up at the suggestion she dine before she retired to her rooms. And paid for it now with a growling stomach and a headache throbbing against her temples.

Poison? Too impractical.

She gave up. Murder took too much energy.

Crying might help to ease the pain in her chest and the tight knot in her throat, but she couldn't do it. Her eyes burned dry and hot, her cheeks flamed, her hands shook with futile self-condemnation. Yet no tears fell.

She'd wept upon hearing of Jeremy's abandonment. She'd shrieked curses to the gods upon the death of her son. The source of that emotion had dried up. She had nothing left for Aidan. She was simply numb.

The rain moved off, leaving a sky streaked with gray and purple and a few struggling stars. She tried sleeping, but couldn't relax.

When she began talking to herself, she knew she'd finally gone 'round the bend.

"It's your own fault, you know," she accused the frowning young woman reflected in the mirror.

"And how is that?" her reflection argued. Willful as always.

Cat shook her head. "You fooled yourself into thinking all that passion meant something. Fell like a sack of bricks for his brooding, masculine intensity. Are you so surprised Aidan turned out to be Jeremy all over again?"

"He's nothing like Jeremy," her reflection denied. "He's the complete opposite of Jeremy. The anti-Jeremy."

"You slept with him." Cat ticked off a point on her finger.

"Yes."

"You trusted him." Ticked off a second point.

"Well . . . I suppose so," her reflection wavered.

"And he stomped all over that trust." Third finger. "I'll repeat, he's Jeremy all over again."

Her reflection bit her lip, her gaze anxious and unsure, a line appearing between the curve of her brows. "You're overreacting. Aidan was startled. He said so himself."

"Startled, my eye," Cat shot back, weary of arguing with an obviously deluded female. "He was shocked. Appalled. Disgusted. You not only fucked a man you weren't married to, but you bore his child."

The woman in the mirror winced. "Don't use that word. It wasn't like that, and you know it."

"I know exactly what it was like. Remember? I was there. You're as fallen and shameless as they get." Her voice rose. "A harlot. A slut. Your child naught but the bastard son of a whore." By now she was shouting.

Her reflection pressed her hands to her ears. Fell back from the mirror with an anguished moan. "Never refer to my son like that. Ever. Do you hear?"

Cat fell back too. Sprawled across the bed. Dragging the pillow to her chest for comfort. Her eyes dry and hot, her skin clammy. "I only speak the truth," she whispered.

Her reflection had the last word. "Then from now on, keep your damned mouth shut."

Aidan stood at the southwest boundary of Belfoyle. Concentrated on the cool, mossy feel of the ward stone beneath his hand. The loamy smell of the earth. The warbling of a chaffinch flitting through the bushes. This focus on his surroundings helped to center him. Controlled the wild maelstrom of magic torching his blood. Even so, singeing heat smoldered along his veins. A boiling ache concentrated bone deep. Sweat streaked his brow. Only one more stone after this. One more possibility of instant incineration.

Wards must be managed like any fence line. Checked for strength. Repairs made as the mage energy warped and waned over the passage of time. In the years after his father's death, he'd let them falter. Why bother? Magic and the *Fey* world had been his father's life. Not his.

No longer.

Slapping the hair out of his eyes, he tilted his face to the drizzle. The rain had moved on, leaving a milky, damp twilight. Within the shimmering mist, the band of mage energy shown rainbow pure. Extended outward from the ward stone—east toward the high fields, west toward the cliffs—before dissolving.

Stretching stiffening muscles, he started toward the final stone, set just off the west cliff path. His strides lengthening as he crossed the park. Climbed a stile. Passed through the sunken road that would dump him out below the meadow where the ward stone stood permanent sentinel.

The gloaming lingered, the sea flat and oily as the sun sank through sooty clouds edged in blood. A sailor's delight. So why did he shiver with premonitions of looming tragedy?

The ward stone erupted from the earth of the cliffs. Weathered. Gold veined. As ageless as the *Fey* themselves in their hidden kingdom. Did they know of Máelodor's plans to bring a return of the Lost Days when the races of faery and mortal mingled? When magic blossomed unlooked for and unexpected from peasant hovels to castle solars? Did they care?

Some *Fey* enjoyed mankind and spent more time than not among the mortal world. The warrior queen Scathach, head of the brotherhood of *Amhas-draoi*, was one such. Creating heroes from those *Other* with the talent and the will to follow her. But most *Fey* remained aloof and disdainful of their lesser relations. Looked upon them with thinly veiled contempt bordering at times on outright hostility.

Unclaimed by either race. Neither fish nor fowl.

He grunted his disgust. No, he'd get no assistance from the *Fey*. They'd relish a war between *Duinedon* and *Other* like a spectator sport. Lay odds. Cast wagers. And care not who emerged the victor as long as they were left alone.

At the first touch of flesh to stone, mage energy shot through his fingers and up his arm in a jerky shock that left him reeling. *Damn.* He shook off the twitchy muscles. Tried again. Taking his time. Bracing himself for the mule kick of magic that met his attempt.

Inhaling, he dove beneath the surface panic. Caught and held fast to that part of him where magic lived. A source of great power, misshapen and blighted though it was. Drawing it forth was like harnessing the power of the stars. A vast spinning whirlpool of energy and light and fire. It dazzled the vision. Set his heart galloping. Trembled already fatigued limbs.

"*Dor. Ebrenn.*"

The gathered energy released in a lightning arc between stone and flesh.

"*Dowr. Tanyow.*"

The inferno ignited. A thousand fires set throughout his body. A human torch.

"*Menhir. Junya.*"

The charge swelled until it threatened to consume him with the force of a funeral pyre. He cried out. Yanked his hands from the ward stone, dropping to his knees with a shuddering moan.

"Damn it all to hell," he ground out through gritted teeth, his arms hanging numb at his sides. Head lowered.

But safe. For now.

Cliffs. Wind. The blind malevolence of a creature born of smoke and wind. The shine off Father's knife. And the bone-splintering plummet to the rocks below.

As always Aidan woke just before he hit. Sheets drenched. Heart racing. Every muscle taut as a pulled bow.

Tonight he sought comfort in the play of the moon across the ceiling. The sorrowful call of an owl. A faraway answer. The muted roar of the ocean. But though hours passed, relief was denied him.

As was sleep.

# twenty-two

"The tapestry's hiding place is in there somewhere"—he tapped the cover of the diary—"I'm sure of it. Why else would Máelodor send that creature after it?"

Jack looked to the door. At least the tenth time he'd done so in the past two hours.

"Stop obsessing over Miss Roseingrave and pay attention. If she returns at all, it will probably be an ambush in the middle of the night. *Amhas-draoi* modus operandi."

Caught, Jack straightened in his chair. Cast a scathing look in Aidan's direction. "You know, what you refer to as cold-blooded murder, others term justifiable homicide."

The jab slid beneath his guard with stomach-crunching power. He closed his eyes, letting the truth of the strike pass before he faced his cousin. "I deserved that."

"Yes, you did," Jack grumbled. "About time you realized it."

Putting aside the diary, Aidan crossed his arms over his chest. Leaned against the desk. "Do you want to get it off your chest?"

"Do you?" Jack parried.

"I asked you first."

"Very well." As if working up his courage, Jack threw himself from his seat. Paced the floor. Reached for then dismissed the sherry decanter. Swung around, head high and on the attack. "Helena Roseingrave is an amazing woman. Smart. Beautiful. Courageous. Strong. A highly developed sense of the ironic."

"And the problem is?"

Jack deflated. Surrendered to the sherry. "She's says I'm a sweet fellow, but not her type. What's that supposed to mean?"

Aidan might have been amused had his own woman troubles been less dire. Instead, he felt a sense of fellowship with his wronged cousin. Joined him at the sherry. "It means she's *Amhas-draoi* and your only talent is the devil's own luck." They toasted their shared frustration.

Jack downed his sherry. Slumped against the table. "So I'm not some Herculean super-*Other*. I'm hardly negligible."

"Compared to what she's used to, you are."

"Thanks for the kind words." He rambled back to his seat. Fell into it with a defeatist glower. "Now it's your turn to be cut down to size. Fire away."

Aidan placed his empty glass on the nearest table. Pulled a cheroot from his pocket, bending to light it. "Cat still refuses to speak with me. She sent my note back unopened. And I couldn't get the poor maid to repeat her verbal message. Said her mother had taught her better than to use those sorts of words."

Jack gave a bark of laughter, quickly stifled by Aidan's sharp look. "Can't imagine why she's not licking your slippers, old man. You kidnapped her. Brought her here against her will, locked her in a room until she surrenders. Any other crimes I've missed?"

"You can lose the sarcasm. You're supposed to be helping."

"Just pointing out the obvious conflict. But if you want advice, I say go up there and wrestle it out with her."

He inhaled on a relaxing drag. "Good thought, but I'm a bit bruised from the last time we wrestled."

"You're going to have to come to some kind of understanding. You tried seduction. That used to have the women eating out of your hand. Must be out of practice." He quickly changed tack at Aidan's glower. "Anyway, that's failed. Perhaps if you—"

Aidan crushed out the stub. "That's not how it happened."

"No?" Jack's brows rose in a look of mock confusion that had Aidan itching to hit him. Hard. "You're honestly going to tell me there was more than sweet talk and good sex between you? I just assumed, Miss O'Connell being who she is. You being who you are—"

Aidan straightened, fists at the ready. "You can shove your damned assumptions right up your—"

"Easy, coz," Jack said. "Let me remind you of your plans to secure your financial future with a hearty helping of Miss Osborne's dowry. What the hell would people say if you turned around and married a woman you found breaking into your home? A woman whose sordid past banishes her from polite society? One they could never receive. Never acknowledge. You'd be a laughingstock. More of an oddity than you already are." He paused. "And that's saying something."

"Is that all you can think about? Miss Osborne's damned money? What people would say? I've wealth enough. And you said it yourself, polite society already associates the Earls of Kilronan with wild unpredictability bordering on eccentricity. If I want to make Cat a part of my life, what's one more bizarre twist in this already insane story?"

Jack sat back, satisfaction dancing in his eyes. "You tell me."

"Wipe that damned smile off your face. You're a bloody pain in my ass."

"Likewise."

Sometime in the night, a key turned in her door. When she finally tried it, the latch clicked easily. The hinges silent. Peering up and down the corridor, she spied a kneeling maid polishing the floor who looked on Cat with a darting shift of her eyes. Beyond that, the way was clear.

She descended the first staircase she found. A narrow stone spiral spitting her out at one end of a long, barrel vaulted gallery. Thick carpets covered the flagstone floor, yet did little to muffle the cavernous feel or relieve the chill in the air.

On the opposite wall, an enormous tapestry hung in the place of honor behind a carved stone balustrade. An armored knight kneeling before a robed and diademed woman. The weaver rendering the *Fey* aura—for even without the recognizable dolmen behind her it was obvious the woman was one of the faery folk—worked in a mix of gold and silver threads.

"It used to be a chapel before the Douglases of Belfoyle chose expediency over faith." Jack stepped around the tapestry from what must have been a door tucked discreetly out of sight in the curve of the stonework. Hands clasped behind his back, face harlequined by the watery light from a set of narrow windows. "They've always known how to thread the vagaries of politics and stay on the right side of any issue. Back a solid winner and all that. At least until the last earl. His lapse was spectacularly un-Douglas-like."

"I suppose tossing in your lot with a bunch looking to resurrect King Arthur would be placing yourself out on a rather shaky limb." Ignoring Jack's penetrating gaze, she approached the tapestry. Motioned toward the kneeling knight. "Who is he?"

"Sir Archibald Douglas?" Jack glanced up before resuming his steady scrutiny. "An illustrious forebearer. He's said to have visited the faery kingdom of *Ynys Avalenn*. Remained there for three years as the lover of a *Fey* queen. Lucky man if half the rumors are true."

He flashed a smile, but his eyes remained fixed upon her as if trying to piece her thoughts. "When he finally returned to the mortal world, the queen offered him a gift to remember her by."

"What sort of gift?"

His mouth twitched. "That part's a bit vague. Some said it was a vial containing a potion for eternal youth. Other stories have it that it was a key to the kingdom of *Ynys Avalenn*, a way back to his love if he chose to return. And there's a third story swearing it was a jewel that would protect its wearer against all *Fey* magic."

"Which theory do you subscribe to?"

"Well, since Sir Archibald's tomb at last check was full of Sir Archibald, I'd say eternal youth is out. And the jewel idea is nice, but hardly very loverlike."

"So you think it was a key to return to *Ynys Avalenn*?"

Jack's earlier lightheartedness turned serious. "They say Sir Archibald died a desolate and broken man. Regretted leaving his *Fey* lover and spent the whole rest of his life trying to find the way back to the summer kingdom and the woman he'd left behind."

"Then all your assumptions are wrong."

A frown settled over his usual open features. "Perhaps yours are too, Cat."

She stiffened. She'd walked right into that little ambush. "Thank you for the genealogy lesson, Mr. O'Gara. But while you're looking to puncture assumptions, it might be best to start with your cousin's."

Jack stared past her into the shadows of the stairwell. "I'm one step ahead of you, Miss O'Connell."

Rolling her eyes, she turned to retrace her steps. Reached the stairs just as Aidan stepped off the bottom riser. How long had he been standing there? How much had he heard? She struggled to look anywhere but into those penetrating, bronze brown eyes. Feel nothing but the churning maelstrom of her own anger and ill usage.

Lines of exhaustion shadowed his drawn, pale face. His arms hung stiffly at his sides as if it took all his will to keep from reaching for her.

"Catriona?" Her name rose soft as a sigh between them.

She closed her eyes on his appeal. If only she could close her heart as easily. "What I did was wrong, but not what came of it. My son was a gift. Not a penance."

He said nothing.

When she looked on him again, she sensed the fettered restraint. It vibrated through him. Shivered the air between them. "I'm frightened," she said quietly.

This time he did reach for her. No more than a skim of her arm with his fingers but it was enough to send need licking like a wildfire through her. "So am I."

"Of what will happen if you love me?"

"No, *a chuisle*, of what will happen if I don't."

They were alone together. Jack finding a feeble excuse to disappear shortly after dinner. And still they remained as clumsy and shy with one another as if surrounded by inhibiting company. Too much said on both sides to overcome easily. Still they tried. Fumbled through a half dozen attempts to bridge the tortured, miserable silence.

Aidan paused in his nervous pacing. "I never had a chance to tell you. I've had an update from Dublin. Still no sign of your friend Geordie, I'm afraid."

Her partner's fate lay buried beneath a mountain of more recent calamities, yet never completely obscured. Cat's hands tightened on her skirts. "He'll turn up. I'm sure of it."

Aidan toyed with a bowl upon a shelf. Straightened an already straight picture. "He means a lot to you."

How did she quantify Geordie's influence on her? His selfless generosity, his healing patience, his good-humored affection. He'd been her family. His loss was like a bruise upon her heart.

"He showed me how to stitch a life together from the merest scraps. For that, I can never repay him."

Aidan met this statement with a look of grim determination. "We'll discover what happened, Cat. If he lives, we'll find him."

She lifted her gaze to his. The shadows lurking in his gold-flecked eyes. The remnants of illness in the sharp bones and sunken hollows of his face, the thick auburn hair brushing his collar, the set of his shoulders, the boundless energy barely contained within the rangy, muscled frame.

So much had become so precious in such a short time.

Her throat constricted. "Scraps can always be rewoven, Aidan. Geordie's taught me that much."

The same charged silence fell between them. But a silence fraught with monumental shifts and decisions made. He crossed the room in angry strides. Shocked her by dropping to his knees at her feet.

"And if I ask you to remain with me? Here at Belfoyle? What would you answer?" His words came hasty and stumbling. His face bearing a fevered flush of color.

She tensed, looking to humor to turn aside a question she dared not ponder too long. "I would say you've suffered a relapse. Are out of your mind?"

His gaze fell to her stomach. "And if you carry my child? Have you thought of that?"

She sat poker straight, shoulders back. Chin up. "I have."

"And if that's so? If you've conceived? Will you stay then?" His voice softened though retaining a hint of tempered steel. He'd not take "no" for an answer. And it would be so easy to say yes.

"The child that died," he asked. "Did Jeremy know?" A change of tack that had her flailing for firmer ground. A way to bolster her crumbling resolve.

"He did."

"And what did he do when he found out?"

"There was naught he could do. He had promised another. And his family saw to it he fulfilled that earlier oath. He left for England and his bride three months before his son was born. I never heard from him again."

Fury flared briefly before the light within his eyes flickered and went out. "What was he called?"

Her heart fluttered as if trying to escape her chest. "Who?"

"Your son. Tell me. I want to know. Tell me everything."

Warmth filled every part of her as if she'd suddenly come from darkness into brightest sunshine. The image of her son drew anew on a mind freed at last from the shame of remembering, and she smiled. "I called him after my father. William."

The moon washed Cat's skin in luminous silver. Her eyes black pools where thoughts lay hidden. Blankets and sheets had been kicked aside or entangled beneath them. He lay spooned beside her, their bodies cooling in the chilly room, their hearts pounding as they recovered.

The dam breeched, Cat's past had spilled out of her in a torrent of festering memories. Aidan had allowed her to unburden herself. Listening in silence. At the end, holding her while she wept. The calm that had followed like the peace after a storm. Sweet. Untainted. Alive with potential.

Cat reached for a blanket, just that slight movement of skin on skin enough to stir him back to life. He pulled her close, his thumb rubbing the puckered nipple he encountered. A hiss of pleasure as she rolled to face him. Breasts flattened to his damp chest. A slender leg thrown across his hip. His now very alert cock nested in the junction created.

She skimmed his stubbled jaw. Kissed him with lips velvety warm, his tongue dipping deep to taste more of her. She sighed into his mouth, grinding against him, causing every inch of his body to stand at attention.

Her hand dropped to curve around him. Her fingers cool. Her touch exquisite. Groaning, he jumped at the caress. "You're far too good at this, *a chuisle*," he murmured, combing his fingers through her hair, gliding them along the curve of her jaw.

Her body stilled, and she lifted troubled eyes to his. Bottom lip caught between her teeth.

He quirked his mouth in a wry smile. "I've stepped in something somewhere. Though the gods only know what," he said, half joking. Their bed remained littered with caltrops. A misstep could spell the end of repairing the damage he'd done with his thoughtless words. His unthinking actions.

She lay back against the pillows, the ebony ribbon of her hair fanned against the cream of her skin. His muscles went from jumping to rock hard. Gods, did she know what kind of a picture she created? As erotic as that bloody damned statue of Leda. He'd almost taken her there. That day. He'd been hard and half-crazed with lust. And she not knowing what the hell she'd sparked with one look from those bright jade green eyes. He'd not surrendered to it then. But now, here, no such scruples forestalled him.

"Cat?"

Her gaze flickered. Died. "Someone told me once men don't want to know they come second to a woman's bed." She paused on a shuddery gulp of air. "That no man wants to think he's being compared to another and found wanting."

He let out the breath he'd been holding. That was it? That was the worry bringing bleak misery to a face so recently awash with ecstasy? He bit back his initial one-word response. Took better aim to diffuse her fears.

His hand stroked the line of her ribs. Traced the curve of her breasts. Drifted to skim the flat of her stomach, pleased with the shiver that met his agile fingers. "And what of the world's widows? Are they doomed to never know another man's touch without worry they're thought of as soiled goods?"

"No, but it's not the same and well you know it." Her gasps came faster now. Threaded with a shaky excitement. His own body felt electrically charged. A touch from her all it would take to shoot him to the moon.

"No, it's not. You're right. You weren't wed with love as you should have been. Nor left with a widow's resources. But if I come second or thirty-second to your bed, Cat, I shall consider myself lucky. For were you any other than I found you, you'd have had the men buzzing like honey wasps and me with nary a chance."

His lips found her neck, the swirl of her earlobe, her lips. His hands stroked her legs, her inner thighs. Brushed ever so enticingly at the folds of her mound, flicking out to barely caress the sensitive nub hidden within. She was wet for him. Heat rose from her body, and the tangy sweet scent of sex.

She whimpered, desire glazing her eyes. A smile tipping the beautiful corners of her very kissable mouth. "You're mad."

He felt the slick, moist fire of her center. His body aching to plunge himself to the hilt. Take her until she screamed his name.

He held back. Chained the brutish desire to possess. Stake his claim. Instead, he took his tortured time. Heightening the pleasure. A wild churn curling along his veins with almost as withering an inferno as the combustion that met his use of magic.

"Besides," he growled, "I think my vanity can handle any amount of comparison."

Pulling himself to his knees between her legs, he licked

his slow and seductive way downward. Lapped at her with his best scoundrel's moves. Resurrected the rake he'd been once upon a lifetime ago to pleasure her senseless. He'd drive that bloody bastard Jeremy right out of her dazed and satisfied brain. She'd forget the damned ass ever existed. It would be Aidan she'd see. Aidan she'd feel. Aidan she'd remember forever.

By now they both labored, whimpers and moans mingling in a bed suddenly far too small for the gyrations of two sweat slicked, writhing bodies in the throes of a passion that had moved beyond mere lovemaking. It had become a battle. A challenge they meant to win. A desperate struggle to exorcise a phantasm played out with pillows.

At one point he found himself on his back, eyes closed, a woman's lips around his member, his body throbbing as spasms built. He wanted to explode. To shout her name. To hold her and never let her go.

His reaction was sharp. Decisive.

An expert twist. A flash of smile. And his shaft lay buried within her. Their eyes met as he rocked forward. As she rose to meet him, taking as much of him as she could, the slide of her muscles goading his body onward.

The rhythm increased. The tempo stretching to a breaking point. He felt her climax. Head thrown back, neck arched, the ripples of inner muscles as he drove into her again and again.

Her hips came off the bed, her body arced like a bow, the moon washing her skin to pearl. Spasms wracked him. He threw himself forward. Thrust. And thrust again. Pumping himself into her. His seed spilling sticky and hot. Giving himself to her. Praying it might hold her when all else he'd tried had failed. For she'd never given him an answer. Never spoken the words he sought to wring from her with his pleasuring: Yes, Aidan. I will stay.

She watched him as he slept. The broad shoulder sloping down into the long, clean line of his collarbone. The slant of ribs, starkly visible with every breath he took. The powerful, sinewy legs. There was a new boiled-down toughness to his body, as if the unessential bits of him had been burned off in the struggle for his soul. Fine lines lay at the edges of his eyes, deep creases carved into the corners of his mouth where none had been before. And one hand fell defensively across his chest, where the long ugly slash of a new scar marred the sleek musculature.

It had been a night of discovery. The two of them finding each other in the dark. Holding on as they stepped over a new threshold into unmarked territory. Thoughts revealed. Plans dreamt. Bodies explored until they lay spent and bedazzled, their skin damp with lovemaking, their breaths quick and shuddering. Holding all the potential for permanence.

But she wasn't blind. Belfoyle bore the same signs of neglect as had Kilronan House. Yet here among the ancient family heirlooms and Douglas legends, thick as furze, the sense of patient waiting seemed almost tangible. An expectation of a turned corner. A new beginning that might bring the old house back to life.

Yet a new beginning meant new money. And even as the tolerated stepdaughter, she'd not held a dowry large enough to tempt a wealthy financier's son, much less a peer of the realm. She hated to admit it, but Aidan needed Miss Osborne. Someone with the right family ties and a sterling reputation. A woman Aidan could be proud of and who in turn would be proud to reside upon the arm of the Earl of Kilronan.

She brushed a strand of auburn hair off his brow. Skimmed a cheek shadowed with stubble. Kissed the sensual line of his mouth.

Her actions carrying the grief of a parting.

She'd fantasized. Of course she had. And Aidan had nurtured the dream with his whispered promises tonight. But deep in her heart, she knew better. Only this time the naive child who'd shattered with Jeremy's abandonment bore a strength she'd only achieved over the last hardscrabble years.

She bent but she did not break.

And her time with Aidan would carry her through a thousand empty days.

From a night of fantasy had sprung a gift beyond measure. A serenity she'd never expected to feel. And a head full of memories no longer bearing the stain of her sins. Her son had come back to her. Every breath he'd taken, every glance from slate blue newborn eyes, every feeble cry as he struggled against the inevitable.

Aidan had taken from her. But he'd also given back. And even if it had been unintentional, she'd give credit where credit was due.

She had her son again. And she knew now he would remain a part of her forever. She leaned over. Whispered in Aidan's ear so that only he might hear: "Thank you."

# twenty-three ◦➤

Aidan stood upon the thin strip of beach at the bottom of the cliff. Shaded his eyes as he estimated the climb. A good three hundred feet. Nothing like the sheer ascent of the cliffs to the south, but still a challenge.

He'd accomplished it twice. Once with his father on that long-ago birthday. The second time in the months following his parents' deaths, when physical exhaustion had been the only way to dull the devastating grief and ease the frustrated desire for vengeance.

It was that same kind of need bringing him here this morning. He'd brought his gear. Leather harness. Ropes. A thin-bladed axe. Hammer. Steel anchors.

Scrambling up the initial part of the ascent, he hammered the first anchor into the rock face. Knotted his rope around it. Attached that rope to the harness at his waist. From here, the way steepened to almost vertical, though at one point, a buttress of rock created a solid handhold at

the top. A perfect place to wedge the next anchor into position. Knot the second rope.

The next stretch grew more demanding. No outcrop-
pings or spurs for easy positioning. He found and dug
his fingers into a narrow crevice. Pulled himself up. Wind
tugged at him. Slapped the cliffs in sea-salty gusts, whining
through his ropes. Nesting seabirds squawked threats from
their ledges and beat their wings to warn him off.

Aidan's shoulders strained as he pulled himself up,
sweat leaking into his eyes. The harness cut into his waist.
His fingers grew slippery and cramped. Breathing harsh
with fatigue.

Fumbling with the next anchor, he dropped it. The
metallic plink as it bounced off the rock and the crash of
sliding shale startled the birds to a fresh round of squawking.

Training took over.

Climb. Hammer. Release. Clip. Repeat.

Clouds moved in from the west. Flattened, bellies black
and licked with lightning. The wind became a tempest, the
rain arriving in icy sheets.

A voice slithered up out of the torrent. A vicious hissing drowning out the sounds of the storm, the squawk of
birds, the rumble of a surging ocean.

A crushing squall tore him from the cliff. He dangled
one handed over the precipice, his shoulder screaming as
tendons stretched to the breaking point. Then, his hold
collapsing, he plummeted earthward, the ground rushing to
meet him. No time for panic. No time for regret.

And just as in the dream when he woke before he
struck, the rope caught, strained against the anchor, his
harness jerking him to a stop with a bone-rattling jolt.

Rain sluiced over his face. Soaked him to the skin. He

squinted up into the downpour. Into the flickering clouds. And swore he saw the ghost of a shape upon the cliff's edge. The gleam of a blade.

His scar burned as if someone had jammed his frozen axe head into it, and he gasped against the glacial agony, tears gathering at the corners of his eyes as he fought back a scream.

The wind laughed at his pain. *"Skoa."*

Soon.

"There's nothing here, Aidan. Not even a veiled reference."

Cat pressed the heels of her hands to her eyes, but the imprint of the words remained etched on the backs of her eyelids. Sharp as if they'd been penned in blood.

Arthur's return figured more and more among the pages now, as if the unfocused ambitions of the group slowly coalesced to a single goal. And sprinkled throughout, references to the tapestry and the stone, both items inextricably linked to this resurrection. Yet nowhere was any mention of the whereabouts of either object. If old Kilronan had recorded it anywhere within the pages of his diary, he'd been too clever for her.

She closed the book, sickness dogging her, a malaise sucking at her like soggy ground. Making every thought, every breath as exhausting as if she'd fought a battle. Ended on the losing side. Pushing the book farther away as if distance might ease the worst of it, she made her decision. "I'm finished, Aidan. I can't do this anymore."

Aidan peeled himself from the shadows. He'd been skulking all day. A simmering anger to his words. A brewing violence to his actions. A new restless purpose, as if he knew Belfoyle's sanctuary would buy them only so much time.

"Fair enough. Give it to me." He held out a hand, a shuttered expression in his eyes.

She checked a quick breath, her hand instinctively curling around the book. "What are you going to do with it?"

"Lazarus is after the diary. Why? Because he's been ordered to retrieve it for Máelodor. Why is Máelodor after it? Because he thinks—or knows—it contains the location of the tapestry and the stone. They'll kill for it. And I'm tired of the two of us being their number one target. They can have the diary. I'm through with it. I've learned all I want to of my father's crazed and ruthless ambitions."

"Lazarus will never let you live. He'll tear you apart, leaving less than enough to fill a canvas sack."

"Perhaps. Perhaps not. I have a few tricks that may surprise."

"Aidan, you can't think you're a match for—or perhaps you do. After all, you did it once, didn't you?"

He turned toward her with slow deliberation. Tracking her with a stare that had naught of the lover in it, but instead a savagery as relentless as the parasitic *Unseelie*. An image assailed her. The glimpse she'd caught long weeks ago upon her first reading of the diary of Kilronan as ironfisted conqueror. Sword upraised. Streaked with gore. A mythic, battle-maddened demon.

She forced herself to remain still beneath his fathomless gaze despite the panic assailing her. Had Aidan been forever altered by the sinister shadows? Was this what she'd been witnessing in the stretched and uneasy hours? Daz had referred to it as an addiction. A craving for the beast that would live within Aidan as a splinter of dark mage energy. Tempting him always. Luring him with clawed hands toward the chasm.

"I've grappled with every angle, Cat. If Máelodor wants

the tapestry, who am I to stop him? Let him have it. Let him try his madness. What is it to me?"

"It's everything. It makes him one step closer to succeeding. To resurrecting Arthur as a slave born *Domnuathi*. Using him to sway the world of *Other* to Máelodor's side. Can you imagine the horrors a war between *Duinedon* and *Other* would bring to the world? It can't be allowed to get that far."

He fell into a chair. Closed his eyes. When he opened them again, the creature had receded into the darkest corner of Aidan's soul. This time his stare burned clear of shadows. Made his words all the more frightening.

"Did you ever think, Cat, that the war has already started?"

She cast a quick glance around the darkened room, the furniture no more than black shapes against the gloom. But this time she knew where she was going. There was no hesitation. And only one or two second thoughts. The ones that had escaped her earlier exorcism.

Aidan wouldn't like what she planned. But Aidan wasn't here to stop her. She'd left him sleeping. Finally.

It had taken hours of tortured pacing—his limp growing more pronounced with every pass, his brow growing heavier with unspoken troubles—before he finally fell into an exhausted doze.

Hours in which she'd hatched her plan. Worked up her courage. Hardened herself to her purpose.

Her talent for languages had begun her involvement. Her talent for thievery would end it.

Conjuring flame to candle, she set an unerring course. Left her coal bucket at the hearth. Crossed to a low chest opposite a high tester bed.

Sinking to her haunches, she worked the lock with the flat of a knife she'd cadged from dinner. One snick of a sprung catch, and she was in.

Within the chest, a bundle of letters tied with a frayed ribbon. A deteriorating set of bound Shakespeare. A fan with one broken stick. A folded length of watered silk. A second of muslin in a pale green. A bouquet of dried flowers.

She placed each item aside as she searched, trying not to think of the woman who once owned this chest. A woman whose life had been torn apart in the initial struggle to bring Arthur back. Now, six years later, Cat refused to let one more Douglas be sacrificed to the obsession. Not if she could prevent it.

A book lay at the bottom of the drawer. Cloth wrapped. Heavy with secrets.

Her heart galloped as she withdrew it, palms moist, fingers trembling. She drew in a steadying breath as the cloth fell away. Tracing the spread-winged bird perched atop its crooked sword, she mouthed the Douglas motto like a mantra—luck favors the strong.

Carrying it to the hearth, she knelt before the grate. Placed paper at the bottom. Added kindling. A few choice pieces of coal from the bucket.

This was it, then. She could taste success.

Again she called forth the mage energy swimming within her blood. A magic passed down from her ancestors in a continuous timeline of *Other*. Sons and daughters who'd tread the dangerous line between the worlds of Mortal and *Fey*.

The kindling caught, snapping sparks up the black chimney.

Would she ever hold another child of her own and know she had become a link in a chain stretching into the past? Reaching into the future? Or would her father's *Other* blood end with her death? No one left to remember.

The coal caught next. Smoke stinging her nose. Flames licking up over the grate. Reflecting off the gothic irons. Burning high.

She closed her eyes, seeing William's blue-tipped features, the tiny clenched fists. His name and his face no longer holding the haze of old memory. But new and clean as if she'd only just stepped away from his cradle.

Aidan's gift to her.

Fed by magic, the inferno raged, the light throwing wicked shadows over the bedchamber walls. Heat burning her cheeks. Watering her eyes.

The diary seemed to writhe beneath her fingers as if it fought its destruction, a thousand screams beating the insides of her skull. Scraping along her jangled nerves. She tried swallowing, but her mouth had gone dry.

"Cat?" The sleepy baritone voice startled her to action.

And before he could stop her, she cast Kilronan's diary into the heart of the fire.

Aidan's knees buckled, a chorus of millions battering his brain, leaving no space to think. Even the act of filling his lungs and pushing blood through the chambers of his heart seemed a monumental effort.

The screams faded, leaving one lone voice torching the edges of his mind. A voice he knew as well as his own and one he'd last heard blown on the sour edges of a coastal wind. His father's ghost shattering him piece by damaged piece.

"Disappointment," the voice raged. "Failure."

The accusations slammed into him with the force of a lifetime's knowledge behind them.

"Worthless."

"Cat," he muttered, his throat closing. His fingers curled against the lit fuse making its way to his center along veins dipped in acid. "The diary."

He closed his eyes against the gut-churning sickness as the earth gave way, sending him plunging through the darkness. Cat's screams spiraling after.


"He wants to see you."

Still in her nightclothes, reeking of smoke, and gripping the smoldering diary, Cat rose from her seat to follow Jack.

He bowed her into Aidan's chambers, his polished courtier airs carrying decidedly rumpled overtones.

"Go easy on her, coz," his parting words before he closed the door, leaving her and Aidan alone.

He wasn't in bed. Instead he sat in a cushioned window embrasure, moonlight throwing shadows beneath his dark eyes, glints of glimmering copper into his hair. His expression unreadable.

"You look just as you did when I first met you," he said. "Like a cornered animal. All prickles and fangs."

No hint of his mood in the tone of his voice. Weary, but nothing more.

She tried relaxing, but it was as if a steel band pressed her ribs. She couldn't breathe, waiting for the explosion. "I never meant for you to be hurt. I only wanted—"

"It didn't work, did it?"

The gentleness of the question pained her more than

any harsh accusation. Burnt, broken leather and melted binding crackled as her fingers dug into the diary's velvet wrapping. "You knew it wouldn't burn?"

His shoulder dipped in a vague shrug. "More a feeling than a certainty. My father intended this diary to last beyond him. His wards were created to be sure it did just that."

"But why did my attempt to destroy it affect you and not me?"

He stood, reaching a hand out. A hand she chose to ignore. She couldn't. Not if she wanted to box her way free of this stranglehold he had on her.

Seeing her reluctance, he dropped his hand to his side. Again came the half shrug. A long, unreadable stare into the dark. "I'm bound to that book by blood. By family. By failed hopes and unrealized dreams. It's a part of me. As I'm a part of it. Father knew I'd find it eventually. And knew once I did I'd have no choice but to translate it."

It was her turn to wince. Not a good time to tell him what she'd discovered. But it was now or never. "I can't read it any more."

"But you said—" he put a hand out again. This time she acquiesced. Handed him the book.

"Something happened when I burned it. The words themselves, they're like a poison in my head."

Laying the diary in his lap, Aidan folded back the velvet. The cover had withered to a bubbled warped mess, the gold leaf of the Douglas family crest burned away. But when he opened the broken binding, the pages remained unaffected by the flames. The writing's slippery curves and slicing lines as vibrant as if they'd been penned yesterday.

Immediately, the steel band tightened, cutting off her

breath while her head exploded in a sunburst of pain. Shredding her thoughts. Blinding her. A voice snaked up her spine. Coiled into the base of her brain.

She snatched the diary back. Slammed it closed, ignoring the crumbling sooty mess coming away on her fingers. "I can't—"

His features held the same waxen pallor, spasms jerking his shoulders as he fought back sickness. His eyes black with despair. "Did you hear him?"

"A voice. Nothing more."

"It was him. I've failed. Again." He lay back against the embrasure, his fist rolling the knotted muscles of his thigh. His gaze unseeing into the night beyond the window.

"It wasn't your fault, Aidan. I burned the book. I ruined your chance to find the tapestry and the stone. Not you."

"It makes no difference." He fell silent, his stare trained on a past invisible to her. "How do I separate the father I loved from the *Other* I fear? It's impossible. I try, and it all comes apart in my grasp. Leaves me holding nothing but death."

Curses she'd expected. Fury that would pierce with hate-filled scorn. Not the quiet misery of a man brought to despair by a ghost he could never satisfy. How to answer such a tangled question?

She bit her lip. Fumbled to find the words hidden among the confusion of her thoughts. Tried to offer him back the same precious wisdom he'd given her. "My son signified a loss of everything I'd known. Everything I'd been. But he was also a treasure beyond price. It was up to me to come to grips with the weaving of good and bad." She paused, but he said nothing. And she blazoned on. "In the same way, your father isn't wholly the saint or the sinner. It may take years, but you'll one day look upon him as the real man—warts and all. And be proud of who you are. Where you come from. And know he loved you."

As if wrenching himself back to the present, he turned his gold-flecked stare upon her, the depth enough to drown in. His hand found hers. Callused. Strong. Warm. A glimmer of amusement in the curve of his mouth. "Philosophy from a thief?"

"No," she answered, a sweet honeyed heat running through her. Hope fluttering like a caged bird in her chest. "Truth from a lover."

He rose, drawing her into his arms. Slanted his mouth on hers, threading his fingers through her hair. His actions needful. Desperate. As if her surety might pass to him in the melding of their bodies.

She clung, loving the taste of him. The feel of his carved, muscled body. The thunderous pounding of his heart matching her own. His chained emotion like a vibration beneath his skin.

It took all her will to ease out of his reach and away from the need engulfing her.

He frowned. His gaze troubled, his hands open and reaching. "Why?"

She gave him a brave smile. "Because you and I are a dream. But it's time to wake from that dream. And time for me to surrender the field to Miss Osborne."

His brows drew into a heavy frown, the line of his jaw sharp as a blade. "Isn't that for me to decide?"

"I lost the right to your love three years ago in a Dublin garret with another man's name on my lips. Had I known you lay still in my future—" she shrugged. "I'm sorry, Aidan."

"And if I choose to overlook it?" His words held an

edge of irritation. His eyes flicking to her waist before meeting her stare for stare.

Hand splayed on the flat of her stomach, she smiled through a haze of tears. "You'd never be allowed to. Not for one minute. Look around you, Aidan. You need a wife who can bring more to the marriage than gossip and side-long glances. You were right to court Miss Osborne. She's the woman who can restore your fortune and your home. She's your future."

He reached for her again, but she evaded him with a move that sent her across the room. Safe from his grip. Safe from her indecision.

"I told you once I wouldn't let you fall, Cat," he argued. "Trust me."

She opened the door. The cold solidity of the knob like an anchor against the persuasive, silken voice. She wanted to believe. Wanted to imagine a future beyond that of cosseted mistress. Sharing his body. His heart. His life.

"No, Aidan," she answered. "In this, you must trust me."

# twenty-four

The sea shone like rubbed pewter, the line of the horizon indistinguishable from the gray skies above. Clouds flat and wide. A wind carrying the threat of rain to come.

He'd dreamt again. The *Unseelie* presence hovering. Building. Gaining strength.

Waking, he'd felt the frozen burn of his scar licking at his muscles. Throbbing with an ache drilling to the center of his bones. Luring him toward a face-off he knew he'd lose.

Had he meant what he'd told Cat? Did it matter whether Máelodor gained the diary? Found the sacred objects and brought Arthur back for another go at uniting the *Other* into a glittering magical army? Or would a world founded in *Duinedon* blood be a world worth having at all? Would his race have sacrificed their humanity in a vain attempt to grasp at a universe that had never existed except in story? The Lost Days not merely lost, but imagined?

The playing pieces had been gathered by his father—the Rywlkoth Tapestry, the Sh'vad Tual.

The game set into motion with the discovery of the diary. Cat's translations.

Now he must choose a side.

He'd come here this morning, bleary and thick. Empty handed. No ropes. No axe. No anchors. No desire to attempt the cliff ascent. Instead, he plucked stones from the rocky strand. Tossed them out across the waves, seeking answers in the infinite ocean's tides.

But even that effort had been abandoned by the time Jack found him propped against a fist of slippery rock revealed by the tide's ebb. Spray silvered his hair. Crusted his cheeks like dried tears.

His cousin's shadow stretched across the beach. Scattered the blennies skimming the tide pool's surface. "Is it true? You plan on handing the diary over to Lazarus?"

He drummed his fingers against his thigh. "You've been speaking with Cat."

"She's worried."

"She's given up the right to worry, hasn't she?" he snapped.

Jack sidestepped the loaded comment by ignoring it completely. "If you're correct about what the diary contains, letting Máelodor gain possession of it would be catastrophic."

Aidan rounded on him. "Weren't you the one harping on *Duinedon* crimes against *Other*? Of the mortal world's mounting mistrust and fear of any who possess *Fey* blood?"

Jack offered a shrug in response. "That doesn't mean I condone war. The Lost Days are just that—lost. We can't go back. Don't know if I'd want to. Magic's well and good, but I don't know how comfortable I'd be with it around every corner."

Aidan fed his remaining stones to the waves. Wiped his hands on his breeches. Stalked the beach, ignoring the painful stretch of knotted muscles as he worked off his mounting frustration. "Then we let the mortal world continue to label us demon spawn? Continue to drive us from our homes? Slaughter us?" He wheeled around. "With none to say enough?"

It all just rolled off Jack like water from a damned duck. "It didn't work when your father and his friends tried it. It won't work now. The *Amhas-draoi* will put a stop to it just as they did then." He paused, his usual carefree gaze cutting with knifelike precision. "If you don't put a stop to it first."

A charged hush fell between them. The wind dying as if they stood within the hurricane's eye. A sense that Jack was not the only one awaiting his decision.

Voices purred through his consciousness. A twining skein of emotions and opinions. Father's pride. Mother's patience. Sabrina's conciliation. And drowning them out, Brendan's forceful outrage. He'd surrendered his future to keep the Nine from launching their war. Could Aidan forfeit that sacrifice and hand the diary over without a fight? Render everything he'd done worthless?

Aidan fumbled in his coat pocket. Came up empty. No cheroot to stave off the nerves jumping beneath his skin. Bereft without the comfort of the habit. "Do you think the *Amhas-draoi* are right? Do you think Brendan is still alive?"

Jack cocked his head in thought. "He could always finagle his way out of the tightest corners. A bit of the *Fey* luck about him perhaps." He laughed. "I like to think he's somewhere out there."

Aidan paced, reflections of the cloudy sky in every

windswept rock pool. Inhaled the mingled aromas of sea and salt and stone and earth.

Reaching a dripping outcropping of rock, he retraced his steps, his decision made. "Whatever happens, I want Cat gone. Today. Immediately."

"You truly mean to let her go?"

Aidan kept his eyes upon the sea. Off the sympathetic concern he'd find in his cousin's eyes. "There's no reason for her to stay, is there?"

"There's you."

"No, Cat's correct." He faced Jack. Just as he'd suspected. Sympathetic concern by the bucket load. It set his teeth on edge. "I need money. Connections. Standing. All the things Miss Osborne can provide."

"She'll make a good wife," Jack encouraged.

"*Hmph.*" The best he could muster.

"She's beautiful. Clever. Sweet tempered."

"The sale's been made," he groused. "You can stop hawking her like an auctioneer at Tattersalls."

"You know in your heart there's no future in Dublin for Cat. Nor anywhere. Not as your wife." Jack continued to state the obvious. Almost as if he was trying to convince himself as much as Aidan. "They'd shred her for an evening's entertainment. She'd be made to look ridiculous. Or shunned outright."

An argument Aidan had already hashed out within his own mind. Still he raged. It kept him from facing the hole yawning wide as an open grave at his feet. Cat's departure toeing him ever closer to the crumbling edge. "Can we stop speaking about her? When all this is over—"

When?

What was he talking about?

Try if.

If he defeated Lazarus. If he still lived. If the world had not toppled into anarchy. An awful lot of ifs between now and a future seeming almost as obscure as that far horizon.

He tried again. "When all this is over, I'll pay a groveling call on Sir Humphrey Osborne. No doubt an earl's suit, even an impoverished earl's suit, will be looked upon with favor."

Jack slanted a skeptical look in his direction. "Don't sound so enthusiastic."

Fire ate at his belly. Clawed its way up his throat. "Damn it, Jack. You can take your thrice-damned enthusiasm and——" he breathed slowly. Gained control over the threatening fury. "Enough about my potential nuptials. Will you accompany Cat back to Dublin? See she arrives safely?"

"You aren't——"

"Yes or no," he snarled. "That's all I need. Yes or no. Will you see her safe to Dublin?"

His cousin offered a curt nod. "I'll see her safe."

They gripped hands. Shook on it.

"Do you think she'll agree to go?" Jack asked.

"No. I don't."

"Then how do you plan on convincing her?"

Aidan hated even thinking about it. "Leave that to me."

"Fine, but once she's settled, I'll be back," Jack declared.

He would have laughed at this show of solidarity—so serious, so solemn, so completely un-Jack-like—if he didn't know his cousin would be dead within seconds of any meeting with the soldier of Domnu.

"I'll need more than luck, Jack."

"You can't face Lazarus alone."

He stooped to snag a rock from the beach. Tumbled it in his hand. Drew his arm back just as a dolphin's glistening dorsal cut the waves like a blade. "I won't be alone."

"You'll summon the *Ambas-draoi*?"

With a heave, he chucked the stone as far as it would go. Watched it spin and skip before striking the water and disappearing. "Let's hope they're the only force I need to summon."

He sat at his desk, withdrawing a sheet of foolscap from the drawer. Dipped his pen in the ink, drops spattering the paper like blood.

Once he made up his mind, the words had come quickly. A hasty recounting of all that had happened since fleeing Henry Street. All that might happen if Lazarus gained the diary.

Satisfied, he placed the pen back in its tray. Sanded the letter. Shook it dry. Folded and sealed it, scrawling the direction across the front. Stood to ring for a servant.

Ten minutes to swallow six years of hate and mistrust.

But would it be enough? And would it be in time?

She'd found the burial ground quite by chance. A small square of green amid the sprawling stonework of Belfoyle. Sunken graves bore witness to the earliest Douglas arrivals to this rocky Irish coastline. Most of the stones had been scoured clean over time, a date barely visible here. A name there. She settled herself in front of a rough-cut block of scarred marble, green with moss, chipped at one corner.

Newer than the others. More personal—"beloved infant."

As she bent to trace the crudely wrought inscription,

the air seemed to crystallize around her, an oppressive weight as threatening as the approaching storm.

"I've ordered maids to have you packed and ready to leave within the hour."

She rose and turned in one sweeping regal gesture. Faced Aidan's flat and unyielding gaze. A body braced for the fight he knew must come.

"You're sending me away?"

"If you're no longer able to decipher the diary, your presence is no longer required. I release you from our agreement. Jack will return you to Dublin."

"I don't want to go to Dublin."

"I don't believe I asked."

"The roads are dangerous."

"Belfoyle's more so."

"And if I refuse to leave you here to face who knows what?"

Anger flashed in his eyes. "I brought you to Belfoyle in bonds. You can depart the same way."

"You wouldn't dare."

"Try me."

Tempting, but she decided against it. He looked more than ready to carry out any and all threats. She retreated. "Fine, but once Jack's delivered me to the city, then what?"

"I've sent him with instructions for my banker. The money will see you settled."

"Settled as what?"

A storm boiled in his stare. "Any damned thing you please, Cat. Just go the hell away, and leave me be."

It took her like a punch to the stomach. Quick. Fierce. She fisted her hands at her sides. "Why are you doing this?" she asked quietly.

The storm broke, his rage burning her body like lightning. His glare holding the tempest's lash, a horrible gale fury pulsing the air. Shaking the blood in her veins.

And then it was over. His icy control regained as if the animal had never been loosed. A glacial freeze that had her shivering despite the late spring warmth.

"Good-bye, Miss Catriona O'Connell."

He spun on his heel to cross the grass, the arrow line of his shoulders, the gimp in his stride, the copper gleam of his hair etched eternally on her memory. The sleek arrogance of his body, the soul-touching thrust of his sex etched eternally on her flesh.

"You didn't answer my question," she called after him. "Why are you doing this?"

He never turned. Never slowed. But his voice drifted back to her, cold as death. "Because I love you."

Hugging her shaking body, she sank to her knees beside the forgotten child's stone. Sorry she asked.

She folded a gown. Half and then half again.

Stupid, pigheaded, stubborn man. Sending her away like a child. Dismissing her as if she hadn't survived two clashes with Lazarus. Wasn't involved up to her neck.

That wasn't right. She shook it out. Started again. Longways. Bring the hem up.

Did he think she could simply turn off her heart like snuffing a candle. Not worry herself sick over what she left behind?

*Blast.* The sleeves—that wasn't it either.

Fine. She understood his reasoning. Even understood his anger. But to arrogantly brush her off onto Jack felt too much like another rebuff. Another rejection.

She'd rejected him first, but that was beside the point.

She crumpled the exasperating gown up and stuffed it into the traveling case with one of her father's choicest oaths. "Bollocks the poxy gown."

"Is that any way to be treatin' such fine material? They'll be naught left at all but a ragpicker's windfall."

She turned to be met with Maude's imperious warrior bulk filling the doorway. Gapped yellow teeth. Creases within creases. And hair a frizzed hennaed horror beneath a stained mobcap, her striped yellow and red gown stretched to breaking beneath a pink apron.

The most horrible, beautiful sight Cat had laid eyes on.

She threw herself into the old woman's arms. To hell with 'take it as you find it.' To her mind, it was bloody damn awful.

"It's like that, is it?" Maude snuffled into a huge handkerchief. Wiped at a suspicious speck in a corner of her eye. "You're a great fool, Cat O'Connell. And no mistake."

Not exactly what she expected to hear. Not after Maude's past advice.

"But I can't be his wife. And I'll not be his mistress."

"Are you so full of prospects you can be turning your nose up at the idea of pleasuring the man without benefit of clergy? Not as if you haven't been doing it thus far, is it?"

"It's not that. But—"

"Go on. Spill it, child. I'm no namby-pamby milquetoast what can't be hit with a hard truth without wilting."

"I won't share him, Maude. I can't. Not with another woman. I want all of him. All or none."

"You'd cut off your nose to spite your face."

"I can't separate my life into pieces. A part with him. A part without him."

"Fair enough. And probably smarter than me. I should have done the same years ago. But I'm an easy woman, and it's been too long, and I don't take to change at all. Can't just leave at my age, can I? No." She sighed. "Ahern needs me. Needs a strong hand and a sound mind when he's gone wandering."

"Is Mr. Ahern all right?"

"As right as ever. Downstairs with His Lordship and Mr. O'Gara. Kilronan sent us to Dublin to stay at his town house, but we got there to find—no house. Couldn't go back to Knockniry. Couldn't stay in Dublin. Ahern started going a bit bats with all the hustle and worry. So we come here."

"No house? What are you talking about?"

"Whole place naught but a whopping charred hole in the ground."

"Lazarus," Cat breathed. Had to be. "Did Aidan say anything about what he'll do? Where he'll go?"

"To my way of thinking, that would be a question for your asking."

Cat picked up the next gown in the stack, counting the tiny pearl buttons. Running a finger over the side seam. Pulling free a loose thread at the neck. Tiny pointless motions as she breathed past the weight upon her chest. Struggled through it to find the warrior within. The one who wouldn't be sent on her way without a fight. "It's none of my concern, is it? He's sending me away."

Maude pulled the gown from Cat's unresisting fingers. "Perhaps he feels he's doing what you want."

"Oh, Maude. That's just it. I don't even know what I want."

"Then how is he to know?"

———o———

She ran him to earth in the dim chill of the old chapel, staring up at the woven rendering of parting lovers. A solemn Sir Archibald receiving a final gift. The woman's icy perfection not complete enough to hide the sorrow upon her frozen features.

An idyll at an end.

She stepped forward, her boots loud upon the stone floor. "Jack's ready to leave."

Aidan turned, a new oaken strength to his features. A new flinty hardness steeling the warmth of his gaze. "We've said our farewells."

"Please, Aidan. Let me stay. I know I can—"

"It's over, Cat." He stood carved and expressionless as the busts lining Belfoyle's south drawing room. There would be no return to the nuzzled spooning of bodies, the whispered endearments in the dark.

"But—" she tried one last time.

This time his face twisted into a mask of animal rage. Frightening. Furious. "What don't you comprehend? There's no reason for you to stay. Every reason for you to get out before this place goes up like a damned crate of explosives. We've made our decisions," he snarled. "We have to live with them. That means good-bye."

He was right. She fumbled her way back toward the staircase, blood pounding in her ears, mouth dry.

A strangled moan followed her up the curl of stairs. Killing her slowly.

A desire to be with him. To stay here forever and the world be damned sank its way past all her strongest defenses. Her steps dragged.

*Beg. Plead. Persuade. Call me back and refuse to let me go. Make me see past my fears. Make me stay, Aidan. Tell me now before it's too late.*

———o———

He opened his mouth to call out. Swallowed the plea before it left his lips. She'd made up her mind. He sank down upon the stone floor. Cast his eyes to the lovers' grief. Strength of mind replacing the broken shards of his heart.

*Let her go, Aidan. Let her go before it's too late.*

# twenty-five

The storm that had threatened all day caught up with them a mile beyond Belfoyle's walled boundary. Slowing the coach. Turning bad roads impassable. Twice they were required to get out and walk while the coachman alternately scolded and cajoled the team through rim-high mud.

By nightfall they'd only managed another four sloppy miles with the coachman complaining the horses were exhausted. Light was gone. The road ahead steeped in danger for a lone coach with only one armed groom upon the box.

Jack raised his eyes heavenward. Stretched his long legs in front of him as he checked his watch. "Seven-thirty." Shoved it back into his waistcoat pocket. "We could have walked to Kilfenora quicker than it's taken us to drive there."

Cat had kept silent through most of the afternoon, staring out the window at the bleak spring rain, the stripped branches, the muddy, beaten fields. Now she focused on her companion. Noted for the first time his own strained patience, a frustration that had not all to do with their lack of progress.

"He's not alone. Mr. Ahern is there," she offered, though she'd told herself this a thousand times already and it certainly hadn't made her feel any better.

Jack seemed to be of the same mind, if the skeptical twist of his mouth was any indication. "And that's supposed to console me?"

"Looks can be deceiving. Ahern saved him once already."

Jack's glower remained unwavering. "He shouldn't need saving. He shouldn't be mixed up in this business at all. He's no bloody warrior. Lazarus will have him for breakfast. Make bloody sausage of him."

She threaded her hands in her lap to keep them from around Jack's neck. "Thank you. I didn't think it was possible, but you've actually made me feel worse."

He flashed her a disarming O'Gara smile. "It's a gift."

Cat opened her mouth to parry that contention when the coach lurched wildly. Jack fell against the door, jarring his shoulder, which he grasped with a grunt of pain. Cat was tossed from her seat in a tangle of skirts.

The coach lurched again and, with a crack of breaking lumber, came to a stop, the rear wheels in a ditch, a heavy hedge pressed against the glass.

Jack threw himself out the door, a pistol held tight to his body. Cat right behind. The coachman was cutting the left leader free from a tangle of harness, swearing as he did so. Of the groom there was no sign.

"What happened?"

"I couldn't say, sir. I were barely moving when a great shape slunk among the trees. Appeared in the road afearing the horses. They bolted with nary a thing I could do to stop them. Took the turn too sharp."

"Where's our friend with his musket?"

The coachman scanned the wreckage. "Don't know. He was here a moment ago."

In answer, a shot sounded from the woods. Then a silence pregnant with possibilities. All of them horrible.

"Cat," Jack barked, "get back inside. No arguments."

By now he and the coachman were nervously searching the trees.

"Your man speaks sense, my lady." A dark shape. A shiver of drawn steel. "Useless though it is."

A voice she recognized from nightmare. The deep throaty rasp as if words came difficult. The scorn underlying that hateful title by which he insisted on addressing her.

She fumbled uselessly with the door handle.

The shape moved into the meager light from the coach's lamps, standing astride the road like a black colossus. His face in shadow, only the wicked gleam of his eyes alive within the darkness.

Jack's pistol rose, steadied, and erupted with a sharp report and a flare lighting up the heavy lines of Lazarus's face.

Thirty feet away. No way Jack could miss.

But Lazarus's movements came fluid and unerring. He dodged with a feint that had him at Jack's throat, his dagger slammed hilt deep into the slighter man's stomach.

Cat screamed. The coachman swore. And Jack crumpled to the ground, his face registering shock as blood spread over his waistcoat. Dripped from between his fingers.

Lazarus never even spared a glance for his victim. Instead his empty stare fell on her. "We've a meeting to keep."

He swung her unresisting body over his shoulder. Strode back into the wood.

Grief snapped her free of her daze. Shrieking and cursing and pummeling and kicking, she struggled. His steps never slowed, his body absorbing her blows without a mark. Finally the woods closed around them, cutting off her view of the broken coach, of Jack's sprawled, bleeding body.

"You killed him," she cried.

Lazarus's grip around her tightened. "Lucky man."

"Damn." Aidan crushed the note in his fist. Eased himself back from the brink of complete and unrecoverable panic. That would get him nowhere except killed that much faster. He needed to think. Plan. Work the scenarios. But time stood against him.

One hour. The message delivered to his door by a terrified peasant boy warned Aidan he had one bloody hour to bring the diary to the gatehouse. Exchange it for Cat. He tried not to dwell on the "or else." Lazarus had left that to his vivid imagination. And what it conjured only made him more desperate.

What had happened to Jack? Did he still live, or had Lazarus already claimed his first victim? And how did Cat fare? Alone? Afraid? As terrified as he was?

"You can't let that scoundrel have the diary, Aidan." Daz sat sunk in an armchair, huge gnarled hands clutching a shawl to his stooped shoulders, up to his ankles in a steaming bucket of salt water. A moth-eaten cap perched atop his wispy, balding head. Only his eyes shone stern with determination. "Not if what you suspect is true and Máelodor seeks the tapestry and stone. I knew the man once, and I don't expect he's improved with age."

Aidan lit a nerve-steadying cheroot. Dragged on the thick tobacco flavor, hoping it would calm his shaking hands. Ease the tension threading his body like coiled wire. It didn't. He tossed it on the grate with another oath.

"If I don't, Cat dies." Hated the fear quivering the edges of his voice.

"For all you know she may already be dead, and this just a bluff to flush you from Belfoyle's protections."

Please don't let it be so. Please don't let his last image of Cat be grief-stricken resignation as he'd shoved her out of his life. What he'd give for one more chance—

"Even if she lives still and you surrender the Kilronan diary to Lazarus, do you truly think he'll allow either of you to remain alive? She's dead either way."

"Not if I win."

Daz's features grew ferret sharp. "And how do you think you'll manage that? I didn't save you from the *Unseelie* once so you could try again, boy."

"If I can defeat Máelodor's *Domnuathi*—even if I can delay him—the *Amhas-draoi* will arrive. They'll take control of the diary. See that Máelodor never gets his hands on it."

"And lose yourself in the process?"

"Maybe. Maybe not."

His hand went to his chest where his scar prickled with a frozen burn. The vessels surrounding the buried *Unseelie* splinter pulsing like a second heart.

His only hope for success lay in summoning the dark force stirring within him. Drawing on it to combat Máelodor's unstoppable killer. Manipulating the violent flow of mage energy without being consumed by it. Avoiding complete conflagration.

Simple.

———o———

Lazarus stood just inside the door to the gatehouse, a ramshackle building empty save for a nest of mice whose droppings could be seen strewn across the dusty floors and piled in untidy heaps by the wainscoting. The walled front garden held almost as much discarded refuse. Overgrown bracken cleared and never removed. A broken barrel. An old set of lumber left to rot in the weather by some former tenant.

Cat watched her captor as he watched for Aidan. He rested at his ease on the door's porch, but she sensed he was neither resting nor at ease. Once or twice his hand strayed to the scabbard at his waist, to the pommel of the well-used sword, his fingers stroking the rounded knob ornamenting the hilt. A few barely whispered words hanging on a breath: *"Roedd hi'n noson fel hwn."*

It was a night like this one.

Did he know she understood Welsh? Was it meant for her ears or simply thought given voice?

He'd not tied her. No doubt assuming she'd be too terrified to run. Too weak to make trouble.

He was right on both counts. Add to that nauseous, cotton mouthed, and heartbroken.

Old sorrows.

Her family. Jeremy. Her son.

Fresh tragedies.

Geordie. And now Jack.

They mingled in her mind like so much flotsam. Broke against the edges of her awareness. Piling one upon another until she drowned beneath them all. Silent, unbidden tears wet her cheeks.

Wind rattled the window, and she glanced out to search

the night. Strained for the sound of an approaching rider. Yearning for it. Dreading it.

Would Aidan fall to Jack's same sudden fate? Would he wear a look of surprise as his life drained away? Would Lazarus's gaze as his blade slammed home remain as empty as an open grave? His *Domnuathi*'s ruthless composure creating stone where once a real heart beat?

"What happens if Lord Kilronan refuses to agree to your terms?" she brazened.

Did she really want to know? Not by the look Lazarus settled on her.

"If he refuses, my lady, he's not worth your tears."

Unable to tolerate the solemn, heavy stare another second, she turned away. Her fingers finding the cool glass of a window pane. Tracing a final message in the dust.

I love you too.

A high whinny startled her fingers from their work. Lazarus's mount called to another.

Aidan was coming.


The shrill welcome of a horse shredded the silence. His own animal returning the greeting with a clarion call of his own.

So much for surprise.

Dismounting within the sheltering woods, Aidan tethered the bay to a tree. Pulled the velvet-swathed Kilronan diary from the saddlebag.

He'd toyed with the idea of offering Lazarus a fake. If he and Cat could no longer read his father's gibberish, it was doubtful Lazarus would be able to do so either. But the limits of the *Domnuathi*'s abilities remained elusive. And Aidan refused to risk Cat's life. Were it just his own? Perhaps he'd have given it a go.

He knelt in the protection of the tree line. Scanned the gatehouse. It looked empty.

Wait. There. He narrowed his gaze.

A glint that could be the moon in a broken pane of glass or the reflection of readied steel. A skitter of movement that might be some innocent nocturnal prowler or could be the shifting of a much larger and more deadly predator.

He straightened, but as yet made no move beyond the sheltering trees. "Bring her out where I can see her!" he shouted through cupped hands.

Another shifting of bodies. Words exchanged. And the door opened on a screech of hinges. Cat stepping into the faint spreading light of the moon. Hair loose down her back in a tangled ebony wave. Soaking up the midnight. Eyes bright in an otherwise impassive mask.

"Has he harmed you?" Aidan asked.

"No, but Jack—" her voice constricted with weeping.

Lazarus cut her off. "The diary, Kilronan. Bring it forward into the clearing."

His scar burned. His whole shoulder on fire. A deepening well of heat digging roots into the soil. Burrowing far into the bones of the earth where the creatures of the void waited. "And what's my guarantee you won't kill me as soon as I do?"

A silence followed, Cat's figure a wavering flicker of light, her clasped hands, her posture as defiant as if she strode to the scaffold.

His hand found the pistols he'd strapped to his chest. The knife at his waist. Closed around the sword at his side.

Finally, the voice rolled out from the well of the house with the answer Aidan expected: "No guarantee."

Even as the scar's spreading arctic plunge numbed his

body, his mind sharpened to diamond clarity. He inhaled a lung-filling breath and stepped into the breach.

*"Dwi'n cofio hwn."* I remember this.

Again the words in that sorrowful language of lost causes. Spoken just before Lazarus stepped in front of her. Drew his sword on a high metallic note.

Aidan moved from the trees with a stiff gait and a stiffer expression.

Lazarus's eyes focused on the wrapped bundle Aidan carried in his left hand. Ignoring the aimed pistol in his right, he gestured toward the low stone wall. "Place it there and back away."

Aidan did as instructed, and only after did Lazarus's attention drift from the diary to the man.

"Now free the girl," Aidan's voice edgy and dangerous.

"The girl?" Surprise colored Lazarus's words. "You speak of her as if she were the horse or the dog. My lady has a name, does she not?"

Aidan's breath sharpened in his throat. "Gallantry from a deathless monster? What would something like you know of it?"

Did Lazarus flinch against the insult? She couldn't tell in the uncertain light. But his shoulders squared, his sharp-featured face holding an ancient warrior arrogance. Raising an empty palm, he shook his head. "Nothing at all anymore."

The pistol shot caught him square in the chest, knocking him backwards. Aidan drew again. And a second pistol roared, this one just as well aimed. Just as deadly.

Lazarus lurched backward, knocking into Cat, reaching for her as he fell. Their fingers barely brushing.

Aidan crossed the space between. Stared down at the bloodied body. Kicked aside the man's sword with a spat curse before drawing his own.

"Run, Cat."

That voice. Echoes of another overlaid the rich baritone. Slippery. Discordant. Malevolent.

She shook her head. Saw the glimmer of Lazarus's gaze. Watching. Waiting. "He's not dead."

Aidan's face flared with a hate-filled ecstasy. "He soon will be."

"But—"

Lazarus closed his eyes. Breath expended on a sigh. "Go, my lady."

Two handed, Aidan lifted the sword high. "Or watch me take him apart piece by unholy piece."

Panic, long held in check, released itself on his snarled threat. She grabbed up her skirts. Began to run for the wood's edge. Slowing only briefly at the plunge of steel meeting flesh. A raw scream of agony. And again. Repeated.

How many wounds would it take to destroy the soldier of Domnu? How much of Aidan would be lost amid the slick spilling of blood upon the ground?

Another terrible scream burst against her ears.

No way to tell whether it was Lazarus or Aidan whose suffering shredded the night.

Hate hazed his vision. His body crawled with malicious glee. Blood streaked his clothes. Splattered his face. Dark. Sticky. Tasting of iron and salt and offal. His sword arm ached with strain but never faltered. Every downward slice of the cavalry saber another nail in Lazarus's coffin. His father. The *Amhas-draoi*. Brendan. Daz. Máelodor. Cat.

Lazarus became the focal point of all Aidan's anger and despair, grief and rage.

Raising his sword high for the final stroke, he aimed for the neck. Swung.

A bloodied hand caught the sword's pommel. Yielded but did not collapse. And the death-bringing thrust was turned aside.

Aidan screamed his fury. Found himself staring down into eyes hell bleak. A face as grim and gore soaked as his own. And one as bent on annihilation.

The battle had only now begun.

# twenty-six

Cat squatted in the heavy underbrush. She couldn't move. Frozen to this small patch of earth. Hands over her ears. Eyes squeezed shut. It didn't work. The battle filtered through her closed senses. The smell of blood and struggle and horror just beyond the trees.

"Cat!"

The tormented shout battered through her pressed hands. Shot her to her feet without thinking.

Aidan was down. Lying amid Lazarus's blood, spasming against the burn of battle magic. Lazarus stood over him. Shaky. Wavering. But alive and in command.

He leaned to pluck his discarded sword from the ground. Raised it high in a horrible reversal of roles.

"No!"

The scream tore up from her chest. She threw herself from the wood to scramble for the only thing that might delay Lazarus for a life-altering second.

The diary.

She snatched it up. Held it high. "Kill him, and I destroy Kilronan's diary."

Would he believe her bluff? Or tear her apart bit by bit with his soul-destroying dark magic? It was now or never.

Glancing at the dry brush and tumbled deadwood by the gatehouse wall, she mumbled the household magic through lips dry and rubbery. Prayed for enough concentration to prove her point.

Flames appeared. Slivers of red and yellow seeping up through the kindling. Snapping to life. Fed by the wind and dry, fire-ready branches.

"Don't, my lady."

He did believe her. She smiled as she held the book over the flames. "Back away from him," she commanded through chattering teeth.

Lazarus offered her a solemn, heavy stare. Took a step back. And in a move defying sight, whipped a dagger free. Hurled it, spearing the diary and knocking it out of Cat's hand to lie dusty, pages fluttering in the breeze. Safe from her futile threat.

The wind picked up. Embers rose. Wafted toward the gatehouse roof. Smoldered. Caught.

Lazarus's gaze followed them.

And Aidan rolled up and to a crouch. His voice slow and steady on a summoning.

Numbness gripped his body, beginning above his heart where the scar seared him with a frozen heat. Needles of ice ran along veins and arteries. Lungs crushed beneath a constricting shell of frost. His fingers stiff. His movements slow as glaciers. But he called forth the magic of the Dark Court.

*Soon*, the creature had promised.

Soon had become now.

The diary would remain free of Máelodor. Cat would remain alive. Anything beyond that, he would put aside as wishful thinking.

"Don't, Kilronan," Lazarus warned.

"Too late," he sneered, already feeling the *Unseelie's* approach in the thickening of the air, the narrowing of his vision. Or was that the fire?

Flames rippled along the gatehouse roofline. Ash drifting and mingling with smoke. A horse's scream came from somewhere behind him.

His fingers fell onto the sword's grip. Easily. Without thought. As if another worked through him. Someone used to war. To survival. To death.

Lazarus accepted the challenge. "So be it."

And the clash of metal rang in a crescendo of sparks and the singing of steel.

The *Domnuathi's* skills were battle honed. Even bearing the wounds of Aidan's previous attempts, he fought with incredible finesse. Parrying every thrust. Attacking upon every opening.

Aidan called forth the *Unseelie* magic. Felt it like a million latching claws into his skin. Biting. Tearing. Pushing its way through him. Taking him over bit by rabid bit. Heat met ice in a boiling fog of thought and action. Another controlling him. Another matching Lazarus move for move with snarling ferocity.

Aidan connected with a sliding blow to the *Domnuathi's* ribs. Lazarus responded with a slash into Aidan's off shoulder, deadening his fingers. Followed it with a spell that overwhelmed him. Crushed him with a mountain's weight of stone. Dropped him to the ground, his mouth filling with blood. His lungs useless.

Aidan drew deeper into the demon's well of power. The raw *Unseelie* magic dropping him through the void. He fell and fell without end, the passage littered with wraiths. But within that abyss there was strength and cunning and survival—of a kind.

Hands reached for him. Voices jeered. He caught a glimpse of the blind-eyed, faceless monster of his dreams laughing. Drawing him down. *"Erelth,"* it called. "Join with me."

His mind screamed against the overthrow. But Aidan ignored it as he ignored the slow thieving of his will and then his body. The demon saw with his eyes. Spoke with his voice. Fought with his limbs. With every push of blood through their shared body, the bond between them solidified until the horizon between man and monster blurred and then disappeared. The abyss dragged Aidan on with the strength of a vortex. Pulling him farther into the darkness where eternity awaited with dripping jaws.

Death without the mercy of dying. An end that would be endless.

No. He wouldn't give in. Let it control him. He rebelled. Crawling from the black. Heaving himself through the inky veil of shadows. The nothing that was the Dark Court's abode. The *Unseelie* shrieked its curses. Sank its talons deep. Its fangs deeper, until Aidan screamed against the pain and the burning cold sliding through his veins on its inexorable path to his heart. And the fight became twofold. A physical contest with Lazarus. An inner struggle against a demon who craved his body for its own.

He couldn't stand against both. Slowly he gave ground.

His arms growing feebler with every blow. Panting. Sweat stinging his eyes. Streaming off his body.

Lazarus backed him toward the gatehouse where fire now licked along the beams. Curled down walls. The trapped horse's terror jolting along Aidan's spine with clawing shrieks. Echoed by the inner vengeful demonic scream of the *Unseelie.*

Embers fell onto his coat. Singed his hair. The heat and smoke grew oppressive. He couldn't see. Couldn't hear.

Lazarus fought harder, strengthened by an internal drive rivaling and surpassing even the *Unseelie* hatred. He herded Aidan. Closer. Closer. Up the path. Into the shadow of the building, where fire leapt high from every window.

Aidan sought to evade the guiding point of the sword, but every blow was parried. Every attack defended.

He stumbled upon the threshold. A wall of flame taking over his vision. Curtains of it running like water across every surface.

Lazarus took that one clumsy moment to pounce. Slammed his sword home. The bite of the blade like the kick of a horse. Or a heavy fist against Aidan's chest.

He felt nothing but empty. With a final keening wail, the *Unseelie* fled. He was a man. Alone. Defenseless. Dying.

He dropped to the floor. Stared up into the red gold burn of the world. Locked on the behemoth in black. Waited for the enveloping darkness that would signal the end.

Cat flung herself between them. Stood her ground though her heart hammered against her ribs and every second within the gatehouse was like a second within hell. Flame. Smoke. Ash. She coughed, her lungs seared with the heat, her throat parched and sore. The horse's screams had long since become one note among a symphony of destruction.

"It's over! He's dead! Just take the diary and go," she croaked. "Go!"

Lazarus faltered. The inferno's glow reflected in his dark, endless gaze.

"You've won!" She closed her eyes, averting her face from his. Shoulders back. Head up. Steeling herself for the sword thrust.

Let it be swift. Let it be clean. And let her find the ones she'd lost on the other side.

The mage energy held him. Crushed him. Tightened its serpent coils around him until he suffocated. Couldn't think. It wanted to strike. Wanted blood. Wanted to swallow him whole until hate and killing and death were all he remembered. All he knew.

He hadn't always been like this. Had once known more than murder. Had shared laughter with friends. Pleasured a woman. Honored a king.

The dark magics sustaining him doubled in force. Sank their fangs into him like spears to the brain. The Great One commanded. His orders had been clear—end it. No witnesses. No one left behind who knew the truth. Kill them all. He, Lazarus, was death undone. He must obey.

He cried out. Fought back. Fed the evil. And in the tiny cracks of his mind, a memory evolved. A night like this. Dark. Starless. Damp with rain and a wind off the sea. Men fighting for their lives. Dying around him as the ambush played itself out amid the summer cool of a Welsh wood.

He had slipped. Fallen. And a figure in steel helmet and leather hauberk—faceless behind a bent nose guard, ageless within the armor of war—had delivered the death blow. A killing stroke that tore through his belly. Another slashing his heart. He'd been dead before his last thought had floated on a frothy breath. Remember me. Remember me. . . .

He strained to capture that last crystal moment of another age. Another existence. But the name was gone. Her name. His link to a past that dissolved like cloud every time he reached for it.

Only the woman remained fresh in his mind.

Dark. Slight. Eyes blue as gentians.

He held her image like a talisman. Lowered his sword.

Offered the lovers before him a second chance. One he'd never been given.

Lazarus disappeared into the heart of the house. Through flame and rolling smoke.

What caused him to back down? What had she done to sway the ruthless mage-spawned creature? Or had it been something he'd done? A battle just as violent within that she'd not been privy to?

A beam snapped. Fell in a sheet of flame. Broke her from her useless musing. Did it matter? He was gone. She lived. For now. But every second sent new flames leaping high. New sparks igniting new fires throughout.

Cat gripped Aidan under the arms. Struggled against his deadweight as she slid him through ash thick as a carpet upon the floor. He caught upon a board. His coat snagged and tore against a nail. He never helped. Never made a sound. But his eyes, brown and gold and crackling with reflected light, burned through her.

Glass shattered. Smoke coated her lungs. Breathing became gasping became held breath.

And then they were free. On the step. In the yard. A pyre blazing behind them. The diary gone. The horse's screams no longer knifing the air.

She cradled his head in her lap. Brushed his hair from his brow. Kissed his soot-blackened face. Threaded her fingers through his.

"Aidan?" she choked through weeping. Tasting the salt of her tears as they curved into the corners of her mouth. "Please don't die. Please don't leave me."

"Saved . . . saved me . . ."

Hysterical teary laughter staved off the pain. "You saved me first."

His gaze flickered. His hand moved in hers. And a question rose from bloody lips. "Stay?"

Anything. She'd offer anything to keep him with her. "Yes, Aidan. I'll stay. I promise."

He closed his eyes. His body stilled. But his heart kept beating.

# twenty-seven

*July 1815*

The three men stood in various poses of uncomfortable impatience around the drawing room. All bore themselves with military precision. Confident stances. Prideful, level gazes. Arrogant swaggers, even at rest.

Aidan smoldered against their presence even as he knew he must suffer through it if he was to do anything to clear Brendan's name with the *Amhas-draoi*.

He sat upright in a chair. A victory against gravity. Against the stream of visitors who'd shaken their heads and counted his hours. Hours stretching to days then weeks as he fought the surrender of a body whose only remaining sense had been pain. The memory of that battle remained in the reflection staring back at him every morning from his mirror.

Scarecrows bore more elegance than he. Gaunt body. Deep grooves cut into the sides of his mouth. An emptiness in his eyes. Silver threading his thick auburn hair. His impression borne up by three sets of cynical gazes.

"About"—he glanced at his pocket watch—"two months late, aren't you?"

The eldest of the *Amhas-draoi*—a man who'd introduced himself with the one-word sobriquet Garrick—barely flickered an eyelid. "We've had much to concern us of late, Lord Kilronan. We came as events allowed."

"You make it sound as if I invited you to a bloody summer fete. Did you read my letter?" He held his temper by the merest of threads.

"Do you mean this letter, my lord?" Garrick pulled free a heavy sheet of foolscap from his coat. Folded and refolded. Stained. Smeared. But still recognizable. The letter he'd sent by express rider to the *Amhas-draoi*. To the only address he'd had. Duke Street. Dublin. To a woman Jack once claimed had a developed sense of the ironic.

Was she laughing now? Or had Jack's death meant more to her than one more victim to Máelodor's ambitions? He didn't know. He'd yet to see Miss Roseingrave. His missive to her had yielded only these three stone-faced gentleman.

"We read it. And we understand your concern. Your late father's diary could be a powerful weapon in the wrong hands. Had we known of it at the time of our last . . . visit to your home here—"

"Let's not coat the memory in sugar," Aidan answered, his throat aching against the words he wished to say. "Had you known, you'd have grabbed it when you murdered my father."

"A regrettable oversight on our part." Garrick waved away the past with a breezy flip of his hand. "But let's talk of the present. We've come seeking more information because well, frankly, we find it hard to believe what you've written."

Aidan's hands upon the chair arms tightened. His spine stiffening. "How so?"

"You state Máelodor is at the heart of this new threat. That he works to re-create the Nine's network of *Other*. That he commands a soldier of Domnu. And that he plots to bring about a resurrection of Arthur." So calm. So even. So bloody cold. "But you see, that's impossible."

"You'd be amazed at what's possible." Aidan's voice matched and bettered the arrogance offered him.

The gentleman's brows raised as if he seemed to see Aidan for the first time. As if he caught the whiff of naked *Unseelie* power still seeping from the pores of Aidan's skin. A souvenir of survival. A memento of all he'd gained and lost that May night.

While Garrick struggled with this new and more formidable Lord Kilronan, his companion stepped into the silence. He wore the midnight visage of the Celt. Shock of black hair. Dark arched brows. A slash of snide mouth.

"Máelodor is dead."

Aidan jerked upright. Choked on a muttered "damn" before easing himself back into his seat. "When?"

"The man was tracked down in Paris and executed. Three years ago."

Aidan shook his head, drumming his fingers on the arm of his chair as he sought to make sense of it all. "You're mistaken."

Garrick found his voice. Reasserting his authority, he gestured to the third gentleman. "St. John was one of the force sent to execute him. He can guarantee it."

The man stepped to the fore. Blond. Lithe. And too damned young. What was he? Twenty-one? Twenty-two? Gods, Aidan felt old. "It's true, my lord." St. John's accent held a subtle hint of some foreign tongue. "Máelodor died in a Paris lodging house. His body burned."

Garrick leaned nonchalantly against the mantel as if he were the host and Aidan the unwelcome visitor. Looked down on Aidan from beneath hooded lids. "It's admirable to seek good in a brother who brings nothing but shame to a family already steeped in tragedy."

Aidan set his jaw. Rose to stiff attention. Unwilling to play the delusional, coddled invalid another moment. "My brother is not part of this hellish plot. Ask Ahern. Ask Miss O'Connell. Both of them can confirm what I set down in that letter."

"We spoke to Mr. Ahern, and I'm sorry to say received very little intelligible among the gibberish. Miss O'Connell could only relate to us assumptions based on her translation of the diary. A diary we find no longer in your possession."

"A diary I nearly died to protect." Anger licked at him. A bit of what he'd almost become in the heat blistering his body. The rage torching that hollow place he still carried.

He lifted his gaze back to the man. Saw Garrick's flicker of recognition, then retreat, though he clamored to bolster his superior stance.

"A diary that, had you handed it over when the chance was offered, would even now be secure. Your wounds, as well as your cousin's death, were no more than your own fault."

"My cousin's death!" he sputtered. "Do you want to know about my cousin's death? I sent men to search for his body. They came back with nothing. Not one bone to bury."

"Unfortunate, I'm sure."

The man was a massive, self-important prick. Locking his knees against a sudden case of dizziness, Aidan pointed toward the door. "Out. This conversation is over. Get off my land, and get the hell out of my sight!"

Garrick merely offered a thin chilly smile. "If your brother contacts you, send word immediately." His gaze traveled over Aidan with a despairing lift of his shoulders. "You've been fortunate once, Lord Kilronan. You may not fare so well a second time."

Fortunate? Did they call having his insides stirred with a sword fortunate? He called it a bloody damned pain in the thrice-cursed ass. Had he an ounce of strength he'd have kicked the man to the courtyard and tossed his compatriots after.

Garrick propped a white calling card upon a long rosewood table. Bowed his way out, his flunkies trailing.

Aidan grabbed up a heavy bookend. Drew it back to throw, chest heaving. Anger narrowing his gaze to a pinpoint. "Here's what you can bloody do with your damned card," he seethed before dropping his arm to his side. Slapping his hair out of his eyes. Falling back into his seat to fish for a cheroot. Lighting it with shaking hands.

They hunted Brendan. How long could his brother hide? They were relentless. Dogged. A pack of damned scent hounds hot on a trail.

Killed, the man had claimed. The body burned.

The blond man's voice rose to haunt him.

Would that be Brendan's fate? Could one misstep or one betrayal send him into the same trap that had been laid for their father? Aidan found himself trained on an inner vision where his brother fought for his life. For his honor. For his innocence.

He ground out the cheroot untasted. If the *Amhas-draoi* could hunt the lost Kilronan heir, so could he. Brendan would not fight alone.

Cat watched from a window as the men swung their horses around in the cobbled courtyard, cantered back through Belfoyle's arched tower. She remained long minutes after, content to rest here unnoticed. Unobserved. Alone.

She'd had few chances for such solitude during Aidan's recovery. Too much of her energy had been spent nursing him through the worst of his injuries. Watching him progress from fevered delirium where every second he lived they claimed as a gift. Through infinitesimal improvements as wounds closed. Fresh scars overlaying the old. A slash of puckered red severing the silver *Unseelie* brand. An angry welt across his ribs. A fainter mark drawing the eye to his upper arm. His shoulders. And a new flinty hardness chilling the warmth of his gaze.

He'd spoken no more of his desire for her to stay. And she'd not brought it up again. That time felt more like a dream every day. One she'd conjured to carry her through the horrors. Even the memory of his touch, his kisses, the feel of him thrusting deep within her took on the misty glow of unreality.

She unfolded the missive and read it again just to be sure she'd not imagined it. But no, the words remained unchanging. A heavy black scrawl. The slanted loops of letters. The information lifting a hidden burden from her shoulders.

Geordie lived.

He was in Dublin. Well. And wishing her home.

A choice lay before her. Could she truly find happiness

as Aidan's mistress, knowing he left her bed for another's arms? That any children she bore would carry their father's blood but not his name? That she must continue always in the corners of his life?

She bit her lip. Traced once more the words upon a window—"I love you."

But this glass held no coating of dust. Her pledge disappeared as if it had never been.


Sweat stung his eyes. Slicked his bare back. Dampened his hands where they gripped the rock face. The harness chafed his legs, straining muscles still weak from months of inertia.

Squinting into the overcast, he measured the distance to the top. Another fifty yards. May as well be five hundred. He'd never make it. He closed his eyes, but the burn of the wide cloud-flattened sky remained upon the backs of his lids. The distant roll of an ebb tide and the squawks of flustered puffins echoed in his ears.

Opening his eyes, he steeled his body for the next move. Adjusted his grip. Picked out the next handhold. Judged the distance. Climbed.

Tendons screamed. Bones grated against one another in movements difficult when healthy. Damn near impossible when not. But he'd needed this challenge. A focus for the gnawing rage. A way to assuage the *Unseelie* fury to a manageable whisper. Already he felt the attack easing. Sloughing off him with the drenching sweat.

Inches, then feet, passed beneath him as he picked his way up the cliffs. Time sliding away as the sun passed overhead. As the tide turned and rose again.

He'd delayed decision making as long as he dared.

Bankers summoned him. Estate managers from his properties in Cambridgshire, Wicklow, and Donegal sent increasingly frantic letters. Fellow investors scolded. Relatives fawned or chastised depending upon their income. But he'd put them all aside as he worked to understand his father's life. His death. His guilt. To knit whole a man woven from so many disparate and contrasting threads.

How would his life have been different if the fourth Earl of Kilronan had been truly the man of Aidan's memories? Would Aidan have remained forever a sauntering, pleasure-seeking rake hopping from scrape to scrape and bed to bed? Gliding through life on a nobleman's entrée and his own good looks until marriage settled him to a more sober existence?

Would he have ever known Cat?

Would he have ever allowed himself to dream of a life with her? To love her?

These thoughts squeezed a heart beating frantically in his chest. Cat had stayed as she'd promised. And yet there was distance between them. A fear within them both that didn't allow hope to blossom.

He understood her reluctance.

He despised his own.

The wind kicked up. Whistled through the ropes. Raised gooseflesh on his overheated back.

He made his next creeping move upward. Gritted his teeth against the pain.

Ten yards—and no more—lay between him and the cliff edge.

Almost there.

His father had been guilty of crimes uncounted. Death unmeasured. An ambition that drove others to share in his bloody and terrifying new world vision. The name Kilronan had become synonymous with ruthless power. Arrogant brutality. Unmatched tragedy.

Against such sins, how did simply loving someone compare?

He scrambled the final yards toward the edge, pebbles cascading below. Scree broken and sliding to shatter against the rocks below.

And that's when it happened.

The rope pulled free of its last anchor, the weighted spike dropping to swing uselessly against the cliffs. Jerking him free of his handhold. He scrambled against the outcropping, his feet slipping, his arms burning with stress as he fumbled to keep himself from falling.

"Hold on." A shadow blotted out the sun. A hand clutched his wrist. "I'll not let you fall."

Seconds stretched forever as he clambered to regain his footing. Drag himself the last feet over the lip of the cliff to lie gasping upon the turf. Above him, the shadow dissolved into a woman, staring down at him from a pair of spring green brilliant eyes, her mouth turned up in a hesitant smile, her curves barely concealed beneath a light summer gown of dotted muslin.

She knelt silently beside him as if she'd not spoken those heartrending words only a second before. Words carrying the punch of a sword thrust. Scalding him with a clarity of purpose he'd last felt upon the threshold of death. He knew what he wanted. Cared not the consequences. They would weather whatever the future held together.

Now if only she'd agree.

He rolled himself up onto his knees in front of her.

Cupped her face. Brushed his lips against hers. Cool. Soft. Restrained. Like kissing a statue.

"Marry me," he said.

That did it. She blinked her shock, eyes shining, mouth rounded in surprise. "But I can't. I wouldn't . . . Miss Osborne—"

"Can't? Wouldn't? You've battled a soldier of Domnu, fought back against an *Unseelie* possession, saved my sorry ass. Four times if you count just now. After all that, what's a few narrow-minded, top-lofty cranks to contend with?" His heart lifted at the amusement in her eyes. The smile playing at the edges of her lips. "Damn it, Catriona O'Connell. I love you. I need you. Marry me. Be my wife. And to hell with Miss Osborne. To hell with them all. "

Beneath him, her breathing quickened. A shiver ran through her. He once again traced the fine line of her scar, almost invisible against the ghostly pallor of her skin.

"Say you will, Cat."

Still she didn't answer.

Desire quickened. The chill of her body against the heat of his skin, the nerve-searing rush of the cliff ascent, the explosion of his certainty all aroused him so that his touch grew bolder, his kisses longer.

He pushed her back onto the grass to lie spooned in the crook of his arm. "Marry me, *a chuisle.* Say 'yes.' I beg you."

His voice shuddered on the plea. He swallowed back another. She would agree, or she would leave.

Long seconds passed as he held her gaze. He counted them in his head, even as the shallowest breath she drew acted like a spur to his growing excitement. He desired her. Ached to bury himself inside her. Ride the frenzied heat of their joining to orgasm, knowing she would always be his. If she pulled away—if she looked away—it would be over.

A smile spread slowly over features gilded by breaking sun. Her arms lifted to his neck. Her kiss, hot and sweet and eager. Her body welcoming him.

"Well, when you say it all out like that." She laughed. "Aye, Aidan Douglas. I must be mad, but I shall marry you," she answered.

He closed his eyes, sent up a silent prayer of thanksgiving even as his hand skimmed her side, caressed the exposed curve of her breasts. Seduction a few popped buttons and a raised petticoat away.

"Out here? Now you're the one who's lost his senses," she squeaked, casting a hesitant glance around her, though the wicked gleam in her eyes gave her away.

He laughed. Clamped his arms around her. Rolled them both over so she lay upon his chest, her hair falling from its pins. Curtaining them in a black, silken river. "May as well be hanged for an old sheep than a young lamb. And if we're going to cause a scandal anyway—"

She dropped a kiss upon his chin. His nose. His forehead. Grinned a sparkling invitation. "As you say," she purred in that sexy, smoky murmur of hers, guaranteed to shoot him over the moon. "To hell with them all.

Turn the page for a sneak peek at

*Lady of Shadows*

The next book in Alix Rickloff's
thrilling Heirs of Kilronan series

*Off the Southwest Coast of Ireland*
*November 1815*

He'd prayed the storm would kill him. One solid lightning strike to splinter his body into so many pieces no amount of mage energy could fit him back together.

A vain prayer. He'd moved far beyond the reach of any god's aid.

The ocean had calmed from the froth of hurricane swells to a slick of black, rolling water. Good for inducing nausea, but not death. Clouds passed eastward, taking their lightning with them, leaving a sky shimmering with frozen stars, full moon hanging low on the horizon. Picturesque, yet his mood longed for a cyclone's destruction to match the chaotic madness infecting his mind.

The storm had pushed them off course. He'd heard the sailors mutter and witnessed the captain's frown as he prowled the quarterdeck. Behind schedule. Battered and in need of repairs. And Cobh harbor another day and a half away if the winds held.

So if the gods had deserted him, it fell to his own devices to find oblivion.

He'd been denied a split second's painless annihilation. But there were other paths to *Annwn*. Trackless dark ways that led just as surely to the land of the dead.

He only needed to discover them.

Leaning against the rail, he scanned the sea, his answer written upon every wave. But could he go through with it? Would the wards keeping him alive and untouchable unravel within Lir's cold fathoms, bringing the solace he craved? Or would the attempt result in endless suffering of a different kind within the clawing pull of the ocean tides?

The stars above rippled gold and silver upon the surface of the sea. Curled and eddied as if a hand drew shapes with light and water. Turned moonlight to a woman's pale face. The ocean's foam drifting across her features like a spill of dark hair, she breathed her love across the separating veil. Shone luminous in a world blanketed by shadows.

Had she been conjured from his tattered memories or was she mere dream? Impossible to distinguish. Names and faces drifted through his consciousness like ghosts. Sometimes as vivid as the existence he found himself trapped within. At others times, only emptiness met his probing efforts to remember. And he was left alone to fight the demonic rage that burned through him like acid. The fury of the damned.

He expected her to dissolve back into the waves at any second, but she remained. Her eyes gleamed blue as cornflowers. Her smile brightening for a moment the hopelessness pressing against his heart, and he knew he must take the course offered. Now. Here. Before she vanished. Before she was beaten back by the howling viciousness, and he was once again left bereft of memories or even the comfort of memories. At least this way he wouldn't face the uncertainty of death alone.

Slinging a leg over the gunwale, he glanced to be sure none watched. But no, the deck remained quiet. He'd not get a better chance.

With a hard shove to propel him out of the ship's shadow, he plunged into the water. Arrowed far down below the waves.

The water jolted him alert. A stomach punch of icy pain, stabbing needles of agony through every nerve. Releasing his breath on a cloud of bubbles, he dropped deeper. Lungs burning and muscles cramping as he fought the instinctual need to breathe. To live.

He struggled against the claustrophobic crush of water, but the seeping drugged cold of the sea made every movement excruciating. And then impossible.

The woman's smile urged him deeper.

Water filled his lungs. His body surrendered. Death came like a lover.

He answered her smile. And stepping through the curtain between them, embraced her at last.


"Sabrina! Where have you gotten yourself? Answer, or so help me——"

Normally such a threat would have shot Lady Sabrina Douglas from her hiding place like a bullet from a gun. Not so today. Today was different. It was the sixteenth of the month. Seven years ago on this date, her world had been turned upside down, and nothing had ever been the same since.

It wasn't like her to spend time reminiscing about the

past. The head of the sisters of High Danu said it was useless spinning what-ifs in your head. One could lose one's self in the infinite possibilities of action and consequence until reality grew dangerously frayed. Madness lay in second-guessing.

But today, Sabrina courted madness. She'd forced herself to remember all that had occurred on that long-ago November day from beginning to end. Let it flow from her brain to her journal in a mad scrawl. And at Sister Brigh's first shout was only as far along as noon.

"You ungrateful, undisciplined hooligan, come out this moment."

When Sister Brigh scolded, Sabrina felt more like a disobedient ten-year-old than the woman of twenty-two she was. But then Sister Brigh considered anyone younger than herself to be a recalcitrant child, which included almost the entire *bandraoi* community. The woman was a hundred if she was a day. Only Sister Ainnir rivaled her in age. The two like mossy twin holdovers from centuries past.

"Sabrina Douglas! I know you can hear me!"

Sister Brigh by far the mossier. And the louder.

Sabrina sighed, closing her journal on the pen marking her place.

November sixteenth, 1808, would have to wait.

November sixteenth, 1815, was calling.

The priestess's clamoring faded as she left the barn. Turned her search to the nearby outbuildings—creamery, laundry, gardener's shed. The convent was large. It would take the head of novices ages to check everywhere.

Sabrina rose from her hiding place behind the stacked straw bales and grain bins, dusting the grime from her skirts. Straightening her apron and the kerchief covering her hair before slipping back into the bustle of the order's life. And right into Sister Brigh's ambush.

"Gotcha." Her talons sank through the heavy wool of Sabrina's sleeve. Squeezed with enough force to bring hot tears to her eyes. "*Ard-siúr's* had me searching for you this hour and more. And here you are, hiding as if there weren't honest work to be done." She snatched the journal away. "Are you scribbling in that silly book again? You've been warned more than once about frittering away your time unwisely."

Sabrina stiffened, giving Sister Brigh her best quelling look. "I wasn't frittering. And I wasn't hiding."

It passed unnoticed. "*Hmph.* Come along. You've kept *Ard-siúr* waiting long enough."

As they passed through the sheltered cloister, a group gathered at the front gates. Voices raised in surprise and confusion, drawing even the determined Sister Brigh's eye from her purpose.

Sabrina craned her neck to peer over the crowd. "What's happening?"

Sister Brigh responded with a scornful huff. "No doubt a lot of stuff and nonsense. Wouldn't have happened in my day, you can be sure of that."

Her day being sometime during the last ice age. Sister Brigh dressed in furs and sporting a club, no doubt.

She tightened her hold on Sabrina. Doubled her pace. Up the steps. Throwing the door wide with barely a word. Slamming it closed with a whisper equally as effective.

The old priestess's sanity might be in doubt, but her magic was irrefutable.

The temperature plummeted once they stepped inside and out of the bleak afternoon sun. Frost hung in the passage leading to *Ard-siúr*'s office, causing Sabrina's nervous breath to cloud the chilly air. The cold seeped through her heavy stockings and the double layer of petticoats she'd donned beneath her gown.

It wasn't even winter yet and already she longed for spring. Spring and a release from scratchy underclothes and chilblains and runny noses and afternoon dusk and drafty passages. At this moment, she'd sell her soul for warmth and light and, well . . . something different.

So little varied within the order that any change, even the gradual shifting of seasons, seemed an adventure. But perhaps that was only because the genuine change she longed for still eluded her and would continue to do so if Sister Brigh had her grumpy way.

As they were shown through the antechamber to *Ard-siúr*'s office, Sister Anne waved a cheery hello. Received a bulldog scowl from Sister Brigh. A wan smile from Sabrina.

Compared to the chilly atmosphere of the outside corridor, *Ard-siúr*'s office seemed an absolute tropical paradise. A small stove put out heat enough to keep the tiny room comfortably cozy, and thick rugs on the floor and bright wall hangings cheered the stark color-draining stone. Add to that *Ard-siúr*'s cluttered desk, complete with purring cat and the slow tick of a tall-case clock in a far corner, and Sabrina's taut nerves began to relax.

The atmosphere seemed to have the opposite effect on Sister Brigh. Her eyes darted around the room with fuming disapproval as she drew up in a quivering pose of long sufferance, only now releasing her death grip on Sabrina's arm.

*Ard-siúr* put up a restraining hand while she finished her

thought, her pen scribbling across the page, her lip caught girlishly between her teeth as she worked.

The head of the Sisters of High Danu seemed as eternal as the ancient standing stones guarding a nearby clifftop meadow. Tall. Broad. A face weathered by years, yet eyes that remained clear and bright and full of humor. Her powers as a *bandraoi* and sorceress seemed to rival those of the *Fey*, as did her air of regal self-containment. But Sabrina knew it took every ounce of her gifts, both innate and learned, to preside over an order of *Other* while concealing their true nature from a distrustful *Duinedon* world.

To all beyond the walls of the order's demesne, they were merely a reclusive house of contemplative religious women. It fell to *Ard-siúr* to see it remained that way. An unenviable task. Though, come to think of it, there was one who envied it very much.

Sister Brigh breathed heavily though her nose like a kettle letting off steam.

Finally, *Ard-siúr* placed her pen in its tray. Scattered sand across the page. Shook it clean. Folded it. And cast her penetrating gaze upon the pair standing silently before her.

"Thank you, Sister Brigh, for locating Sabrina."

Her acknowledgment clearly meant as a signal for the head of novices to depart.

Instead Sister Brigh barreled ahead with a list of grievances. They rolled off her tongue as if she'd prepared them ahead of time: "Three times in three days, *Ard-siúr*. Three times I've caught her with her head in the clouds when she should be working. That or she's scribbling in that diary of hers. You can't keep brushing it under the rug. It only encourages her to feel she's above the rules.

The lord's daughter she once was rather than the aspiring *bandraoi* priestess she's supposed to be."

The sarcastic emphasis Sister Brigh placed on "aspiring" had Sabrina bristling, but one look from *Ard-siúr* and she subsided without argument.

"Is this true, Sabrina? Do you feel above the rules? That your family's station in life entitles you to special consideration?"

"No, ma'am, of course not, but—"

Sister Brigh slammed the journal on *Ard-siúr*'s desk, sending the cat leaping for cover with a hiss. "Sabrina's lack of devotion and her failure to abide by our way of living undermine her candidacy. And I, for one, believe she would be better off leaving the order and returning to her family."

*Ard-siúr* turned her gaze upon Sabrina at last. "Sister Brigh brings up serious charges. Could it be that you aren't as committed to a life among us as you think? That you begin to yearn for the life you might have led but for tragic circumstance?"

Sabrina blinked. Had *Ard-siúr* brought that up on purpose? Did she know what Sabrina had been writing in her diary? Or had the mention been mere coincidence? Always difficult to know with the head of their order. She seemed to have a canny knack for discerning all manner of things. Especially the bits one didn't want known.

Perhaps forcing her mind back to that long-ago November day hadn't been such a good idea after all. She'd dredged up memories long buried. Forgotten how much they hurt.

"I'm more than ready to take up my full duties as *bandraoi*." She shot an offended glance Sister Brigh's way. "And

I didn't mean to make you wait, *Ard-siúr*. I was trying . . . you see, I needed . . . it happened today seven years ago, *Ard-siúr*. And I felt as if I needed to remember it clearly before it slipped away."

*Ard-siúr* gave a slow nod. "Ah yes, your father's death."

"His murder," she clarified. "It was seven years ago today the *Amhas-draoi* attacked and killed my father, ma'am."

"And for good reason, if half the stories are true," Sister Brigh mumbled. "*Ard-siúr*, even if it's not enough for you that Sabrina shirks her duties and carries on as if she were queen of the manor, you must see that her presence brings the order unwanted attention. Never in our history was one of our priestesses interrogated by the *Amhas-draoi*."

"It's not my fault they wanted to speak with me. I didn't tell them anything."

"Keeping secrets from the very brotherhood sworn to protect us? Worse and worse."

"That's not what I meant. You're twisting my words."

"Enough." *Ard-siúr* lifted a hand.

Momentum behind her, Sister Brigh barreled on. "A father working the demon arts. A fugitive brother running from the *Amhas-draoi*. The family of Douglas is cursed. And the sooner you're gone from here, the better for the order."

Sabrina turned a hot gaze on the elderly nun.

"I said enough." The whip crack of *Ard-siúr*'s voice finally silenced Sister Brigh, though she remained red faced and glaring with suppressed fury. "This is neither the time nor place. If you have valid arguments to make, bring them to me at another meeting and we can discuss it further."

Turning her attention to Sabrina, *Ard-siúr* smiled. "My dear, I requested your presence merely to deliver a letter that's come for you by messenger."

How did one simple sentence drop the bottom out of her stomach and create an immediate need to draw nonexistent covers over her head? In her experience, letters never boded well. Like holding an unexploded bomb in your hand.

The door burst open on the flustered face of Sister Anne. "*Ard-siúr*, Sabrina's needed in the infirmary right away. A man's been brought in. Found half-drowned on the beach below the village."

"May I go?" Sabrina cast beseeching eyes in *Ard-siúr*'s direction.

Sister Brigh looked as though she chewed nails, but the head of the order dismissed Sabrina with an imperious wave of her hand. "Go. Sister Ainnir needs your skills. The letter will await your return."

Plucking up her skirts, Sabrina dashed from the room in Sister Anne's wake. She could kiss the unlucky fisherman who'd rescued her. Saved in the nick of time.

It was only fair to return the favor.

Tremors shuddered through him, chattering his teeth, turning fingers numb and jittery. Even his skull ached as if his brain had rattled itself loose. He tried swallowing, but his throat felt scraped raw, his tongue swollen and useless. He tried opening his eyes. Squinted against a piercing glare as if he stood within the sun. Golden yellow. Blinding. Sending new shocks of pain through his sloshy, scattered mind.

Slowly his sight acclimated. His surroundings coalescing into a cell-like room lined with cupboards, a low shelf running the perimeter. A sink with a pump. His pallet jammed into one corner. Beside him sat a small bench holding a pitcher and basin and three stoppered bottles.

A cane-backed chair drawn up close. Sunlight streamed in from a high window, and a three-legged brazier had been placed in the middle of the room, giving off a thin stream of smoke and just enough heat to keep him from freezing.

He burrowed deeper into the blankets in a vain attempt to get warm. A vainer attempt to figure out where he was. How he'd come to be here.

He remembered endless black. Crushing pressure. Cold so intense it tore him apart one frozen inch at a time. But when he sought the reasons for these sensations, he came up against a barrier. A wall beyond which lay a vast emptiness.

He pushed harder, but the barrenness extended outward in all directions. Any attempt to concentrate only made his head hurt worse. Still he struggled, panic quickly replacing confusion, until the shudders wracking his body had less to do with cold and more to do with sheer terror. The only memory he managed to squeeze from a brain scrambled as an egg was a woman's face, though her identity eluded him.

If he rose. Walked around. Perhaps that would help. He fought to stand. Lasted five seconds. The room dipped and whirled like a ship caught in a storm, his stomach rebelling with a gut-knifing retch that left him doubled over and heaving.

Collapsing back onto the lumpy mattress, he stared up at the crumbling plaster ceiling, gripping the thin wool of his blanket. Clenching his teeth against a moan of pure animal fear.

Someone would come. They would tell him what had happened. Why he was here.

Who he was.

The latch lifted, the door swinging open on a figure

shrouded by the dim light of the corridor beyond. Stepping into the room, she paused.

And he caught his breath on a startled oath.

Vivid blue eyes. Dark brown hair escaping its kerchief to frame a narrow face. And a figure that managed to defy her shapeless gray gown.

Here stood the woman. His one and only memory.

She was called—he blanked.

"Please. What's your name?" he croaked, praying she wouldn't be insulted he couldn't remember.

Instead she smiled, turning her solemn face into something iridescent, and, crossing to sit beside him, placed the tray she carried on the bench. "I'm Sabrina. But, actually, I was rather hoping you could tell me your name."

Oh gods, she didn't know him. She couldn't fill in the holes. The truth kicked his last hopes out from under him. He was alone. On his own. And he hadn't a damned idea who he was.

She stared, head tilted, expectant, eager.

He shook his head, hating to disappoint. Hating the sick, horrible dread pressing him with a weight as crushing as the oblivion that preceded it. "I don't remember."

# LOVE HAS A MAGIC
## ALL ITS OWN...
### Bestselling Paranormal Romance from Pocket Books!

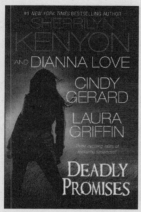

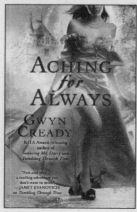

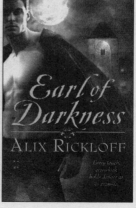

# Passion is stronger
## *after dark.*

Bestselling Paranormal Romance from Pocket Books!

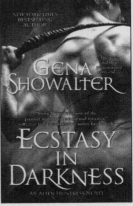

# The darkness hungers...

## Bestselling Paranormal Romance from Pocket Books!

### KRESLEY COLE
# PLEASURE OF A DARK PRINCE

**An *Immortals After Dark* Novel**

Her only weakness…is his pleasure.

---

### ALEXIS MORGAN
# Defeat the Darkness

**A *Paladin* Novel**

Can one woman's love bring a warrior's spirit back to life?

---

And don't miss these sizzling novels
by *New York Times* bestselling author
Jayne Ann Krentz writing as

## JAYNE CASTLE
# Amaryllis  Zinnia
# Orchid

Available wherever books are sold
or at www.simonandschuster.com

POCKET BOOKS
A Division of Simon & Schuster
A CBS COMPANY

POCKET STAR BOOKS
A Division of Simon & Schuster
A CBS COMPANY

23519